SONS OF MAN

Phillip Lawrence

Copyright © 2025 Phillip Lawrence

All rights reserved

The characters and events portrayed in this book are fictitious. Any similarity to real persons, living or dead, is coincidental and not intended by the author.

No part of this book may be reproduced, stored in a retrieval system, or transmitted in any form or by any means, electronic, mechanical, photocopying, recording, or otherwise, without the express written permission of the publisher.

Printed in the United States of America

To my exceedingly patient and beautiful wife, I couldn't have done this without your support. So I guess it's your fault. I love you-BSP

And there we saw the giants, the sons of Anak, which come of the giants: and we were in our own sight as grasshoppers, and so we were in their sight.

NUMBERS 13:33

CONTENTS

Title Page
Copyright
Dedication
Epigraph
Prologue
ONE   1
TWO   48
THREE   79
FOUR   121
FIVE   214
SIX   257
SEVEN   284
EIGHT   313
NINE   377
TEN   378

PROLOGUE

2037

The gunsight settled on the target's head. Rhett's finger, outside the trigger guard, tapped the lower receiver—soft and drumming. He imagined the head popping, the body slumping. He shifted his weight, crossed his legs, and leaned forward. He'd been in the hide site for what felt like a week but, in reality, was only two days. Dense, woven creeper vines buried him in the high thicket—blending him into the valley's wall. The blending of Rhett into anything was quite a task. The man was large. At six feet five, he blotted out what little sun managed to trickle into the observation post. Carved into the steep bank, covered in heat-reflective blankets, the entrance was shrouded with area greenery.

They were a good ways up the hillside. The target he'd observed throughout the night was maybe three-hundred-fifty yards away. He guessed out loud, "It's about three-forty-two." He lifted the digital reticle to his eyes. Readouts scrolled at the top right corner. The distance read: *351 yards*. Placing the reticle on his lap, he smiled. His dirty face seemed to crack. "Glass says three-fifty-one." There was no response from the dark space behind him. "You hear me, Daniel?"

"I heard ya."

Rhett's eyes dipped in consideration; he felt ignored. "I guessed three-forty-two. The glass said three-fifty-one."

"Yeah."

"Well, that's a pretty good guess, I'd say."

"*You'd* say? You say all kinds a' stuff. You *never stop* sayin' stuff. Every once in a while you're gonna get somethin' close to right."

Rhett nodded. It made sense. "Whatcha reckon it's been doin' down there?"

"Just how in God's name am I s'posed to know that?"

Rhett cocked his head and eyed the target as he'd been doing since they dropped it on the road two days ago. "It's blind, ain't it?"

Daniel sighed.

Rhett said, "I'm just askin'." He softened his tone to deflect some of Daniel's surliness. "'Cause it ain't moved. It's just been sittin' there. All night."

Daniel said, "It doesn't matter if it's blind or not; its brain wasn't done cookin' when we got ahold of it. It wouldn't know *where* to go, even if it knew that it needed to go somewhere."

Rhett considered the thing deeply—the Skin. He asked, "You think it believes it's a person—I mean that it's alive?"

Daniel slipped up beside his large friend. He pulled the reticle from him and motioned to the back of the hide. Rhett slid past him, agile for a man his size.

Daniel put the glass to his face. "Skins ain't alive—none of 'em. Even the ones that think they are."

The Newborn sat naked in the dirt, legs crossed. His back ramrod straight, arms rested on his knees. His face, the skin of it, gleamed chemically. A mixture clung to the developing dermis, allowing his pigment to culminate. His current tone: bloodless. He sat, covered in the stuff, on the edge of the road.

Having just been upgraded from the tanks, his flesh had attained the third phase of growth. He existed that way for a brief time, outside the tank, stashed in a cold, metal folder. His skin, in the early stages of stratification, still maintained its sleek, waxy appearance.

He'd experienced very little in the way of stimuli until the event which unfolded two days ago. After lifting him from the culture on forks, still wet from the cellular stew, the techs had wrapped him in a stereostatic cocoon; his body had been bombarded with a mixture of buffering agents and antibiotics.

By that point, his internals—brain, liver, and lungs—were capable of supporting his functions. He understood these things, even though he'd never spoken a word or had had a word spoken to him. It all seemed to sit inside his skull:

imprinted knowledge. He was in the early stages of the actualization process—when psycho-resilience stressors were to be applied.

He'd been on a transport, or as the Oldborn techs called it: *A body haul*. Something catastrophic had occurred. There was a loud clap on the truck's outer shell. A concussive wave rolled through the hauler, crippling the storage system responsible for life support. His oxygen supply plummeted; loud, sharp explosions erupted all around. The screaming voices of the Oldborns filled the gaps.

The doors were wrenched apart, and he was pulled from his bag. He felt, for the first time, dirt on his skin. Unfiltered air in his lungs. Dragged and tossed into a rough, metal compartment, he rumbled about for hours and then was stiffly deposited where he sat.

Blind, yet the fibers, muscles, and nerves of his eyes functioned. The optic pathway, due to developmental priorities, was slow-baked over several weeks. This was scheduled to transpire within his buffering bag. But as a result of the catastrophe that had befallen him—for which he had no frame of reference—he was outside his cozy envelope, sitting on what he understood from overheard conversations to be a thing called Virginia.

He didn't trouble about it, though; he had no notion of *troubling*. He had no concept of the future and, as such, was unperturbed despite the violent disruption.

As each developmental milestone passed, the explanation of it unlocked itself inside his mind—a dissociated scavenger hunt of sorts. And as each of these "unlockings" occurred, his disposition became ever so slightly more clear in his mind.

Trepidation was not in his nature. Although, while sitting on what he took to be Virginia, he felt as if nothing more would reveal itself. Throughout those dark, uncomfortable hours, an inkling had grown within him. Things had gone awry. The process had been disrupted to the point that, short of a dramatic correction, he would learn nothing new. Had he the capacity for expectation, he might well have felt lonely, or disappointed. But as an incomplete being—non-actualized—he felt neither.

And, of course, he had no idea that someone was coming for him. And that was, in fact, the reason he sat in the dirt—to bring them to that spot of earth.

Daniel reviewed his preparations. The burn bombs were in place. Simple things—he didn't nerd out over demolitions. He liked them to be easy and reliable. This rig was just that: backup fuel cells, taken from first-gen hovercraft—pretty easy to get your hands on, stockyards were full of them, lined up, unguarded, about fifteen minutes' worth of work would get them loose. There were three of them—a triangle of death as arranged—daisy-chained together, set to go off at the initiation of the main. The wire-operated trigger consisted of a line that ran from the initiator to his hide site. It terminated in a booger knot tied around a sawed-off Sweetgum branch.

Rhett stirred from his nap, rustled for a minute, and asked, "Why are you so particular about using those burn bombs?"

Daniel stared at the Skin, rigid and unmoving on the roadside. "Because fuck them."

Rhett stretched his arms as far as he could in the cramped space, yawned. "That checks out. How long we gonna sit here, wait on this guy to show up?"

Daniel said, "We'll give it another twenty-four. If he don't show by then, we'll cook this'n and take off."

"Sounds good. You think—"

"You think maybe you could internalize a thought here or there?"

Rhett chuckled. "What, you didn't get breakfast today, old man?"

Old man.

Daniel opened his mouth to take a jab at his partner but shut it as the hover slid over the top of their position. The gravidic propulsion modules dotting the skids just above the treetops—the thing flew in fast and low. It dropped down into the valley, disrupting the hardwoods; leaves were shredded loose, came down in showers.

Daniel said, "Pack it up. It's just about go-time."

Rhett hurried, gathering the packs and stuffing away what little gear lay outside them.

Daniel lifted the branch connected to the tripwire

with a light touch. He held it in his hand, the other sliding forward over it, denting the line from the tension, playing with it... waiting for the right moment...

He held his eyes even, his breath the same. As Rhett behind him scrambled, emitting nerves, Daniel saw the scene with cold eyes, gallium-filled veins. He barely raised a hair at the knowledge of what he was about to do.

The hover didn't dance about. It ripped once around, scanning, just above the level of the hide site. Once done, it dropped out of the sky on its extended legs, settling hard. The clear blast door slid back and the ramp dropped.

Daniel narrowed his eyes. Rhett came forward, his bearded head looming over Daniel's shoulder. Without a trace of irritation, like ice, Daniel said, "Get off me." Rhett backed away but managed to keep the hover in sight.

The Special Forces team came down the ramp. Daniel lifted the reticle. He scanned the operators as they disembarked, fanned out and formed a perimeter around the slick, naked Skin. They wore the latest skeins, optical headsets synched over a command net—fancy guys with fancy gear. He studied them—moving where he thought they would, acting within their operating procedures, and aligning themselves near perfectly with his predictions. As each operator fell on the perimeter, he emitted a simple grunt of satisfaction.

Then, he saw him. "There he is."

The man walked down the ramp, in command. He consulted his heads-up display and spoke into a radio. He pointed, gave directions, and the perimeter tightened up.

Rhett said, "He *is* a persistent sumbitch. I'll give him that."

They sat in silence and watched their subject step off the ramp into the trap.

Rhett said, "Good ole Tommy boy—been waitin' a while for this."

Tommy approached the Skin, stopped in front of it, studying it. Attempting to communicate, he waved his hand in the Skin's face. He scanned up and around the valley. His posture shifted; agitation crawled into his spine. A creeping suspicion worked its way in there, inside his eyes. He pulled a couple of his men from the perimeter, gave them anxious directions, grabbed his radio, and started talking.

Daniel said, "He's gettin' the heebs. Startin' to dance a little."

"Stop wastin' time. Burn 'em."

Daniel didn't need much more convincing. The whole detachment of operators sat inside his kill zone. He yanked the branch over his shoulder, reaching as far back as possible. His free hand slid the length of the line, snatched it and he grunted as he jerked it past his hip.

What followed was the overwhelming sound of nothing. The Skin, the operators, Tommy, all of them went about their business in the kill zone.

"What the fuck?" Rhett's voice had an edge. "Yank

it again."

Daniel dropped the line. "It's compromised—caught on a stump or somethin'."

The perimeter began to collapse with several of the operators moving to the ramp. Two of them had the Skin in their hands, lifting it, dragging it. Tommy's eyes were birdlike, darting black dots. Daniel knew how he felt, realizing you'd walked your guys into a trap; it was overwhelming, threatened to unmoor you from your instincts.

They were moving fast, escaping the kill zone in an orderly fashion. The hover began to hum as it came online.

Daniel said, "Hit the clacker."

Every plan has contingencies. The alternate initiation process was a radio frequency detonation. Most Special Forces commanders carried body-bound RF disruptors. If Tommy had his switched on, the clacker wouldn't work.

Rhett grabbed the thing from the ground. "Prob'ly jammed." He hit the lever—again, nothing. The prey continued to escape, a couple of guys on the ramp now, looking up into the valley wall, guns up.

The third contingency required a level of exposure. Daniel grunted and plucked his rifle from the wall of the hide site. "If this don't work, you know what to do." He slid out from under the heat reflective blanket, understanding the signature that he created on the hillside.

The question here—as it always seemed to be—was *who's gonna see who first?* Well aware of the sensor platforms on assault carriers, Daniel knew he'd have several moments before the scanner would pick up his presence. Once detected, the belly gunner would receive notification. It was a simple matter of execution at that point—traverse, aim, shoot.

Daniel slid on his stomach down the sharp incline, in a wallowed-out path that led to his designated point. From there he had a clear site line to the primary fuel cell. Marked with a small piece of orange cellophane, it was no more than fifteen feet away when the belly gunner opened up on him. The rounds traced over his head, slapping the hillside, splintering the tangled roots.

No choice but to continue, he buried his face in the muck and snaked forward, reaching the tape. Behind him, from the hide site, he heard a rocket blast and caught the smoky tail as it sliced down toward the hover. He propped his rifle into a Y-shaped branch. The rocket burst, harmless as a gnat, against the armored hull. The belly gun swung away toward the hide site.

He placed the aimpoint of his rifle on the fuel cell. He took a breath as he settled into the shot. The belly gun warmed up, getting ready to hose Rhett.

His finger produced six pounds of pressure.

The entire valley floor bleeped out of existence for a moment in a blast so glaring it clipped the sound. The tripped fuel cells unleashed hundreds of thousands of pounds of pressurized flame, charring everything in a white-hot eruption. The air in the valley sucked down toward the hell of it, the treetops yielding. Half inside the zone of fire, the hover's landing gear collapsed under the shifting weight of its melting frame.

The conflagration lasted about ten seconds, then burned out, and the charred spot of earth was blackened to chalk. The operators, the Skin, and Tommy were all gone—intermingled, indiscernible ash. The trees along the hillside burned: the heat had relocated their molecules outside their bodies, spontaneously igniting. Half the valley wall was either burning or thinking about it.

Daniel took a deep breath, looked over his shoulder at Rhett. He yelled above the roaring fire, "You ready?"

Rhett smiled like a boy. "We should prob'ly get."

Daniel jumped up, ran back to the hide site. "Leave the shit bucket, let it burn."

Rhett nodded. They slipped into the rising smoke. Daniel led them over the spine of the ridge, stopped, and looked back. "They'll be comin' for us now."

Rhett hadn't stopped smiling. "Let 'em come."

Daniel peered through a break in the smoke. The hover, wholly plagued by flame—nothing down there but the ash of all those men and that one thing.

He looked at Rhett. "You say that now. Wait till they find us. See how you feel about it then."

They disappeared into the wilderness.

XVIII

The White Room

The memory faded around the edges, scarred onto the white wall. Years of trauma and drug-induced hallucinations spoiled the edges of it. The center of the picture—the moving part—lived for him as often as he wished to see it.

Lori lay before him again, in his mind, on the ground. The tall grass sloped away from him. They pointed toward her but did not look into his eyes, because they knew what he'd find. It would be too much for him.

He moved to her. The wind came down, stirred the grass, then the leaves. Her hand reached for him.

Her body had been stripped of clothes, the cuts and burns worked into her skin. Drained of life, the juice of her gone, leaving this violated thing. It was not her. It did not sit proud, as she had.

It was not her.

He touched her hand and it was cold like meat. The eyes sat open, two beads staring into the unflinching sun.

What must she have thought of him toward the end of it? Had she waited for him to arrive and save her?

She didn't deserve this.

He painted this place on the white wall and visited it many times. He spoke to her but she never answered, always the sun beating into those still, glass beads.

He fell to his knees over and again, begging a God who didn't care. He begged a God invisible to him.

Now the white seeped through, threatening to spoil the memory.

The goddamned white.

He stood ashamed in the face of his failure. He imagined her struggle. Had she forgiven him? The state of her body encouraged dark imagining, and so he did. His mind worked through the possibilities, the endless debasements. How long did she tolerate it?

Then, the same cold blackness opened beneath his feet and he felt hell below him. His chest shuddered, and it was fair and right for him to go down into it.

Something moved near him, off to his left. It tugged at his awareness, vague and distant, yet waiting. No matter how often he told himself he deserved death and hell and every other thing, he always ran from it.

The movement near him was subtle. He could feel the person, or the thing waiting for him to pull his eyes from the wall, to rejoin his body and be present along with it. So, he did. He left her in the grass in her pale, naked body. She'd be there for him when he returned.

ONE

2041

*The cloak of earth covered my Master
I then parted with my torment
The seas, the trees, the roll of the rivers
could not answer it, the seeking heart.*
—The Dawnbringer's Chronicle

The patrol left out two days before. The temperature wavered, hot in the day and cold at night—October in the mountains. The terrain billowed like giant, green waves across the endless Appalachians. The low ground was dark, filled with the claiming things. Every vine equipped with spikes: some straight, others barbed. Hidden until the skin dragged the stem and the million needles drew blood. The grapplers flourished in the soft soil, clustering upon them, delaying them, sapping them.

They labored to make the high ground where the trees grew sparse and the ground was rocky, less fruitful. A man could walk upright and take a breath. The sun on his face for a few minutes, all the while, the whispering maw waited beneath him. He stumbled into its teeth again and climbed out. This he repeated until the thorns engraved his arms and his lungs burned with the smell of sweet vines in the mountain air.

Through this, Daniel led the patrol—*his* patrol. He was accurate and on time, as was his custom. He knelt on a ridgetop, somewhere in the hills of Virginia. His lean face carried a layer of sweat in the midday sun. He scanned the area with his hard, close-set eyes.

There were no roads, no buildings for miles, only the green angles and ridges of the hills. Spinal processes etched eternally in the crawling mist. They expanded before him, disappearing in the afternoon haze.

He compared the distant landmarks to the lines on his map. He knew where he stood. He understood the truth of the world—every hill and crevice served as a waypoint. He traipsed across it like he owned it. He carried himself on stout legs. Yet the grinding from his knees had grown in volume over the years.

He would have a last day, a final patrol, but not today. Someday his body would refuse. It would quit on him, but not today. Today he would see to his business. The world within his reach would again smell the metallic tang of revenge and soak in the sulfur of his hatred.

Daniel had developed a philosophy of war, and he ensured his junior leaders were indoctrinated. His words echoed in their ears during the quiet, painful moments on patrol.

When it comes to killin' men who don't wanna be killed, preparation is well over half the gig. Maybe, fellas, it's the whole shebang.

On his back, the heavy rucksack stood. It sat on his spine and wicked away his essence like a giant, green tick. Over his shoulder, a long gun hung, taped and camouflaged, ready to be put into play.

Above him, in a crux of limbs, a man peered at the valley through his digital reticles. He locked eyes with Daniel. The two exchanged a series of hand signals, intricate and silent. Daniel nodded and waved him down.

His patrol knelt in positions alongside the trail. They were young, teens and early twenties. They shifted to and fro, gritting under the weight of their patrol rucks. They were vigilant, looking for signs of trouble. They were good boys.

For instance, if the men you wanna kill should happen to be a great distance away, you might need a level of endurance appropriate for the task. This doesn't happen overnight. Killin' men as a routine matter necessitates consideration. There are the bullets, which must be lugged. There is whatever food and water is needed to sustain the effort. But there is, foremost to all other considerations, the mind of the man tasked with the job. Never assume he is ready to kill. You won't know his mind until you see him act.

Daniel stowed his map and gazed at the young men, most of them not old enough to have lived, in any significant sense, a life of their own. The wars had chewed up their families. Many of them had grown up under his guidance. He knew most of their fathers—most of their fathers, now dead. They were old friends who lived like ghosts among the trees. He could hear their voices sometimes when it got rough and the green tick was working him over.

The proper leverage must be found and applied. The appropriate grievance, skillfully kindled. The button, so to speak, must be pushed.

The lookout in the tree slid the last ten feet to the trail. A thin, fit young man, twenty years Daniel's junior. His name was Carl. The point man on the patrol, he possessed an unusual ability for land navigation.

"We're good, boss. The road is about a klick, straight down there. Half-hour to the rally point."

"Alright." The boy's waited, obedient in the afternoon sun.

This vulnerability, one that all men have, has gotta be cultivated particular to each man. It requires attentiveness. It requires empathy. It requires love, and it's better if that love is genuine. Let him know that killin' for you is killin' on his own behalf. Convince him that killin' for you is the only answer to his personal injury. That's why you've taken him in, a lost soul, and taught him, and fed him and loved him. So that you could stand beside him and watch as your shared demons are burnt to dust.

They waited for his orders, commitment written in their eyes. He'd earned that by walking them to the door of death. They came out on the right side of it more often than not. His talent in the hot moments and the ease with which he made quick decisions endeared them to his leadership.

War was not fought with machines. It was fought with the minds of men, and Daniel didn't lie about it to himself or anyone else. He cultivated this creature for over a decade—the monster in the woods.

A man expected to endure hardships in the cause of hunting other men, must be ready to do so when the moment arises. It should not be debated at the time of the doing.

Most of his fighters had lost their families during the early atrocities. They were in search of a reckoning, and Daniel brought them to the place with regularity. He never raised an eyebrow at the brutality of it all, and he was well aware of the impact this had on his men. They spoke of him in secret. He was their icon of retribution. It was as natural as breathing for him. His thirst to drag the enemy down like a wild animal, bleed him, and drain him of life was unmatched in their eyes.

Daniel lived as a vengeful revenant. He called them forward into battle, to wash their hands in fountains of blood, born from the veins of their tormentors.

This issue of whether or not he will kill must become an afterthought. If you've done it right, this last, little piece will be just that, an afterthought. You would in fact prefer it that way... It being the only thing better to think of after.

The heads of the patrol turned to him. It was a quiet, expectant moment, and it reminded him of a truth: This savagery would eventually kill them all. No amount of skill would save them, even the best of them.

"When we get set in, make sure everything is right on the assault line. Everybody's eyes are open, doin' their job."

Carl nodded.

"Haven't lost anybody in a while and I don't wanna start tonight."

Carl nodded again. Daniel knew his point man. He understood his mind. Carl was already considering the movement to the rally point, from which the two would reconnoiter the objective.

"Pick up your guys. Lead us out." Daniel patted his shoulder.

Carl shuffled away, waving his hands as he moved through the formation. The men stood and relieved their aching knees. They bent over and cinched their straps.

Daniel pulled his canteen, held it to his lips, and scanned the rear of his formation. There, on the sun-beamed trail, sat his gun team.

Selection for the gun team on a combat patrol was an honor nobody wanted. Heavy and relentless, the gun was the deadliest weapon system on patrol. It would remind the gunner of that fact through a ceaseless application of pain.

Curtis, a man of nineteen years, knelt behind the thing referred to as the Beast or the Pig. An ancient device, placed into service a hundred years ago, the Beast had two characteristics: loud and heavy. A short belt of ammunition hung from the chamber.

The worn-out, sweat-soaked gunner viewed the world through dark eyes. The only thing he can remember is that he is not yet finished and that he has many more miles to go. With every step, the Pig reminds him to feel honored.

Maggie stood next to Curtis; she was his ammo bearer. She hunched under the weight of a ruck bulging with linked 7.62-millimeter rounds. The heavy tripod for the machine gun sat on top. Having languished under the ruck for days, she patrolled without fear or tactical awareness. The straps burned into her shoulders, and the weight compressed her spine. She didn't care about anything but her own misery. As if she'd discovered a torment novel in its nature.

Daniel narrowed his eyes and spit. He delivered a short, sharp whistle. Curtis lifted his head. Maggie didn't bother.

Daniel motioned them forward, and Curtis stood with a grunt. He lifted the gun across his shoulder and moved out. Maggie followed like a suffering mouse, legs trembling. She negotiated the uneven terrain with weary steps.

It had been a decade since he'd seen the girl. She was six years old when he'd shut her into a smuggling compartment in the bed of a plumbing truck. Her eyes were ripe with tears as she clung to his arm. Fear creased her face as she recognized his betrayal.

Inside Daniel, all the normal machinery was done for, the gears stripped and useless. He couldn't see her in front of him, the need of the girl. He lost the capability of caring. He'd made a tactical decision.

Maggie would be safe where she was going. She'd grow up in a world of safety and predictability. The girl would sleep in beds, ride in cars, go to school, and make friends.

There was no place for her where he was going. What he planned was retribution, ruthless and inhuman. He did not bother about dying in the pursuit of it. It would claim every piece of him. There was no time for the girl. There was no place for the girl. Yet, once the sun had fallen on the hills, she sat before him, having returned from her careful exile.

She stayed busy, arranging and rearranging the belts of ammunition. She cleared debris, twigs, and pine needles from the links. She organized them so the beast could be fed when the time came. She did this with a nervousness that annoyed Daniel. "How long you gonna do that?" His voice was low and grumbling, out of the darkness behind her.

"I just want to make sure it's right."

"It's right. Stop fuckin' with it."

Curtis smiled and shook his head. He sat behind the gun, mounted on the tripod, and surveyed the land below him. A steep slope led to a paved road that ran toward his gun and then bent at ninety degrees to the right, one hundred meters below. "What's your left limit?" Daniel asked him.

"The funky tree off that rock." Curtis pointed to illustrate.

Daniel agreed. "When this thing kicks off, make sure you lean into it. Just like you been taught. That pig'll jump up on ya."

"Yes sir."

"Watch your rounds. Make 'em count."

"Yes sir."

Daniel's tone was laid back and easy, as if he were giving directions to a grocery store.

Maggie said, "Will we be able to hit them all from here?"

Curtis shook his head again and chuckled. He kept to minding his own business with the gun.

"Why in the hell would we set up here, if we couldn't hit 'em all?" Daniel was losing patience with the girl.

Maggie's voice grew tight with strain. "Alright. After it's over—"

"You should know the plan. Why don't you work on bein' quiet?"

Maggie turned her head and stared at the ground. Her shoulders shot high with tension, noticeable even in the darkening day.

It had been two weeks since she showed up with a supply run, orders in hand from Command. She had been assigned to Daniel's group. After he'd attempted to persuade her to return to her civilian life and she refused, he'd taken advantage of every opportunity to isolate and aggravate the girl. She would regret her decision. He'd made a bet with himself that he could break her.

Her frustration radiated in the darkness and he was satisfied with his progress.

After a slow and silent time, the groaning of a 6.7-liter turbo diesel engine filled the valley, interrupting the stillness of the deep, bright night. The moon was in its first quarter waxing; the growing white hump of it splashed the road with light enough to distinguish individual rocks alongside it.

During the mission's planning phase, they analyzed and considered the level of illumination, the size and weight of the lead vehicle, and the gradient of the hill. The truck would struggle to maintain its patrol speed while dealing with the incline and sharp turns of the road. This placed the convoy in a precarious position, making it vulnerable to attack.

Daniel sat up and moved to Curtis. They did not speak. The engine grew louder, and its echo bounced around the valley. Daniel lifted a handheld radio to his mouth and pressed a button. "On me."

"Roger." Carl acknowledged the order.

The plan called for the gun to initiate the ambush. Daniel would study the advancing convoy, determine if the target was viable, and when it reached its most vulnerable position within the kill zone.

Vehicles rounded the corner some two hundred meters away. Daniel viewed them in night vision mode through his digitized reticles. In a bath of green light, the device distinguished the type, the distance, and the speed.

A large, armored truck was in the lead. A man sat behind a mounted pulse gun in a turret. Following, two armored SUVs. They were running "lights out" under their night vision systems. A defensive posture to prevent the enemy from seeing their headlamps—on a night with a nearly full moon, it was a waste of time.

Daniel studied the vehicles. His intel had been correct. It was a small, nearly undefended convoy of a low-command element. He spoke into the radio again, "This is a go. I'll kick it off. Have Mushy hit the lead vic with the rocket."

"Roger," Carl flatly responded.

The loud, bulky truck continued to approach. Curtis leaned into the butt stock, steadied his breathing. Maggie stuffed cotton balls into her ears. She picked up the belt of ammunition with trembling hands.

A few more feet and Daniel was satisfied. The armored vehicle was short of the bend in the road. He squeezed Curtis' shoulder. He shouted, "Now!"

Curtis opened up, unleashing a furiously loud series of explosions that shocked the valley walls. Orange flame spewed from the muzzle, and the tracers strung out and down toward the convoy. Every sixth round was illuminated—a combination of strontium and magnesium created a dotted, orange line. The trace lifted over the top of the lead vehicle.

Daniel leaned in. "Get 'em down! Get 'em down!"

Curtis adjusted, ushering another strand onto the armored truck. This burst found its mark. The rounds splashed across the truck's top, exploding in sparks and dismantling the man behind the gun.

There was a crack of light, followed by the smoke-white trace of a rocket from the ambush line. The warhead smashed into the armored vehicle, penetrating the hull. The flames flashed throughout the truck's cabin, which rolled to a stop within a few feet.

"Shift fire to the SUVs!" Daniel screamed at Curtis.

Little flickers of orange and white crackled as the ambush line fired on the SUVs. Their armored bodies spangled with impacts, resisting the onslaught.

Several men spilled from the middle truck, a desperate miscalculation. This must have been the command element, overwhelmed and making stupid decisions, unaccustomed to the heat of enemy fire. They tried to flee the kill zone on foot and found themselves in the bright, naked night.

"Traverse right!"

Daniel pointed, but Curtis had already unspooled his flailing, orange rope into their midst. Some of the men fell and crawled. He dropped clusters of steel into them, methodical as an accountant balancing transactions. Once short of moving targets, he raked the fallen again, as he was taught. A gunner suffers under the Beast and so becomes one as allowed—payment for his efforts.

The killing unfolded, as orchestrated, before Daniel. His face was a tangle of twitching fury. As each man fell, he leaned forward, almost groaning. He had spent an eternity of days and nights in this war, buoyed by hate. These moments were sanctifying.

He still awoke, remembering the horror of finding his wife in the grass—what they had done to her. With every breath, he sought vengeance. *This is what you get, motherfuckers.*

Another rocket fired from the assault line, into the last SUV, splitting it in half. Shards of metal and glass ripped the sky in all directions. The heavy chassis flipped in separate parts into the opposing ditch. The fuel tank erupted and soaked the chert rock bank with persistent fire.

Daniel lifted his radio. "Cease fire. Cease fire."

Along the ambush line, Carl echoed his order. "Cease fire!"

Daniel allowed the world to be silent for a moment. The suffering on the road beneath lilted up to his ears.

Carl interrupted. "Mags!"

The fighters on the ambush line reloaded their weapons. Carl moved among the men and collected information. He yelled to Daniel, "We're up."

Daniel stood and raised the radio. He spoke with a quiet calm. "Assault."

Carl echoed the command with a yell, and his men stood and maneuvered toward the kill zone. They moved orderly and stayed online, conscious of each other's location and careful with their weapons. They were well-trained boys.

Daniel tapped Curtis's shoulder and pointed away from the trucks toward the road as it continued past the curve. "Move the gun. Cover that road. Anybody approaches, light 'em the fuck up."

"Yes sir." Curtis did as he was told.

Maggie fumbled with the ammunition belts, but Daniel grabbed her. He said, "You're with me." His voice like a bag of rocks. He grabbed his pack and slid down the slope.

She picked up her long gun and stumbled after him. The angle was steep but negotiable. Maggie sat on her rear and did as her father did. She slid behind him, approaching the road.

In the ditch, on the near side of the kill zone, Daniel caught Maggie's eyes and unclipped a sawed-off shotgun from under his pack. He cracked the breech and loaded two twelve-gauge buckshot rounds. He sealed it, gazing through her as if he were looking at some remote goal in the smoke-filled darkness only known to him. "Carl, you up?"

"Up!"

"Wait here," he said.

His eyes, to her, were terrible. She nodded and opened her mouth to speak but changed her mind at the sight of them.

He skulked away into the acrid smoke, a force of darkness soaking up the moonlight around him.

Next to her were the remnants of the armored vehicle. The back hatch lay open, and a charred arm dangled—a failed escape. Maggie imagined the man inside, taken by flame for no reason. His death served no purpose, righted no wrong. It was pointless.

She winced, then the smell of it hit her amidst the generalized odors of death: burnt rubber, gun smoke, charred flesh. She squatted, the assaulters on the other side of the road. She was isolated, walled off in the smoky night.

Carl spotted Daniel heading toward him, crouched, shotgun cradled. He'd seen him like this before and anticipated what was coming. He blinked and shook his head, trying to convince his boss to consider some options. "We got two left alive. One of 'em's pretty fucked up. The other we might be able to—"

"Let me see."

Carl glanced at the shotgun. *It was going to go that way.* He turned and led Daniel into the wood line past the torn bodies.

They passed two of Carl's fighters, who were rifling through the pockets and packs of the slain men, collecting intelligence. They wore heavy rubber gloves up to their elbows to insulate them from the gore. Another pair moved behind them, rounding up weapons into a long duffel, ammunition into a separate bag.

<----- • • ----->

In the tree line, two soldiers lay stripped of their equipment and under guard. One shuttered when he drew wind and wheezed in the effort, the results of a jagged hole in his chest. The other, leg shot; judging by the size and type of damage, perpetrated by Curtis's Beast. The shattered bone broke through the skin. Someone had applied a tourniquet.

He rocked side to side, held back tears, and pleaded to the night sky. No one would meet his eyes. Silent, dark murderers were all around him, watching him die. He scanned up to Daniel, who met his gaze and held it.

Daniel asked him, "What is your unit? How many men?"

By his reaction, he knew who and what Daniel was: *the Monster in the Hills*. He wept. "Please."

"Unit. Number of men." The words were a

placeholder, preliminary to the inevitable. Daniel's thumb was already blanched against the exposed hammers of the shotgun. He applied steady pressure, drawing the hammers back and eliciting the distinctive clicks.

The soldier's eyes filled with dread. "Please. I just —" He gasped as the shotgun was placed against his comrade's forehead.

Daniel buried his face into the crook of his elbow and pulled the dual triggers.

The resultant mess—blood and bone—flowered the soldier. Stunned, he blinked and moaned in a low voice. His hands fumbled at the grisly brew on his face.

"Jesus. Gimme a heads-up, at least." Carl keyed up his radio. "Hold your positions. We're good. That was an internal shot."

Daniel reloaded. "Settle down," he said to Carl over his shoulder. His eyes bore into the remaining prisoner as the barrels rested against his leg. He asked again without words.

The soldier released any claim he had to life. His shoulders sagged, and his body trembled, jolting his breath—stilted utterances of dry air.

Daniel covered his face again and pulled the triggers, nearly severing the man's leg. The shot captured the femoral artery, and hot blood rushed into the dirt.

The soldier screamed and rolled over onto his side. He reached down with his hand, feebly trying to aid himself. The spigot refused to slow.

Exasperated, Carl said, "We mighta got somethin' from—"

"He was a private. He didn't know shit."

The man whimpered and leaked into the dirt.

Daniel lost interest. He turned to Carl. "You worried about that *thing*? You need to worry about the mission. Get us off the X." He moved back into the smoke.

Carl sneered. "Let's go! Let's go! Rally point!"

◄─────••─────►

Daniel approached Maggie through the vehicles. The stinging smoke broke away and wrapped itself along his shoulders and back, trailing him, an orange vapor in the flames. She focused on his eyes, seeking some commonality or connection.

"What was that? What did you do?"

Daniel trudged past her, silent, his face dark. He watched his step under the hazy moonlight, content in his own thoughts until he had climbed several feet. He turned to her. "You comin'?"

On the radio, Carl called out, "Internal shot."

A single rifle shot cracked off on the far side of the road, behind the vehicles, through the smoke.

Maggie stood, hesitated, and gazed upon her father in disbelief.

The soldiers spilled past her from the opposite side of the kill zone. They hustled over the ditch and up the hillside, heading to a designated point, efficient and trained. She filed in behind them and worked her way up the hill.

It had been nearly six hours since the ambush, and they had not stopped moving. The patrol toiled up a steep incline.

In fact, if a patrol did anything with more regularity than toiled, I wouldn't have the slightest idea what that would be.

Shafts of early morning sun crackled through black spruce branches. Body heat rose in waves off their necks. Their eyes told a miserable story: sleep-deprived and suffering.

The incline was sharp. Daniel slipped to the back of the column and waited on his slow-moving gun team. Maggie and Curtis, having fallen so far behind, were in danger of separating from the group.

She dragged her boots and stumbled over rocks, her load equal to her body weight. Staring at the ground in front of her feet, she was lost in the delirium. This was not uncommon for long-range events. Nonetheless, it was a sign that the patrol needed to slow down.

Daniel grabbed the radio. "Carl, let's do ten."

After a slight delay, Carl responded between breaths, "Sounds good. This leg is a bitch."

"Yep." Daniel tilted his head and studied Maggie. "Take ten, you two."

"Yessir." Curtis stood still.

"Curtis. Take that load off, get your feet up."

"Afraid I might not get back up, sir."

Daniel laughed. "Life a' the gunner, man. Life a' the gunner."

The color had drained out of Maggie's face, into her boots, and she was angry. She dropped the ruck onto the ground with a thud. Near tears, she choked them down at the sight of her father's eyes. She pulled a canteen, glared at Daniel, then sat on the ruck and faced away from him.

Her shoulders slumped; he could see her heartbeat through her thin frame. The wet shirt clung to her narrow back.

Until a couple of weeks ago, she lived in a cul-de-sac.

Now she sleeps in ditches and shits in holes. Why is she here?

He pulled his canteen, tilted it, and dragged the sloshing contents from the bottom.

◄──••──►

The patrol plodded toward Hillcamp. They passed a line of wire through layers of booby-trapped footpaths. The last steps of a patrol were always the worst. The joints burned and the blisters cracked open, letting the fresh meat beneath rub against the soles of the boots. They stood tall and leaned against it, proving to themselves and their comrades they were up to it because, in the end, this was all that mattered. Could you do it? Could you be counted on when it got shitty?

The camp was buried underneath a thick canopy of spruce, marked by mounds of dirt on the perimeter. Each mound connected to a fighting position, covered in pine straw and branches. They served as subterranean quarters. The doors were made of braided saplings woven together with Virginia creeper.

Unencumbered by gear, young men from the camp approached and mingled into the patrol as it re-entered the wire. Their exhaustion gave way to laughter. There was the customary retelling of patrol stories—*Somebody fell in a hole... Somebody shit himself*—that kind of thing.

They passed around mason jars filled with clear, glinting moonshine. Glad to be done with it, they laughed to calm themselves, slapped each other's backs, and gripped forearms. The booze warmed them inside and papered over the pain for a moment.

Daniel turned to Curtis and Maggie. "Go to your hole. Get some chow. Clean your weapons. Grab some rack."

"Yessir." Curtis didn't wait around. He moved like an old man, the Pig bending him into a stooped shuffle.

Maggie stood as tall as possible under her burden. The edges of her eyes and mouth were tight and downturned.

"You got somethin' to say?" Daniel looked down his nose at her.

"Those two soldiers back there..." She hesitated.

"So, what they say, what I always heard is true?"

"Don't know what they say." He lied. "Don't care either. You're lookin' for sunshine in the shade, girl. Need to go look somewhere else."

He turned and left her to languish.

She held him in her eyes as he walked away. Her body revolted in tremors. She wanted to say more to him but limped toward her hole instead.

◂─────•●•─────▸

Daniel knelt beside a trough. Clear water flowed from a pump over his hands. The reddish-brown stains of the recent exertions spilled into the basin, filling it with cloudy trail residue. He paused a moment, took stock of his odor, and wrinkled his face. He pulled his shirt free and dunked it in the waiting trough. The water turned red and surrounded his fingers up to his elbows.

He pulled the shirt out and ringed it. He studied his pants and found speckles of flesh. Dark, crimson prills dotted the fabric. He stood and loosened his belt, dropped the pants into the receptacle, and cranked the pump with a fury. The water receded. He scrubbed the pants against a washboard.

He was naked in the daylight, working the gore away.

◂─────•●•─────▸

Daniel sat at a small, rough-hewn table inside his dwelling. An oil lamp burned at his feet, casting angular shadows across his face. Saplings were lashed and interwoven with fern and mud, buttressed by a heavy, jointed mesh of timbers, creating the roof. The floor was natural clay. Along the walls, an assortment of weaponry leaned in their places, oiled and ready. A small, ruggedized computer sat in a corner, and a field phone rested on its large, green receiver. A heavy nylon cable ran up the slate rock steps from the phone, disappearing under the thatched door.

He ate a steaming meal of root vegetables and a chicken leg. He chuckled at Rhett, sitting on a small, rough stool—a hulk with a beard, overgrown and unkempt to a comical degree. He sat quietly and smiled like a friend. He leaned to his right. A bullet had claimed his left buttock, causing him to shy from the point of his hip.

Daniel recalled the day Rhett lost half his ass. He'd dragged him from the middle of an ambush, lifting him over his shoulder. He fell twice before Rhett screamed, "I can run. Leave me be, Daniel." Then, they ran out of the kill zone together—Rhett with a hitch in his step, explained by having half an ass. This memory, shared between them, like most of these terrible things, was humorous now.

"Heard it went well." Rhett smiled.

"Went okay, I guess," Daniel said.

"That walk back wasn't no fun. Was it, old man?"

Daniel swallowed and grinned at the question. "Well, to tell the truth—I feel like a sack a' smashed assholes."

Rhett laughed at that. "You suppose you're gonna be done with all this someday?"

"Suppose I will."

"You factor you'll be alive for your retirement party, or—"

Daniel interrupted, "I don't do much factorin' on the future. I can come up with at least a dozen better ways to waste my time."

Rhett agreed with a beaming smile. "Well, factor this… John's here."

Daniel's face pinched in like the chicken leg suddenly spoiled. "What? What for?"

Rhett shrugged. "Don't know. Must be important though, if he's gonna give up his bed and hot shower, come all this way."

Daniel sneered at his food and dropped the chicken leg onto the plate. "That fuckin' guy."

Rhett twisted his face with curiosity. "Look, brother, I know you hate him. You've never been shy about that, but you think it might be time to let that shit go?"

"I still draw breath."

"Come on, Daniel. He's almost as much of a legend as you are." Rhett smiled to himself when he said it, a knowing smile like he was poking fun.

Daniel sat the uneaten food on the table and wiped the grease on his pants. "He's a fuckin' bureaucrat, which means he's useless. Also means he looks out for himself over everybody else."

Rhett interjected, "He's got hundreds of ops under his belt. He pulled his hitch. Now, he's outta the field… *promoted*. Maybe you ought to think about it."

Daniel eyed him hard. Somewhere, deep in, he winced at the comment. He brought Rhett into the field and taught him everything he knew.

Big, dumb, fuck.

"You think I'm done?"

Rhett shook his head and smiled. It was one thing to think it, and another thing to tell Daniel to his face. "We all gotta be done someday." He leaned back and waved his hands like shooing a fly. There wasn't much point, but he said it anyway. "You're still good. Someday you won't be anymore, you'll zig when you shoulda zagged and that'll be the end of it."

"Then," Daniel said with some steam brewing in his eyes. "That'll be the end of it, I guess."

"I guess." Rhett passed Daniel a toothy grin. "You know they'll be runnin' up and down these hills long after your old knees are shot to pieces. It's like every trigger you ever pulled didn't happen."

"Well, why don't you take off, thinkin' like that?"

Rhett raised his voice. "I'm thinkin' the way you taught me to think. Remember? 'Don't lie about what's coming.' How many times have you told me that?"

Daniel was quiet for a moment. Regaining his appetite, he picked up the plate. A smile slid across his face. "I understand it if you have to go, Rhett."

Rhett stood and crouched to the entrance of the hole. He was resigned to the fate of Daniel. The man would never stop. "John wants to see us later. You good? Need anything?"

Daniel did not turn. He grinned and spoke with his mouth full. "I appreciate the concern."

Rhett stopped at the door, shoulders sagged. "Get some rest, brother."

Daniel shrugged and dealt with the chicken leg. Rhett opened the door and climbed the short steps.

◄———••———►

The hole was full, packed to capacity. Rhett and half the company, shoulder to shoulder, lined the walls of the cramped compartment. Daniel leaned back in a rough-hewn chair, arms crossed. He eyeballed his visitor with a tense, doubtful glare.

Across from him, a low table between them, John sat hunched forward. He looked the worse for the wear, with a short, gray beard and sagging lines on his face. He smiled at Daniel, acknowledging the tension, accepting the unease of the situation and seeking to drain some of it away.

John was the odd man, everyone fit and ready, except him. The paunch of retirement hung heavy over his leather belt. His eyes were hollowed with exhaustion. He had hung up his patrolling boots long ago, yet here he sat in the middle of the hills. The ashy skin on his face told the story—way too much comfort in his life nowadays.

There was a reason for John to be sitting in that seat. The trek was long and difficult. Daniel's questions were always the same with the higher-ups: *What did they want, and how much would it cut into his operations?*

"Glad you could see me, Daniel." John tried to be professional. He turned to the assembled insurgents and understood their presence, the power on display.

"Don't got any choice, now do I? You come all the way out here. What do you want?"

John made a show of looking over his shoulder at the assembled men. "You think we can do this in private?"

Daniel laughed. "You got something delicate to talk about? You gonna fire me?"

"Of course not. Why can't we just—"

"Why can't you just tell me what you want?"

Daniel enjoyed the upper hand. This was not Greensboro or Charlotte. This was not some urbanized outfit where John's word carried water. He was in the sticks and standing on ground to which he had no claim outside his rank. The people who put stock in that were very far away.

John straightened in his chair, took in some air, and held it. He worked at controlling his temper. "Alright." He smiled like a politician. "Alright. We have something coming up, and we need your help."

"In my AO?"

"No, Newbern."

Daniel rolled his eyes. "Sounds like Newbern's problem."

"They can't handle this."

"Don't know what to tell ya. We just came off a mission. Out for a week. Need to rest, recover, refit

—"

"I'm not asking you, Daniel."

Daniel made a slight move, near imperceptible, and was towering forward. The table between them became all the tinier. The veins in his neck engorged. His eyes narrowed. "You think 'cause you walked out here, I'm more likely to do you a favor?"

"I think—" John didn't shy from it. He leaned in as well. His ashen face filled with color. "I think you know good and well there's a chain of command. I follow it, just like you follow it. And while it's true we give you a lot of leeway on your missions, we are the ones who resupply you. So, keep fucking with me and see how long you last without beans or bullets."

John leaned back and swallowed some of the stale air. Talking this way to a man like Daniel in front of his men was risky, and it showed in his eyes.

Daniel calculated the threat. It was an effective ultimatum. No matter the disdain he held for John or the rest of the city dwellers, he would dry up and die if his supply lines were cut. Dealing with higher-ups was always a game of pushing the line farther until you'd pushed it too far.

He broke the silence with a nod. "What do you need from me?"

Some of the tension drained from John's cheeks. Gamesmanship with a lunatic has specific perils. He grinned. "An HVT is doing a facility visit outside of Newbern in a few days. I want you to lead a specialist in—"

"You talkin' about that little guy?" Daniel pointed

over John's shoulder.

A thin, handsome Latino kid was crammed into the midst of Daniel's men. He smiled upon being recognized—the type of smile that worked hard to win you over. A young face, he carried himself with a cool air. He ruffled his shoulders forward through the crush of fighters lined against the wall.

"Yeah. That's Rudy. He's the specialist."

"What is he, fifteen?" Daniel studied Rudy with a wagging disapproval.

"Nineteen." Rudy's smile beamed across the hole, nearly eradicating the mood's darkness.

Daniel canted his head, skeptical. He shared his doubts with John.

"He's good. He's been running since he was twelve. He trained out in Colorado with Bathgate."

"What's he so *special* at?"

"Sniper, demo, psychotropics."

"Psychotropics?" Daniel sneered at Rudy. "You gonna party with him, son?"

"No, but I can mess with his head pretty hard if he becomes some sort of a problem. Depending on what you want, of course." Rudy tilted his head to Daniel, a show of respect.

"Of course." Daniel re-engaged John. "Who is this HVT? Why's he too big for Newbern?"

A grin crawled across John's cracked face. The room was impatient but silent. "It's Brue Carnell."

He let it sit, allowing for its impact. Everyone in the hole knew the name, the architect of the future, the new age conjurer. The abuse and the atrocities had been attributed to him, whether he deserved the responsibility or not. Brue Carnell was one of many who the mountain people would bleed out given the chance and then dance around a fire to celebrate.

Daniel sneered. "What's a guy like that doin' in Newbern?"

"Like I said, facility visit."

"What kinda facility?"

It was tiresome for John to have his intel called into question, a fact of which Daniel was well aware. If he could bug John and make his time unpleasant, he would do it.

"It's R and D for the Skins. It has something to do with a new line."

"New line? They been tryin' that shit forever. Still got these half-bred idiots runnin' around out here."

"Well, apparently they're getting better at it, because—"

"How do you know?"

"I have guys on the inside—contractors."

The thought of a mission relying on people who were already traitors didn't sit well with Daniel. He shook his head, another piece of the puzzle. He didn't like the picture it was making.

John sensed it. "I know your disdain for contractors, but these guys are solid. You have to trust me on this, Daniel."

"Trust you?" Daniel curled his mouth.

John averted his eyes. There was an ancient wound between the two men, a topic he was unwilling to broach.

"If I do this, it's *my* mission. I make the calls. Got it?"

"Of course, that's why I came out here. Only one thing needs to be understood before we move forward." John waited for Daniel to ask, but he received a nonchalant glare instead. "Alright. When we take this guy, absolutely under no circumstances whatsoever are you to lay a hand on him. Do you understand?"

"What are you worried about?"

"You're cold-hearted, Daniel, more than anyone I've ever seen or heard of. That's what I'm worried about. We have a plan for him and it's going to accomplish a hell of a lot. Certainly more than you getting your rocks off bleeding him out in the dirt."

"Don't worry about it." The conversation over, Daniel waved the masses, including John, out of his dwelling.

"I need to hear you say it." John crossed his arms and refused to move.

"How about I say *fuck off*?"

John studied Daniel's face with interest, then spoke his mind. "You know, when Maggie asked to come out here, we debated it vigorously."

"Did ya now?" Daniel became even in his tone. His eyes went flat.

"We did. Some thought she might help *domesticate* you, in a sense."

Daniel smiled. "And I suppose you voted in favor?"

John shrugged. "Why keep a girl from her Daddy?"

Daniel reached into his boot and pulled a small

flask. He twisted it open, took his time, and pulled a long drag. Once finished, he offered it to John, who took it and tilted it back.

He pulled it from his lips with disgust. "Jesus, what is that shit?"

Cool as the wind, Daniel said, "Appalachian stump brew."

John coughed, wanting to scrape the substance from his tongue. It burned behind his lungs as it crawled down his throat.

John had outplayed him. Maggie was an intentional Achilles heel, sent out to weaken his position. Daniel had been a thorn in the side of the higher-ups for a long time, and he knew it well. Her presence created vulnerability.

Daniel smiled. "I'll take the night to toss it around. Let you know tomorrow."

John handed the flask back. "This isn't a request."

"Look around. I don't see nothin' but you and that skinny kid."

Daniel eyed him with contempt as if he were looking for a reason to do something drastic. Years of resentment bubbled in his mind. He leaned forward, ready to go whichever way John called it.

John scanned the faces of the young men. Their allegiance was unquestioned. He had overcorrected in his effort to ensure guarantees from Daniel and played his hand a little too hard. "Alright. Let's talk tomorrow."

Maggie sat on the floor of her dwelling, a wool blanket covering the hard clay. The meeting at Daniel's was ongoing, and she had obstinately decided to clean her weapon. Unnecessary because she'd not been invited to the meeting and neither had Curtis, which was fine by him. He slept on his side, a blanket pulled over his head.

She worked at cleaning her rifle. She'd pulled the takedown pin and shot-gunned the upper receiver. The bolt assembly was spread out on an oilcloth. She rubbed lubricant onto the parts and scrubbed some invisible carbon loose.

Curtis stirred as Maggie slammed the lower receiver onto her sleeping mat. He pulled the blanket down, his eyes squinting in the small light of the lantern. "Whatchu doin'?"

"What's it look like?"

"Dude. It feels like we walked a thousand miles. Get some sleep, weirdo. You didn't even shoot the damn thing." He pulled the blanket back over his face, done with the madness.

Maggie scrubbed, ignoring him. The events at the ambush gnawed at her. The exhaustion and pain from the patrol only served to amplify her disposition. Her father, who'd loomed in her mind since her earliest memories, had been a steady disruption to her happiness, to the alleged normalcy of her life.

The civilians she'd grown up around tossed about this image of him—a monster. In her early childhood, they were careful not to speak about him in her presence. Then his legend grew, and the stories became more outlandish, grotesque, and mindlessly violent. They looked at her with pity in their eyes and treated her with cautious kindness. She'd been raised among them, never truly fitting in. She was an orphan from a different tribe.

A foolish idea took root in her fifteen-year-old mind. She would discover the truth about her father and clear up the misunderstandings. She was driven to contact him with a relentlessness that John and the other commanders found challenging to ignore.

They told her: *This is a bad idea. You should stay where you are.* Finishing her sophomore year, she had nearly made a friend or two. *Who knows, maybe you'll forget about him and move on with your life.* This was the core of their argument.

She smirked a little at the memory of those old men, thinking they were allowed to decide what was best for her. She had a plan, and she knew in her bones it was going to work.

What Daniel did at the ambush, or what she suspected he did, wrecked that plan and her chance to sleep. It reinforced the whispers she'd heard as a child and the silent recriminations she'd faced among the decent people. It made clear that every time someone passed judgment on her and her family, on the very blood beating through her veins, the anger she felt was, in fact, misplaced.

She deserved the isolation and the doubt she received from the civilians. The legends weren't simply words or stories. They were true. Daniel *was* a monster, and they had every right to keep her at arm's distance.

She asked, "Is it always like that?"

"What?" Curtis spoke from under his blanket.

"The missions."

"Well, no. Sometimes you sit there for a couple days, and nothin' happens. Freeze your ass off, and you don't hear shit but your guts growlin'. Then you traipse on back here."

"That's not what I mean. Does he..." She thought about it and worried over the recklessness of the question. "Does he always murder them?"

She had his attention now. He sat up, smirking.

"Murder? Are you sure you understand what's goin' on out here? It's called a war. And fuck them, anyway."

"Doesn't matter what you call it. He murdered them."

"I personally don't care what he does." Curtis laid back down. "Long as he keeps me alive. And for your information, he's pretty good at that. I ain't dead yet. Probably ought to be, but I ain't."

Maggie reassembled her weapon with trembling anger. She clamped the thing shut and reset the pin. The gun was placed on her sleeping mat. She made her way to the steps and headed outside.

It was ink-black in the early night. The thick canopy overhead muted any potential starlight.

Once the braided sapling door was shut, burying the dim, orange glow of her quarters, she could see nothing. She was night blind.

She stood still, waiting for her eyes to adjust. Irritation had taken hold of her and, along with it, impatience. The more she thought about her *mission* in the hills, the more foolish she felt. She didn't want to admit or own up to her miscalculation.

In the last days of her exile, she'd taken to arguing with anyone who dared to engage. She'd become downright unpleasant. She told them they were wrong about her father. Those were stories. They were lies. She became overbearing. Yet they still tolerated her and cared for her needs. But they walled her off, away from their circles of trust, all but reinforcing her isolation and anger.

When they told her to let go of ever seeing Daniel, she developed a pigheadedness, which they ultimately conceded to, stating that there was no separating her from the person she very clearly resembled in temperament and patience.

She saw it in their eyes and heard it in their tone. She would prove them wrong. It became an obsession.

Her eyes were not yet adjusted to the light, but she took an unsteady step nonetheless.

"Give your eyes time to adjust," Daniel said in a low and condescending tone.

Maggie, startled, said, "Shit!"

She took another step and rolled her foot over a large stone, then recovered her balance. "I did."

"Is that why you didn't see me standin' three feet from ya?" It was more of an accusation than a question.

Maggie had worked herself into a deep anger over the preceding hours. The thought of Daniel correcting her was a hot poker in the guts. "I get your point. What do you want?"

"I think it's time for you to go back to Raleigh. You don't belong out here. You know that now."

There was a fair touch of relief in his voice, as if he'd been waiting for the right moment to say it. Now, she'd seen its brutality, heard, and smelled it. She'd feel alienated. He spoke like he was doing her a favor, as if the timing lined up with some internal clock.

"What if I don't give a shit what you think?"

Daniel breathed in, reached forward, and grabbed Maggie's collar. He pulled her close to his face and whispered in a husky, angry tone, "You better watch your mouth. This ain't your little neighborhood. I run this place. Bein' my daughter don't mean shit—"

Maggie shoved his hands away. "Oh really?" Her eyes filled up in mock surprise. "You think that's a mystery to me? That you don't give a damn about me?"

Who is this bastard, to stuff me in a hole and forget about me?

Daniel released her collar like it was on fire. He stumbled like a fighter, shocked with a right hand, and languished momentarily on the ropes. He fumbled his words. "Not that—I didn't mean—"

"No delusions, here. I know where I stand."

"That's not how I meant it. I meant—"

"I know what you meant. For your information, I don't care what you think." Her voice increased in volume, animated like raging flood waters after an upriver dam had broken. "Did you know I was passed around from family to family? Huh?"

Growing now, the bitterness, biting into every word.

In the dark, Daniel could see her face, its indignation. He pulled his eyes away from her to the black canopy undulating in the evening breeze. "Those were all good people. I knew where you was, and who you's with."

"You know what it's like being your daughter? All the things they said—"

"Fuck this." Daniel turned and walked away.

Maggie caught up with him, spitting whispered venom at his back. "Talking about all the people you killed—women and children—like a wild dog."

Daniel didn't turn to her; he leaned into his retreat.

"People lookin' at me. Wondering if I'm a psycho, like my old man."

He didn't grab her collar this time. As he wheeled on her, his hand was out, an empty vice. He scooped her throat into it and pulled her close.

Maggie's face twitched. For a moment, she couldn't breathe. She pried at his thick fingers. His features were lowered in the darkness, the light scattered on his forehead, and his eyes sunk into an abyss. She thought it possible she might die for a moment.

Then, he released her. She wobbled a step back, holding her throat, stroking her windpipe.

He hid his eyes again, the light now shining down into the holes of him, and he was hurt and confused. He breathed in puffs through his nostrils, forcing it back inside.

"You wanna stay out here?"

Maggie nodded, as defiant as she had ever been. The pain from his hand on her throat was nothing. She'd been preparing for worse than that as long as she could remember.

"Then you do what I say when I say it. I don't want to hear a fuckin' word outta you till I say you can talk, you got that?"

She nodded again, the fear leaving her eyes.

Daniel checked over his shoulders, spinning his head about to see if anyone had witnessed his unraveling. He took a deep breath and stomped away to his hole.

Maggie rubbed her throat. The dim, orange glow of his quarters disappeared as the door closed and the blackness of Hillcamp was restored.

She stood in the dull night air, wrangling with the memory of Daniel's face when he'd pushed her into the hidden compartment of the truck and the image of his confused eyes moments ago. She saw something in there—her chance. She became, once again, obsessed with her plan.

She turned back to her dwelling now that her eyes

had adjusted, able to see the ground before her.

The sun broke through in slats of light. Near the water trough, young men huddled, taking turns scrubbing their clothes. They passed the time the way young men would: harshly joking at the expense of each other and laughing at their compatriots' minor misfortunes. Rough pecking orders had long since been established, an ongoing activity since the beginning of time.

Two younger ones had settled a dispute with a crisp and decisive fistfight. One had decided to challenge the order. He sat outside the group now, bloodied and reconsidering his choices. The winner washed his knuckles under the pump, receiving congratulations as he chatted off the adrenaline.

The morning was brisk, and the fog from their breaths flittered about their heads. Their mood beneath the wavy boughs was unwithered.

Below, in a tight, subterranean space, two young men sat before a table. On top was an array of ruggedized laptop computers. The computers were made of thick, shockproof plastic, with rubber gaskets coating any openings. They were attached to heavy cables that ran up the slate steps and out of the hole.

The cables ran two kilometers and were attached

to the base station of a tactical antenna array. The field antenna was camouflaged and masked against detection in the RF spectrum.

Between the men, a dark, heavy phone rested on the bench. It was hand-cranked and also connected to a heavy nylon cable. The phone was a relic —so old that communications across the camp could not be detected on any modern observation equipment. Hillcamp could detect the air around it, and communicate internally and externally, with the assurance of invisibility.

One of the men leaned forward and wiped his eyes. The pitch of his voice heightened by immediacy, he squeaked, "Holy shit."

Not taking his eyes off the screen, he flailed at his companion, smacking his arm.

"There's a ball comin'. A ball—inbound!"

He reached for the phone, lifted it, and cranked the handle.

His partner flipped a clear plastic cover over a red switch. He reached for it and checked back over his shoulder, unsure.

The man on the phone said, "Flip the damn switch!"

◂————••————▸

Above, the morning revelry was interrupted by three short, concise beeps from small speakers set about the camp. The group grabbed their clothing and dispersed. Their jovial nature all but evaporated. They made for their holes, slipping on the grass and cursing.

Something was headed toward them, and no one wanted to be above ground when it showed up.

◄———•●•———►

The lemon sun sat a hand's width above a dip in the ridgeline. In the areas outside its influence, the low ground, stubborn pockets of mist clung to rocks in shadow like abandoned climbers. If one sat on a clear patch of grass with a view as morning broke, one would not have seen or heard the ball. It required special instruments to detect its presence, and once it was detected, it offered little time to react.

Three thousand feet above the wide valley, with the sun at its back, an orb flew through the brightening sky. It had no apparent means of propulsion and slid through the air. Just over a meter in diameter, it was sleek, gray, and menacing, and it was headed toward Hillcamp.

The craft stopped on a dime and traversed the horizon in a three-sixty circle. As it rotated, sounds emanated: mechanical, digital chirpings. The thing was taking measurements, estimating the impact of atmospheric pressure and glare upon its instruments. It absorbed the hills, and its algorithm challenged the findings: *a binary representation of the horizon, the hills in relief as the instruments probed. Slow and deliberate, the sensors swept rightward until a small heat signature was detected. The image was refined and the signature was enlarged. It detected an indeterminate shape, a subtle movement.*

The orb reinitiated flight. It corrected course for the discovery of the heat signature and started as it stopped, with no apparent wake or propulsive effort.

◀———••—— ——▶

Daniel sat at his small table, quartering an apple with the phone receiver to his ear. He worked hard to appear cool in front of his visitor.

John could not claim as much. He shifted his weight, side to side, on his seat.

The men in the observation unit reported to Daniel through the field phone. He nodded and said, "Uh huh."

John, who leaned toward him and held his palms outward, asked, "What's going on?"

Daniel crunched an apple slice and chewed it for a moment. "Alright, when it hits twenty klicks out, let the hogs loose."

He hung up the receiver and passed John an arrogant look, expecting the question. He saw that the man had been sweating it since the alarm activated. It was a fair amount of fun to watch him squirm.

John tried an uncomfortable smile. "Hogs?"

Daniel talked around the crunching apple. "Similar size and shape profile to a man. If the ball caught somethin' and came to check it out, we'll give it somethin' to look at."

John nodded, flop sweat on his lips. "Hogs. What if it doesn't buy it?"

"Then it's gonna get loud. Real loud."

Daniel popped another chunk of apple in his mouth and went to work on it.

"How much damage can one of them do?"

Daniel's eyes got big. He sighed. "As much as it needs. Fuck us up pretty good. Electromagnetic attacks. Of course, that's not too big a deal for us, but it would knock out our RF soak capability."

"You mean we—"

"Wouldn't be able to see it anymore, yeah. Also, they standard load twenty Pranashi rockets. Fucking twenty of 'em."

"How do they fit—"

"Pranashis are about the diameter of a ten-gauge shotgun shell, maybe five inches long. Punches through armor, airbursts, clusters—pretty much whatever you want it to do. The ball programs 'em based on the target set."

John's skin turned white. He worked to swallow some spit but couldn't manage any.

"Yeah. Pretty much don't wanna be on the wrong side of it." Daniel finished, enjoying John's discomfort. Every word he said was true, but watching a rear-echelon type like John afraid for his life was a great source of entertainment for him.

John pulled his pistol and racked the slide to seat a round in the chamber.

Daniel screwed up his face. "What do you plan on

doin' with that?"

John said, "Look, I've been out of the game for a minute."

"No shit?"

"Fuck off, Daniel."

"Well, you can run out there and shoot it if you want, Doc Holliday. You do outrank me." Daniel chuckled to humiliate him. He could see it worked. John sat there holding his pistol like a jackass.

"I tell you what, why don't you take my mind off it? Why don't you tell me if you're going to take the mission?"

Daniel stared at him, worked another chunk of apple in his mouth, and chewed with a sneer. The phone rang. He picked it up, never losing eye contact with John. "Good copy." He hung the phone up and waited for the question.

"What was that?"

"Hogs are loose."

◂────•●•────▸

The ball rived through the air, above the valley. It calculated and tabulated the data. It made decisions. These things could be controlled remotely, but the bulk of the inventory was set to roam and was operated by internal algorithms. If it were to discover some living thing that did not correspond to a range of signatures, the ball could interdict independently. It did not require permission to engage. Balls were deployed over troubled areas, and it reduced lag time in the approval process. Quite often, a simple hunter, fisherman, or hiker found his or her legs and arms scattered across the top of a ridgeline due to an algorithmic decision made by a floating machine.

Digitized foothills. The frame slid to the left. A heat signature was detected. The camera refined its inputs, and the signature was enlarged. Two hogs meandered down a shallow draw.

<hr />

Daniel finished off the apple. He raked the core and seeds into a bowl. "I'll do your thing. But you gotta do somethin' for me."

John shook his head. "That's not the way this works."

"Near as I can figure it, you don't have an element large enough or capable enough to do this thing. Your timeline's tighter than an altar boy's ass. That's why you came all the way out here. You're hittin' when the dealer's showin' ten." Daniel straightened up, a little proud of himself. "Least that's how I figure it."

John nodded at the not-unexpected gambit from Daniel. He slid his pistol back into its holster, looking a little embarrassed to have pulled it out. He curled his lips into a slight smile. "Alright, what do you want?"

"Take her back to Raleigh when this thing's done."

John, wary of agreeing too soon, cocked his head

to the side, waiting for more.

"Then, cut her loose so she can't ever find you again." Daniel looked away.

John, surprised, said, "Daniel, are you sure Lori would want—"

"Don't you ever mention my wife's name again." Daniel's tone was cold, dead. John winced and nodded.

"Alright. If you're sure this is what you want."

The old phone's electromagnetic speaker shrieked as the caller from the other side of Hillcamp cranked the handle. Daniel lifted the phone to his ear, listened, and nodded. "Good copy." He reset the receiver. "And if you ever involve her in anything again, you're gonna need more than that pistol. Understand?"

"I understand."

Daniel crouched to the slate steps, ascended to the thatched door, held the handle for a moment, turned to John, and said, "The coast is clear."

He pushed the door up and was outside.

TWO

They spoke in those days of the Overman.
Barely conceived, their minds failed the task...
Certainly, they quaked in the shadow of the new day.
. . . an intellection, leaving behind them the ways of old.
—The Dawnbringer's Chronicle

Brue tapped the glass with his impeccable fingernails. They were cured with a resin to strengthen them. It was neither ostentatious nor overbearing. They were clear, orderly, and, most importantly, all the same length, and they would stay that way.

He was a tall, thin man wearing a suit with immaculate lines indicating an uncommon seriousness of character. His face was built out as a wedge, starting from his nose and angling back to his ears. A thick, dark mane of swept hair sat atop his head. His gaze took him out over the Hudson River. He looked down from the ninety-third floor of One World Trade Center.

Behind him was a sleek conference room. A long, glass table occupied the center, on top of frosted glass floors, lighted from beneath. The entire wall of the room before Brue, all fifteen feet of its height, was glass. His eyes were locked on the brownish-green water.

He scanned the Newport Waterfront area. To his left sat Ellis Island, with its last ferry churning away, engorged with humans from across the globe. Above the traditional ferry routes, hovercraft lanes of traffic also carried humans to and from. In the late evening sun, the lights twinkled in constant motion before him.

The room was filled with silent souls whose meekness and patience inferred, if not insignificance, then indeed a secondary nature. Monitors blazed, spread across the top of the long table. Three thousand miles away, the patient faces waited for Brue to speak.

Few in this assembly would have intervened to disrupt the silence. These were mathematicians, biologists, geneticists, and accountants. They were not imbued with adversarial dispositions. They would sit still for as long as it took, waiting for the issue of funding and getting their slice of the pie handed out.

One man in the back of the room, a sandy blond with a mustache handle-barred down his cheeks, didn't seem to harbor such a nature. Affixed to his face was a dedicated smirk. His head was blockish and sat on a thick neck. His shoulders were firm and tall. He leaned back against the wall in his chair, looking the part of a bored teenager. He was the type who would prefer to be almost anywhere, doing nearly anything other than this. The type who despised the tiny rooms filled with 'leaf-eating' chumps. His large, rough hands fiddled into his suit and withdrew a pocket watch, an ancient thing, refurbished. He studied it, placed it back where it belonged, and sighed.

He wasn't going to say anything, either.

Brue tapped the glass. "Pro—" There was detectable motion in the room, a shuffling as he spoke. People pulled themselves back, their minds having drifted to other problems. This pause was something he enjoyed, pulling a crowd to the edge of their seats and making them wait. "—creation."

He turned to the people. They shrank into their seats a little, even on the monitors.

"I'm not talking about the act of it, the copulation. I'm talking about passing another life into this world. *This* world." Their faces were solemn, concerned. "This world which has lost the ability to support them. I'm talking about the rumble in their bellies from a lack of food, the shivering of their bones from the bitterness that descends half the year. Frozen, starving, diseased, dying human beings. That, to me, is the product of the act of procreation."

Brue stepped to the table and picked up a small, flat piece of sculpted glass that came alive with lights as he handled it.

"As you all know, I was tasked with the solution to this problem. I found you all, recruited you all and assigned you commensurate duties based on your skill sets."

He swiped the light board and studied the glass. "Seminal vesicles, functional. Ovarian development." He lifted his head and engaged a young woman with an elastic sensibility. "Fiona, what is the status on One Eight Three?"

Activated like a prim automaton, the woman swiped her light board and began reading. "You are reading the due-outs from One Eight Three, sir. Anticipated alterations in sexual function will be minimal at best."

Brue grumbled and exhaled. "Velshi, cognitive issues?"

A middle-aged African man piped up, his voice blatting the speakers in his monitor. His face was careworn. There was an edge to his tone. "One Eight Three and subsequent series are experiencing the same issues. Reduced critical thought parameters, but improvement in spatial relations..."

Brue, unimpressed with the notes on spatial relations, asked a simple, acerbic question: "Superstitions?" Brue said the word with contempt as if it were a personal preoccupation.

Velshi nodded and sucked a little air before he spoke, knowing he was about to dive into rough waters. "The limbic conditioning has been minimal. We haven't yet been able to isolate and halt the vesicular monoamine transmitter's ability to produce the necessary proteins. Without this, we can't package the neurotransmitters and release the signaling chemicals into the neuronal synapses—"

"Are you trying to piss me off?" Brue was abrupt. His face was a growing mixture of differently motivated anger.

Velshi was disoriented. "Not at all. I simply wanted to remind you that these structures are congenitally linked to not only religious belief..." Velshi made air quotes with his fingers when he said the word *religious*, "...but all levels and inferences to transcendental events within the human experience. The job of diminishing one without interfering with the other is not easy."

"Do I have the right person in your seat, Velshi?"

"Do you..." Velshi restrained himself. He tightened his lips and caught himself with a silent sigh.

"We identified the structures that caused us to point at the sky and invent myths to explain the seasons quite a while back. In fact, I believe I read a paper you published about the subject some twenty years ago. I'm not talking about structures with you. I will never talk about structures with you. I'm talking about that little spark of god that has dragged us all to the brink of extinction time and again. I'm talking about the future of the human race moving forward in an orderly and rational manner. Do you understand what I am talking about?"

Velshi nodded. He had nothing more to say. One more sentence, and he could be sent back to conduct personality experiments on chimpanzee models in the sweltering heat of Dubai.

"The next time I ask you a simple question and find myself inundated in your technobabble bullshit will be the last time you sit in front of that camera. Do I need to find a neurogeneticist who takes this project seriously?"

"You do not." Velshi had been tamed.

"See to it that the issue is resolved." Brue scanned the others in the room with the same admonishing eyes. "That goes for all of you. I am tired of putting out your fires and clarifying your messaging. I pulled you in for a reason. I expect results."

The heads bobbed in the room and on the monitors.

"Fiona, send a message to the vats: Discontinue One Eight Three and subsequent pools."

Brue turned with metered violence toward the window and discovered the pinpricks of light floating, traversing the dark-hued vista.

"We can't keep delaying. The money does not come from an eternal source. It will dry up, and so will humanity's chances. We have stalled as long as we can. We need the breakthrough. Do your jobs."

Brue waved his hand behind him, dismissing the assembled group. They stood and shuffled toward the doors. The monitors went black.

Fiona moved to Brue's side, stood motionless, and waited for him to speak.

The mustached man languished in his chair, the apparition of boredom. He pulled his watch and pressed his lips together in a tight seal, perhaps to keep himself from speaking. He had someplace he'd like to be.

"Cleary," Brue said as he tried to squeeze some irritation from his voice.

The man stood and walked toward the window. He was straight and bulky in a tight-fitting suit. There was a nature about his walk as if he were politely stalking. His steps were deceptively quiet for a man his size.

Brue observed him in the glass. "How're things?"

Cleary inspected the question and caught Brue's reflection. "Better 'n some. Worse 'n others."

Brue had grown accustomed to Cleary's wordplay, his diminutive attitude toward whatever anyone else found important. He smiled at it. "Maybe a few more details."

Cleary shrugged, stepped alongside Brue, and studied the hovercraft and their obscenely bright, flashy affectations. He pointed at them. "You ever wonder why these guys have to put on such a high-falutin' display. From up here, it's annoyin'. Underneath 'em, it's damn near headache-inducing. Don't see how you people live under it."

Cleary spoke with more than a hint of a Scottish brogue, lurking just beneath an indeterminate time and distance.

Brue chuckled and said, "I'll bring it up the next time I'm at a city council meeting."

Cleary smiled. He clearly enjoyed wasting Brue's time.

"But for now, the threat report, if you don't mind."

"Well, if you're lookin' for the biggest numbers, it's

still in the Midwest. Colorado is filled with assholes, but there are about four hundred fewer of them after the recent run of ops. Remember, if you would, they are seasonal. Winter rolls in, they button up pretty tight. Until then, it's the same as it ever was..."

He glanced at Brue to see if he recognized the song lyric. He did not.

"Small-scale hit and runs on mineral facilities. You know all that shit, with your fancy rocks."

"Cerium, erbium, praseodymium—you mean?"

"Yeah, all that shit. Small potatoes, really. Only reason they exist. Now, if you're looking for the most dedicated, that would be the hillbillies in the East Coast Mountains. Those are the hard cores. Ideological. Dedicated. Numbers sittin' about the same. More of a nuisance than anything else, presently. Ambushes, hit and run shit."

"Aren't they fairly well isolated?"

Cleary grunted. "Takes 'em days to get anywhere. They gotta be on foot in the hills, so not exactly a rapid strike force. Plus, with all your *little balls* floatin' around down there…"

Cleary nodded at Brue with a smile.

"So, nothing to worry about, then."

"I didn't say that."

"Of course, you didn't and never would. If there were nothing to worry about—"

"I might have to get a real job." Cleary increased the intensity of his smile. He tried it on Fiona, whose brows furrowed together, strengthening the angle of aloofness she'd adopted as soon as he joined them by the window.

Brue gave it some thought. "Run some attrition operations. I like the numbers out of Colorado. Let's give Information Operations a win for the Eastern division."

"You just want me to go drop a bunch of bombs on the foothills?"

"Well, I don't know, Cleary. I can tell you how to do *my* job."

Fiona snickered.

Cleary's eyes pinched into slits, but it didn't deter his broad smile. He nodded. "As you wish." He caught Fiona's glare, and she looked away, eager to ignore him. "By the by, did you get my recommendation for your personal protective detail?"

"I reviewed it."

"And?"

"I enjoy having a small footprint when I'm on site. It communicates something to the underlings."

Cleary said, "Oh, it communicates somethin' alright." He pivoted and walked toward the door.

Brue turned to him and exhaled loudly through his nose. He was rigid, with his hands clasped behind his back.

Cleary stopped and glanced up at the ceiling, seeking patience. He turned. "Is that all, sir?"

Brue narrowed his eyes. "What is the status of the Gen Ones in the pipeline?"

Cleary's smile and laugh were cutting. "Oh. The Skins?"

Brue's brow twitched.

"Just jokin' there, boss." Cleary put his hand forward, palm up, begging for some grace. It was well-known how much Brue despised the nickname. "Your Gen Ones can't think their way out of a paper poke. Plus, they seem to lack the proper motivation to meet the challenge, I don't know. Not exactly hard chargers, like the regular candidates."

"Regular?"

Cleary's smile faded. "You know what I mean."

Brue cocked his head. "Is the problem the student or the teacher?"

Cleary thought about his next words. "Let me put it like this. They have no motivation to do the job. It's not an easy job, and it's dangerous. Hell, they didn't even exist till a few months ago. They have no connection to a land, a people, or an ideology. They got no... reason."

Cleary leaned in close and whispered. This was pure show, as they stood in one of the most secure rooms on the planet. "You see, I think, when you went to monkeyin' around in their brains, you took somethin' from 'em. Now, I don't know what that would be, but it seems to be somethin' important." He tried to soothe the taste of the medicine. "They seem to work alright on the conventional side of the house, you know, long as you got some solid people over 'em. Line 'em up. Dress 'em the same. Give 'em the same job over and over."

Brue didn't seem soothed.

"So you *really* don't want 'em to believe in..."

Cleary looked up, and Brue followed his eyes.

"The ceiling, Cleary? I don't want them to believe in ceilings?"

Cleary's smile became so broad that it was in danger of engulfing his entire face. He nodded, conciliatory. "That's right, sir. We can't have them believin' in such nonsense as ceilings and whatnot." Cleary waved his hands, shooing away the thought. "I'll leave it to you or your lovely assistant here to read the latest from the Special Warfare School to get the details. I'm sure you'll find it illuminating. But I'd put it like this: If I had a choice to run an op with one of your Gen Ones, completely trained, or some random bawbag off the street, me and that bawbag would get to know each other. The odds he could make a lucid decision under pressure, I'd put at one in three… your boys?"

Cleary straightened up and winked at Fiona, who reacted with a flat stare. "With your permission, sir."

Brue gave it some consideration. "Have a good night, Cleary." He turned back to the window, and Cleary made his way out.

Fiona's eyes followed him. When the door closed, she turned to Brue. "What do you have for me, sir?"

Brue, sensing the room had been cleared of potential threats, large and small, rubbed his forehead and sighed. "Tell Velshi I—tell him—"

Fiona interrupted, "I think he heard what he needed to hear."

Brue straightened himself and pulled his hand from his face. The stalwart Fiona had wrenched him free from his moment of exhaustion.

He negotiated difficult terrain, dealing with governing bodies across the globe, spending his days assuaging the fears of beleaguered bureaucracies. His hands delved into the political, economic, scientific, and militaristic worlds. He occupied a rarefied space, operating outside the confines of the global politico-corporate structures yet needing their support. He often felt the undertow of their continuous scheming, their continuous malevolence.

The Earth was dying, and it needed saving. A clear vision for its salvation had been proposed. He was aware that this thing was outside himself, larger than he would ever be, and that it was just and righteous. There were moments when he would have happily handed it to someone else, but not today.

He tugged his suit coat and reset the lines. He took to peering at the hovercraft and paying attention to the light shows, each trying to attract eyes. A young industry, a young technology enticed wealthy city folk looking for the fastest route to and from work. On the weekends, the business became "party flights." Young people crammed into them as the city passed beneath, got drunk, and got high.

"We need to work on the messaging. The readouts from reproductive compliance aren't great."

"They are better than they were," Fiona said.

Brue smiled at her. "At this rate, we will be replacement neutral in eighty years. It's unacceptable."

"It shouldn't be a choice," Fiona said before she could stop herself.

Brue passed her a stern look. The idea of involuntary sterilization had been introduced through unofficial channels too soon. It was an idea that wasn't curated or massaged before it leaked into the public consciousness. It was a definite non-starter for most.

There was not yet a solution to the progeny issue, no solution to the biological impulse to make another human, to carry your flame into eternity. His solution was being built, a relief valve for all that pressure. He curled his lips and stared back out over the water.

In the silence, Fiona dutifully stared at him from below his left shoulder. She was not interested in the view.

He turned to her. "Call Roma. Set something up. Tell her I want to have the *breeder* conversation."

Fiona raised an eyebrow. "That language hasn't been approved, officially."

Brue nodded, mollifying her. "It was introduced over a decade ago. About time it was formally adopted. If it makes you feel better, drop it in Farchat. Keep it off the discoverable wavelengths."

Fiona nodded, making notes on her light board and turning to the door.

"Fiona." She stopped and turned back to him. "During the Gen Two facility trip—that's when I want to see Roma."

"So, we'll be staying overnight, then?"

"Yes. We will."

"Got it. Anything else, sir?"

"Go home, Fiona."

"Yes, sir." She turned to the glass doors and exited the conference room with the same crisp decisiveness with which she performed all other tasks.

Brue was a *vistas* person. He turned back to the large window wall. The sun had almost set, and the lights were finding their place. He focused on the horizon. The black outlines of the buildings and the water beneath, which glittered in every imaginable and phony color, sunk below his view.

His eyes were out beyond all that and into the growing night. He took the time to place it into memory, a thing he'd done since childhood.

You never know when you're looking at the last one you'll ever see.

◄———••———►

The helicopter beat the air into submission as it slipped over the ridgeline and dropped into the bowl west of Old Rag Mountain. Tremulous and buffeted by cross winds, the old-fashioned bird nosed down into the valley.

Brue sat with Fiona, harness-strapped into their seats. He perused his light board, unbothered. Fiona, in distress, held the cross straps of her harness. She disliked these machines and might even be described as terrified of them, but he refused to hover unless necessary.

Across from them, a small contingent of personal security was arrayed throughout the compartment. These were serious men, attired in dark suits and bulky in angles, which didn't hide their concealed weapons very well.

Brue waved at Fiona, catching her attention, then pushed a button on the side of his headset. "Is Roma going to make the meeting?"

Fiona nodded, then pried her hand away from the false comfort of her harness and pushed her button. "She should already be here. At least that is what I was tracking before we got into this death trap."

She followed her comment with a stinging glare at Brue, and he smiled in response.

He said, "I think you mean this precision-built mode of transportation."

Fiona's hand flew back to the button. Her voice trembled with the airframe. "No. I meant overly loud, oily rattlebox." She reinstated her death grip on the harness and locked her eyes on the floor, not interested in having a conversation.

Brue turned to the window. Up ahead and to the left, he could see the spine of Old Ragtop approaching, notable due to the large granite protrusions along the summit approach. The surrounding hills were shrouded in an assortment of Eastern evergreens, creating the appearance of a luxuriant carpet from this altitude.

At the bottom of the bowl, the bird flared to slow

its descent. They hovered toward a tan building, multi-storied with sharp angles and brutally minimal. A high, razor-wire fence ran the expanse of the perimeter. A small crowd of men dressed in sterile coveralls gathered on a gray tarmac.

The helicopter slowed to a hover, and the men's coveralls fluttered as the rotor wash battered them. The craft touched down and the light above the door turned green. A member of the security detail opened the door.

One of the greeting party leaned into the stinging winds, protecting his face with his hands. Brue hopped out and met him halfway. They shook hands in the tsunami and moved off the pad.

◀———••———▶

Brue led the group from apparatus to apparatus inside a large, sterile room lined with all manner of medical-grade equipment. His hands were pinned behind his back. He wore a rebreathing mask, eyes scanning the equipment and the faces of the technicians.

Fitted with a look of boredom and bemusement, he leaned into the task with resolve. He nodded on occasion. The technicians followed, swimming around him. They stayed away from his jaws like pale, jump-suited remora. Each one interjected as his topic of specialty was broached.

One exuberant technician, proud of his new gadget, spoke to Brue. "So, sir, as you've been briefed, we are excited about these new fiber matrix facilitators." He laid his hand on a component of a large tank. "These have managed to—"

"Speed up gestation time by approximately twenty-nine percent, if memory serves." Brue checked his memory with Fiona. She nodded and studied his attitude. He took the exchange as an opportunity to express to her his impatience.

A second technician said, "That is impressive, sir. With all the details of this campaign, you can recall such—"

Fiona interjected, bulldogging the man out of the way. She raised her voice and turned her back on him, cutting him out of the circle.

"Alright. That's enough of the tour. We have a meeting scheduled with the facility manager in ten minutes. How about we do that now."

Her question lacked a question mark. She stared at the technicians, waiting for someone to step up and take charge of the gaggle. No one grabbed the helm. Fiona rolled her eyes. Technical people were a sheepish lot.

After an awkward few moments, the last technician, whom she had stepped on, tapped her shoulder. "Excuse me. Do you mind?"

Fiona moved to the side so he could address the group. "We are in conference room 209. Let's all make our way there."

He turned to Brue with a strange look. His excited, gregarious air evaporated. He attached an oddly disappointed look to his face. Then, he regretted the display as a glitch and recycled a smile that was beginning to look somewhat plastic.

Brue noted it and told himself to look into the guy later. He seemed a bit off.

<hr>

In conference room 209, baskets of fruit, a bowl of ice, and bottled drinks covered a long table. Otherwise, the room was as bland as you'd expect to find in any manufacturing plant. A long window overlooked the facility floor. The steady, mechanistic drumbeat of the goings-on beneath hummed into the room, muted by the insulated glass.

Brue walked in, still listening to the technicians' data points, which had not slowed. He had endured enough, but years into the job, he'd developed an impressive forbearance for the little people. He'd developed techniques to make them all feel appreciated, as if his interest was bottomless and they had captured it.

Across the room, he caught sight of her.

Roma leaned against the back wall. She held her light board in one hand, and the other rested on her hip. Her figure was drawn out in a dark dress, which cut impressive curves into the drab wall. It caught Brue's eye, and he experienced the sensation of homesickness—the way one felt rounding a bend after a long drive, gazing upon a familiar place.

He smiled without reservation, and the voices

of the techs faded away. Roma was in her early thirties, of Spanish descent, and elegant beyond Brue's ability to articulate. She returned his smile and straightened her body, still full and swaying. She walked to the table to take a seat as Fiona took charge of the room. Her eyes never left Brue, and the heat from them crawled up his chest and into his face.

"Alright, let's all have a seat, please. Mr. Carnell has limited time on site. Please, let's all cut the chit-chat."

Fiona smiled briskly at Roma and moved around the table, seating the technicians like a babysitter dealing with unsure toddlers.

Once seated, Brue scanned the assembly and said, "Well. What's so important that I couldn't get this in an up-rep?"

The technicians commiserated in silence with doubtful shrugs. No one wanted to speak. On the edge of frustration, Brue eyed Fiona. She opened her mouth to speak but was interrupted by the presumptuous technician from earlier.

"We have a prototype." He said it with dispassion.

Brue leaned forward, his eyes wide. He passed a shocked glance at Fiona, who had begun to swipe her light board without mercy. "You have—"

"A Gen Two prototype—fully actuated." The tech finished his sentence, a little put out at having to do it.

Brue had endured eleven years of trials and mistrials to actuate the Gen Ones, and two more to work out the kinks in the production cycle. That process became a very public pendulum that swung from adulation to humiliation and back.

He recalled the meager beginnings, the birth of the concept. In his initial trials at the University of Wisconsin as a PhD candidate, he revolutionized the field of genomics. He had discovered a way to make life from basic carbon blocks, strung together. They were designated compounds serving as scaffolding, supporting the construction of a new organism. There was no donor in his process, so the life he created was new. He had become a god, a laughingstock, a god again, and now, a bureaucrat.

The Gen Two program had gone into effect two years prior, and if he were honest with himself, there hadn't been a lot coming out of it. He'd been consumed by his Gen One program, with its setbacks and looming deadlines. He found it difficult to lift his head long enough to see what had been going on in the hills of Pennsylvania.

At odds with this thought is that he received regular briefs from the program. He'd visited this building and its sister facility in Newbern several times. It was inexplicable that he should be caught off guard by this.

"Just why in the hell didn't anyone update me on the—"

The technician interrupted him. "Institutional policy. A separate line of funding. Provided by the governing body to—"

"Who is responsible for this?"

"The governing body." The technician allowed a discouraged look to cross his face, which he replaced with a suspicious grin.

What the hell is wrong with this guy?

Brue glanced at Roma, who withdrew into her chair. Where had she been on this? Her primary function was to provide insights into the governing body. She was his beautiful mole. Her lips were pressed tight. Many words were behind them, but the time wasn't yet right to speak them.

He turned to Fiona, who paused her rapid-fire tapping and swiping to acknowledge her complete ignorance with a deep shrug.

Brue was *in the weeds*, as his fellow genomic students used to say when dealing with a knowledge deficit. This type of disadvantage was not new to him. Who would be undermining him at this point? Whom had he provoked, by action or inaction that had the power to slip this past him? Forces have been at work behind his back.

The question was: "Why loop me in on this now?" he said.

The technician responded. "Because you have been assigned operational control of this line." He followed it up with an unhelpful smile.

Brue sat back in his chair, reset the lines of his suit, and cleared his throat. He issued a long, slow breath and felt the tension subside, his body falling into line. He forced his features to exude poise.

"And the demonstration?"

The technician pushed back from the table and

sauntered toward Brue. He stood above him and offered his hand. "My name is Jakob."

This made more sense. Brue accepted the handshake. "You're the prototype."

Jakob looked down on Brue. He stood close. "Yes, the demo began—"

"As soon as I entered the building, I suppose."

"Yes." Jakob waved his hand across the room. "Maybe we should find a more suitable place to continue?"

Brue stood, leaning away from the looming, immovable Jakob. He buttoned his coat. "Let's do just that."

◄―――――••―――――►

As before, the technicians floated just outside his eyeline, careful to avoid his smoldering anger. They hovered about his flanks, observing him as Jakob performed.

The large room's ceilings were latticed with various obstacles and ladders. Jakob cruised between beams, bars, and ropes. His movements were not quite inhuman, more akin to those of a world-class gymnast.

Brue leaned his head, kept his eyes on Jakob, and spoke over his shoulder. "He's only been actuated for three weeks?"

The technician skulking off his shoulder, said, "Yes. He came out of the tube at this level. It's all in the up-reps."

Brue burned a hole through the man with his eyes. "The up-reps I received, or the up-reps you intentionally withheld from me?"

The tech broke eye contact and sucked a little air. "We were—there were restrictions in place."

Brue waved the man away. "How is the limbic situation?"

A tech approached, unsure of his footing, as if on ice.

Without turning around, Brue repeated, "How is the limbic issue?"

The man breathed and smiled. "Resolved, we think. It's not exactly clear. We don't have the same facilities as Velshi, and since the program was not on the same funding lines, we couldn't contact him."

The man had nothing to add, so he waited for a response. He received the customary wave-off. As he walked away, the tech thought he could make out the beginnings of a smile.

Brue said, "Send all the readouts to Fiona." He glanced at her. "Since this was a separate program, she'll handle all the classification issues."

"Absolutely, sir, but this demonstration is not complete until you see Jakob in action."

Brue raised his eyebrows. There was more to this breakthrough than met the eye. After all, he'd witnessed the latest Gen Ones demonstrate exceptional motor skill advancements, so there had to be more to Jakob to warrant such an extravagant expenditure of his time.

The man continued. "While his physical

attributes are impressive, it's the intellectual realm where he shines."

He took a tentative step toward Brue, holding his hands in front like a mouse working a crumb. "In actuality, he is assisting us in the program."

"Assisting?"

"Yes. The fiber matrix tanks—that, uh, was his project. He walked the floor last week and, um, spotted the need."

Brue was incredulous. "Just spotted the need, did he? Just intuitively came up with the solution to a problem that's plagued you for two years."

"Well, yes. You have to witness this."

The technician turned and snapped at an assistant who rolled a table with a wide glass screen on top toward them. He then turned to Jakob.

"Jakob, could you join us, please?"

Hanging ten feet up on a ladder, he let go and landed gracefully. He walked toward the group, smiling at the technician. "What will it be today, Father?"

The technician chuckled and passed a nervous glance at Brue. "That's his, uh, sense of humor."

Brue turned to Jakob. "Is it?"

Jakob, unaffected by his exertions, smiled. "Apologies. I just find some things funny that others do not." He paused and contemplated for a moment. "In my defense, I am surrounded by technicians."

He offered Brue a smile, inviting kinship with him, but he was met with a wall of doubt.

"I want you to consider the limbic system and its

role in regulating transcendent human experience." Brue lifted his light board and tapped it a few times. He moved to the large glass screen and swiped his board toward it. The glass erupted with charts and figures.

"Transcendence." Jakob turned to the tech. "This is the work of your friend Velshi." He rubbed his hands together. "Well, let's take a look, shall we?" He turned to the glass and scrolled through the documentation alarmingly fast.

The technician's nervousness rose to new heights. This was a demo. Demos are controlled events where the inputs and outputs are crafted to produce specific results.

"Are you sure you don't want to see him, say, settle the Reimann hypothesis? He did so the other day, by the way. We've submitted the paperwork to Cambridge for acknowledgment, but our mathematics team here insists that he got it—"

"I get the picture." Jakob interrupted. He turned to Brue. "Is this a problem for you?"

"It's a problem for every man and woman on Earth." Brue paused. "An eternal problem, apparently." He frowned at the technicians.

Jakob studied the screen and wrinkled his brow. "Structure is the issue with your man Velshi, which makes sense from a conventional point of view. I get what he was trying to do. I believe he might have more success if he concentrated on processes."

"What do you mean?" Brue asked. Interested now, he passed a look at a wanting Roma and scuttled it before she could meet his eyes. She held her thoughts under a pout, to which he couldn't currently devote any time. There had been subterfuge and scheming. He'd been purposefully left out of significant decision points in a program he established and toiled like a madman to keep afloat. A program she was supposed to work to protect on a geopolitical level through access he did not have. He'd deal with her soon enough.

"You've played around in genomics. Yes?"

Brue appeared entertained. *Was that a joke?* "Yes. You could say I played around in the field."

"Good, then you'll understand the solution should probably be sought through neurochemistry."

Brue turned to the technician and then back to Jakob. "How's that?"

"These processes are the issue. Not the structures. The structures shouldn't be touched. I don't know much about the other project, but based on what I've read, I would imagine you've gotten some pretty substandard results. I would suspect your Gen Ones are—lacking something. Motivation or direction. Am I right?"

Brue responded with a cold stare.

Jakob continued, "The availability of certain signalers to initiate certain processes should be adjusted or even canceled on the genomic level. The signals should... You know what? I'll write it up for you." Jakob turned to the light screen, swiped it clean, opened a new document, and started typing.

Brue studied Roma. She stared at Jakob in awe. His

eyes softened toward her. He would hear her out, see what she had to say for herself.

He turned to Jakob. "How do you account for the problem?"

Jakob stopped typing, sensing Brue was no longer asking about limbic processes or transcendence. He didn't turn around. He stared over the top of his screen. "How do you *define* the problem?"

Brue, for the first time, appeared hesitant to speak.

"There are too many humans. We starve by the millions. The resources necessary to support fewer than those who now exist will disappear within fifty years. Expulsions produced in the process of providing for them pollute exponentially." Brue again struggled to voice his problem, as if it had only existed inside his mind until that moment.

Jakob ruptured the ensuing silence. "And the problem?"

"How do I—*we* convince humanity to ensure its future by denying certain biological imperatives, namely procreation? How do we convince ourselves, through technology and progress, to move forward sustainably?"

Jakob leaned back. He spun his chair to face Brue. After some thought, he said, "Some species live in extreme environments and utilize collective breeding. Are you familiar?"

Brue shook his head.

Jakob continued. "It's an evolutionary technique in which a dominant pairing is essentially freed up to breed in overdrive, while the less selective members of the community assume the role of nurturers. It increases the percentage of overall species survival in the face of environs so harsh that migration would be the only other solution. *It improves the stock*, I suppose. Since the migration of humanity would require technology that doesn't yet exist to move to a place whose suitability is yet to be determined, yours would seem to be a reasonable approach. To forego biological impulses for a time: long enough to switch the population model to a sustainable one." He paused and smiled at Brue in his disturbing way. "Of course, from what I've read of us, it's inevitable that there would be malcontents." He turned back to his screen. "But that is a different kind of issue, one in which the task of convincing becomes crucial to the success or failure of the endeavor. It seems to me you understand the problem and have acted logically. Whether or not the species will accept it is another story."

Brue narrowed his eyes. "To what species are you referring?"

Jakob didn't turn. He paused while a slim smile transited over his lips and then disappeared. "Ours."

Brue stood still for a long moment. He turned to Fiona. "You stay. Establish the classification priorities. Open up a new protected chat channel with the director." He pointed at the technician, then turned to Roma. "Do you have a moment to speak offline?"

She nodded her head, demure.

Brue didn't return to Jakob and didn't look at him again. He walked past Roma, who followed him from the room.

<hr />

The facility's courtyard was as emotionless as the structure that encompassed it. Benches were arrayed in an equilateral way. Cobbled concrete walks with rough, intermittent grass patches were arranged to subdue the pneuma of artful hearts. The first floor's windows were blacked out. The bricks, tan and ugly, jutted inwards on them; all in all, it was a terrible spot to take lunch.

The sun had passed its apex, and so they stood in shadow. They stood close. They were alone. Brue's protective detail had dispersed to cover the entrances to the courtyard. He held his hands pinned behind his back. His shoulders were high, and he did not look at her or see her ardent, hungry eyes.

"In light of very recent developments," Brue waved back toward the demonstration room, "I find your specialty to be of heightened importance. We are at a crucial juncture."

Roma said, "Agreed. Absolutely."

"I especially need your connections, your knowledge of the governing body."

"I am here to help you with whatever you need."

The anger spread through his chest and he wanted her to touch him—to pull him tight and listen as his heart calmed.

"This maneuver, with the alternate line of funding…" The distant, hidden pain of betrayal flared when he looked at her.

Roma couldn't stop herself. She reached out, pulled the elbow of his coat, and held it. "There was never any convincing evidence you were in danger."

Technological ideologies had descended upon science. Brue was the object of derision or veneration, a heretic or a prophet. The entire venture hung on his ability to know the ground around him, to know the players.

He pulled his arm away. "Why didn't you tell me? Were you waiting to see how it played?"

She withdrew. Her eyes ringed with moisture. "No. I would never do that to you."

He'd been in this game for a long time—a listless genius who woke up one day and discovered the future of humanity. His meteoric rise into the ranks of the elite thinkers and policymakers had been unforgiving, fraught with reputational danger and required attention beyond the lab. He was still in the game because he had discovered a talent for the bruising world of politics and money, and trusted no one. This woman represented his first vulnerability in twenty years.

"Why didn't you tell me?"

"Listen to me." Roma attempted to avert a disaster. "There was a struggle for control of this. *You* won. Does that mean nothing to you?"

"But how—"

"Because there are people who speak for you when you are not in the room." She lifted her eyes to him.

Brue exhaled. In her closeness, Roma could feel his breath on her face. She leaned into the comfort of it.

"You made this happen?" Brue sensed her body inching closer.

She shook her head. "*You* made this happen."

He gathered up her hand.

"Our futures are intertwined. Can't you see that?" Roma said and smiled with relief.

Brue leaned in, pretense gone. He pulled her face close to his and pressed his lips onto hers.

THREE

Generally speaking, the way of the warrior is resolute acceptance of death.
—The Book of Five Rings

Cleary, installed in the chair behind the desk, rested his feet on the windowpane. One flight down, the floor was filled with workstations. The electroluminescence of the monitors created a warm, soft glow. Technicians hunched over the screens. They cranked away at some problem buried deep within the ever-expanding vision of the centralized governing authorities.

The office door opened. A man stopped in the entryway and deflated at the sight of Cleary sitting in the seat as if he owned it. There was a silent protest on his face and a simultaneous sense of resignation.

He was the lead technician of the Global Observation Unit, the largest autonomous vehicle program ever devised and implemented. His division controlled most of the Union of American States, and his technicians processed hundreds of petabytes of data daily.

That is to say, the algorithm processed it, flagged what it found worthy of examination, and passed it to the techs. They then scoured the footage for potential errors and glitches, which could cause false positives—the telltale signs of suspicious activity that had pinged the machines' radar. They applied filters and extraneous programs against the footage and passed it along to intelligence analysts, who would then cross-reference geolocations with significant events and known suspicious characters. The whole process ended up as "Rolled-Out-Feedback" and would land on the work desk at the Operational Cell.

The leader of the Operational Cell happened to be the man sitting in the chair with his feet kicked up, smudging the window. The tech straightened his shoulders before entering the room. "Mr. Cleary, how very nice to see you again. What can I do for you?" The words were spoken through tight, impatient lips.

Cleary pointed through the window, down at the techs. "How many people you got workin' here?"

"Twenty-nine."

Cleary's eyes got big. "Twenty-nine? Twenty-nine people to watch over machines that are s'posed to watch over themselves?"

The Tech hoped Cleary couldn't hear his quiet sigh. "Technical support for several hundred Unmanned Aerial Observation Units is not as easy—"

"So anyway, the boss wants us to drag some skulls down in hillbilly country. Do me a favor and send me the observed incidents in the Northern Appalachians for the last forty-eight hours." Cleary leaned forward and tapped the monitor on the man's desk. "Send 'em right here, if you don't mind."

The man gritted his teeth and turned to leave when Cleary stopped him. "Listen, I don't want a bunch a' bullshit. Don't care about all the farmers and hikers that you people murder down there. I want post-analysis, unresolved instances with a probability of fifty percent or greater."

The man nodded. "Got it." He closed the door and walked back down the stairs.

Cleary leaned back in the chair and took stock of the room. It was small, unremarkable, and crowded with mementos. Brue had visited the tech several times. There were pictures of the two standing alongside orbs in various states of development. A proud papa, or maybe uncle of the program. Who knew?

The clear glass monitor blinked, and four small boxes filled the screen, each a paused video clip with metadata printed beneath. Cleary sat down and tapped the first video. He scrutinized the ball footage, made note of the highlighted aberration, and manipulated the screen to zoom in and pull out. His brow creased. He wasn't convinced.

The door opened again, and the tech walked in. "These are the only four that meet your criteria in the last forty-eight."

Cleary looked up from the screen and said, "Thank you so much." He swiped away from the first video, tapped the second video, and leaned into it.

"Hmmm. This one's interesting," Cleary said.

The tech moved to his side and studied the footage. "Ah, yes. This is a new TTP."

Cleary raised his eyebrows, his finger hovering over the screen.

The tech said, "I mean the hogs. We started getting hits on hogs last month in association with higher-probability instances. Then we cross-referenced with the human intelligence guys, and apparently, it's a thing they do when they think a ball spotted something. We're tweaking the algorithm right now."

Cleary pointed at the video. "Check out the canopy on that grove of spruce. That's where I'd be if I was hidin' from your little balls."

The tech wagged his head. "Makes sense."

Cleary pulled his light board, tapped it several times, and held it to his ear. "Hey, mate. Wait one." He pointed at the screen. To the tech, he said, "Forward all the data related to this one over to the OPCEN."

The tech nodded and leaned over to handle the request from the monitor on his desk. He was awkward about it, brushing Cleary's massive shoulder.

Cleary glared at him. "Get the fuck off me. Wait till I leave."

The tech stood and thought it over two seconds

before backing up, mouthing silent curses.

Cleary lifted the light board to his ear again. "I got somethin' comin' up to you guys. Start the workup. I'll be in later." He tapped and pocketed his light board.

Cleary studied the video. He stared at the canopy that protected Hillcamp from observation. It created a dark and unknown slice of the world. The type of place snakes and rats lived. The hogs spilled out from under the trees, rooting through a thick draw west of the hilltop. He was impressed at the creature's agility, being so large.

"Whatta you think those hogs weigh?"

The tech leaned in, unsure. "Um, I couldn't make an accurate estimate without some calculations."

"Jesus, you guys. Never can just have a conversation, can you?" He shook his head and walked toward the door. "Just tryin' to have a conversation." He closed the door without looking back.

The tech stared at the monitor and sighed.

◀──────•●•──────▶

Curtis and Maggie sat in the shade on the edge of Hillcamp in the warming, early daylight. Between them, a small, ruggedized laptop sat, hinged open. Sturdy enough you could throw it off a cliff, and it would still function. Multiple cables spooled off toward a short, stout antenna.

Curtis touched the screen. "So, you don't see

nothin' here. That's cause nothin' is flyin' right now."

Maggie spun the small screen toward her, on it were graphical illustrations and rolling charts. "This is how you see the balls?"

Curtis snickered. "Or you could just ask nicely."

She smacked his arm, full force, pushing his shoulder back.

"Okay, sorry, I'll keep it on point here."

Curtis was nineteen years old, born in a Boston suburb, and dragged to the hills of North Carolina at seven before he knew what was happening. Then, the wars jumped off and he spent his life living off the grid. Matriculating in guerilla camps, his complete understanding of human interaction was focused on killing, surviving, and ball-busting.

He'd been nothing but a friend to Maggie when she showed up, fresh from the suburbs of Raleigh. She didn't have a clue what she was in for, and Curtis helped her adjust as best he could. He'd kept the wolves away from her, the others with their lusty eyes. She caught him tussling with two of them, not jokingly. A boy got his lip split wide open, and Curtis stood over them to remind them how gentlemen should behave.

"Yes, this is how we see anything flying overhead. If it's got an RF signal, this antenna picks it up and displays it on screen."

"You can see anything flying?"

"Yes." He pressed the button on a small earbud. "This is how I get notified if there's a hit when the screen is closed. I'll get a ping in my ear."

Maggie acknowledged with a nod. "When that happens…"

Daniel walked up, loomed over, and studied them. Maggie tried to catch his eye with an awkward smile. He didn't consider her, buried in thought, barely there.

Curtis asked, "You need somethin', sir?"

Daniel shook his head. "Pack that shit up, move to the center. Apparently, we're gettin' some new gear." He stomped away.

Maggie reached for the computer, but Curtis put his hand out, stopping her. "You go ahead. I'll pack this up. Just get me whatever they're handin' out. Long as it ain't heavy."

Maggie hopped up and dusted her pants. She gave Curtis a playful wink and nod, then took off after Daniel. "Hey, wait up."

Daniel did not wait up.

Maggie lengthened her steps. Her feet were still tender from the miserable patrol two days earlier. "Wait up. I want to talk to you."

This did not affect him. His pace increased, if anything. His neck pitched toward the center of camp as if she weren't following. She figured he was occupied with the concerns of command, problems that had plagued him for years: how to make mission and keep everyone alive.

Maggie caught up and plucked at his sleeve.

"What do you want, Maggie?"

She smiled at him. It took some effort. "Two things: I've thought about it a lot, and I want to apologize for giving you so much shit about the... you know, those guys."

Daniel gave her an understanding nod of his head. Distracted, he stepped past her when she put her hand on his chest.

"I also wanted to thank you for choosing me for this mission."

Daniel's mouth fell flat. "Well, that is one of my utmost concerns as a commander. Making sure my ammo bearer is gettin' the most outta life."

Maggie bit her tongue. Her eyes scrolled with possible retorts. She restrained herself. "Why can't you just treat me like you treat everyone else?"

Daniel smiled. "Alright. Shut up and pack your shit."

"You know what? Fuck you." She'd had enough of being nice.

"That's more like it." Daniel smiled and resumed his walk, having rubbed away the thin veneer of Maggie's civility.

She followed him. "You know you don't have to be such a jerk. Just treat me like you treat everybody else." She stumbled behind him, matching his pace on her aching feet.

Daniel shook his head. "I'm tryin'."

He reached the center of camp with Maggie on his heels. Several soldiers were gathered on their knees, watching a demonstration.

Rudy stood before them, holding what appeared to be a folding, nylon chair collapsed to a small square.

John spoke. "So what we brought for you guys is brand new. They're called bump tents. They deflect heat just like the old blankets but have nanotech, which indefinitely dissipates. So you don't have to worry about burping the heat out. Also, it's refractory or some shit. Meaning it blends you into the surroundings. So, it's good against direct observation as well."

The assembled fighters were impressed. They grumbled to each other about the pains of sleeping on patrol in the summer, of sleeping on patrol in the winter, and that they often wouldn't sleep on patrol at all.

The autonomous orbs presented significant problems. Moving around without detection was becoming more complex. Often, the patrol would be forced to "dome up" under their heat-reflective blankets for hours, even days, while waiting for the drones to loiter out of the area. They would even relieve themselves inside their tents to avoid detection.

Maggie tapped Daniel's shoulder. "We should talk."

He shooed her away with a brushing hand. She caught the gesture, the intent of it, and made a quick decision not to let it get at her. She had a mission. In her mind, they needed some common ground. Searching for it right then and there wasn't beyond the pale for her.

For his part, Daniel wanted nothing to do with it.

John told the group, "This thing weighs maybe

one pound, so it's a fourth of the weight of your old blankets. Plus, it deploys and packs up easy and fast."

Rudy popped a couple of buckles, and it deployed into a small, dome-shaped tent.

The assembled fighters were impressed. This seemed like something that would make life better and scrape a tiny edge off the suffering.

Rudy looked up from his work and saw Maggie for the first time. His eyes softened and his jaw slackened. Maggie paused her assault on Daniel and noted the boy's eyes—like a little puppy. It made her smile.

She was tall for a girl, slim in the waist and strong through the shoulders. She'd had no trouble attracting boys back in her civilian life. Sitting in the sunshine of Rudy's gaze, she became somewhat conscious of the fact that she hadn't showered in days. She pulled her eyes away from him and resumed tapping Daniel's shoulder rather violently, all the while aware of Rudy and the awkwardness of a boy in the middle of everything happening.

She told Daniel, "You can't ignore me for the rest of your life."

"Out here?" Daniel perused the environment as if he were just now noticing that he was in the middle of a war. "You never know." He walked away from her, approaching John.

Maggie glanced again at Rudy, her face becoming flush with anger. He hadn't pulled his eyes away from her—or closed his mouth.

Daniel spoke to John. "You guys about done?"

John said, "Why? You ready to go."

"Whatta *you* think?" Every interaction with John and Daniel's fuse burned a little shorter.

John shook his head with exasperation. "Give me twenty minutes."

"You got ten," Daniel said, turning to the assembled fighters. "Get this shit packed up! We roll in ten mikes."

The fighters ditched the chit-chat, grabbed their tents, and shuffled toward their patrol packs. Maggie noted the speed with which the fighters accomplished tasks was directly correlated to the level of irritation in Daniel's voice.

Daniel turned to Rudy, who was staring, trying to unlock the mystery of a beautiful girl. "Gimme that thing." He snatched a bump tent from Rudy's distracted hands and fiddled with the latches.

Rudy held out a tent to Maggie. "Are you gonna need one of these?" He spoke with a lot of air. She didn't even hear him.

Maggie pressed on with Daniel. "Let's just sit down for a few minutes."

Daniel struggled with the tent. He couldn't get the latches to open. His thick, gnarled fingers slipped over the activator. Steam could have issued with his tight breath.

Rudy reached to guide him. "Just push these two right—"

Daniel tossed the tent on the ground. "Piece a' shit. Been usin' a blanket for twelve years. No need to switch now."

"Are you gonna talk to me or not?" Frustrated, angry tears verged on Maggie's eyelids.

"Yeah, are you gonna talk to her or not?" Rudy spoke before he thought. It was a deep instinct, a reflex at the sight of her anxiety. His prefrontal gyrus kidnapped his tongue.

Its effect could be compared to that of "rapid deceleration syndrome." Maggie, John, and anyone in the area stopped what they were doing to see how it would play out. It was a singular event.

Daniel lost interest in other matters. He turned to Rudy and spent considerable energy engaging him. "The fuck you just say?" Daniel's tone was restrained, the way barbed wire restrains a bull.

It was important for Rudy, withering under those eyes, to get his following words correct. "I, um—the lady wanted you to—"

"Lady?"

Maggie interjected, "I take it back. Don't treat me like you treat everyone else." She rolled her eyes.

Daniel ignored her. He angled over Rudy. "She's sixteen." His eyes asked a silent question: *Do you understand me?*

Rudy said, "Yes. Yes."

Maggie shook her head at Daniel. "You're unbelievable." She stepped toward Rudy with her hand out. "Hello, I'm Maggie. I don't believe we've met."

Daniel snatched her arm and walked away. She stumbled behind him, prying his grip with no luck. "What is your deal?"

She tried to plant her feet but slid across the grass. He dragged her away from the camp center and headed toward the line of waiting patrol packs.

Maggie realized if there was any hope of a breakthrough today, it would have to wait. While they were on the patrol, they could talk things through. Her father was a violent, mule-headed asshole, but he was hers. She intended to have it out with him.

She just needed the right time and place.

◄──────•••──────►

Rudy turned to John, who had leaned back against a tree working a toothpick, the slightest hint of a smile. "You like making friends, huh?"

"How was I supposed to know?"

◄──────•••──────►

The morning fog had burned away from the low areas. A distant haze floated above the faraway ridges, but the sun was up and strong. Daniel believed he could cover eight klicks a day in straight-line distance. The straighter the line, the higher the pain level: the patrol would gain and lose a lot of altitude. He believed it was manageable.

They filed out of Hillcamp. Carl nodded as Daniel counted him out of the perimeter. He was 'on point' with a laminated map attached by line to his lapel. Following him was the hand-selected crew for the mission—twenty fighters in total, counting John and his man Rudy.

The loadouts were lighter, and the packs smaller. This was a slimmed-down contingent compared to the regular combat patrol. Speed was an issue, and they decided during the planning session to leave the Pig behind. Curtis and Maggie were heartened by this decision.

Rhett stood beside Daniel as the slow cavalcade proceeded off the hill into the draw.

Daniel said, "Probably not a secret here, but I don't like this shit."

Rhett acknowledged and spit a dark sphere of tobacco juice onto the ground. "Kinda figured. Better you than me, buddy." He grinned.

Daniel thought it over for a moment. "Yeah, you're right. It *is* better. Probably has a chance to succeed this way."

Rhett chuckled in mock pain. "That's hurtful."

John walked past, hunched under his ruck, carrying a new weapon. He'd stolen a pulse rifle from a government armory—wasted in his hands, in Daniel's opinion. He passed Rhett a heads-up greeting.

Daniel twisted his face. "That fuckin' guy."

More patrol members filed past. Maggie, adjusting her ruck, smiled at Rhett.

He said, "Take care, little girl."

"*You* take care." She glanced hopefully at her father, who didn't seem to notice her.

Curtis ambled past, unburdened without the heavy machine gun. Daniel smiled. "You miss the

Pig, Curtis?"

"Not in the least little bit."

"Well, you might."

As the column flowed out of camp, Daniel turned to Rhett. "Not gonna try to get comms with you till midnight in the first window."

Rhett nodded. "I got twenty-one leaving, heading to Newbern. I expect to be there in thirty-six hours, give or take. Comms windows are established. If I don't hear from you, I'm drivin' on. If you don't hear from me, it was nice knowin' ya. If I make enemy contact, I'm bounding out and away from you till I can reach out safely. If you make contact, zeek all comms with us and fall back to your alternate locations... and God be with you."

Daniel delivered the contingency brief with a customary touch of fear lacing into his heart. He feared that he would never see Rhett or his boys again. He feared that the movement and activity would arouse observation of the camp and cause trouble. He feared death, being run down through the hills by an army of unforgiving Skins. He had accepted this path—the possibilities. None of them were safe at any time and probably never would be again.

Rhett said, "We got our ears on, brother. You take care."

"Yeah." Daniel nodded at his friend. He cinched his pack and flowed in behind the patrol onto the rough ground with its spruce roots sliding through the grass like wooden snakes.

The patrol halted along the top of a ridgeline maned with pine and mountain hardwoods. The trees' high crowns allowed the fighters to see into the low ground and into the distance. The hills rolled away, haphazard and green.

The fighters were arrayed alongside a trail, spaced out, watching the approaches in all directions. They knelt and scanned through the scattered, early fall foliage.

John sat on his rear, his ruck propped against the trunk of a long-leaf pine tree. He faced the trail and poured a canteen over his head.

The movement had been intense. There was a lot of ground to cover and little time to do it. Daniel had prepared everyone during the mission briefing, saying, "We gotta move out like scalded dogs if we're gonna make this hit time."

John, along with everyone else, nodded, acknowledging the implications. But, unlike everyone else, John wasn't prepared to move with such haste under ruck weight. His body had forgotten the ups and downs of patrolling, the endlessness of it.

He caught his breath whenever they stopped for their map checks. With hundreds of patrols under his belt, he'd earned a break. Daniel's men were well trained. Let them pull security.

Daniel consorted with Carl. The two exchanged

the relevant information without speaking. Daniel knew what he was doing and that Carl was a good man on point. They'd no need of his input. He would catch his breath and let them handle it.

Carl moved to the front of the column, whispering, "Grab some water. We move in five mikes."

Curtis knelt next to Daniel with the small laptop on the ground. He held the fat antenna up toward a break in the trees. He shook his head and smiled at Daniel. "All clear."

"Alright, pack it up. Keep the antenna out and your ears on. Let me know if you hit a ping."

"Roger that." Curtis opened his pack to stow the computer.

Daniel turned his head and caught sight of John. His face wrinkled. He moved to him, stuffing his map away. When he got there, he hovered. "Seem to recall, back in the day, nobody sat on their ass during a security halt."

Covered in sweat, John got the notion that Daniel didn't believe he'd earned that break. He slid the canteen into its pouch and rolled over. He pushed himself up onto a knee, and it crunched like it was full of sand. "You happy now?"

"You'll be back in your comfy bed with your hot showers before you know it." Daniel scanned the valley floor through the branches.

The pain of the movement, the exhaustion, caught up with John. His diplomatic nature took a hit. "You got a problem with me?" The question had an obvious answer.

"See all these kids?" Daniel swept his hand in the direction of a couple of his fighters. "You need to set the right example." He stared at John, and his eyes burned. "Always."

"That's not your problem, and you know it." John's eyes were wide. "It's Lori. It's always been Lori."

He opened the wound which sat between them for ten years. He reached right into the meat of it and pried it open with his sweaty fingers. He'd had enough of this shit, and decided right there on that ridgetop to air it out.

"That night was the lowest night of my life, Daniel."

Daniel glowered over him, his lips as unmovable as his soul.

John tried again. "I've beaten myself up over it every day since."

"Good to know." Daniel was steel-eyed.

John's mind flashed to the moment they found Lori. They called it out over the radio. She was in the tall grass. He'd been rightfully afraid to accompany the search parties, afraid someone would kill him in his sleep. He heard the reports before they returned with her body. Those hours waiting for them, he considered ending himself.

When they entered the camp, they carried her wrapped in a sheet, and the men were quiet. Daniel was in a state, wide-eyed and disconnected.

He said, "Listen, I've thought about it a million times. I don't know how they got in."

"They crawled in like they'd crawled in over at the Tomscott's. It's what they were doin'. You didn't see 'em 'cause you went to sleep."

And there it was. The forever accusation that no one said out loud but everyone accepted as fact. There had been an investigation. The higher-ups believed John was out on the edge of the perimeter, responding to a motion sensor when the infiltration occurred. That's what he'd told them. The sensors maintained a log of all alerts, and the area he referenced provided proof to support his claims. Nonetheless, the suspicion over his actions that night had never abated.

He'd grown weary of the endless penance. His entire career as a fighter was distilled to one miscalculation. He'd left his post too long, believing he'd heard something. He stayed too long and should have gone back sooner. But he didn't fucking fall asleep. He would never have done that.

The Skins slipped in on their bellies and dragged the women from their dwellings in perfect silence. They filled them with psychoactives. The victims crawled out behind them, lambs to slaughter.

Only one was found. Lori.

John said, "Sometimes I wish you would have just killed me. But I didn't do what you think I did."

Daniel leaned in. "I don't give a fuck what you think you did or didn't do. You never had the dignity to go off and suck-start a pistol, so far be it from me to do the job for you. Just do your job. Don't mention my wife again."

John had more to say, but he kept it to himself. A man can only be expected to take so much. For now, he would tolerate him. Nobody could better move a patrol through the woods, and his men were well-trained.

The success of this mission would draw blood from a beast with no weakness. John gritted and swallowed the words he felt like saying. He scanned the woodline, looking away from Daniel, pulling security like he was supposed to. It was better to concentrate on the task at hand.

The sun slid through the sky. The patrol made good time, busting the draws and climbing the fingers. Daniel kept his word, and they walked the dreaded "straight line." In a security halt, Daniel and Carl knelt over a map. *How far had they moved? How much farther should they go? What was the best-looking place to call it for the night?*

Satisfied with their deliberations, Daniel spied the rear of the patrol. Rudy had wormed his way to the back of the column during the break and sidled up next to Maggie. He leaned into her, and her shoulders chuckled.

He stowed his canteen, moved to them, and took a knee. This had a chilling effect on the conversation.

"What's so funny, Rudy?" Daniel stared down at the steep edge of the ridge.

Like a suspect in an interrogation cell, Rudy said,

"Nothing, I—"

"Grab some water. We move in five mikes." He stood, paused, and then, with some gravity, said, "Rudy."

"Yes." His voice cracked.

Daniel pointed to the front of the patrol. "Get back in your element. Up front, right behind Carl, and stay there."

"Yessir." Rudy bounced up in that cartilage-rich way teenagers bounced and moved out quickly.

Maggie curled her lips and shook her head at Daniel. "Really? All the sudden you care about who takes me to the prom?"

"It's not like that. You don't even know that guy."

"You don't know me. I could've been a pole dancer, for all you know."

"Yeah."

Daniel was unimpressed. She looked like an angry little mouse trying to pick a fight with a jackal.

"You wanted to be included. Well, here you are. Pullin' security is the gig. We do the work—we stay alive. We joke around—we get dead. Now shut up and keep your eyes and ears open."

Daniel walked away, leaving Maggie to simmer. She couldn't argue with him. His words were plain and obvious truth.

He was getting better at this father business.

◄———••———►

Cleary sat in the troop compartment of a Special

Forces hovercraft. Gone was the fine, tailored suit. He wore tactical gear for operations on the Eastern Appalachian Trail. Muted green, camouflaged kit with pouches and weapons adorned his large frame. It was a natural look for him, the same as the other operators on board, save the ridiculous blond handlebar mustache shagging up his face.

He leaned over a computer, next to the young, thin-framed captain of the Special Forces team. They studied the images on the screen which had shifted from a fuzzy white to crisp and clear.

"All the money in the world and they wouldn't redirect a satellite until today. Stinkin' bean counters."

With the advent of the Gen One Soldier Initiative, many professional warriors were repurposed in their careers. Infantrymen found themselves earning college degrees or working dead-end jobs.

The Special Forces detachment in the cabin with Cleary was a serious group, serious about their job. Being some of the few remaining "Oldborns" allowed to do it, they always intended to do it well.

The planning process had been frustrated by the lack of real-time imagery. Now they scooted along the air, approaching a location Cleary had identified on a hunch. There had been no human intelligence to support this as an enemy camp, but there had been an ambush some eight miles away in recent days—again, just a hunch.

The captain didn't like it and had made that evident to Cleary. "We'll have four drones over the target synchronized one minute before hit time so we don't spook them away."

Cleary nodded and looked out a large, clear door—a monofilament, projectile-resistant glass covering to the troop bay. The hills rolled past. He smiled. That little place inside him felt the tickle again.

"We'll stick with the plan, yeah? Hit the offset, a couple klicks out." Cleary tapped the screen at the infiltration point. "Set out the S and O points. Get feedback. If they're there, go fuck up their day. Sound good, son?"

The Captain grimaced at the false affection from Cleary. "Roger."

Active-duty operators didn't care for contractors, especially when they usurped their command on ground operations. Cleary felt fine about it. Let the captain boil a little; it would keep him sharp throughout.

Cleary stared into the rolling valleys. He touched his gear, a ritual developed long ago when he came up as a hitter. He started at the left shoulder, touched all the essential components, and called them out in his mind. *GPS. Bangers. Flares. HUD. Watch. Clinch Pick. Pistol. Mags. Smoke.* He ended the routine on his right shoulder. It comforted him.

He never knew what he would get in this job, so he needed to know something for certain. This helped him stay sane. It connected him to reality, the bench he sat on, and the pompous little boy next to him. His job was to instill order amid chaos.

Cleary was in his element again.

Brue wanted scalps. He wanted a win in the hills, in the media, and in the boardrooms. The right man was on the job. A man who saw things the way they were and didn't lie to himself about what needed doing. A man who could get to the objective and get off it with a win in his hands.

The hills rolled by.

◆——————•●•——————▶

Daniel's patrol dug into the leeward side of the ridge. The last ounces of orange light slid up the opposite side of the draw. The location was dark, wet, and growing cold.

Daniel and Maggie squatted next to each other, digging. They used collapsible shovels to rake away mud and debris from a small shelf dug in the hillside. The roots and rocks were a problem. The pair worked in silence.

The patrol had broken into buddy teams and spread out through the draw, preparing their bivouac sites. Some bump tents were already up, and the inhabitants changed into clean, dry clothes.

Daniel pulled a thick blanket from his ruck. One side was shiny and metallic, and the other was rusty brown, flat, and non-reflective. Maggie continued to work at the carve-out. She pulled branches that had been cut into short poles and shoved them into the mud to create a frame.

Daniel studied her. Her hair was matted down with sweat and filth. "You ready to set the roof?"

She nodded and wiped her face, leaving a dark gray mud streak on her cheek.

He handed her the blanket, and the shiny side went down. They draped it over the top of the frame and weighted the edges with stones. Daniel placed large sections of moss peeled from the surroundings on the roof of the heat tent.

Maggie sat back for a moment and caught her breath, looking at the buddy teams inside their tents, cozy and warm. "Exactly how is this better than a bump tent?"

Daniel knelt beside his ruck, the roof now covered in moss. He picked up his rifle. "Everything's better till it ain't." He stood.

"What does that even mean?"

"I gotta check with Curtis, make sure he got the RF up." Daniel scrambled up the slope out of her sight.

She grabbed her pack, shoved it into the makeshift tent, and crawled in on her hands and knees. Once inside, she plopped down on her rear onto the cold mud. She studied her fingernails: dark crescents. She was exhausted, cold, and wet. On her skin, the sweat and dirt created a slurry she could feel all over. She asked quiet, bitter questions. "How does sand, having traveled the course of a person's body throughout the day, settle itself the place you least want it?"

Her breath fogged before her, and she had a quiet moment of contemplative misery. In fact, she couldn't recall a time during her sixteen years in which she felt as completely wretched as that moment. The nighttime audio of the mountains flipped on like a switch, buzzing around her, and she was alone in it. Her body shivered.

She heard noises outside, someone approaching. The blanket peeled back, and Daniel squatted in the dying light. He handed her his rifle and then followed his pack. He shoved it into the opposite corner and crawled in.

"I can hear your knees crackin'. My lord," Maggie said, and she meant it. It was a complicated mix of grinding and snapping. She could only wonder at the mechanisms of dysfunction within those joints.

"Yeah." He grunted. "Got some miles on 'em."

Daniel situated himself and laid his rifle across his lap. Then, he exhaled long and slow for what must have been the first time that day. He pulled his canteen and finished it.

"Remind me to have everybody top off water from the stream tomorrow before we move out."

Maggie agreed with a silent nod.

"We're on fifty percent security, so go ahead and get some sleep. I'll wake you in a couple hours."

"You don't wanna talk to me?" Maggie's voice was soft, hopeful.

"Talk about what, your pole dancin' career?"

She grew quiet. She'd waited for this moment as long as she could remember. She drew a blank. There had been a million things. "Why didn't you even visit me?"

The question landed hard on Daniel. Maybe it was exhaustion from the movement or the quiet closeness of the moment, but it hit him. He had no idea how to respond, and it showed in the small, nearly inaudible click in his throat.

"Why didn't you ever send for me?" Maggie asked.

"Because your mama wouldn't have ever wanted that."

"Would she have wanted you to become... *this*?"

"This what?" There was a hot angle to his tone.

Was he irritated or insecure? She didn't know him well enough.

"These people that you're killing—"

"They're not people."

She glanced at him. His eyes were filled with uncertainty. Maggie thought she'd caught him in a trap. In all his preparations, the careful selections of the appropriate courses of action, the war gaming, the contingency planning... he had failed to account for this very moment. He had failed to prepare himself for the questions she had every right to ask.

She said, "They're close enough to people for it to leave a mark on you."

"Bullshit."

"How many of them have you killed?"

He thought about it. "Don't know."

"Were they frightened when you did it?"

"You know they killed her, right? Whatever the hell they are. They killed your mama."

"Don't pretend you're doing this for her." Maggie was emboldened. Many of her long-held thoughts were coming back into focus, and she had some points to make.

"Why the hell else would I be doin' this?"

"I remember when I was little. You'd pull me into bed with you and Mama when I couldn't sleep. Sing me songs till I went to sleep. I don't know if that was the person I expected to see out here, or not. I thought, all that time, what they said about you was bullshit. Just rumors from people's stupid imaginations. But then I came out here, and now I can't believe you're the same person."

If that hurt Daniel, he didn't show it. His breathing slowed, and he became more measured and less angry. He was regaining control of himself. Like any ambush, if you could survive the first thirty seconds of it, you had a good chance of making it out alive. "You grew up in a different world, Maggie. That's the way I wanted it. That's the way she would have wanted it."

"Stop talking for her. She's dead."

The words sucked the air out of the tent for a moment. They both sat silently in the vacuum.

"I'm sorry for any hurt I caused ya. But you're better off without all this," he said.

"All this?" She laughed, a tight, bitter sound. "All this is your doing. None of these people would even be out here if it weren't for you. All these *boys*. You should hear the way they talk about you. Curtis— Curtis should be in school somewhere flirting with girls, not out here in all this craziness."

Daniel sighed deeply. "I can't help any a' that."

"You *can* help it. You can walk away from it. Don't you think you've done enough? Haven't you collected enough skulls?"

The more Daniel withdrew into his isolated, quiet tones, the more agitated she became.

"I don't know." He said it, and she knew he had slipped away from her. She felt his apprehension for a few brief seconds, which caught him, the real man, her father, in a moment of uncertainty.

"What about me? Huh? What about me?" She asked. Her voice was as hollow as her insides, as empty as all the birthdays with the well-meaning strangers.

Daniel had flipped the switch. He was back in control, numb to it all again. "You were never supposed to be here. Go back to Raleigh. Live your life."

"So, you're going to run around out here and fix everything? Right all the wrongs? I just don't get to have a father?"

"If your mama hadn't been killed, I mighta seen this for what it is."

Her eyes were getting wet on the edges. The liquid drained from the socket, smearing the lids against her will. She didn't want him to see that—didn't want him to see the cavern inside her guts. "What is it, then?"

Daniel's voice let go of the gravel of him. It filled with air. "A giant tidal wave that nobody's ever gonna stop. One that's gonna wipe us all off the face of the planet."

He grabbed his bootlaces and scrubbed the drying mud loose from them. "Sometimes I think I coulda gone off and lived a life, you know? If I'd chose different that day, maybe we coulda gone off, you and me."

He let his shoelaces loose. His face hardened. "But, there ain't nothin' for me now. They ain't gonna stop, and neither am I."

He checked with her to see if she understood. His desolate eyes, hid behind the same cold wall he'd affixed to his face since the day she'd arrived in the camp. It was too much for her, the embodiment of failure, a lost life. She didn't want him to see her tears.

"You ain't had a father for a long time."

Maggie wiped her face. She pulled her hood down and leaned away from him. The close moment he'd almost cracked in that cold draw had passed. If she could have kept the pressure up, chosen the right words...

But, in all those years, in all those dreams, she had never created a creature as hard and empty as Daniel to practice her arguments against. She wasn't prepared. She had wasted her time, and the shuddering knowledge of it was too much to bear.

His ghosts held sway over him in ways she would never be able to compete against. She gave him up to his ghosts.

Cleary walked through Hillcamp. A lazy smoke, held captive by the remaining canopy, drifted across his face. The dwellings had been uprooted and smoldering, echoes of the extreme violence visited upon them. Splintered timbers, junked furniture, clothing, weapons, and indiscernible body parts were strewn across the ground. He sauntered through the wreckage, pleased with himself.

The Special Forces detachment moved between the remaining intact dwellings. The shooters spied into the low entryways, yelling at the occupants. Their pulse rifles at the ready, bright lights penetrating the holes.

"Get out here! Put your hands up! Get your fuckin' hands up! Come out, or we'll burn you out!"

Cleary and his detachment had won the brief firefight, if it could be called such a thing. The orbs came on station moments after they had established overwatch of the camp.

The camp alarms sounded, and the fighters fled toward their holes. The operators lit them up with volleys of controlled and accurate fire. Blue-white tracers from their pulse rifles streaked throughout the camp. The young men fell. They died running. They died hiding. The crossfire was efficient, death coming at them from every angle. There was no place to hide—no spot of ground free from the operator's sights.

The orbs fired their Pranashi rockets through the canopy, directed by the operator's laser-selected coordinates. The dwellings mushroomed in fire and smoke.

Both of Rhett's legs were shot through—his femurs shattered, his thighs engorged. Swollen to twice their normal size, the bones leaked blood and sanguineous fluid into the tissues. Each movement was accompanied by exquisite pain. He reached for his pistol. These bastards would have to come into the camp, whoever they were. If he had any spark left in him, he'd put down as many as he could.

A rocket slipped through the canopy and splashed nearby. The blast flung him in the air. Aware, vaguely, he noted the new pains accompanying his flight. His back had been the recipient of dozens of small, hot fragments.

He landed in a smoking crater. This *lucky bounce* placed him where he was protected from the pulse rifles. Shielded in the shallow pit, he searched for his pistol and cursed through gritted teeth as he realized it had been blown free.

He dragged himself to the edge of the hole. With every movement, the pain overwhelmed him, blinding him. He rolled back to the bottom of the crater as the bombardment continued.

Smoking debris showered down on him. His men screamed as they died. He stared at the dark canopy and wished his pistol had not been blown free. *Not a terrible view*, he thought. The breeze rolled through the tight-knit work of spruce boughs. In the blue sky above, he caught glimpses of the gray orbs with their dead eyes, floating. His hearing had grown fuzzy from the explosions. The voices and the movements all became distant. It was as if he observed everything from the bottom of a fish tank.

Was he not dead? *God has one last job for me*, he thought. To listen to his boys be ripped apart and bled out, alone on the grass, a million miles from their mothers. Rhett was never a suitable replacement for their mothers. And now they were dying all around as he floated in some faraway substance, listening to it, unable to help them.

The soldiers cleared the camp. They moved ever closer to where he lay. He looked around—there was nothing he could use to end himself.

Was he not dead?

He heard the voice before he saw the man. "Well, well, well. Who's this, I wonder?" The voice had a slight brogue to it.

Rhett looked up onto the edge of his crater.

Cleary stood, one leg on a broken timber, his hand resting on his thigh. He leaned over Rhett with his pistol lazily canted. Then, a look of recognition crossed his face. Cleary holstered his pistol, put his hand on his utility belt, and winked. "I know you."

◄───••───►

Rhett woke up in the troop compartment of the hovercraft. They floated a thousand feet above the remnants of Hillcamp. He shook his head and tried to loosen the fog of the drug they'd pumped into him. Beside him were two young fighters from camp. They appeared a little scuffed up but unharmed. They were bound and gagged, hog-tied with their hands tied to their ankles behind their backs.

Lining the bay walls, the operators sat, leaning forward, dark apelike faces. They maintained their equipment—gruff men speaking in earthly tones—death and laughter. They scrubbed their weapons, not a care in the world.

How many had they killed? Twenty? Rhett tried to think through the haze of the drug. Daniel's patrol had been reworked up to the last minute, and he couldn't remember how many had stepped off with him.

What kind of a leader was he to forget such a thing?

A young medical tech sat next to Rhett, working the problem. The big man had multiple severe wounds. The medic smiled at Cleary and said, "He's back."

Cleary stopped tapping on his light board and looked at Rhett. "Is he now?"

"We can keep him stable as long as you want."

The medic was happy about his performance. Rhett's legs were encased in an inflated cast. It was a transparent composite that braced his legs and wrapped up over his hips. The surface of the cast had an intricate touch screen. Vital signs chirped and displayed themselves in bright lights across his abdomen.

Cleary knelt beside him. "Rhett, do you remember

me?"

Rhett nodded and passed a worried glance at his men, both young, like all of them. They wouldn't survive this. There was hope in their eyes, and he hated himself for his part in planting it there. Every single thing he had ever said or done to convince these kids to take up this war ran up his throat like bile. "I remember you."

"Good. You remember when—"

"I remember killin' your piece a' shit brother." Rhett was deep in Cleary's eyes when he said it.

Cleary blinked and nodded at two of his men. They put down their weapons and cleaning solutions. Like nonchalant bulls, they lumbered over to one of Rhett's boys, lifting him like a bag of wriggling cats.

The kid didn't make it easy. He fought them as best he could, blind with terror. The bindings on his face couldn't suppress his shrieking.

One of Cleary's robots punched a button, and the bay door slid open. They turned to their boss, who tilted his head.

The young insurgent was thrown from the entryway into the darkening day. He hung there for a slice of a second, the evening breeze ruffling his clothes before he dropped out of sight, still fighting against his lashings.

Cleary turned to Rhett. "You can clip all that bullshit, mate. I know you didn't kill my Tommy alone. You had a friend. What was his name?" Cleary enjoyed this.

"Lil Tommy burned to death if I recall. That's a shit way to go." Rhett was set on his course of action: poke them and get it over with.

"We know you have a patrol out. The head count doesn't match the bed count. I'll give you credit; you zeeked the comms, so we don't have an RF trail. We saw where the patrol started, but we lost the sign. So, you let me know where your buddy Daniel is, and —"

"Daniel's dead."

Cleary laughed. "And so were you till an hour ago." He nodded and patted Rhett's inflatable cast. He motioned over to the executioners, and they grabbed the other boy and dragged him away.

"Where are they goin', Rhett?"

Rhett locked eyes with the boy and nodded his head. He said, "It's alright. It's alright, you did alright."

I'm not your father. I got no right to do to you what I did.

The boy stopped struggling. He closed his eyes and started praying.

Cleary sneered. "Do you people ever doubt your own bullshit?"

Rhett turned to face Cleary, and met his eyes. "It shouldn't be debated at the time of the doin'."

Cleary absorbed the comment, stood, and shrugged his shoulders. "I don't get you people." He turned to his men, and the boy was sent sailing.

Rhett's eyes filled up.

Cleary told the medic, "Gork his ass. We got drugs

back in the rear." He turned to Rhett. "You hear that, mate? You killed your boys for nothin'. When I get you back, you're gonna ride the dim train. You'll tell me anything I want to know."

Rhett smiled through his tears. "Your brother died screaming."

Cleary didn't respond to him. He gave the medic a nod with a smile stretched tightly at the edges.

The medic pushed a few buttons on the touchscreen display, and Rhett fell unconscious.

Cleary stared at him a moment, then walked to his seat and buckled in. He grabbed a headset, put it on, and pressed the talk button. "Let's get outta here."

The hovercraft tilted and slid through the air, headed northeast to New York.

He thought of his brother, Tommy. He hadn't thought about him in a while. He had assumed, back during those days when the insurgency was raging across the nation, the ones who killed his brother had died along with him. He'd unraveled the networks and dissected the attack. He'd recovered DNA evidence and checked it against the databases. All signs indicated the men responsible were most likely dead.

He pulled the headphones off—didn't need to speak to anyone else. He had become familiar with Daniel, his face, and his actions years ago—how he walked and talked. There was a time when he'd been consumed by him, the desire to find him, if he still lived.

If that son of a bitch was alive and operating in the

hills, he would burn the fucking hills down to get at him.

Some hurdles needed jumping, and some red tape required cutting, but Cleary was about to unleash the full force of his wrath on whoever was roaming around Appalachia looking for trouble.

◂——•●•——▸

His office was on the ninety-fourth floor. The flickering night filled his window wall. He leaned back in his chair and relaxed for a moment. He allowed himself a couple of minutes of this every day—a restful period of nothingness.

Refreshed, Brue swiped his desktop, and across the room, a large wall monitor blinked and turned on. He checked his watch and touched the desk again, and the volume increased.

A celebrity interview show blared on the screen. A holographic image of the city floated as a background to the simple set. The host sat cross-legged in a green chair, his hair a ridiculous, black pompadour. Roma sat opposite him on a couch. Her dress was tight, with a slit up her thigh. She was easy about it, absolute comfort in this role, in her skin. She was the kind of woman that caused a man to doubt himself, and she was the kind of woman who knew it.

The host laughed and beamed a plastic smile at her. "Are you saying they knew what they were doing?"

He was expectant. It was the setup to a cheap punch line.

"Well, I suppose you could look at it that way, I mean—"

"What other way is there?" The host laughed first, followed by the crowd. Roma played it coy and pretended to be embarrassed.

She leaned in, touched his hand, and lowered her voice, "It's not like there was a bunch of *breeders* hanging out around the place all night."

This drew a tremendous laugh, a collective guffaw. Something said that hadn't been allowed until that moment. It was as if Roma had lifted some unspoken yoke from their enlightened shoulders, and the people couldn't have loved it more. It was revelry.

Brue smiled to himself. "Always on message."

Fiona walked into the room holding her light board. She lifted her eyes to the monitor. "Oh. She did Byrne tonight." She was delighted. "I love Byrne, he's hilarious."

"He's a dickhead." Brue tapped the desk, and the monitor went mute.

Fiona re-engaged her board to verify a timeline, nodded, and said, "The council is up. Everybody's ready—waiting for you."

Brue tapped the desktop, and on the opposite wall, smaller monitors cracked on. Each one was labeled on the bottom: *Afri-Corp*, *Asia-Corp*, *Euro-Corp*, and so on. Each continent was represented. On each screen, an individual sat at a uniform distance from their camera, dressed in a monotone color with similar backdrops—expressionless functionaries.

Brue sighed, then swiped again to activate his camera. "I appreciate your time, ladies and gentlemen. I believe you have all received the latest up-rep on our 'directed evolution' program?"

Brue checked with Fiona, who nodded. All the monitors were muted, so they responded by nodding.

"Outstanding. I've been assured the decision to move to Phase Five has been agreed upon, and there won't be any surprises at the General Assembly tomorrow?"

Again, the routine with the nodding heads.

"We have sent the messaging campaigns to your information divisions as of this morning and expect to see your proposals by next week."

Brue stared at the monitor across the room, distracted by Roma. She held her arms above her head, and her tight dress stretched along the curvy course of her body. She stepped to an inaudible beat, and her hips swayed with shy restraint. *Is she dancing?*

"Does anyone have any questions?" His hand inched toward the swipe controls on the desk.

Roma sat down again. She pulled some deep breaths, rosy in her cheeks, body on full display. He'd seen her like this, excited around the eyes, breasts heaving over the top of the neckline.

It was difficult to concentrate.

The monitor marked *Euro-Corp* activated its

microphone. The face opened its mouth to speak.

Brue said, "Thank you for attending." Then he swiped the monitors black. He leaned back in his chair, staring at her—the magnificent flesh of her.

Fiona said, "Well, that was a short meeting."

"I think they got the point." Brue turned up the volume.

Roma spoke earnestly, and Byrne did his best to pretend he was interviewing a cultural personality. After all, this was merely entertainment and not an information operation.

"... I mean, we've worked too hard to get where we are." She implored the crowd. "Together."

The people applauded, pliant, and grateful to be included. A crowd is controlled in different fashions, dependent upon the organism's intercellular nature. What motivates the tissues? What substitutes itself for oxygen?

"Just imagine where we'll be in twenty years. No more diseases or birth defects. No more inequality. Humanity is in harmony with the Earth. And that's the difference—harmony."

As she spoke, her voice changed in depth and pitch. She signaled the crowd with the corners of her eyes, and they articulated with her. She pressed her points with powerful gestures, and they gushed, self-aware and proud to be there at that moment. There was a cooing sameness to the organism's emanations. She fed them. She owned them.

Brue turned the monitor off and spun his chair to face his twinkling vista.

"Do you want to—"

"Go home, Fiona. I only want to be right here, right now."

He looked out into the night, pleased for the first time in a long while. Things were lining up: the Gen Two solution to a Gen One problem, the world governing body was about to begin the most advanced and comprehensive messaging campaign humanity had ever experienced, and after all these years of isolation, he had the comfort of a woman he could trust.

Yes, he wanted to be where he was at that moment. Tomorrow and its bullshit could wait.

FOUR

*Give them not praise. For, deaf, how should they know
It is not curses heaped on each gashed head?
Nor tears. Their blind eyes see not your tears flow.
Nor honour. It is easy to be dead.*
—When You See Millions of the Mouthless Dead

The clearing sat adjacent to a large, flat field. Knee-high goldenrod blooms swayed in the warm afternoon breeze. The orb had experienced a malfunction, and its automated return mechanism misfired. It landed, nestled on the edge of the plush, yellow expanse. Managing to transmit its coordinates for retrieval, it was otherwise unresponsive to remote attempts at control.

The small crew of Gen Ones had been called out to the field to recover the orb. The techs in the global control center were confident the Gen Ones could conduct the physical reboot and get the orb back online.

The trip into the hills took five hours, much of it on the road, but the last couple spent slogging through thick brush and stinging nettles. They left their vehicle far behind.

Sweating under a steady afternoon sun, the Gen Ones were in foul spirits. They worked on the problem, but none were happy about it.

Two soldiers sat and faced the orb. A third stared at a large glass board and waited for a connection to the drone's neural processing unit. He said, "This is a shit job."

His companion fidgeted with the stalks of goldenrod, deeply troubled. "Why do they send us out here alone like this? Those crazies are probably watching us right now."

The light board operator chuckled. "I wouldn't worry about it. It's a big area, and there aren't very many of them."

The soldier said, "We should have driven behind the compound and hid for the day. We should have called them up and told them we couldn't find it. Instead, here we are—and they're probably watching us."

The interface process completed. The soldier opened a folder containing the reboot steps. He read off the glass and said, "You guys pick it up. Hold it at your waist. It says no more than three feet. Hold it for a minute."

The two picked up the ball and stared at each other, shaking their heads.

"This thing is heavy."

Soldiers have done nothing throughout the history of conflict more than complain. These soldiers were no exception.

"This is bullshit... probably watching us right now."

◀———•●•———▶

Carl lay still as a stone, above the flowers, on the far side of the field. He held digital reticles to his eyes. On the screen, he observed the Gen One repair crew working on the drone, the distance and direction displayed on the bottom. They lifted the ball and held it at their waists.

Carl turned to Daniel, who squatted ten feet behind him. He gestured a string of hand signals.

Daniel nodded in reply, then turned and pointed at Rudy, waving him forward.

Rudy crawled on his belly, dragging his pack, his long gun on his back.

Daniel said, "Three Skins, four hundred yards in the open. They're about to launch a ball. Can you get 'em?"

Rudy smiled. "Four hundred yards is like sittin' in the same room."

"Don't brag about it till you do it." Daniel pushed him forward. "Carl's got eyes on. Hurry up. Get it done."

Rudy slid forward on his stomach, moving faster now.

Daniel pulled the radio from his belt, pushed the button. "Everybody hunker down. Prep your bump tents for a possible ball launch."

Along the patrol's line, the members sat flat and

quiet. They pulled their tents free, prepared to hunker down or run for their lives.

Rudy slid next to Carl. "What you got, man?"

"Four hundred, ten yards out. Clearing at one-five-nine. Three pax, prepping a ball."

Rudy popped the bipod legs on his long gun. He nestled the cheek rest and touched the nobs on the scope. He lifted his eyes above the tube, checked the direction off his wrist compass, and then reset his eye to the scope. "Alright. I got 'em."

"Take the one with the command module," Carl said.

"No shit." Rudy chuckled.

"What are you zeroed at?"

"One hundred yards."

Carl cycled through functions on his reticle. "Stand by for solution."

"Roger."

"Up, nine point five zero from your MOA."

"Roger, up nine dot five."

Carl said, "I have a slight wind from right to left. Dial in right, one MOA."

Rudy made the adjustment. "Roger."

Carl said, "Send it."

◂─────•●•─────▸

Among the yellow blooms, the Gen Ones continued their work. The day had been long. The ball was heavy. They had a shitty walk to get back to their truck. Could they get the thing back online? If not, they were expected to carry it, to hump the metal monster with its dead brain, back through the nettles and brush.

This was a shit job.

"Think about it. When's the last time anybody talked to you about the end of your service requirement?" said a soldier, tired of holding the heavy drone.

His companion looked away, disgusted. "They don't care about us."

"It's almost up, guys. Just another—hold on. Let go of it." The soldier on the command module smiled with expectation.

They released the ball, and it floated, making some chirping sounds. When the propulsion mechanism came online, their uniforms matted to their skin. Their guts crooned on a molecular level, and their skin tingled to the point of burning.

"What the hell?" A soldier touched it, and pulled his hand away, numbed. They stepped back, uncomfortable in the field of disruption.

The soldier closed the light board and said, "Told you it'd only take a minute. Now we need to—"

His head whipped with a sudden smack. Behind him, the tracing bullet deposited dark, red blood across the yellow blooms. His body slumped over to the ground.

One soldier dropped, flattened, and reached for his rifle. He heard a slap as another round found flesh. His companion fell, a hole in his stomach. Landing on his rear, he sat still before the next shot opened his skull, mottling the surface of the ball with brain and bone.

The last soldier's rifle erupted in long, random bursts. Blue tracers slipped across the open field as he stumbled back toward the tree line. The final shot was clean, through his left eye. He fell like a marionette with its strings cut.

The ball continued to float—the noises from within chirped, whirred, and rattled around its electric soul. The thing was waking up.

◄─────••─────►

Rudy panned his scope across the target area, looking for signs of movement. There was none. He smiled and cocked his head back toward Daniel. "They're down."

"Status on the ball." Daniel was holding his applause.

Carl gave him the report. "It's up, but it's only floating there. I don't know if it's online or not. Don't see any lights."

"Fuck!" The ball could wreck every one of them within moments of lighting up. The skins had either gotten it online or activated an internal repair algorithm. Either way, he needed to make a call and make it quick.

Rudy asked, "Want me to take it out?"

Carl said, "You'd just piss it off."

Daniel popped up to a knee and cycled through his options. They were in the open, no canopy. If the ball launched, or *when* it launched, his people would have to dome up, if they could even do that in time. They would then be at the mercy of the drone's loiter time, which could be days. With fresh, dead skins half a klick out, more forces would be sent to recover them. It was a bad situation.

"Fuck." He hissed into his radio. "Everybody up. Move. Move. Move." To Carl, he said, "Move us out fast. ERP fourteen. Let's go!"

Along the patrol, fighters cinched up their packs and started moving. Carl jumped up in a flash, his map out, running.

The element poured past Daniel. It was a hell of a racket. A patrol endeavored to be quiet almost above all things—as near silent as possible. Right then, his main concern was putting distance between the ball and his people, and if the effort created noise, so be it.

The rattling din lumbered past him. His skin crawled. If the ball launched, they'd be dead. He would have killed them all with his decision.

He had a contingency in mind, and if they moved fast enough, it could get them off the grid and away from the eyes in the sky.

But they would have to run like scalded dogs.

◄──────•●•──────►

The patrol scurried from ridge to ridge. They poured down into the bowls and trudged up the inclines. Carl had elected to stay on trails for speed, a decision

Daniel had no problem with. The main issue was getting clear of the damned ball.

Daniel sucked for air, covered in sweat. As the patrol leader, he was required to run forward and back down the line, ensuring his men kept moving. He studied their faces as he passed, looking for the signs of dehydration or exhaustion.

Having established a miserable cadence, the noise echoed through the trees, and steam wafted off their necks in the cooling air. They were like a large, grunting caterpillar inching along in the dying light of the mountains.

The orb buzzed three feet above the blood-soaked flowers. The occasional breeze stirred it, but it held its place and chirped. Beneath it, the goldenrod was pressed flat by its propulsive field.

A remote command found it. The neural processing unit received its directive. A loud ping echoed across the field. The curved surface flashed. Vibrant colors waved across the globe. After the display, it returned to the flat, gray color. Several clicking sounds emitted from its cold body.

Then, like a buoy held deep beneath the ocean's surface, suddenly freed, the ball shot straight up into the evening sky.

The patrol stopped after two grueling hours. Daniel

stood on a large granite slab, catching his breath and working hard at it. The trail ended at the face of a cliff. From his vantage point, he surveyed the surrounding valleys. Carl knelt beside him, working to get oxygen into his lungs.

Daniel turned to Curtis, who had stopped a few yards away. "Get the antenna up."

Curtis nodded and opened his pack. He rooted through the contents.

John was splayed out near Daniel. He didn't bother to remove his ruck before he fell onto his side. His chest heaved, and he wheezed as he lifted himself onto his rear. He leaned against his ruck, desperate, pale, and worn out.

Daniel called out, "Everybody give me a perimeter. Get security up!" His voice broke as he managed his breathing.

The fighters tightened up the perimeter, feeling the heaviness of their blood-gorged legs. They stumbled into positions and pointed their eyes outward. Individual plumes of steam rose, showcasing the trace of the patrol.

Daniel glanced at John.

"Don't even think… about it." John struggled to speak.

Daniel pulled out his map and showed it to Carl. "There's a cave complex on the face of this incline." He pointed over the edge of the granite cap. "It's about a hundred meters down. We could probably scramble it, but everybody's tired, so let's get the rope team up here and set some anchors."

Carl stood on wobbly legs and started toward the perimeter.

"Umm, boss. I don't... uh." Curtis rummaged his pack, jerking open pockets and inspecting them, then moving on to the next. His tone matched his frantic hands.

"What's up, Curtis?"

"I can't find the antenna."

This was not good news. Daniel immediately scanned the dusky sky. It was pointless. He would never see the ball if it were up there.

Curtis said, "It musta fell out when I was runnin'. I thought I had it tied down." He ransacked his ruck. His eyes were shot through with shame.

"Not much we can do about that now. When Carl gets back, help the rope teams set the anchors so we can get low."

Daniel glanced across the clear granite shelf. Maggie sat beside Rudy. He'd pulled out his canteen and shared it with her. They sat on the edge of a rock, which was lipped up at an angle, like they were on a hiking date. He shook his head. He didn't like it, but he was too exhausted to raise the issue.

John spoke up. "A cave isn't going to help much if they've got eyes on us already."

Daniel had finally caught his breath. He explained, "It's a complex—runs through all these ridges." He waved his hand over the surrounding area. "It's good. I've used it before. Gets a little tight in there at some points, but it'll take us most of the way to Newbern."

Daniel heard the sound first, the subtle, angry whisper of rockets. Then, the earth opened up around the edges of the patrol as explosions blossomed. One after another, the shots claimed their victims. Pressure waves followed the blasts and forced him back. He stumbled under a low hang of granite.

The rockets walked along the perimeter. Each explosion destroyed another of his men. Their bodies were rendered to pieces and distributed, along with their equipment, about the area.

Daniel, stunned by the attack's speed, was overwhelmed. He'd experienced mortar fire, sustained and effective, but nothing like this. Every incoming shot was bound to a victim.

His eyes followed the black lines of smoke back to their origin. The ball, the matte gray demon gliding like a dancer, destroyed everything around him.

He remembered Maggie. Rudy had pulled her under his body, protecting her. They had climbed beneath their rock bench—their soft bodies waiting for some red-hot shard to find them under it.

The attack paused. Orbs could simultaneously mark and engage five separate targets. At the end of the cycle, the machine had to reset its parameters and adjust for smoke and heat over the target. The barrage would renew within moments.

More was coming, yet Daniel's feet were cemented to the rock. He was frozen, and even as he perceived the humiliation of that fact, he could do no more about it than he could stop the drone above him.

Carl sprinted across the open area, wrangling ropes over his shoulders. He was on a mission, undeterred by the carnage. He worked to complete the last task he'd been given.

His rocket found him as he lurched over a crest of granite. It burst ten feet over his head, raining shrapnel down. Curtis found himself inside that same ring of death. Angles of steel pulped their bodies.

Ricochets glanced in all directions from the rock's surface, flashing past Daniel's face. He had experienced that before—*hot shrapnel*. His body woke up and reacted on autopilot. He dropped to his pack and lifted his eyes. Carl and Curtis were broken open, dead.

The shots continued along the edges, and Daniel became aware of his legs again, along with his breath. The acrid smell of explosives burned in his nose. Smoke began accumulating on the granite tip, sterile in the evening doldrums.

Rudy screamed at him. "Daniel! What do we do?"

His voice cut through the thickness, pulled Daniel's eyes away from the massacre, and helped wrench him back to his wits. The boy had been ready to sacrifice himself for Maggie. The sight of it simplified things. Explosions blunted into background noise. He was able to put a hasty plan together.

It was a simple one.

He grabbed his pack straps and screamed, "Follow me!"

He lifted the pack in one hand, turned to the cliff face, and slipped over the side.

The angle was steep but not impossible. He slid until he felt himself leaving the surface of the rock. He smeared his hands against the cliff, trying to create enough friction to slow down. His body continued to float away, and a deep pit opened in his stomach. He pawed at the slab, trying to stick.

Finally, a thick lip jutted into his clawing hands. He locked onto it. His body, on a fulcrum, slammed into the granite face. The impact nearly dislodged his hold. His feet slid and kicked, trying to find some purchase. Every sinew in his torso burned from the effort, worked at one purpose. Beneath him, a three hundred-foot drop before his body would hit the treetops.

A sound pulled his attention upward—John slid toward him, his belly and face catching the rock.

Daniel dropped several feet and stopped on a pronounced edge. John above him was still barreling down. Daniel could only watch as the man fell toward him.

John left plenty of skin on the rock, flattening his legs against the slab and spreading his arms wide above his head. The friction caused him to slow, his body burning. The rough, lined granite stopped streaking past his face. Shaking, he summoned the courage to investigate his situation, looking down past his feet. Daniel stood on a diagonal lip.

"Let me move, then drop down here," Daniel said. He grabbed a handful of sloped rock and wedged his fingers into a crack. He stepped off to John's right and left the tiny ledge open.

John grabbed what he could and lowered himself to the ledge.

Above them, the rockets continued to pummel the ridgeline. Daniel waited to see his daughter follow, but she didn't show.

"Where is this fucking cave? We hang out here too long…"

John's voice quivered from the adrenaline and pain. He gripped whatever bumps and slopes were available. His body smashed against the rock face; he avoided looking beyond his feet.

Daniel studied the area, got his bearings, and spotted the cave entrance. Its dark mouth sat open twenty meters down to his right. "We gotta down-climb. It's not easy," he said to John.

"As opposed to this?" John was hanging on, his eyes pinched shut.

"Hey!" Daniel got his attention.

John glanced his way, careful not to look past him at the deep drop beyond him. Daniel pointed down to his right.

"You're gonna need to watch me so you see the route."

John was wide-eyed. Daniel tried again.

"Watch me so you can—"

"Yeah. Yeah. Just go." John's voice was threaded with stress.

Daniel began the climb down with John cursing a few feet above him. They struggled to negotiate the cracks and small edges of the rock. They descended toward the dark safety of the opening.

◄———••———►

Daniel squatted in the cave's entrance. He craned his head out, scanning the rock face. "Rudy, Maggie, come in. Come in." The radio was stagnant, not even a squelch.

John was sprawled against the rock floor, his lungs seizing as much air as possible. His pack was strewn to the side. This was much more than he was prepared to handle. He said, "It's probably jamming comms."

"Rudy, Maggie, come in." Daniel leaned back out of the entrance, his face a maze of deep worry. In all his years and operations, he'd never been devastated this way. His patrol had been destroyed before his eyes. There was nothing he could do to stop it once it began.

He froze in the face of it, and that gnawed at him, but what tore his soul in half was his daughter not following him over the edge. He could imagine a couple of reasons, and neither of them was good.

John mustered enough energy to say, "Get your head back in here. You're going give us away. They can slip one of those rockets right in here."

Daniel ignored him and squinted his eyes in the new evening. He sighed. "Rudy, Maggie... Fuck it."

He dropped the radio on the ground and leaned out of the hole. His hands reached up and cupped a slope. Then he was up and out of the entrance, his feet resting on the bottom.

"Daniel." John sat up and pushed his rear off the cavern floor, but his exhaustion took over. He sat back and waved his hand. "Whatever. I get it."

Daniel found some footholds and began the ascent.

The attack didn't last long: it had finished minutes ago. He did the math in his head. He reckoned the drone had fired all its rockets. He figured it was observing the area until another drone could come on station. Without an accurate round count, he was acting on instinct, on a hunch. Still, he was willing to take the chance. It had been his experience that, when one of the balls started killing, it just kept on going, blasting and mutilating the bodies under it until its wired heart was satiated.

He climbed on, reaching for another sloped rock, heading toward Maggie.

◀——•●•——▶

On top, the slab at the peak had provided all the cover and concealment that Rudy and Maggie needed. He'd dragged her underneath the overhang when the barrage began, utilizing the drifting smoke as cover. Once wedged beneath the angled rock, he pulled their packs against the opening, hoping it would dissipate their heat signature.

Above, the ball circled, studying the kill zone with its cold, liquid eyes. Its algorithm confused Rudy and Maggie with blast spillover among the blinding, white carnage beneath it. As it was programmed, the ball concentrated its rockets on viable and distinguishable targets. Now, it circled, idle, observing the terrain.

Maggie was stunned and silent. It had been close and gruesome. Curtis had been dismantled in front of her, gored by shrapnel—disassembled. His violent end was running on a loop in her mind. The grotesque display wedged into her thoughts.

Rudy pulled her tight. "I think it's outta ammo."

"How do you know that?"

"Well, it'd be a bit of a guess. I didn't start counting 'til we got under here. But I counted fourteen rockets. They carry twenty. So, I think it's dry."

"What does that mean, exactly?"

"It means we got maybe eight, ten minutes till another one shows up. So if we're gonna get, we better start gettin'."

"It's still up there watching us?" The idea of stepping out from cover under the eyes of that flying thing was terrifying.

"Listen, I think it's empty. I'm sure it is."

Rudy wedged his hand up to his throat, rolled his balaclava over his face, and adjusted the eye pocket. "Cover your face unless you wanna end up enrolled in their database. It's gonna get us on video."

Maggie covered her face, her hands trembling.

"You ready?" Rudy asked with a slight quiver in his voice.

"What are we going to do?"

Nothing in her life had prepared her for this. She thought of her father for the first time since the explosions began. After he jumped over the cliff edge, Rudy had held her close, shielding her from the chaos. What a shame if she would never see him again. What a shame the whole thing was, all the killing. All these young men had been cut down for ideas that had no hold on her. It didn't make any sense.

"We're gonna grab them ropes off Carl, anchor 'em off this rock, and slide down. We'll find that cave. If we're fast, we can get it done before the next one shows up."

"Wait." She touched his hand as it reached for a pack. She pointed to the sky. "What if that one isn't empty?"

He started to speak, then changed his mind. His eyes got soft. "We gotta go."

Rudy pushed the pack out of the opening and slid out. He ran to the ropes, checked them for damage, sliding his hands along the length, looking for compromises. He worked fast. Satisfied, he dragged the rope to the rock and coiled it—found the midpoint and tossed the line over the angled slab.

He turned to Maggie.

She stood, staring at Curtis's body. She

remembered him alive and smiling. His body now—his face, pale and broken, didn't seem to be real. He'd been a friend to her. This was a cruelty. It was senseless. There was nothing fair about any of it.

Rudy dropped his rope and moved to her. "Hey. Hey. Best not to look at that stuff, okay."

He touched her face and pulled it to his eyes. He shook his head. "Keep that shit outta your brain. Now let's go."

She leaned into him and took a shuddering breath. Though she'd spent much time ignoring and contradicting Daniel, some of his words had taken root.

When you find yourself surrounded by madness, take control of the only thing you can: yourself.

She nodded and took a deep breath. "I'm good. Let's go."

She moved to the packs and lifted them. Rudy looped the rope over a jagged outcropping and slid it deep into a crevice. A noise from the cliff's edge got their attention. Rudy pulled his side arm and held it at his waist. Maggie slid her pack on and picked up her rifle. She steadied herself.

An arm popped over the lip of the cliff, the hand searching for a grip—then, another hand. Daniel lugged himself up on top. He took a knee and looked at the two of them. His smile was weary but relieved. He waved them over.

They ran to him, Rudy dragging the rope behind.

"We need to get down now." Daniel was tired; it was in his eyes. He reached out and touched Maggie's face.

She grabbed his hand and leaned her cheek against it. Chewed up from the rough granite, his fingers scraped her skin. He'd come back for her.

Rudy interjected, pointing at the rock. "The anchor's set. We can go."

Daniel said, "Alright, no time for a harness; it's about a seventy-five-degree slope. So, we're gonna do a body rappel. Go down one at a time. I'll go first so you know the way. Got it?"

They nodded.

Daniel stood, slipped the rope between his legs, wrapped it back around his left hip, and then over the opposite shoulder. He held the rope underhanded with his left hand. He leaned back, tested the anchor, nodded at them, and walked backward down the rock face. The line fed through his grip to control his descent.

Maggie said, "I've never done this."

Rudy shrugged. "It's easy. Watch him, and then I'll set you up real quick. You good?"

Maggie scanned the area behind her. In the settling darkness, she saw the stains of the attack and the glistening remains of her friends.

"Yeah. I'm good."

◂━━━•●•━━━▸

Brue walked from the kitchen of his luxury penthouse apartment carrying two tumblers of bourbon. The glasses tinkled with ice and promise.

He was naked save for a fluffy, ornate bathrobe open down to his abdomen. As he stepped, the floor beneath his feet splashed in multi-colored clouds. It was a nanotech feature—an upgrade. He installed it after he was appointed global project lead. For all the suffering in the world, some people still walked on clouds.

He stepped into the entertainment room. Roma sat on the far side of the couch. Her naked shoulders drew him closer. Her soft back rounded inward toward her hips. When he cleared the sofa's edge, he took her in fully, and it called for a moment of appreciation. He stopped and said, "Whew."

She turned and smiled, reaching for her glass.

On the wall monitor, the Planetary General Assembly was amid a vote, made evident by a digitized tally displayed on the lower right-hand of the screen.

"How's it going?" He asked.

"Like it's supposed to," Roma grinned. She held the glass flat and leaned her nose over the lip. She made a face. The bourbon was bitter and complicated, and she never got the point of it.

"Well, it looks good." He pointed at the counter.

The screen read: *Amendment to Prop. 10857, Yea: 102, Nay: 47*

As he spoke, the camera focused on a heated argument between two members of Euro-Corp. An older man, sputtering and red-faced, laid into a young blonde woman. The blonde stood cocky with her arms crossed, shaking her head in a slow, deliberate disagreement. This enhanced the man's agitation, which in turn intensified the woman's unbending attitude.

Roma's eyes narrowed. "I hate that bitch."

Brue's eyes widened. Taken aback, he asked, "The blonde?"

"No. The old man." Her laugh was sarcastic but not biting. "Of course, the blonde. That's Phillip she's arguing with. He's solid, from Denmark. Very reliable."

"What's her deal?"

"She wants something. She always wants something." A hint of exhaustion slid into her voice as she eyed the screen. It had been several days of non-stop negotiating. A fair amount of political capital had been expended to get this vote.

"Is she a problem?"

Roma stood. She stepped in front of him. Her pubic hair grazed his lips. "No." She grabbed him beneath his jawline and lifted him to her mouth. "She's just a bitch."

They embraced and pressed their lips together. Brue grabbed her waist and slid his arms up her back. He pulled her tight against himself.

The vote counter shifted, and one more vote entered the "Yea" column.

◄——••——►

The bedroom's opulence was heightened by the fifteen-foot window wall. Brue sat at the edge of the bed. He stared out into the blinking city. He tilted a glass of bourbon, no ice. There was no more need for ice. The bottle sat close to empty at his feet on the floor. A purple halo floated around it.

He sighed. The world had its places of joy. This room had been joyful since the first night Roma came to him. She showed up unannounced after he had endured a brutal interrogation before a board of inquiry.

A mishap at a factory producing a growth medium poisoned an upstate New York water supply. Some whitish fluid leaked into the groundwater. It was no real concern until he discovered a senior senator's mother lived in the town.

He sat at the table for fourteen hours over two days, convinced that he was finished as the lead researcher. He might even be removed from the project. The public committee had been packed with media. There were the requisite onlookers and one beautiful woman who sat in the back. She made it a point to catch his eye from time to time.

The night she showed up at his doorstep, she told him she could help. She had nuanced her familial connections into a vast, growing politico-corporate influence operation. She said she could reach deep into the apparatus. She'd seen him speak once and had been moved by his passion. Her eyes were downcast, almost reverent, as she talked to him. She told him she knew people who could help him if he would let her in.

He did, and she hadn't left him since.

Behind him, the bed sheets shuffled. He drained his glass—a little more drunk now. She was about to ask the things she always asked. He would say the things he always said. He would show his jugular to her, and she would kiss his skin, rub his chest, and talk with her body. Soon, his worries would be forgotten, drowsily floating in a pool of hormones.

"Why do you always do this?" Roma yawned as she spoke.

"Do what?" He reached for the bottle and worked at the cork.

Roma sat up. "Do you think you are the Dios del Futuro?"

Brue stopped fidgeting with the bourbon cork and gave it some quick and serious thought. "I don't know. If I don't sleep, there is no future. Only the now. See?" He continued twisting the cork top. "When you fell asleep—*so rudely, I might add*—this, now was the future for you. It has only been the now for me. Do you understand?"

Roma placed her soft hands on his and rested the attempt to unseal the bottle. "I understand you have had enough to drink." She kissed his shoulder. "Why don't you come to bed with me? We can have some more fun." She dragged her fingernails across his lower back.

"I wonder if I could stop it, you know? If I needed to."

The nagging, distant worry, formless and forbidden, often reared its head in his quiet moments. Brue's mind leaped to risk mitigation, but he was far too drunk to peel that onion. If the enterprise were to get away from him... there were stop gaps.

He had ensured he wouldn't play the part of some evil overlord. The project would succeed, and the dignity of humanity would be upheld. But there were quarters of the world from which no amount of convincing had been, or would be, enough.

When the god freaks came after him, with their asinine misunderstandings, the project was new, and its success or failure relied on his ability to paint them as what they were: fools paralyzed by archaic and illogical dictums. This, indeed a slow process, had accounted for, in his estimation, his greatest accomplishment—the marginalization of the hardcore adherents and the co-opting of the more amenable.

The fanatics condemned him for years, and it wasn't until they traded their words for weapons that he was allowed to actually deal with them. Every country, of every color and creed, they were dealt with, and the populations were cured... for the most part.

Yet, the prophecies still rattled around in his head—inane, reactionary screeds. In these naked moments, he entertained them. He recalled the interrogations, the men who suffered untold pain instead of recanting. Their eyes, all the way to the end, possessed a certainty that haunted him.

What had them so convinced? Had he overlooked it?

"Stop what?" Roma kissed his neck. "Why would you stop anything?"

Brue shrugged. "You never know."

But he knew her warmth, and the fullness of her breasts pressing against his arm. The distant concern floated away into the recesses of his mind, replaced by a surge of oxytocin.

"Why sit here alone all night?"

"Because if I don't..." Brue fell to his back on the bed as if in surrender. "If I don't, who will?"

Roma mounted him, her breasts inches from his face.

He opened his mouth and craned his neck, but she pinned his shoulders and laughed. She egged him on with her eyes. She shook herself in front of his drunken face. He struggled with her for a moment and then gave up. His head fell back to the pillow, and he closed his eyes.

She slid her arms underneath him and rested her head on his chest, listening to his heartbeat.

"You were amazing on that clod's show tonight." Brue stroked her hair.

"Byrne is nice."

"Everyone's nice to you. Byrne is a clod." He smiled. "They really do seem to love you, don't they?"

"I don't know." Roma shrugged her shoulders like a girl.

"I do. I see it every time you do the public."

Roma kissed his chest. She rubbed her body against his and listened to his heart rate increase.

"You know I've had the procedure, right?" he said it, out of place as it was. He recognized that she wanted him, sensed her weakness. It was a good time to capitalize.

She stopped, lifted her eyes to him, and said, with a sweet sadness, "I know."

"Last year." He nodded to himself. "It was the right thing to do—for the future. A responsibility, you know?"

Roma's grip weakened, and she lost some air. "I know." She had stopped moving her hips into him. Her body hinted at sadness.

Brue grabbed her, bridged his hips, and reversed their position. Now lying on top, he discovered her body. Roma laughed, happy to have his eyes on her.

He gazed at her and breathed. "Do you trust me?"

◆———••———▶

The hovercraft had not yet stopped when the heavy, clear door opened. As it came to rest, Cleary stepped out. The medic followed with Rhett strapped into an automated litter. The operators piled out, slipped past the two, and headed to their team room for the showers and beds.

Cleary paused the medic and pulled him to the side before entering the building.

"Listen, mate. Don't hand him off to the infirmary just yet. Keep treating him. I got a call from the drone fellas, and apparently, there's somethin' for me to see. If I like it, I'll simply call you and give you my condolences for your patient. You follow?"

The medic was puzzled. "His blood pressure is stable in this—"

Cleary interrupted with agonized patience. The kid wasn't getting it. "So, this is going to go one of two ways. I'll either *want* to talk to him again, or he *won't* make it. You know? His blood pressure will drop dangerously low. Like, zero-low. Does that make more sense?"

Cleary was saying something without saying it. *Do you like working with the teams?* or maybe, *Nice career you have there. It'd be a shame if something happened to it.*

The medic got the picture. He scanned the area to see if anyone had overheard. He glanced up at the cameras mounted over the entrance.

Cleary sensed his misgivings. He took his patrol cap off and wiped his brow, chuckling. "You know, back in the good ole days, as they say, we could pretty much do whatever we needed to do." Cleary glanced about, sharing the medic's suspicions. "I mean, nobody was countin' these guys. The gloves were off, as they also say. My point bein', I haven't even called this guy in. There's no report in which he exists. Do you understand?" He gave the young medic a probing stare.

The medic got the point, gave him a terse nod, and wheeled Rhett away.

Cleary pulled his light board and swiped and tapped it. He held it to his ear. "Just landed. Be there in five."

Cleary burst into the lead technician's office. He powered his way to the live, active monitor with the joyfulness that followed successful operations. He was expectant, and the force of his movements showed it.

The tech surrendered his seat to avoid being thrown from it.

Cleary studied the screen with impatience. "What am I looking at?"

The tech leaned over from the edge of the desk and pointed at the screen. "Twelve minutes ago, two orbs responded to an action in Romeo Hotel, Five-Three. It was an autonomous action that ended by the time our guys were on stream."

Cleary gave him some hard eyes. "Where is the action?"

The tech swiped the screen, pulled up a recorded feed, and rolled it back ten minutes.

The granite peak of the ridgeline and the heat signatures of twenty people came into focus. The outline of their weapons glaringly blazed in white. Dispersed across the ridge's peak, arranged in what Cleary took as a patrol halt, they constituted a military formation.

Several had been designated with small, digital squares surrounding their heads. Micro-calculations filled the data boxes, and the drone made its final decision.

The feed wiggled and blurred with smoke as the rockets launched. On the edges of the patrol, people disappeared in white hot flashes or cartwheeled through the air, their limbs flying off in different directions. After the first five rockets, the drone restarted its designation and calculation routine.

The heat-based feed dazzled with debris as it rained down across the rocks.

"Has this been fully analyzed?" Cleary asked.

"Well, it's been ten minutes, so—"

"Who is that?" Cleary pointed at two figures as they slipped over the face of the ridge top. "Where did they go?"

The tech hesitated. "The orb was—"

"Call it a fuckin' ball, would ya?"

"Yes, um, the ball was in the principal engagement phase, not focused on runners."

"Yeah?"

"But, they come back." The tech offered as a consolation prize.

"They come back up?"

The tech said, "Well, one of them does, after the ball is Winchester. He came back for two members of his team."

"Let me see."

The tech swiped the feed-forward through the waves of butchery. A man scaled the rock and covered the lip of the cliff. Cleary studied him. The nighttime feed and radiance of the impacted area fuzzed the footage and made it difficult to identify him. "Facial recognition?"

"Tough in this spectrum, too close to the heat signatures. But we'll use multiple identifying markers—height, weight, and posture—during full analysis. If he's in the dataset, we should get an identity for you."

Cleary studied the man, his movements, his bearing. He waited for the knowledge to rattle loose. He didn't want to force it, didn't want to cloud his judgment with bias. There were indicators in the images: the straightness of the shoulders and back, a quality unique amongst men who carried heavy weights for years, the thickset chest, short neck, the cant of the head, and the coolness of a guy whose patrol had been decimated moments before. He carried the hallmarks of the man he had chased years ago. He grabbed a pen and paper, wrote on it, and slid it to the tech. "This is the guy. Do your comparisons, but I know who it is." He pulled his light board, held it to his ear, and waited until someone answered.

"Sorry about your patient."

◆———••———▶

Their whispered voices echoed inside the tight cavern. Mud laced the floor and walls.

The survivors cloistered together, their clothes caked in silty, tan mud. Much of their movement required them to crawl on their bellies and squeeze through the tight joints of the cave system. A single chemical light burned bright blue. They squatted in the center of the cavern, working through the problem.

Maggie sat in a corner, holding a small lantern, lost in her thoughts.

Daniel drained his canteen. He looked at John, the vacant, spent look in his eyes. He pointed at the map on the floor.

"So, like I said, these are the exits." He used the blue chem light to point at several spots on the map. "If we get moving, we should pop out before they expand their search rings."

"Where will we come out?" John repressed a yawn.

"Honestly, I can't remember. It's been a while. But any of 'em are close enough to make the hit time." Daniel eyed the map.

"Hit time?" John was incredulous. "What are you talking about? There's only four of us."

"You're not planning on flakin' out on me, are ya?"

This was a proposal John wasn't prepared to entertain. "Daniel, I understand that—"

"Do you know how long it's been since I lost anyone on a patrol?" Daniel's voice grew strained. He worked to control his temper. John had access to the resources he needed, and it was doubtful that he could strong-arm him. He anticipated John's reluctance to continue, knowing the man well. "This thing was a huge waste of my men if we drop it."

"Don't worry. I'll hold up my end. I'll honor my agreement." John nodded at Maggie when he said it.

She caught the attention and wondered aloud,

"What agreement?"

"Stop trying to muddy the waters here, John." Daniel was losing his patience. His voice flared. "You think you're gonna get all my men killed and waltz off like nothin' happened?" Now, he was screaming. "Cuz you're not—you're not gonna do that!"

Rudy yelled, "Hey! Can I propose something, or would you two like to crack each other's heads open in this cave?"

Daniel dipped his head to Rudy, and he sucked in some stale air, trying to get control of himself.

John shook his head and threw up his hands. "Might as well."

Rudy rummaged through his pack and withdrew a small metal canister. He set it on the map and twisted it from the top. Once open, he pulled two syringes out and laid them flat, holding the blue light above them.

He held his hand out to John as if to slow him down. "Hear me out. These are two doses of a psychotomimetic drug called BZ. It's not actually BZ—that shit would kill you at this dose—but it falls into the same class." Rudy smiled. "This has a real smooth impact and lasts longer."

John was irritated. "You trying to make a point here?"

"Yes, sorry. Listen, if I can get close enough to this guy, we won't need to shoot our way out. He can hit the net and reroute security. He can escort *us* off the X, if you get me?"

Daniel leaned in. "It doesn't make him crazy?"

He'd heard of these drugs causing targets to go off the rails, start inventing languages, and jump out of hovercrafts at ten thousand feet.

"No, that would be useless to us. Like I said, this is the good shit. He'll be fully on board with whatever I tell him to do. He won't fight, won't complain. Just comply."

Daniel wagged his head, smiling. "Shut down security protocols with override codes. Send his detail packin'." He implored John. "What do you think about that?"

Rudy spoke up. "According to the intel packet, this guy has a four-man detail. Some heavy hitters for sure, but I don't care how good you are, you can't cover everything with a crew that small."

"Sounds like a fuckin' do-er to me." Daniel warmed to the idea, his voice picking up steam. "We need a way in. What about your contractors?"

John nodded. "I've definitely got some infrastructure in and around Newbern. Got a guy with a chemical removal contract. He can maybe get us in. Maybe."

Daniel held his words. He worked through the problem and the possible solutions, and conducted a hasty risk evaluation. He was no fan of taking long shots, but he wasn't about to let his men die in vain. It made sense: the small security detail, the psychoactive drugs. Were he honest with himself, he'd acknowledge his desire for vengeance, that his judgment might be compromised. But as he mulled it over, he became acutely aware there wasn't enough time. The decision needed to be made now.

He said, "Let's grab that piece a' shit."

John looked around the cavern at the faces of the 'assault force.' "I'll need to make contact with my man. It'll be last minute, so no guarantees."

"Sounds like we got the beginning of a plan." He asked Maggie, "Can you drive?"

She didn't respond, her face flat in the thinning, blue light. "What agreement?"

◄─────•●•─────►

Cleary pocketed his light board, having attempted to contact Brue for the fourth time. He sat at the tech's desk, fingers forming a triangle in front of his chin. His boss wasn't great with communication. The tragedy of genius is disorganization in all matters unrelated to genius.

He pulled the board out, swiped, tapped, and held it out in front of his mouth.

The link occurred, and a curt "Yes?" issued from the speaker. The voice was not welcoming, but Cleary smiled anyway. "Fiona." He was happy to hear her. "How are you today?"

There was silence on the other end. A moment passed. "Yes?"

Cleary's optimism dipped. He'd dealt with Fiona a bit and found her to be tiresome, yet something about her physical form pleased him. He enjoyed baiting her into anger. "So, I've had some trouble reaching the boss. Do you—"

"If he wanted to talk to you, he would."

The word *frigid* jumped to the front of Cleary's mind.

"Yes, I get that, but darlin'"—an audible groan from the speaker made Cleary's eyes light up with mirth—"I *am* his head of operational security, and if he doesn't take my call, it could actually be dangerous for him."

The condescension in his voice was palpable, and he grimaced, wishing he could take it back. As entertaining as it was to irritate Fiona, he needed something from her.

"What is the query? Maybe I could answer it for you."

That's more like it, thought Cleary. "What are the boss's travel plans for the next few days?"

"The schedule has been synched with your team."

Icebox.

"But you guys are always runnin' off to places that aren't on the schedule."

"If it's not on the schedule, then you're not read-on to the classification status."

"Again, darlin', I'm tryin' to do my job here."

"Submit your report."

"Does he read them, though?"

"He reads what he reads."

Cleary had to take a breath. She had turned the tables. He took a moment to appreciate her as a tactician. "Then, maybe you could pass somethin' along for me?"

Fiona did not respond, leaving him to hold his

silent light board in the air like a beggar.

"Alright," he said. "Tell him the operations in Virginia have gone well. But he needs to be aware that a man is on the loose down there—currently."

"Currently?" Fiona was skeptical.

"Yeah. We got a line on him but don't currently have him in hand."

"You used that word again."

She was enjoying herself, as indicated by the lilt at the end of her words. Cleary could almost see the smile on her face. "So, if you would, let your boss know if he's on some super-secret squirrel mission to the area that he might want to cancel, or—"

"Cancel? Because you can't keep hold of one of your hillbillies?"

"Well, this one can be a problem for—"

"Currently, he's your problem."

Cleary let it sit for a moment. "Could you please—"

"Is that all?"

"Yes."

Cleary's light board went dark as the connection was cut. He dropped it on the desk and ran his fingers through his hair, exasperated. A five-foot, two-inch woman who weighs a hundred pounds just ate his lunch—just took it out of his hands and ate it.

Still, he had to smile.

◂———•••———▸

People crowded the sidewalk, jammed together, leaning over barricades. The police security line in front of the public health clinic was strained by the exuberance. Media companies dotted the street with their trucks and drone cameras.

The clinic doors opened, and the crowd leaned closer, gaping to see. Roma walked out onto the landing and into the acclamation. She waved and was greeted with obsessed eyes staring back, awestruck. Her fans cried, waved, and shouted for her attention.

The cops pushed them back, and the hectic tug-of-war created an undulation of humanity. The flimsy barricades were caught in the ebb, the path collapsing and respawning.

Roma kept her head up. She stepped into the human quag—pawed at like a thing. An interview station waited, and she pushed her way toward it.

The police wrestled the followers away. A slow-moving grind, she negotiated it with a tight smile.

She reached the waiting reporter and concealed herself under the warmth of a practiced facsimile. Millions of people tuned into the proceedings on monitors around the country.

"First of all, let me say, I—no, *we*—are proud of you. We are floored by your commitment and are inspired." The reporter was a good actor.

Roma went with it. She reached out and touched the woman's hand. "I think if we all considered it, we'd see that it's the only way forward." She poured her eyes into the camera. "The only way."

Inside the armored utility vehicle, Brue sat, twisted toward the rear window. His shoulders and neck were marked with tension. He absorbed the scene with as much patience as he could muster as the mad crowd crushed in on Roma.

She stood at the interview station, the floating cameras with their lights glaring onto her fine skin. She smiled throughout.

The crowd, now tamed, had been wrenched from her path. Brue would have some choice words for the police commissioner about his lack of foresight with the security preparations.

Roma's hand sought those reaching out and gripped them. She scanned the crowd but looked in no one's eyes. Brue felt pulled toward her. The overwhelming urge to redeem himself was born inside his guts. There was pain under her pretense. She couldn't hide it from him.

The door was opened. She turned again to her fans, then slid into the vehicle backward and rested on the seat.

The door closed, and the interior filled with silence. A fresh void sat between them, and Brue found it tricky to speak in the face of it. It was a thing he created; he understood that. He, of course, had known there would be a difference in her, in them, but the measure of that silence hinted at something far vaster than he'd expected. It had a weight to it.

She lifted her head and caught her breath. Roma, a woman of devoted optimism, couldn't break her gaze from the seat ahead or peel the lines of pain from her eyes. She exhaled, tremulous and shaking. He reached for her, but she pushed his hand away.

"Not yet."

Brue leaned toward her, concerned. "Are you in pain? They said there was no pain." His voice was tinged with guilt. Asking someone to give up eternity for you was not a light thing. It was not a small promise to fill the void created. He wasn't sure he could do it himself.

"I am not in pain." Soft, little tears spilled across her cheeks. "Only, I don't know why you couldn't be with me."

He grabbed her hands. "Because this was your moment. *Your* statement, not mine." Brue searched his depths to find the enthusiasm to push this on her. "Now, more people will follow us. It had to be this way, don't you see?"

She stopped crying, a good girl—a strong girl. She said, "I did this for you."

Brue nodded and opened his mouth to speak.

She interrupted, "But in there, I felt alone. I was..." She looked at him then, for the first time. "I was conscious, but disconnected—I don't know—like someone standing alone in a dark room. I couldn't even feel their hands on me."

She softened. With her eyes, she let him know that he could hold her.

He pulled her tight into his arms, and she accepted him. She leaned her head on his chest and laid against his electric life as the city rolled past.

This pain would live with her for a while, he told himself. She would accommodate it. This was the hope for the future—she would know it had been the right decision. Brue's body stiffened as he thought of the days to come, the things he must now do.

Roma sensed his tension, and she could feel his attention drift away. She said, "When do you leave?"

"Tomorrow. Early. I can cancel if you want. "

"No." She sat upright and wiped her eyes. She straightened her jacket. "Just go."

Brue touched her hand, and she didn't pull it away, but there was a stiffness to it, an unpliable rejection.

She would overcome this. He would wait for her to come around. There were too many mouths to feed and too much poison belched in the effort. This was the right thing.

She would soften to it.

◂—————••—————▸

The light board vibrated inside its hidey-hole at two in the morning, which was unusual. Tony sat up in bed. He hadn't had a deep night's sleep for a couple of years. Too many things could go wrong at any time of the day or night. There were too many catastrophes in waiting.

His wife, half asleep, said, "Tony, what…?"

"It's okay." He rubbed her back as he felt for the

tiny seam on the varnished oak frame of the bed. "Go back to sleep. It's work."

His fingers found the lip and pressed the concealed compartment cover. It popped open to the side, and he grabbed the light board. It was programmed to turn itself on at random and brief time windows.

They had convinced him to keep the thing by explaining that, as long as it was in the bedframe, shielding it from conventional networks, the authorities couldn't detect it. There were times when Tony questioned his sanity at ever having agreed to such nonsense, believing whatever techno-gobble-de-gook they threw at him. He wasn't an idiot. He had a college degree, after all.

Tony was a good, religious man who had gotten the proper certificates and found himself of use to the burgeoning technocracy. He was skilled at chemical removal, disposal, and neutralization. He'd made wise investments. He owned the only operable facility within one hundred miles—a singular distinction.

After the Ameri-Corp government contracted him to manage the Newbern facility, it was only a matter of time before a person like John would reach out to him.

The contacts came through the church. Tony was a Southern Baptist, as were so many of the early players within the insurgency. He was acquainted with quite a few sympathizers.

The meeting with John was brief and to the point.

He met the man in the youth Bible study room and sized him up as honest. He was given the device. John described the nature of the thing. The way it touched the network was untraceable. He described the time windows, and how and why they were randomized. The money was discussed, and it was less than he'd expected.

The money was increased as soon as his access to the facility was vetted, and he'd proven that his intelligence provided value.

This morning, it would be increased even more.

Tony left the bedroom and lightly tread the hallway, lifting the board to his ear. "Four Two Nine."

In his ear, he heard the return cypher, "Nine Four Two."

"Wait a second," Tony said as he closed the door to his office and sat behind his desk in the dark. "Why you callin'? Couldn't leave a message?"

"Too urgent. I need something extra."

"How extra?"

"Access for four people. Safely into the loading bay."

Tony put the board down on his lap and shook his head. He took a breath, keenly aware of the time window for the conversation. It was closing.

John's voice squeaked in the speaker. He lifted the board to his ear. "That's pretty last minute."

"No choice. Forty thousand."

Tony smiled. That was his magic number. The number to get him out of the country and into the other life he had been preparing for some time. "Forty-five."

"No. Forty."

"Put it in."

There was a brief pause. Tony pulled the board up to his eyes, swiped it, and tapped it. The credit in his account increased by the correct amount. Back on the receiver, "Where and when?"

"Standby for pick up time and location. It's still the alpha rotation for the passwords. Also, send me the latest updated floor plans and guard schedules. You were due those by today anyway." John was all business, about five seconds left in the transmission.

"You'll have it." Tony swiped the call away.

He sat back in his chair and looked out the window. The hint of an early winter dragged the seed balls of his crepe myrtles down in the porch light. He thought about the weather and what he needed to do to prepare his truck for the mission. He thought about his son and wife.

He thought about his new life, somewhere warm, and a smile crossed his lips.

◂—————••—————▸

The twelve-wheeled truck rolled to a stop. Its stenciled logo read *Kensington Chemicals*. The engine was shut down, then turned on again, along with the hazard lights. The morning air was chilly and still. Moisture suspended in a loose cloud transferred onto the windshield with ease. It slicked the mirrors and metal.

After a few moments, John emerged from the thick foliage. He moved through the fog, keeping his head down. He stopped at the front of the truck on the road's edge. The treeline was thirty meters distant when he turned to face it. He produced a cigarette from his pocket, and he lit it with a butane lighter. He flourished with the thing and made a show of it.

The passenger door opened. Tony stepped down to the runner board. He kept the door open and studied John with concerned consideration. He chewed over whether or not to speak. His son sat in the driver's seat in silent wonder, having learned of his father's "side job" hours earlier as they prepped the truck.

Tony gave his boy a nod, raised his eyebrows, and stepped down onto the red dirt of the road. "You lookin' for somethin' out here?"

"Just trying to find my way," John said, then pointed to the trees. "You got room for my friends?"

Tony nodded. "You said four total, right?"

"Four total."

Tony pointed at the truck. "I cleaned out two tanks. Got the facility smocks back there for ya. But I can't get you out. Them tanks'll get filled up."

"We'll cover the exfil."

Tony leaned over and kicked the chert. "You don't mind me sayin'. This seems a little ad hoc for you. Always got the impression you's the careful type who took his time."

John waved at the trees, signaling the others. "Yeah. Let's say that the situation is fluid. There's an opportunity."

"This opportunity of yours gonna blow back on me?" He tilted his head, trying to see inside John's mind, trying to read the man's honesty. It had been some time since they were face to face and then, for a brief few minutes.

"It's a dangerous neighborhood, Tony. Forty thousand should pay for the moving trucks."

John laid it out flat—the cost of doing business. Tony's life would end in about an hour. If he'd followed his training, he'd be prepared for his new one.

Tony's shoulders drooped. "About time to retire anyway, I guess."

Daniel, Rudy, and Maggie reached the road hunched under their packs.

Tony turned and addressed them. "I got rebreathers in back. You need to wear 'em when I lock you in. We scrubbed the tanks, but that shit's pretty noxious. When I open 'em up, you'll have about three to five minutes completely off camera. You'll be in the loading bay, utility level." He turned to John. "You get those floor plans?"

John nodded. "I did. We got a plan."

Tony smiled. "Hope so. Go ahead and hop in."

Daniel turned to Rudy and waved him forward.

He touched Maggie's shoulder as she passed, and she angrily withdrew from him. She batted his hand away, sped past him, and grabbed Rudy's jacket hem.

The two climbed into the opened box truck.

John walked past Daniel, stopped, and said, "You probably shouldn't have told her."

"Didn't have much choice, did I?" Daniel passed a cold stare at John.

He handed his pack to Rudy, then grunted as he pulled himself into the trailer.

John took Tony's hand in a firm grip. He nodded and made eye contact. "You got something lined up?"

Tony cracked a big grin. "Somethin' nice."

John climbed into the trailer and then into the huge tank, which sat open. Rudy handed him a rebreather.

Tony stood over the tank and gave them one last look. He closed the hatch and twisted the bolts. He jumped down from the truck and pushed the door shut after him. He rotated the cam-actioned latch and sank the bolt lock in place.

He turned to the trees, scanned the sky above, and speculated as to who or what had recorded this big party. After executing his bugout, it wouldn't matter, and it was too late to worry about it anyway.

<-------•●•------->

It had been a busy day. The trip down to Newbern on the helicopter was uneventful, aside from rattling Fiona's nerves. Brue conducted the facility inspection and received briefs from technicians, researchers, and administrators. They did what proud techs always do: droned on and on.

Brue learned that, upon Jakob's actuation, he had begun assisting at both Gen Two facilities. As a policy, the newly actuated were restricted to their home facility for at least six months. This allowed for the engendering of indoctrination and the testing of psycho-resilience.

However, Jakob's progress and capabilities were earthshaking. The scientists and technicians requested exemptions from this policy, and it turned out to be a good call.

Due to Jakob's input, both facilities' productivity was expected to quadruple over the next eight months. And there was new promise in the search for category-specific, transcendental neutralization. The scientists sat with Jakob and navigated the genome in ways that had been impossible.

They viewed him as a miracle. Jakob was a carbon-based, general intelligence machine operating at the quantum level. His ability to store and sort data, and run analytical processes against proposed theories significantly reduced the time necessary to address the topic.

Based on experiences with the Gen Ones, diminishing structural pathways was deemed unwise. The new focus centered on neurochemical interactions. Extrinsic actualization would be replaced with an intrinsic understanding of one's place in the enterprise of life and culture.

It was all the better for humanity. The troublesome plague of belief would be a thing of the past within a few generations.

Jakob accompanied Brue and Fiona for the production floor walkthrough. Brue observed a pod of blueish fluid.

Jakob explained, "The issue with chemical divergence was based on the faulty design of the agitators." He smiled. "Funny to think, but appropriately timing the speed and frequency that we *stirred the pudding* was enough to increase yield."

He laughed forcefully. A wrinkled smile climbed across Brue's face. Jakob's sense of humor was often ill-timed and elicited responses well out of proportion to the joke.

Brue looked at Fiona. "Don't we have—"

"Yes." She stepped toward Jakob. "I'm afraid that's all the time we have for the inspection. I forwarded you some requirements for a streaming conference?"

Jakob gave her a quizzical smile. "Yes, you did. You'll find the rest of your team through that door." He swept his hand toward an exit in a theatrical manner.

"Thank you, Jakob." Brue wrinkled his brow, reached for Fiona's shoulder, and guided her away toward the door.

Jakob's smile scuttled as soon as the two of them had stepped away.

Brue leaned over to Fiona and whispered, "He puts me off."

"He does that, indeed," Fiona agreed and checked over her shoulder to find him walking in the opposite direction.

Brue pushed the door open. His security detail was waiting, lined against the hallway. Large men in dark suits, faces fixed with cold expressions. Upon seeing their principal, the team lead gave silent commands, and the four men dropped into formation around Brue and Fiona. It was seamless.

<hr>

Cleary stared at the map projected onto the large glass wall. He studied the dots and put his finger on them. Hillcamp's dot sat in the middle of nowhere. The location of the ambush was disconnected from lines of travel, which made it a sensible location for an ambush. But that was days ago. He hovered his hand over the corner of the glass, and a holographic menu floated beneath his fingers. He manipulated it and specific map layers, such as infrastructure, cycled onto and off the glass. He stopped the process, uneasy, feeling like he was missing something.

His light board buzzed, and he took it out of his pocket, swiped it, and held it to his ear.

"Mr. Cleary." The lead tech of the drone program spoke with a touch of excitement.

"Yeah." Cleary kept studying his map.

"You'll want to find a monitor, log onto it, and link up my portal."

"What's goin' on, mate?"

"We got your guy."

Cleary pocketed his board and almost knocked a

table over in his haste. He made his way out of the OPCEN toward his office, but that was a bit of a walk. He slipped into the first office available. It belonged to a brigade-level officer in charge of logistics.

The man sat on a couch, watching a wall monitor. Some game show host preened on the screen, and lights and the sounds of smiling and frivolous people filled the room.

As the door flew open, Cleary said, "Don't get up." He dismissed the general officer with a wave of his hand.

The man recognized Cleary. A look of distaste set up on his face, and he sat back on the couch. He went back to staring at his monitor but became somewhat self-conscious about it. He shuffled back and forth. His hands were empty. He didn't know what to do with himself but was confident he shouldn't have been watching a game show mid-day.

Cleary swiped the desk monitor and then swiped his wrist chip to commandeer the system. After a few touches, a drone feed displayed on the screen, and the lead tech's voice came through the speaker. "You with me, Mr. Cleary."

"I'm here. Whatchu got?"

"So we broadened the scope of the search in exponential rings and brought on more balls as you requested—built the algorithm to handle all the feeds. We pulled this one from the hopper from about, um, looks like two hours ago."

"What am I lookin' at?"

On the screen, a large, white truck was pulled

to the side of a dirt road. Its hazard lights were blinking, and two men talked at the truck's front.

The tech said, "This flagged because it meets the parameters of a clandestine pickup. The ball would have engaged in the normal course of things, but based on your orders, we discontinued those authorities. So, the drone recorded, flagged, and notified. Notice the people coming from the wood line. I think you'll recognize one of them."

The screen froze, and a zoom was applied. Then, Cleary's monitor filled with Daniel's face. There was no need to hyperpixelate the image. It was crystal clear.

"Yeah. It's him. Who's that truck, and where are they going?"

"The truck is registered to a Tony Furlough out of Newbern. He is a mid-level contractor for government services."

"Military?"

"No. Science and dev."

"Okay, what's the good news?"

The tech's tone lit up. There was nothing a tech liked more than to provide people like Cleary with answers. "He's not on the books that we could find, but the ball followed him to this facility."

The timeline rolled forward quickly, and the screen displayed a large, angular facility surrounded by a high, solid fence.

"So, what's that?" Cleary had never seen the building and was clueless about its use.

"Interestingly, we don't know."

"That's interesting? It would be more interestin' if you knew."

"Well, it's not in our dataset. This means it's that way on purpose, and very few programs could exclude themselves from our dataset. *Which is what makes it interesting.*" The tech's face indicated that he had spoken with a bit more force than he should have and was regretting it.

Cleary ignored him, sat back, and glanced at the general officer watching his game show. "Alright, mate. Good job. Forward this to the detachment."

He swiped the monitor off and pulled his light board. He held it to his ear. "Captain, get your men together—high priority incoming to your screens, full spectrum kit. S-P in ten mikes."

He closed the board and stared at the general officer. The man sat, useless and nervous, the games shining on him from the monitor. He could feel the heat from Cleary's eyes. He turned and faced him.

Cleary's eyes didn't wander, bored right into him.

"This is my office." His voice was weak, almost petulant. It made Cleary smile.

He cocked his head to the side. "Well, let me get outta your hair. Looks like you got some important stuff goin' on in here."

Cleary stood and made his way to the door. He would have knifed the guy with insults if he'd had more time, but he was happy and expectant of the day to come.

Daniel and John wore the tan smocks of maintenance technicians. Daniel brushed his hand along the seams of his outfit, hoping it fit well enough to avoid suspicion at a distance. They moved from the staging room adjacent to the loading dock into the hallway. He said, "Your guy better have his shit together."

John said, "Tony's a good man. If he says this is the schedule, then this is the schedule."

"Like, I'm s'posed to take your word for it." Daniel was preoccupied, fiddling with a special tool he'd stuffed up into his sleeve while they'd changed clothes.

John stopped walking, dropped a stare charged with stress and irritation. "I'm here, ain't I, asshole?"

Daniel stopped and turned to him. He dipped his head—about all he could muster as far as show of appreciation. John didn't want to be there, and in truth, didn't have to be there. He was taking a risk beyond what he'd planned—trying to live up to what he owed for the lives of the patrol and maybe also for Lori.

Daniel nodded and referred to his light board, checked the hallway number and swiped ahead on the pre-planned route. He checked the timeline for the mission, looked at his watch. "Through that door." He pointed straight ahead. "Take the first left and . . ." he checked his watch again. ". . . that should put us on the X. Depending on whether his goons will have him where and when he's supposed to be."

John breathed out through tight lips, trying to calm himself. "They'll have him there. This guy's whole life is planned down to the minute."

<-------•••------->

The security detail surrounded the protectees in a moving box of shoulders and hard stares. They flowed from one hallway to the next. Brue and Fiona swiped at their light boards, unaware of their surroundings or destination, herded through the facility like prey animals.

The detail lead glanced over his right shoulder and made eye contact with his companion. He held his fist up, halting the formation.

"Time hack," the lead said in a flat, monotone, his eyes up and scouting ahead past an office door to his right and toward a doorway at the end of the hall.

His associate checked his watch and replied, "We are plus thirty seconds on this leg. Haven't been able to confirm with next destination—probably structural interference with my transmission."

"Roger, plus thirty. Let's slow our roll a little so you can make comms."

He started the group out again past the office and toward the door.

<-------•••------->

Daniel spotted the detail enter. Knowing the

VIP's routes were designated off-limits to facility personnel, he anticipated a reaction from the security team. The guard in front of the group flipped the edge of his coat back and placed his hand on his sidearm. He continued to walk but slowed his steps, studying Daniel and John.

This is where the disguise is gonna work or it's not.

Daniel whispered, "Keep it together. I'll kick it off."

The bodyguard pointed his thick, calloused finger at them and waved to his left. It was an aggressive gesture that left no room for misinterpretation. To ensure his intention was understood, he said, "Hug the wall." His voice was cold and detached, suggesting consequences for noncompliance.

Daniel smiled and held his hands up, presenting no threat. He bumped John with a nervous elbow. They flattened out, backs against the wall. He glanced at the man's grip on the pistol and averted his eyes, a memetic act of deception. His body tensed, and his nostrils flared. He was selling it.

Apparently satisfied, the lead took his hand off his weapon. As he approached, he kept his eyes on the two mechanics. "You're not supposed to be here." He held eye contact with Daniel as he passed.

Then the moment came. Daniel saw the lead understood, with a flashing regret, that he'd badly misjudged the situation.

Daniel's eyes deadened. His smile tightened at the corners. He produced a metal prod from his sleeve and shoved it against the lead's chest. A loud crack and the smell of burning flesh followed. The prod glowed red and pumped a massive burst of electricity into him. His eyes rolled back, and his body locked, vibrating so tightly that it hummed.

The action caught the guards flat-footed.

The nearest pulled his pistol. John lifted a small handgun, pressed it to his temple, and pulled the trigger. The man fell into an awkward pile.

The guard nearest Carnell shoved him to the floor on the opposite wall. He reached for his weapon as Daniel shoved the prod against his neck. His pistol fell to the floor and he danced. Pink bubbles inflated along his neck, erupting in geysers of blood charred black.

The last guard gripped Carnell's assistant as a shield. John pressed his barrel against her chest. They fired at the same time. John fell back against the wall as the bullet smacked him. His shot went through the woman and into the neck of the guard. The three of them fell into a pile.

The guard's severed carotid pulsed and sprayed. His hand couldn't stem the tide. He fought to pull his pistol from under Carnell's assistant.

John placed his barrel on her chest and emptied his magazine, finishing them both.

The smoldering bodies of Daniel's work piled down on top of the scrum. Carnell sat amid the carnage. The woman's lungs shuddered—their last gasps for air.

The entire event unfolded over mere seconds.

John leaned against the wall. The bullet had passed through the upper lobe of his left lung. Small amounts of air became trapped inside his chest, and every breath acted as a bellows, collapsing his lungs in increments. The internal thoracic artery had been ruptured and was leaking blood. The two forces struggled for space. His wheezed pallor indicated a quick end.

Daniel knelt next to him, their faces close. He'd seen these wounds before. Based on his color alone, he wouldn't make it. No point in dealing with it—there wasn't time.

John reached out to him. He inhaled, and a sick, crackling sound came from his throat.

Daniel shook his head and turned away. He shoved the still smoldering core of the prod in Carnell's face, near to touching his eye. "Get the fuck up, or I'll fry you right here."

Daniel grabbed his collar and ripped him from the jumble of bodies. He launched him down the hall in the direction from which he'd come. Brue landed on his hands and knees, his legs refusing to participate.

Daniel plucked him from the floor and propelled him down the hallway. He glanced over his shoulder before reaching the door.

John's eyes followed him. His jaw sawed, raking his teeth against each other, unable to form words. His skin was blanched. The eyes were the same as every man who'd found himself shutting down. His will to live clawing against the meat of him—the tubes, the fluids all malfunctioning.

There was nothing to be done about it.

Brue's face smashed into the door. He fumbled at the handle.

"Open it. Open it," the angry man hissed at him, smearing his face against the cold metal.

He succeeded at turning the handle, and found himself standing on a loading dock. He was controlled completely by the furious, gnarled hand squeezing his neck below the skull.

A leaf on a raging river—confused and overwhelmed, he'd been paralyzed by the loud, violent struggle that had ignited around him. Fiona had been killed right in front of him, and he had been useless. He'd managed a pathetic whimper, buried in the middle of it all.

Brue couldn't shake the image. Her lifeless eyes sought the ceiling, mouth open. Her shirt had been charred from the blasts of the barrel. The dark flesh of the bullet holes visible beneath.

"Is Fiona alive?" His face twisted in disbelief.

"Shut the fuck up." His handler had neither sympathy nor patience.

Brue's coat was ripped from his flaccid body, and tossed onto the ground.

A young man with dark hair, who seemed to be waiting on him, made eye contact and smiled. He pulled Brue's arm by the wrist and twisted the palm toward the ceiling to expose the crook of his elbow. He grabbed Brue's bicep and squeezed it. The veins jumped up in the light. Then he shoved a needle in and pulled back on the plunger. A dark cloud of red leaked into the amber fluid. Then, the juice flowed into him.

Brue didn't protest. The forces at work against him were far too powerful to resist. His will had crumbled at the sight of pale Fiona, sucking for air with her round, terrified eyes. Like a child, he said, "Maybe she's still alive."

Within moments, he found himself at peace as the psychoactive chemicals hit the miracle of his circulatory system. The molecules bound along the veins' lining, too large to permeate. They butted up against the various substances, crashing to and fro, seeking the specific receptors for which they shared their affinity. With remarkable efficiency, they were delivered to the brain. The tiny explosions happened within the neurotransmitters. The magic took root in his skull.

Brue smiled. The sudden gush of contentment that flooded into the corners of his brain abolished all traces of fear and sadness. "Who are *you* guys?"

His poisoner smiled back. "We're your friends." He reached into a pocket and withdrew Brue's light board. "Alright, buddy. Listen closely, okay?"

Brue pursed his lips. "What else am I going to do?"

He felt really, *really* good about this.

"I like your attitude. I need you to call the security manager and give him the stand-down protocols. Use whichever classification status you need to make that happen. Then I want the guard posts on the east gate emptied within the next five minutes for an unannounced VIP arrival. That includes monitoring. Utilize the gamma clearance protocols. Got it?"

"That sounds easy enough." Brue took the light board and swiped it. He placed it to his ear. He stared at the young man with an easy smile. Brue said, "They'll want the override code."

"Well, give it to them when they ask."

"Of course." Brue went back to his call. He kept the kid in his eyes. There was something about him—he liked him.

◄———••———►

A tiny, red EV slid from a spot and approached the dock.

Rudy swiped Carnell's light board several times, and it went dark. "Board's off the grid now. No tracking."

Daniel nodded, and as the car reached the dock, he shoved his prisoner toward it, who lifted his hands in front, showing no aggression toward his captors. His face was covered in a pleasant smile.

Rudy opened the rear passenger door and entered. Daniel encouraged Carnell to follow him, bumping his head against the door in the process.

"Could you please—" Carnell began.

"Shut the fuck up." Daniel slipped into the passenger seat and said, "Drive. The east gate should be clear."

"*Should* be clear?" Maggie was behind the wheel, adrenaline in her voice.

"They're not supposed to stop us. If they try to stop us..." He lifted his pistol and waved it, reminding her that he had a weapon.

Maggie nodded, working up the courage. "Okay. I drive, you shoot."

"That's the plan."

She put the EV in gear and rolled toward the exit. "Where's John?"

Daniel's eyes were up, scanning the area. "He's dead."

Rudy produced a small, simple box with red and green lights on its surface. He held a button on the side and began sweeping Carnell's body.

Daniel looked back, asked the question with his eyes.

Rudy said, "These assholes usually have trackers implanted—subcutaneous tissue modules. Little radio bugs that get activated after they are reported missing."

The box slid across Brue's abdomen and chest, over his shoulder. The red light activated at a spot on the back of his arm.

Rudy grinned and winked at Daniel. "Check this out."

Daniel asked "What now, we cut it out?"

Carnell said, "I certainly hope not." Then he closed his mouth at the sight of Daniel's tight glare.

Rudy held the button over the spot until the red light dimmed and the green light popped on. "All we gotta do is short it out. See, no more tracker."

Daniel nodded. "Be a lot easier just to pop this piece a' shit."

Rudy took a deep breath. "So, what's the plan? This was John's mission."

"I know where the safe house is. He briefed me on that much. When we get there, we wait. The exchange should happen before dark."

"Before dark." Rudy hated the sound of that.

"Let's just get the hell outta here, then work the problem," Daniel said definitively.

There wasn't time to reconsider the course of action. Unless—he were to turn around and shoot the fucker in the face, dump him in a ditch, and keep rolling. He had a hard moment of contemplation— *the easy road*. But, he remembered what John had wanted, and to his legitimate shock he felt like he owed the man. It was an uncomfortable feeling.

So he sat there thinking through the one thousand ways this could go to shit.

The red EV rolled out of the loading bay into the bright midday sun.

Carnell said, "Where are we going?"

Daniel said, "Shut the fuck up."

◄───── •• ─────►

The hovercraft slipped through the air, and the Appalachian Mountains roiled beneath.

Cleary sat at his laptop and worked the keys. It was unusual. His clearance had been denied access.

Furthermore, his efforts to communicate with the facility in question had been fruitless. Numerous attempts to speak to the security manager had been rebuffed after his authorization was forwarded.

Sorry, but you don't have the clearance, and as such, I'm not at liberty to divulge anything about the operations of this facility, was the very bureaucratic answer he'd received.

Cleary detected more than a touch of disdain from the security manager. A little prick, no doubt, who'd avoided kinetic service like the plague during the wars. It always amazed him how many men he encountered within the bureaucracy who had never fought but had great ideas about how it should be done.

He studied the terrain on the laptop, no surprises. Foothills and thick forests surrounded the facility. The area towns had small populations. If support structures were in place, they would look the same as most isolated networks—infil/exfil routes, safe houses, link-up sites, etc. Cleary assessed all the suitable routes to and from the facility. The narrow roads carved into the steep hillsides had tight canopy coverage. He compared intelligence reports of the insurgent networks operating in the area. How many fighters were there? How motivated were they?

During the flight, he cobbled together an estimation of what Daniel would most likely do. All of this, however, he did in the blind. There was a critical piece of the operational picture that he couldn't see. *What is in that place, and why would Daniel want it?* He closed the lid of his laptop and said, "Guess we're about to find out."

In his earpiece, the pilot said, "We are ten mikes out."

Cleary tapped a button on his chest. "Roger that."

He looked across the troop compartment at the captain of the Special Forces team, nodded, and held up ten fingers. The Captain passed it along to the others, and they began their final preparations.

Cleary touched his kit. He circled across his body and stared out over the rolling hills. *GPS, Bangers...*

◀——•●•——▶

Brue sat on the couch stroking the smooth material with his hand. He found the experience relaxing. He pulled a deep drink from a fresh, cold soda Rudy had scrounged from the refrigerator.

A conclusion jumped into his mind. He hadn't sought out any such thing—any conclusions. Conclusions to what, after all? He didn't remember asking questions or having the slightest interest in anything unrelated to his skin's location, temperature, and relative comfort. Nonetheless, with a palm full of velour, he stumbled upon the realization that his life had become complicated. At that moment, his aspirations seemed distant and worrisome. There was an easy comfort to be found in the sugary drink and the warm, broken-in couch.

He should seek these types of experiences more

often.

His pupils were blown out like miniature coffee saucers. His breathing was controlled but elevated, a match for his heart rate. He tapped his foot softly but rapidly.

He didn't want to disturb the people in the adjoining dining room. He had just met them, and they seemed nice, although they were having an agitated conversation. They kept looking at him and furrowing their brows, having found themselves at some sort of impasse.

Whatever it was, he was confident they would work it out. They were good people. He was sure of that.

◂─────•●•─────▸

Daniel, Rudy, and Maggie huddled around the modest dining room table. They spoke in strained half-whispers. Maggie tapped the wooden top in agitation.

"So, we just sit here, now?" Maggie asked, tapping faster. "Won't they be looking for this guy, like, *really* looking for him?"

Daniel glanced at Rudy. It was a sensible question that hadn't escaped his observation. "We did what John said to do." Daniel waved her question away. "Sometimes sittin' and waitin' is the only thing left."

But still, it felt wrong to be this close to the objective after an operation. It made more sense to move and keep moving. But this was not their area of operations. They had no knowledge of the players in the arena. With the type of heat that was about to arise, it wasn't wise to start making friends, either.

In truth, they had moved a mere three miles from the facility into a small house on the edge of Newbern. The one-story building was the last house on the block, and its backyard butted up against the wood line. Behind it laid hundreds of miles of Virginia hills. Its thickets and monster draws made it easy to get bogged down, encircled, and rounded up.

What were their options? Make for the hills? Not likely to be successful. All the drones in the world would be swarming a twenty-mile circumference of the facility. Get back into the cave complex? The nearest entrance was five miles by crow, longer on the roads, which would be crawling with government forces any minute.

It wasn't an easy problem. *Would've been better to have let it go*, he thought.

Rudy had been silent for a while. He pointed at the prisoner "This guy's gonna get a crazy response as soon as they put it together. How long till they find the bodies, you think?"

"How the hell would I know?" Daniel's eyes zeroed in on Carnell, sitting on the couch in the next room. "But I know what you mean. They're gonna come down like a ton a' shit-bricks when they figure out he's missin'. Every swingin' dick on the Eastern Seaboard's gonna chub up."

Maggie scanned their faces, trying to read their

thoughts. "So what are we waiting for? Let's get outta here."

Daniel nodded his head and turned to Rudy. He'd made a decision. "Gimme his light board. You two take off. That's as far as this is gonna go."

Rudy understood. He pulled the board from his pocket and handed it to Daniel. "You plan on sending him off with a bang?"

"Somethin' like that. How long is he good on this dose?" Daniel checked his watch.

"He should be good for another twenty minutes. Want me to dose him again?"

Daniel eyed his captive with a determined hostility. "No. I want him to know what's happenin' to him. Get the car outta the area and ditch it. Pick up another one. The only chance you got is to get out now. Move and keep movin'. The bubble starts expanding any minute and keeps expanding every minute after. You got any resources in this AO?"

"Nah, I'll make do, though."

Maggie piped up. "What are y'all talking about? Are you staying?" She looked at Daniel.

"Yeah." He pointed at Brue. "Need to send this guy off right."

"Why do you have to do it alone?"

Daniel wagged his head. "Just works better that way. Stop arguin' and—"

"So, you'll get what you want one way or the other, right?" She crossed her arms, and her skin scorched a bright red.

Rudy turned toward the kitchen. It was awkward.

It was an intimate conflict, a family struggle based on an ancient injury, and he had no place in the midst of it.

"Maggie, listen, I need to light this fire on my own. I'll give you two a head start. Gonna turn this on, do a little broadcast, and then I'm out."

"Broadcast, what? Why do you have to do it alone?" Daniel was ignoring Maggie's question—her *real* question.

He couldn't comprehend her problem. "You guys clear out. I'll give you, what, half an hour?" Daniel checked with Rudy, who agreed with a nod.

Maggie laughed with bitterness. "You're such an asshole."

"Yeah. I'll link up with you guys in the next couple a' days."

"No, you won't." She welded her eyes to him like a searchlight on a prisoner in the yard after lights out.

Daniel found it hard to reciprocate. "I will." He looked at the floor, the wall, the ceiling, anything but her eyes.

"Why would you? Even if you make it out of this, you made it clear that you don't want anything to do with me."

Daniel struggled to find words that would soothe the situation. He needed her gone. He couldn't arrive at anything useful. "What do you want from me?"

Maggie closed her eyes, tears forming in the corners. "Nothing."

She walked out of the room into the kitchen past Rudy.

He needed her gone. She wouldn't understand why, not for some time, if ever. The closer she was to Brue, the more danger she was in. She could hate him if she wanted. He accepted that. At least she'd be alive, as long as Rudy could get her out.

He interrogated the boy with his eyes. "You got her?"

"I got her."

"Then get goin'."

Rudy blinked, caught Daniel's gist, and nodded. He understood the task. He turned and followed Maggie through the kitchen into the covered driveway.

Daniel pivoted to his target, who sat with happy, druggy eyes. He rubbed the couch, ground his teeth, and tapped his foot.

Daniel walked into the room and stood next to him, staring.

Carnell caught his eyes and, driven by the drugs, patted the couch like a long-lost friend. "Have a seat."

<------••------>

The hallway was bland, gray, and dim. It was yet another in a twisting, monotonous hive of passageways.

The door opened, and a tech entered. He carried a tight stack of monofilament containers. His eyes were pinched, near closed, and he viewed the world through the muted slits of light. He wore earbuds singing in a high falsetto. After a few steps, he stopped in his tracks. The containers crashed onto the floor, scattering about.

His eyelids jumped open, and he saw the human wreckage sprawled before him in all its bloody glory. Six bodies were twisted among each other, their conditions of death various. The smell of burnt flesh and blood caused him to wretch from his depths.

The odors mingled and hung in an invisible cloud. Dark, sticky crimson pooled beneath the pale bodies. Three of them burnt, unrecognizable—crisp, blackened hands and heads, friable to the touch.

He stumbled out of the hallway and collapsed to his knees. He sucked in fresh air. He slid against the wall, reached up, and pulled an alarm.

Sirens and lights erupted, shattering the dull, mechanical hum of the building.

The tech heaved. His ribs made a move toward his mouth. He heaved again, and this time, a brackish fluid ejected with force and covered his legs.

The sirens screamed.

◆————••————▶

The hovercraft slipped over the valley wall and performed a combat descent. After a moment of hesitation and lightness, explained to the mind as "zero gravity," the thing fell, nose down from the crest of the ridge. The airframe rumbled as it reentered the friction of flight. The maneuver was known to cause the innards to rise in a tickling and disturbing way.

Cleary crunched his core muscles and grabbed the harness. He sat into it with a grunt.

He fought the urge to deposit his lunch onto the floor of the troop bay. It's not the thing to do in front of these types of men.

He pushed the button on his chest and spoke into his headset. "Captain. I got us at two mikes out. Follow my lead when we get there. Haven't had comms since they cleared us to land."

The captain said, "Roger that."

He's a dull kid, thought Cleary. *Like talkin' to a tech.*

He turned to the clear bay door. The trees and rocks hugged the hull and passed by in a blur.

One minute out.

◄────•●•────►

On the hover pad, a long, narrow tent had been erected. Six bodies, atop stereo-static blankets, were arranged on the tarmac. Post-mortem investigators, dressed in containment suits, examined the bodies. They were not allowed in the building due to the facility's security level. Instead, the bodies were brought out and placed in rows. The entire process violated the concept of forensic analysis, but when science and sensitive programs collided, the programs won every time.

Two investigators worked on the electrocuted guards. They lightly scraped at the cindered material, placing the samples in vials of fluid. The bodies were twisted, faces charred away. Alongside them were black chunks of dusty flesh, broken free during relocation.

Another investigator swabbed for chemical residue and photographed the remaining bodies. The dead were naked in the cold evening light. They were placed in studious rows of three, with plenty of space between them for the analysts to do their work.

The hovercraft flared before it touched down and performed an immaculate landing. Short bursts of steam ejected from the chassis as the vehicle off-gassed. Gears and hydraulics clicked and bumped as the thing came to a rest.

The glass door slid open, and Cleary was the first to step on the ramp. A few of the operators stepped down behind him. They strode forward across the landing pad, their eyes swept across the assembly of people.

A heavy-set man in an ill-fitting suit stood before the makeshift, open-air autopsy. He stood with his arms out wide—a human guardrail. There was an air about him. He believed he was in charge.

Cleary smiled at the man and sized him up. He noted the fat roll creeping out of his collar, the red face, and the alcoholic nose. "You must be Preston."

Preston puffed himself up somewhat. "I'm the facility security manager."

"Yeah. I know." Cleary bent down, brushed his arm aside, and slipped into the tent. "You're doin' a helluva job, mate."

Cleary had done his research. Not much was

known about the program or the facility, but as soon as he had received the cold, dismissive rejection for information, he researched the signatory of the response. It didn't take long to crack the nut.

Preston was a career man. Already vested in his pension, he'd worked for the government in some form or fashion for the majority of his life. Given the size and scope of the particular shitstorm in which he found himself, Cleary figured he'd have some decent leverage.

"Listen, I know you were trying to contact me."

"Oh, Preston, I *did* contact you," Cleary said, then stopped cold. He got his first look at Fiona. His eyes narrowed.

"Listen, there are protocols in place to avoid—" Preston had an argument, which clearly he'd been crafting in his mind from the moment the bodies were discovered.

Cleary couldn't turn away from Fiona's dead eyes. "The only thing you need to say to me right now is that you'll cooperate in every way with this recovery mission. I don't have time for the proper authorizations to be sent, signed, and resigned." Cleary turned on him then. His eyes burned. "Or for you and your little keyboard-clickin' pussies to slow me down. Do you *fully* understand me?"

Preston tilted on his axis and caught himself with a back step. Cleary wasn't interested in rank or authority. He might even get violent if his work were interfered with. "You'll have whatever you need."

"Good. For starters, I need you to get away from

me." He pointed at the captain. "He'll tell you what we need transferred to our mobile operations center. Give him whatever he wants."

Preston nodded vigorously, but Cleary had already turned his back. He knelt next to Fiona's body. The bullet holes in her naked, white chest clustered together. The life drained from her, yet the mutilation could not spoil her form. She was beautiful to him in that moment, the vulnerability of it. And the death mask failed to hide her willful nature, evident in the curl of her lip.

A flat, knowing smile crawled across his face. He looked up at the mountains and the trees and knew at once that Daniel was nearby. He could smell him.

◂────••────▸

Brue shook his head, trying to claw the sticky webs from the corners of his mind. He smiled. "So, I—I think it's wearing off."

Daniel, who menaced him across a walnut coffee table, agreed with a cold grin. He pulled Brue's light board from his pocket, waved it at him, then sat it on the arm of his chair. "In a few minutes, you're gonna turn this on and make a statement." Daniel flung a small notebook at him.

Brue tried to catch it, but the notebook hit his chest. He lifted it and squinted his eyes. The text was scrawled and difficult to read. He pinched his brow in concentration. Then his eyes lightened, and he laughed.

"What's so funny?" asked Daniel.

Brue waved him away, smiling. "Oh, nothing. The syntax is challenged. Who wrote this?"

"You fuckin' with me?" Daniel leaned his head back and looked down his nose at Brue.

"Well, no. It's just... listen." Brue read aloud from the notebook. "I accept all the responsibility for the downfall of all men." He shrugged his shoulders. "I did this by myself?"

"Well, it's kind a' hard to get our hands on you people. So, you'll be the one answerin' for it tonight."

Brue dropped the notebook. "You're going to need more of the drug because I'm not reading this." He crossed his arms.

Daniel pulled his pistol. "Fine. Not really my strong suit anyway—all that influence shit. I'm more of a hands-on kinda guy. You know what I mean? Live execution works, too. It gets the same point across... Comprende, dickhead?"

At the sight of the pistol, Brue sunk into the couch — a reflex to create some distance between himself and the barrel. It was an involuntary reaction.

His fear aroused Daniel's aggression. He stood with the gun gripped in his hand. He squeezed the handle and relaxed several times. His index finger traced along the weapon's edge, outside the trigger well. The tendon and muscle worked through the problem—deliberating.

Brue shifted on the couch. Then, he spoke with some sense of confidence. "If I'm not mistaken, your daughter needs another ten minutes or so? Is that about right?" The tactic surprised him as if it sneaked out on its own.

Daniel flinched, confused for a moment. He pointed the pistol at Brue like it was his finger. "You put that together all by yourself?"

The barrel of the pistol appeared cavernous. Brue smiled. "Toward the end of that ride your little friend put me on, I somewhat started to come to my wits. Your interaction with Maggie was—"

"We've been estranged." Daniel interrupted.

It violated operational security for an adversary to gain personal information. In this instance, however, the adversary was minutes away from destruction. So, Daniel let it go. He laughed.

Brue mimicked his wide, loathing smile and his laughter. "If you were to walk out right now, I'd sit right here and wait for them to come find me. You could catch up with her, be with her. Mend those fences."

Daniel's smile straightened but didn't vanish. He checked his watch and shrugged his shoulders, every nerve in his body on edge. He wanted to kill him and be done with it, but John's words about having a greater impact bounced around in his head. The more he thought about it, the more sense it made.

The world was full of sick people, needling their days away with screens in their eyes, endorphins hijacked. They were soft—living their lives in ruts built for them by the controllers of information. They needed a shock to their systems. He'd place a punctuation mark before them in a way they couldn't avoid. Brue would die in front of them in real time. They'd watch him beg and then see the life leave his body. The world was full of sick people. This was their medicine.

He'd estimated it would take Maggie thirty minutes to get clear, which tempered his impulses. Sometimes, the best thing to do was to shut down the lizard brain, sit down like a man, and simply wait. There's nothing wrong with thinking in the midst of chaos.

So, he did. He sat down and rested the pistol on the arm of the chair.

"You're gonna make a statement one way or another."

◀──────•●•──────▶

Cleary, alongside the detachment's captain, sat in the hovering OPCEN. Multiple monitors were spread across a folding desk.

They studied the inputs from the Gen Two facility. There was no video imagery of the attack. The hallway had been selected for a reason: it was a blind spot with no surveillance equipment. However, the red EV was caught driving out the east gate and was fed into the algorithmic search vectors.

They had access to current drone footage. The orbs had been adjusted based on what little was known about the assailants. The red EV had not yet been spotted, so it was reasonable to assume it had already been ditched. Either way, it was a data point, a search feature.

Real-time satellite imagery was made available: analysis was required. Cleary had been doing this for years. He was close to having too many inputs. When there was an overabundance of information, things could get muddy. He was wary of adding analysts to the effort. Often, this could lead to an emergent piece of information being overlooked and judged inconsequential. In his experience, no one could make a clear call like the commander on the ground.

The captain asked, "When will they fix his beacon?"

Cleary, irritated, said, "A program satellite is breaking the horizon in minutes. We should get a ping then."

Cleary's irritation was based on a singular frustration. The homing devices implanted in specific high-ranking VIPs were distributed across live, encrypted networks. The encryption was considered live because it was in a state of perpetual motion—of a sort. The devices were not mere signaling beacons with passwords established to gain access. Instead, they were "living devices" whose sole purpose was to invent and re-invent their encryption process, an evolutionary binary code. This, of course, would be useless without a key to the living code. Far from being a password, the process closely mimicked human agents' exchange of bona fides. This meant the key, as it was understood, was also essentially alive and of the same algorithmic species. When they met, an understanding would be achieved via a process that had evolved beyond the understanding of human analysts. In fact, the network's only need for human input was controlling the satellites and pointing them toward each other.

These satellites were specific to the program, and the key lived inside them. Limiting them this way was an effort to deny malevolent actors the ability to gain access and secure the VIPs' locational data. As it was creating a significant delay in the recovery effort, it was a clear case of a feature being a bug.

The team members prepped their gear and laughed at rough jokes. They checked their weapon systems, tested their communication platforms, and aligned their map sets onto their heads-up displays.

They waited for a grid location, an enemy template, and a target description. After that, they needed their boss to put together a plan, which they would then execute. It was a simple life. It was a good life that left men in good moods—laughing moods.

The computer in front of Cleary updated. He said to the captain, "Looks like three mikes."

The craft hovered, and the killers prepared.

<hr />

Daniel was filthy. His movement through the

mountains had produced no small amount of perspiration, both dried and current, which inspired him with a rich odor. There remained remnants of the cave mud, caked into the crevasses and folds of his clothing. His skin was muted with a cloudy film, the by-product of long-range patrolling. He could not have looked more different than the man who sat opposite him, with his tailored shirt and tie and shiny haircut.

Daniel crossed his legs like a homeless academic, established in the plush armchair. His eyes asked silent questions as he was working on a problem. He had some time to kill.

"How does one man convince an entire species to erase itself?"

Brue's eyes lit up, more than willing to engage. He leaned forward and put his hands together, forming a triangle. "I think you're looking at it all wrong."

"I doubt it."

Brue straightened his tie—nice and flat. "I could try the themes on you, but something tells me you would be less than convinced."

"You mean all that sunshine you pumped up the world's ass?"

"Right. So, let's try this. You must have formed some kind of opinion about the plight of your fellow man. Yes?"

Daniel wrinkled his face. The idea was ridiculous. To worry about people and events on the other side of the globe was a study in conceit.

Brue continued. "The famines, the climate. The

suffering? Nothing?"

"Sounds like you're describin' the natural order."

"So, no then. Never thought about the destruction that we—"

Daniel pointed the pistol, pausing Brue midsentence. "You and me ain't in the same category. Ain't no *we* here."

Brue nodded and smiled. He sat back and recalibrated his approach.

"This *natural order*, as you call it, does that seem like a fair deal to you?"

Daniel chuckled. "Fair? Why's anything gotta be fair?"

"Because it seems to me, the natural order calls for the planet to boil and the dirt to crack. It leaves people starving in dust." Brue was getting into it far beyond messaging; this was conviction, and it showed in his eyes. He continued. "The seas rising, burying a tenth of the arable land—people starving to death."

Daniel got a kick out of Brue's distress. He smiled. "You gonna stop all that? You?" Daniel had developed a habit of using the pistol to point.

Brue acquiesced with a nod. "Fair enough. How many people did you watch die of starvation?"

Daniel checked his watch. "You got maybe five minutes. You wanna spend 'em tryin' to lay a guilt trip on me?"

"It's a horrible thing, starvation. As desperate as death can be in my eyes."

"Do you find this whole approach works on

people? I mean, it must, considering you ain't been strung up by now." Daniel relaxed. He let the pistol dangle over the arm of the chair.

"All this death you're worried about—you watchin' that from your glass tower? With all your money and your fresh water? In your city that's lit up to blind the moon? Gimme a fuckin' break. The world does what it does. Kinda always has if you think about it."

"And you would blame me for trying to help."

"I blame you for pretending you can."

◆———•●•———▶

The hovercraft made good time as it slipped over the rolling valley. The captain tapped and swiped his light board. He touched the mic for his team's internal communications.

"Listen up. We're dropping about three hundred meters from the target building. Check the foot route between. Typical alpha, bravo formation with Cleary on bravo lead. I've changed the special team's loadout, so consult your HUDs. Study the specs of the structure. Be prepared to receive more guidance during movement."

He exchanged a glance with Cleary, who nodded in agreement. Then he keyed up his mic again to talk to the aircrew. "Hotel-Four-Nine, this is Two-Six-Alpha. Offset three hundred meters southeast of the objective location. Sending LZ coordinates, time —now." He swiped his board.

Cleary took a breath.

He was about to meet an old friend.

"Would you blame me for helping a blind man? A sick child?" Brue stretched his arms, his hands open. He continued trying to reason with Daniel.

"Look at you. Brue Carnell. Saved the human race by destroyin' it. What a saint you are. Is that what you want? To be remembered as a saint?"

"I'll never understand you people."

"I don't suspect you will. Don't even understand yourself."

Brue leaned back into the couch. "Oh, I understand myself, alright."

"You don't even know what you are." Daniel smiled, and it infuriated Brue.

"So what am I then?"

"You're just another monkey beatin' a drum. Nice tie, by the way."

Brue was thrown by the comment. "Come again?"

Daniel relaxed into the seat. Three more minutes, he thought.

"We trade masters, see? It's not a thing peculiar to humans, either. You're the alpha right now with all your guns and money. Those of us who don't like it get thrown in a hole. Keep buckin' the system, we get punched so hard that we shit teeth. But if we *keep* gettin' in the way, well then, we get dead. That's the way it's always been."

He wanted Brue to feel the full weight of his following words, so he took his time and pressed deep into his eyes. "But make no mistake, there's gonna be someone who comes after you. They're gonna straighten *you* out. Then, *you* go in the hole, see? And I think if you ruminate on it properly, you'll figure out who that's gonna be."

Brue's face twitched. It was a tiny gesture, and Daniel liked the feeling of it. He didn't know what he'd said to cause it. He relaxed again and checked his watch. He had made his point.

Whatever happened in that room didn't matter. He'd killed too many men to think one more would make a difference. John was wrong, but this was the way of it now. There wasn't any changing it. He'd let it go too far and should have burned this bastard up back in the hallway. Should have moved and kept moving.

"You people... cook up a story to justify what you're doin'. You say, 'It's for the sufferin' ones.' All the while creatin' more sufferin' than you can comprehend."

Daniel checked his watch. It was almost time.

◄───── •• ─────►

The captain squatted on the far side of the tree. Lying prone near him, an operator scanned the house. He was in place behind a long gun with an elaborate scope. The thing was equipped with a long eyepiece. It rested on his brow with form-fitted rubber, blocking the remaining light of the day.

In his eye, the reticle danced in elaborate colors as the device refined its knowledge of the structure. It calculated the type and consistency of its materials. It utilized several spectrums, including audio, mass spectroscopy, temperature, and laser penetration, to see through the walls.

The operator pressed a button. A mass of white and gray blobs refined into discernible shapes. He cycled through the system's options. At one point, he visualized the interior of the room as well as the internal workings of two human beings. Their brains, skeletons, and organs floated in the middle of the digitized space.

"Hold up," he said as he tweaked the buttons, hitting a set point. The device refined the image and filled in the gaps. A perfect three-dimensional rendering of the safe house living room came alive in his scope. There was no color, only gradients of shale and black, but he picked up two people in the room, both seated.

"I have two targets. I need the ping."

The captain said, "Wait one." Then, he waved at Cleary, who was hidden behind a wall of foliage. He nodded and activated his HUD.

He whispered into the device, "This is Two-Six-Alpha. Targets in sight. We need the ping. Repeat, we need the ping."

"At some point, you believed in something." Brue attempted to push the conversation in a different direction.

He stalled. He didn't want to die just yet.

"Oh, I still do," Daniel said with a straight face.

"And what is that? I mean, I don't get the opportunity to speak directly to you people, so maybe entertain mc for a moment."

Daniel glared at him.

"Maybe it's not what, but who?" Brue studied his face, looking for the slightest tell. He believed he detected something. "It *is* a who."

Daniel had spent no effort hiding his emotions over the last decade. His job required him to be frank and upfront. Everyone around him relied on quickly understanding his intentions. As such, he'd devoted no energy toward covering over the cracks in his temper. As Brue poked around, he triggered some tell on Daniel's face—a twitch of the eye, crease on his forehead. It, like this entire conversation, was of no concern. The son of a bitch would be dead soon.

"Who is it you think I took from you?" Brue was excited to have found an inroad. "Your type, the *hard cores* as we call you, you're not that complicated. I bet I could figure it out." Brue leaned forward as Daniel checked his watch. "Give me an extra minute. This might actually be enlightening."

Daniel tipped his head. It would be alright for the man to talk another minute or so. There was nothing he could say to save his own life. So, let him talk.

"Thank you. So, let's see—when the resistance broke out, it was mainly along religious lines. Given this geographical region, I would assume you're Protestant—a common Baptist?"

Daniel smiled. "*Southern* Baptist."

Brue rolled his eyes.

Daniel cocked his head. "What were you raised to be?"

Brue lifted the tip of his tie, which had gone askance, and placed it neatly over his belt buckle. He regained Daniel and said, "Logical."

The whole show made Daniel chuckle. He was going to enjoy putting this guy down.

Brue continued. "You people hung out in your little cloisters, raged about the coming apocalypse, and saw yourselves as the chosen ones. Then you started killing—all in the shadow of your cross." He touched his chin in thought. "It was a woman. Nothing enrages you people like the feeling your property was taken from you. Was it your mother?" Brue cocked his head. He was having fun. "No. It was your wife." He studied Daniel's face.

Daniel lifted Brue's light board and looked at his watch.

Brue persisted. "If she were still alive, would you be—"

Daniel stood. "Time's up, asshole."

"Hmm." Brue leaned forward and spoke with a fresh confidence. "I believe you're right. *This* is your last chance to walk out that door—to live to see Maggie."

Daniel operated in the truth of the world. He estimated outcomes and likelihoods of success or failure. Lives routinely hung in the balance of his decisions, and so he'd developed an attitude toward the truth he once described as: *Loving, yet abusive*.

Once convinced, he executed his plan but always kept his decision loop open to new inputs. Often, plans would need adjusting as the circumstances unfolded. There was only one way to meet new challenges: stay alert and don't bullshit yourself about what's happening.

Something about Brue's tone and mannerisms ignited a sliver of skepticism within him. He pivoted to see the room. He checked the front window—the blinds were drawn. Standing silently, he listened for noise outside the house, hearing nothing. He grinned at Brue flatly.

"You're tryin' too hard."

Brue produced an easy, slick smile. "You're not stupid. You know what we are capable of. You had to know this was all bad, or you wouldn't have sent her away. You know how this goes. Inside, you know."

Daniel moved to the door, then turned back. "How?"

Brue leaned back. "Do you know the thing about intelligence?"

Daniel pointed with the pistol. "Tell me."

"Yes." Brue raised his hand to urge Daniel to lower the pistol, which he did not. "The thing about intelligence is that it can be wrong—devastatingly wrong."

Daniel said, "The tracker implant."

Brue nodded. "Do you think a piece of information as important as that would float around in the air waiting for you rubes to pull it down and use it against us?"

"The one in your arm was a decoy."

Brue nodded with vigor. "Of course it was. I've been online this whole time, so I am offering it again. Just walk out that door. At this point, I can't promise what will happen to you, but I will leave your daughter alone. That, I promise you."

The operator laid still. Slow inspirations raised his shoulders and settled them in increments near undetectable. The soft eyepiece cuffed his orbital pocket. The reticle rested on a space between the two men. They had shifted. One now stood and held a pistol toward the other.

The sniper was in control. His breath and the tension of his finger against the trigger were a matter of simple production. He waited for the ping.

Then, a white dot in the base of the seated man's cranium lit up. It blinked in a rapid pulse. The sniper adjusted the crosshairs onto the standing man. "I have the ping."

The captain referred to his HUD, nodded, and said, "Take the shot."

Daniel lowered the pistol. "So, I walk out that door and you leave her alone?"

Brue agreed, exhaled, and relaxed, melting into the couch. His face pinched in toward his nose, the beginning of a flinch.

Daniel asked, "Why?"

"Because, even though a force is acting on my behalf, what happens in this room is yet up to your determination. Put simply, you have a gun pointed at me. Giving up your daughter to secure my life is an easy decision."

Daniel's mind raced to its inevitable conclusion. He raised the pistol and pointed it at Brue. "Bullshit."

The round cut the thin door and sliced through Daniel's lower spine. Trailed by a blue-white tracer, the projectile continued through the house into the kitchen. It drilled through an appliance, the subsequent wall, and made its way through a tree before becoming lodged into the bank of a steep hill.

Daniel fell straight down, his legs and all sensation of them cut away. The pistol slipped from his fingers and landed nearby.

Brue raised his hands, stepped forward, and kicked the pistol away from Daniel.

The door banged open, and the team entered with their rifles up. They cleared the building like professionals. They flowed through the rooms, covering dead zones and corners.

Brue was pushed to the floor and squatted on by an operator. The others slipped through the house. Calls rang out from the various rooms. "Secure!"

Brue's face was close to Daniel's. He craned his neck so their eyes could meet. He studied him, looking for the slightest hint of pain. His eyes were large with the adrenaline of success. Anger slowly replaced the fear in his eyes. "I'll make sure you live long enough to see what I do to Maggie."

Daniel closed his eyes and rolled his face onto the rug. His arms had been cuffed behind his back. Rage overtook him. His body shuddered with it. He had allowed himself to be strung along. Now, he was laid out, bleeding from his guts.

Cleary entered the room as they lifted Brue from the floor. The two exchanged a long look of doubtful trust.

Brue said, "Your response time was impressive."

Cleary agreed with a smile. "You felt the ping?"

"I felt it."

Cleary, pleased, said, "Good. Good."

He moved to Daniel's side and turned to the medic. "Keep him alive." Looking down as Daniel shuddered, he said, "You seem smaller." A sneer crawled across his face.

Brue spotted the dark affiliation between them. "Do you know him?"

"In a sense." Cleary sighed as you might at the end of a long journey.

With his face smashed into the rough carpet, Daniel drifted off toward unconsciousness. The sudden and violent reversal needed to be reckoned with. How many years had he slid by? How many bullets had missed him?

Rhett had been right, of course. He'd lost a few steps, and it caught up with him. His belly burned above the chasm where his legs had been.

What had he done to Maggie? What kind of life had he inflicted her with? This was the worst outcome. If she would never have come out to him—

Maybe Rudy could get her to safety.

He wanted to die, and he surely would. The question was, how much fire would he walk through beforehand?

FIVE

Be still, inside yourself, rest your minds. The muscle and skin of you, has lasted long, for the length of its days. A call to thought, if you grieve for it, your passing life, remember the world and all within it... all the others.
—The Dawnbringer is Here

The light flashed, bright and sudden, ripping his mind from its chemical sleep.

They jerked Daniel from the litter onto the operating table, his body wrenched and tossed. They cut and stripped his clothing loose and piled it on the floor. He was flipped, covered in sterilizing solution, and then scrubbed like a luau pig.

He opened his eyes and tried to focus. The light burned into his corneas. They flipped him again, his face stuffed into a donut hole on the table. He mumbled in pain as his eyes probed the floor. Sterile, booted feet scuttled about him, kicking away his filthy clothes.

His naked and purple body lay splayed out in the aseptic light. The hole in his lower spine was perfect, small, and round. The meat blossomed from it, swollen at the edges and dried out in the air. Beneath the crusty mouth, the pit looked tender, dark, and warm.

They pushed more drugs, and Daniel slipped away into the darkness of suspended animation.

Brue stood in an observation room. A large window connected him to the procedures. He studied the preparations with some impatience and touched a wall-mounted board. "Is he a suitable candidate?"

Standing beside the nurses, a tall woman in sterile scrubs with a banded eyepiece leaned over the wound. She inspected it, then lowered the digital eyepiece and studied a three-dimensional representation of the bullet's path. She touched the side of the eye screen, and the image synched so that from whichever angle she viewed, the digital representation was superimposed over the wound.

The device highlighted sections of the projectile's canalization. It flashed red and amber over specific structures within the bullet's path and estimated the damage they had sustained.

"I can't say for sure, sir. We're going to have to get in there. It appears there is enough tissue remaining, but we just have to do it. Up until now, it's all been theoretical."

Brue touched the board again. "Well, consider this your first human trial. Take notes. I don't really care if it works as long as I can speak to him again."

She laughed. "Will do. It's going to take some time."

"All the time you need." Brue released the button and left the observatory.

The woman signaled, and an assistant handed her a small torch. She flipped a switch and activated a green plasma flame. She dialed it until the flame tightened to laser focus. She moved the torch toward the perfect hole in Daniel's back.

◂————••————▸

Brue stood in front of the door to his apartment, avoiding Roma. He'd spoken with her the night before. The conversation was brief. He could hear the striction in the back of her throat. She tried to keep it to herself, but her fear flowed through the speaker of his light board.

He wanted a moment in the hallway to brace himself. He'd been surrounded by people without sleep. He'd submitted to debriefings and after-action reports.

A moment of silence—he didn't want to spoil it yet. Besides, he didn't know what he would say to her. It occurred to him that he hadn't really thought about her at all.

He drew a deep and fortifying breath as the door swung open.

She'd been watching him on the security glass and couldn't wait any longer. She poured herself onto him, engulfed him. Emotions kept in check for many hours were let loose, and all he could do was squeeze her. He dropped his bag and wrapped his arms around her.

It had been a nasty near miss.

In that moment, Brue grasped the power he held over her. He could have been snuffed out in an instant, reduced to black emptiness. All he had ever known would have become vapor, but it would spawn a lifetime of sadness for her.

He stood in awe of it, detached from it, an observer. But that wasn't right. He loved her, or he thought he did.

Why was he so numb to it all?

She vibrated against him, the relief pouring out of her.

He stroked her hair and said sweet things that he didn't at the time mean.

◆―――••―――▶

On the couch, the low table before them covered in random takeout food, Brue and Roma lay still in each other's arms. The sun was setting, and the skyline was coming to life. Roma squeezed him.

"My mother asked me what I would do if..." She couldn't complete the sentence.

"She was silently celebrating." Brue made the joke and got the reaction he had hoped for, trying to cut the mood.

She sat up and smacked his shoulder, smiling. "Don't say that. She really wanted to know what I would do. We are a fatalistic family in some ways. In their early life together, she and my father would have lunch dates to discuss various death scenarios and who would take care of what."

"First of all, that's weird. Second, I was missing for less than an hour." Brue reached for a glass of bourbon. "You should have a little more faith in me."

He drained the glass, a happy light in his eyes.

Roma examined him, the line of his nose, the tightness of the lips when he spoke from his heart. Her smile contrasted her melancholy eyes, a sweetness she expressed to him without knowing.

"She said if you died, then I would have given away any chance to find someone else." Her voice trilled at the end of her words like she wanted to say more. She looked down at his bare chest and put her hand over his heart.

Brue stashed his anger under a practiced smile. He placed his hand on hers.

"People of her generation don't understand. They don't get what this is all about. They caused it, in fact. We're going to solve it."

He gripped her hand as he said it. He wanted to reestablish her connection to his truth. In case she had forgotten why this all had to happen. In his absence, her mother had worked against him and tried to sabotage their future.

"My mother brought me into the world to live aside you. She had that power. What power do I have?"

Her mother had indeed been at work. Brue had

grown accustomed to the old lady's ramblings, her old way of thinking.

"You have my life. You are *my* power."

He fell back on the lonely truth of it. He was all she had now and would ever have. She had given more to him than he could ever repay. He wouldn't forget it.

Roma sank into him and hugged his body tight.

"I'm glad you are home."

Brue refilled his glass. He scanned his skyline. He felt untouchable. He was the Dios del Futuro.

Daniel laid on a hyper-realistic version of the carpet from the safe house. The taste of it, the small, bitter fibers that danced into his mouth when he fell on it, were there. It was as real as anything he had ever experienced.

The carpet opened into a pit beneath him. He slipped into it, clawing. The fibers found his fingernails like splinters. Then, the black hole swallowed him. A pinpoint of light above blinked out as the floor closed shut. The sensation of free fall forced his stomach to lurch and rise until its contents spilled over his face and onto the bed.

He tried to breathe and sucked some bile into his trachea. He coughed, spraying the stuff into a mist. In his vision, the color white burned into his corneas as he tried to make sense of himself.

The coughing continued in earnest until two large arms flipped him to his side and smacked his upper back. Several more ejections and the bile worked itself clear of his windpipe.

He shivered in silence for a moment before he opened his eyes again. He found himself in a white room, with a large man tending to him like a smiling mountain. Daniel adjusted through the fog of drugs and the perceptive disruption of the solid white space. His focus drifted from blur to blur until his surroundings clarified.

The giant pulled a white chair close to the bed. He rolled Daniel toward him and peeked over his hips. He checked the dark, red spot on the bottom of Daniel's white shirt. He lifted the shirt to inspect the surgery site. "You're gonna need to take it easy, mate. We got big plans for you."

A look of genuine concern covered his face. He pulled a silk kerchief from his pocket and cleaned the vomit from the corners of Daniel's mouth.

When Daniel tried to speak, his voice gashed, an empty husk. He gnawed at a word but couldn't produce it.

"They say it's gonna be a few weeks before we can have a heart-to-heart. Rest assured, I'll be visitin' with you soon."

"Maggie?" It sounded like a burlap bag dragged across concrete when he spoke.

"What's that?"

Daniel swallowed hard. He was dehydrated. He couldn't reproduce the word.

"I tell ya what. You work on gettin' stronger and leave the little lady to me. How's that sound?"

The big man didn't wait for a response. He moved across the room toward a wall of white. A black rectangle appeared, and he walked through it. The void closed with soundless efficiency, leaving Daniel alone in the harsh fluorescence.

He looked down at his legs, motionless. Their emanations plagued his memory. He recalled their power, imagined himself ascending a steep incline. The muscles and tendons worked, sliding over each other, so much meat. He knew them from the bone out. They wouldn't move, but they were on fire in his mind.

He closed his eyes, and the tears flowed. This wasn't supposed to be the way it ended. Decades of this shit, and he didn't have the luck or the sense to be dead. At least a hundred times, he could have ended up scattered to pieces or burned into the side of some hill overlooking the mountains.

Instead, he was lying on a cot, a gimp. His men, those boys, were all dead. You're as good as your last mission, so what did that make him?

He then was overcome with thoughts of Maggie. Was she alive? Did she make it out? Or was she lying in a room like this, waiting to pay for the sins of her father?

◆───••───▶

The pump station was a holdover, standing for over a hundred years, tucked away in the tip of a steep run of the Appalachians. The walls were brick with patchy white paint, the floors worn linoleum. Under the dingy lights, rows of ultra-processed, packaged foods formed the aisles. Booths were lined along windowless wall in the back. A menu of fried foods hung over a counter. Heated glass boxes displayed hot dogs, chicken, and baked potatoes.

Maggie sat crumpled into the farthest booth from the counter, a Styrofoam box open in front of her. It contained a suspicious-looking sandwich. Rudy sat across from her, studying her expression and posture. He had a mouthful of the same type of sandwich.

"You'm dun wan?"

She looked at him with bemused irritation. "What?"

Rudy took the time to chew his food and swallow it. "I asked if you wanted your sandwich?"

Maggie didn't answer. She slunk deeper into the plastic bench. She iced him out and stared at the wall.

Rudy sighed. He had been on the run with the girl for two weeks while waiting for his support mechanisms to pull them underground.

The first hour of the escape was the most treacherous. The pair left the safe house in the red EV and hurried to the northern edge of Newbern. Rudy drove; his eyes darted in every direction during the short trip, looking for signs they were being tailed. He ditched the car in a machine shop. Then, picked the bio lock on a backcountry rover and wired it up. They spent the next four days taking a circuitous route past Dublin, Staffordshire, and Narrows on unimproved dirt paths before ending up at Rich Creek on the north side of the New River.

This was Rudy's stomping grounds. He knew people—for what that was worth. He activated his emergency alert plan and waited, along with Maggie. They hid in abandoned buildings, leaving no trace, both never sleeping at the same time. They had long since discarded their light boards, drowning them in the New River.

He had received some contacts over secure channels, acquired an untraceable board, and used limited communication windows. The leaders in his network deliberated. Maybe they would pull them in. Maybe they would roll on him to take the heat off. Everything was on the table, and Rudy knew it.

He asked, "You ever wonder if you eat just to be eatin'?"

Maggie stared at him. Throughout the trek, she'd described her anger with Daniel. She talked about the years it took to build the courage to go to him. She felt directionless—didn't know which way was up, didn't know what to do. She'd been rejected again, the same as before, so long ago.

At least that's how she thought of it, and no amount of convincing from Rudy would change her mind. He'd argued on Daniel's behalf. He wasn't sure why. He understood the decision.

It was hard to say what had happened to Daniel. Rudy's contacts were spotty, but the word was he'd been killed in the raid. The government had been reporting his capture, but that didn't mean anything.

"I'm not hungry." She said, sliding the sandwich toward him. Then, she grabbed his free hand and held it tight. "You've been good to me, Rudy. I appreciate it."

Her eyes changed up.

He warmed at her touch and shied from her gaze, smiling. "Well, I'm not gonna leave you on the side of the road."

He got his appetite back and took a big bite.

"Have you thought about what I asked you?" She squeezed again, putting her stamp on him, insisting without words.

Rudy had been too obvious with her, in the way he looked at her. He chastised himself on occasion. It went against his training to be vulnerable to anyone. He couldn't help it with Maggie. He didn't care, either. He never gave a second thought to the way he pulled her underneath his body when the drone attacked.

She had.

He'd noted her closeness since they were on that cliff face together. She had developed a need for him, which Rudy suspected she didn't understand. However, she did understand whose hand she was holding. Rudy's delight reflected in her eyes. She held more than his hand.

And he was fine with it.

He finished his bite. "Listen, you might wanna give it some time before you go makin' a decision like that. Besides, I don't know if they would even agree to plug you in. They'll probably just kick you back down to Raleigh. They haven't even pulled us under yet."

He scanned the store. It was part of his routine in public: spot all the access points and possible exits, sit where you can see them, rotate your eyes through them, and don't get complacent. "We're still flappin' out here. Too hot for them to make a move toward us."

"I know all that. Heard you say it a thousand times. They'll pull us in. What else are they gonna do?"

Rudy spoke with seriousness. "Well, that's just it, see. They could do anything. Or they could do nothin'. They could figure us to be a liability and burn all connections. Just set us to floatin'."

"Why would they do that?"

"You don't know nothin' about this shit. Like I been sayin', you don't know what you're askin' for." Rudy's sandwich fell on the plate. "These are very serious people. They're assumin' that our faces were grabbed somewhere along the line. They know what that means and how much more dangerous it makes us. They just gotta make up their minds."

He sat back into his booth and let go of her hand.

"And believe me when I say, that decision won't be based on how much they like ol' Rudy. It'll be a tactical decision, cold and plain. A risk assessment, that's all."

Maggie stuttered for a brief instant, then

persisted.

"Well." She straightened up in the booth and dragged her sandwich back across. "As far as I see it, whether they let us in or not doesn't make much difference."

"Oh no?"

"I know what I'm gonna do."

"Oh, do ya?" Rudy cocked his head

"I have nothing, no mother, no father. I've lost my whole family to them. They're going to answer for it. Don't know how yet. But they will."

She took a bite of the food.

It had been maybe five or six days since this obsession had claimed her. She'd talk about little else. Rudy had no idea what had sparked it. She went to sleep one night quietly after being in her mind most of the day. The next morning, her life was all laid out in front of her. She was going to set things right. Each night, when they traded guard shifts, she worked her way toward sleep, her eyes on the ceiling. He could only imagine what she was seeing and what sort of calculations were happening.

He thought about it for a moment. "When you say they're gonna answer, who you talkin' about?"

She swallowed hard and chased it with her soda. She appeared to be deciding her answer all the while, the gears churning. "Don't know. Kinda figured you guys would."

Now, he reached for her hand. "You don't know—"

She pulled her hand away. "Don't tell me I don't know what I'm asking for again. I know what I'm asking for, Rudy."

"Do you? You're runnin' on nothin' but hate right now."

"What else is there for me?"

She made sense, and Rudy had learned enough about the girl to doubt his ability to talk her out of it. "You gotta understand somethin'. You can lose yourself in this life. I mean, the person sittin' in this booth right now will be a memory if you go down this road."

Maggie put her sandwich back in the box. She brushed her hands and placed them on the table, ready to do battle.

"I don't like the person sitting in this booth."

Rudy opened his mouth to interject. She held her hand up to silence him.

"This person's weak. She always will be. She's already a memory to me. *I can't use her.*" She opened her hands to him. "*They* made her—been making her since the day she was born. I reject her."

There was a vast and empty space beyond the beautiful, green glass of her eyes.

The conversation had strayed away from plain English, and Rudy wasn't comfortable with it. He scratched the side of his head.

She touched his hand again. "Rudy, I'm going to introduce myself to those who took my family. They need to see what they've created. Don't you think?"

Rudy sighed again. He wasn't equipped to deny her. "Alright. When I make comms tonight, I'll mention it."

Maggie reacted with excitement. She raised her voice. "Seriously?"

Rudy put his finger to his lips, smiling, her exuberance catching on. "Yeah. I'll talk to 'em. But you gotta promise me you're in. You can't turn it off once it's on."

"Oh. I'm in." Maggie peeled some crust from her sandwich and shoved it into her mouth.

"And listen up. If this goes down, your whole life is gonna change. It's a different world from your father's."

"Good. You people have bathrooms, I see." She enjoyed her joke.

Rudy chuckled. "Yeah, we got bathrooms." She excitedly tapped the floor with her foot. Still, he had things to say, and he needed her to hear them. "It's not black and white. It's hard to tell who's who sometimes. Long as you remember who *you* are."

"And *you*." She caught him up in a wide-eyed and trusting gaze. Her eyes danced across his face.

He dipped his head, embarrassed but emboldened. "You don't ever have to worry about who I am."

A corner of her mouth lifted. Yeah, she knew who she was dealing with.

He continued. "Everything is planned to the T. Not just operations but your whole life. You know why Daniel was so good at this stuff?"

"He was a cold-hearted prick?"

"Well, yeah. But he was meticulous with his plans. That thing back there." Rudy waved off toward Newbern and all the destruction and death in that place. "That thing was an aberration. It only takes one mistake."

He waited for an acknowledgment.

She said, "Yeah. Ok."

"Just one shiny thing ended him. You go off half-cocked in this business, let me tell ya—"

"Rudy, I get it." Her rising smile assured him. She grabbed his hand again and pressed it, and he calmed. "Thank you."

He shook his head, looked away, smiling, and checked to ensure he was still in her gaze. He lingered there and ate his sandwich.

◀——••——▶

Brue sat and fiddled with his light board. He crossed his legs and adjusted his coat. The door opened, and an orderly wheeled Daniel into the room. Brue checked his board for the time, then set the thing down and smiled.

Daniel groaned. He narrowed his eyes. His legs ached, lying limp and useless up into his hips. His new truth was less than ideal. He couldn't shit without help. All he could do was complain and feel sorry for himself.

Is this when it starts? Here, in this room?

He figured that Brue wasn't the one who'd do the work. Watch it, maybe, but he wasn't the type to get his suit dirty. Like many, he was incapable of enacting his own desires—he'd need a man of fortitude to do it for him.

"Well, look at us, together again. The last time I saw you on the carpet of that little house, I wasn't so sure we'd meet again. You really look well, Daniel." Brue affected a carefree smile.

"Whatta you want?"

Daniel was cool about it. His position was desperate. He had no leverage that he could think of. His temperament wouldn't allow him to show weakness unless it provided a tactical advantage. In this instance, he could see none. He was fucked. There was no escaping what was headed his way.

"I bet you have questions." Brue's eyes interrogated him. "I know you have them, so go on, ask."

Daniel's ignorance of the world, his complete blackout, was a primary source of Brue's power. He didn't even know where he was—city or state. Yet, he mustered a startling amount of petulance. He lifted himself on the arms of the wheelchair to shift his body weight. His lower back burned.

"I've got some time." Brue leaned back, picked up his board, and swiped it alive.

After another moment of silence, Daniel said, "Maggie."

"Was that a question?" Brue didn't look up from his board.

"Yes," Daniel answered dryly.

Brue became animated. A bright smile covered his face. "Wonderful. I had a bet with Cleary that you'd ask about her first. He seemed to think you'd be more self-concerned. Has a quite a low opinion of you, that guy."

Daniel said, "Maggie."

"She's safe. We have her. It wasn't difficult to lay hands on them. She and that boy were running like little mice." Brue's face twisted along the edges. "Do you make it a habit to work with children often?"

"Should I work with your types instead?"

Brue opened his mouth to reply but stopped as the door to the room opened.

Cleary walked in, nodding. "I know. I know. I'm late."

He stepped toward the orderly and waved him away. The man turned and exited the room. Cleary stood rigid, expectant.

Brue passed him a glance, and he raised his eyebrows and gave him a flat smile, like a stranger passing with nothing to say.

Cleary moved to the wheelchair and placed a hand on Daniel's shoulder.

Brue said, "Maggie is being treated as well as you."

"Why?" *Here's the rub*, thought Daniel.

"Because I would like to convince you of something."

"Would ya now?"

Brue nodded.

Daniel said, "And what would that be?"

"That I'm not the monster you think I am. That everything I've done, I've done for the good of humanity."

Daniel drew deep from his trachea, a hollow, rattling production. His mouth filled with phlegm, and he spat on the floor. It was a crude protest, and it had an effect.

Brue snarled, warping his nose and mouth for a brief instant. Then he regained himself.

"Alright, you need some control to be reasonable, so let me give you some power here." Brue glanced up at Cleary. "It turns out, Daniel, that you and your friend John are some rather notable detractors. Well, in his case, *was* notable. Either way, your names are known, and you have garnered some respect from some of our more bothersome corners."

He paused momentarily to ensure Daniel followed his line of thought. "It's your work. They romanticize it." He swiped his light board and scanned the screen. "Administration bombings, ambushes, assassinations. You've made a name for yourself. And three years ago, when we thought you were killed, you did a good job of maintaining that pretense while still being a sizable thorn in our side. How did you do that, Daniel?"

"By chicken-hawkin' a bunch a' little boys to do his killin' for him." Cleary's words were like razor blades.

Daniel glanced up over his shoulder and, for the first time, without the halo of narcotics, studied Cleary's face. He smiled. "I remember you."

The strike came from his right side, an open-handed smack to his temple and cheek. The flat of the hand found a good amount of skin and encompassed the ear.

Cleary could feel the bones of Daniel's skull

pressed against his palm for an instant. It was brutal, fast, and powerful.

Daniel's head snapped hard, and without the ability to brace himself, he flew from the chair and bounced onto the concrete floor. He lay still, gasping, white dots in his eyes. He shook his head, attempting to clear it. His ears rang.

"We weren't sure you would remember Mr. Cleary." Brue smiled as if an easy warmth was descending through his chest. "Do you happen to remember the cause of his ire?"

Daniel arched his neck toward Brue. "He's got a tiny dick?"

Before Brue could respond, Cleary's large hands were on Daniel. He was lifted and tossed across the room.

Daniel grunted as he landed on the cold, hard floor, biting his tongue in the process. His mouth filled with the taste of hot copper.

Brue lifted his hands to Cleary with a stern face. "You'll have him soon enough."

Cleary stopped in his tracks. He leaned back on his heels, baited, like a twitch snare. He was all potential energy, waiting for the line to be tripped.

Daniel dragged himself to the wall, his forearms flat on the cold floor. He used the wall to roll himself over to face his attackers.

Brue said, "You've killed thousands of our people and—"

"They weren't people," Daniel said, convinced it was the right play to continue antagonizing them.

"Your little test tube freaks. Fuckin' sins against God."

"Whatever you call them, they weren't all Newborns, were they? Plenty of them were what you would call normal people." He nodded at Cleary.

The big man scooped Daniel up in one hand and dragged him back to his chair. He slammed him down in the seat.

Electric bolts of pain shot through him, his breath running away in bursts.

"Everything coming your way, I want you to *really* feel, Daniel. Cleary will represent all of us over the coming days. The rest of humanity, abandoned to your senselessness—your blood lust. You're an animal. You'll answer for your crimes, and the world will witness as you beg its forgiveness."

He walked past Daniel and put his hand on Cleary's shoulder. He whispered, "Cautiously, fully, completely, break him. The next time I see this one, he should avoid my eyes."

Cleary nodded, his nostrils flared. As Brue left the room, he slid gloves over his hands. A dark, rigid plastic rim projected over the knuckles.

Daniel didn't look up at Cleary again. He sat in his chair, attempting to store air before the onslaught. All the pieces were in place now. It would begin within moments, and the question in his mind was, "How long will it last?"

He would break. It was inevitable. There had never been a man who could withstand torture when it was done correctly, and Cleary had the look of a professional.

He thought of Maggie, her blonde hair in the mountain morning and her thin frame drawing deep breaths at the top of a ridgeline. He worried about her.

Cleary's gloves buttoned, he moved to the door and locked it. He reached into his pocket and retrieved a small, bullet-shaped device made of brushed bronze—a plain thing, with a small switch lying flat against one side. He palmed it and turned to Daniel.

Cleary, a man of purposeful, interpersonal deception, no longer disguised his desire.

He was alone with Daniel.

◀——•●•——▶

A bright shock of light pulled Daniel from the shallow pit of sleep. His muscles, tendons, bones, and viscera all burned with an unforgiving agony. It lasted a moment, then evaporated into the air around him. An echoing darkness followed it.

This had become the custom. He would drift away into sleep, then be ripped from it. His intestines lurched and pushed the air from his lungs. He would make gurgling sounds as foam and spit rose in his throat. Then, the force would abate, and he would grow limp.

During the intermissions, he trembled on cold, wet concrete.

The attacks were erratic in nature. It came from

within him—his body was the source. He'd been hijacked, his nervous system. When he made this observation to Cleary, it came with a plea. He needed time to consider the demands. What they had asked of him was too much, and he couldn't possibly think if his neurons continued to randomly burst into flames.

He needed time.

Cleary's argument was solid. Time was immaterial there, in that room. This could last as long as Cleary's finger could flip the switch.

When would the next one come? It did him no good to know.

He was naked and covered in filth, his skin deteriorating into ulcers and infected scabs. His hair was patched, missing in clumps. Vomit and mire decorated the floor about him.

The next shock came, locking his body into a rigid board. His arms twitched and smacked the skin across his legs. Spit danced from his lips on thick, ropey strings. His eyes rolled backward.

The jolt ended, and the cycle began anew—the twitching, naked skin, the feces, the terror of inevitability. His fetid breath exhaled in fits.

A door opened, and a light, filled with the shadow of Cleary, fell across him. Daniel whimpered at the sight, a pathetic, crippled victim.

Cleary walked in, squatted beside him, and kept his hems out of the muck. His eyes looked to have grown weary of it. He said, "Do you fancy yourself a warrior, Daniel?"

Cleary quietly studied him, the vomit on his lips. He pulled a kerchief and wiped the corners clear of the funk. "Were you set loose on a noble mission and then abandoned to us?" He stowed the kerchief. "Do you know how long it's been since you asked about the girl?"

Something fractured inside Daniel at the mention of Maggie. A long, moaning sob emitted from within him. Tears flowed onto his cheeks, creating streaks, the color of his long-unseen skin.

He hadn't asked about her because he couldn't. He couldn't bring himself to face all the decisions which had destroyed his family. So, he would hide in the fitful bursts of shrieking agony. He would hide her from his mind's eye, and as long as he could not see her, she didn't exist. He found places inside himself—he called them "carveouts." He retreated inside them as needed whenever a memory of her entered his mind.

He deserved all this. He kept telling himself he deserved it.

Cleary leaned back away from the display and averted his eyes. Fair amounts of disgust and pity prejudiced his tone. "All that's left of your kind are footprints. Your men are all dead. Rhett is dead. All those boys, cold and in the dirt. Yet, here you lay, begging scraps from a master who has forgotten you."

Cleary narrowed his eyes at the crying, broken man before him—the smell of him.

"You moralize. You murder. You hide behind some

vow, some coat of arms, some *religion*. Whatever you call it, you're still just a murdering savage—a fucking chump."

Cleary rolled him over and inspected the device. A small, ribbed dome, flat metal, and stainless steel, protruded from his lower back. The skin healed around it, pink and beaded like an arc weld.

"You know this thing can basically keep you alive forever, Daniel. It's tapped into your neural net. Knows exactly how much you can take before the lights go out. And as you see, that's quite a lot." Cleary produced the small bronze switch.

Daniel's eyes bulged at the sight of it, and his pupils exploded. Pure fear. He reached a scum-coated hand upward and begged. "Cleary, Clear—No, please, Cleary."

"There's one thing I haven't shown you yet." He stood and flipped the switch.

Daniel grimaced, clamped his teeth shut and moaned. It was a complicated mixture of sound. If desolation could be sung, its tune was familiar to Daniel.

"Shush. This isn't what you think it is."

Daniel stopped groaning. He opened his eyes. Nothing had happened. He unclenched his muscles, breathed again. His hands trembled. Then, confused, he checked with Cleary.

"Can you feel it?" Cleary was smiling.

"Feel what?" Daniel looked down at his legs.

The phantom pains had plagued him for weeks. He'd grown to accept it. But, at that moment, they were absent. He was overcome with the tingle of muscle and bone. He perceived the grime and the cold, wet floor on the skin of his bare legs. Confused, he checked in with Cleary. This didn't make any sense.

"You can feel it." Cleary was entertained. "No shit?"

Daniel moved his toes, and his heart almost stopped in shock. He bent his left knee, dragging it through the filth. He pulled both knees together and used his hips to roll onto his back. He slid to the wall, stopped, and begged Cleary for permission to stand with the look in his eyes.

Cleary dipped his head, happy like an angler whose line was bumped. "Go ahead, buddy."

Daniel slid his feet under him and twisted toward the wall. One foot was up, followed by another. He worked his way, sliding his chest against the cold concrete, using his hands to brace himself. His breath shuddered in anticipation. The pain was never more present, but he overrode it. He forced himself to stand up.

When he was nearly to his feet, nearly standing, Cleary hit the switch. Daniel's legs disappeared as if they had fallen off him. From the waist below, he didn't exist. His body fell into a twisted heap. The force of the collapse bounced him backward and onto his side.

He was finished. This was the last insult. His eyes rolled into a vacant stare as he slid inside one of his deep carve-outs. The wall before him, the pain, and the wet floor all became blurry, as if experienced through smeared petroleum. He locked himself away from that place, knowing his body to be near its end, yet curiously unallowed to die. He protected himself from it but maintained awareness of it.

Cleary lingered behind him. He squatted again, careful not to smudge his clothes with the filth. "What should you do, having been set adrift into the ether of peace?" Cleary held the switch in front of himself. "What would a man like you do without his war? Where are all your guns?"

He hit the switch and Daniel thrashed, slinging slime onto his shoes. Then he stopped the current. "Where are your men? Where is your god?"

Daniel screamed this time. He shrieked as the fire erupted from within. His teeth banged as his jaw pumped open and closed.

Cleary held the switch fully open. "Where are the happy campfires? The sanctuaries that brought you together?"

Daniel twisted in a death spasm. Then he went limp as the device shut itself down.

Cleary held the switch, his finger red against it, trying to force it forward, trying to kill Daniel. He sighed and released it.

Daniel's face was in the muck. He cried, begging with words that made no sound.

Cleary leaned in close and whispered in a hateful voice. "All gone, your kind. Lost forever, victims of your own hate."

He pressed the bullet against Daniel's face and slid

it along through the wet grime. "And now your life has grown terrible with pain"—he paused with his finger over the switch in the corner of Daniel's eye—"and it will never end."

The switch.

The screams.

◄———••———►

Cleary marched down the hallway, a scowl carved into his face. Anyone unaware enough to slow him down was moved aside, their rank and station be damned. He hadn't expected it to last this long, the thing with Daniel. If he weren't under orders, he would have killed him weeks ago. He would have walked into the cell and bled him out with his brother's knife. Or he would've put a simple bullet in the back of his simple head. He was worn from it, the nearly inconceivable fortitude of the man. He'd never known it to last this long, a man to resist this long.

In the deepest parts of him, pity sprouted roots. He hated that fact but acknowledged it. There was no point in lying to himself about it.

There were always intersections in the perspectives of enemy fighters. They spilled the same colored juice on the same patches of dirt. They sought to murder one another and hid from the other in terror. They shit themselves when they died. They came across each other in piles—dysregulated, pale, and shattered. They experienced euphoric highs at the sight of each other's death and then stumbled across quiet moments here and there where they could not hide from the shame of those feelings. The sameness that possessed them was intangible.

Wars had been fought by poor men from the beginning. Poor men were more likely to fall victim to grand ideas. Having no relation to the thought controllers, the well-educated, well-connected, there was no chance they would receive the gentle tap on the shoulder and the whisper of truth: *This is all bullshit*.

The ideas were planted when they were young. Cleary could remember running around with an oak branch cut into the shape of a rifle. He remembered looking down its crooked barrel and sighting it against his buddies, who pointed their sticks at him. The ideas grew in fertile soil. The roots took complicated routes and spread wide and deep inside them.

The old around them were no less its victims. For what it's worth, the old are only versions of themselves with more rust on the hinges. The veterans came creaking down the lane, singing songs of glory and praising the young. Thus, the system was fortified and established long before the poor kid could even pull his own pud.

There was generational perpetuation, and the well-heeled needed only watch and tip their cap from the sidelines on occasion to show solidarity with the poor, simple bastards.

These men didn't have the cheat code. Their opportunities were slim. There was no buffet of options for them when war kicked off. They knew the cold, and they knew the longing for a better life. They picked the system into which they were born to devote themselves because that system had carefully crafted the traditions that allowed them to be steeped in honor.

They laid themselves upon an altar of blood.

As Cleary had learned, after enough killing, they realized the points of intersection were at least as strong as their differences. They began to see each other as the same. The odd paradox was that this knowledge also made them much better at killing each other.

The system had to be admired.

Politicians plied their trade with information. They fixed the minds of civilians with bloodlust, but the soldiers understood each other. It might've taken some time, but they came to an understanding.

Daniel had killed Cleary's brother. His brother was a soldier, like his father and his grandfather, and it was his place to die. As it was Cleary's place and Daniel's. There was a string that tied them all together, and no matter what viciousness they unleashed on each other, the string existed long into the future, long after the killing and dying had happened.

No soldier sees himself as a monster. The monster is what he will give his life to destroy. On occasion, he wakes up and sees himself in full. He turns to his shadow and doesn't recognize the shape of the thing. The people around him won't look into his eyes.

When he tries to remember why he had ever started this business, he finds himself in arrears of his promises as a young fool, donning his helmet and his costume and walking into flames for other people.

Cleary was tired of the routine, the days spent watching Daniel writhe along the floor, shrieking in agony. He wouldn't die. He couldn't, and that didn't seem fair. It strained him to justify it, going well beyond the nameless boundaries of honor—if any such thing still existed.

That he engaged in it at the behest of a pencil-necked drone like Brue didn't sit well with him. The man had no idea what it meant to be mortally engaged with another. He was no warrior. He was a politician, a weasel.

Cleary stopped in the hall for a moment. Maybe it would be him on that floor someday, with some fresh, young monster standing over him, watching him through the glass; the newest of warriors, boyishly applying his torment, unquestioning because he'd not been made to question.

He shook his head and entered the elevator. It was guarded, so he showed his badge and wrist to the scanner. The lights turned green, and the doors closed. The lift pulsed upward at a fast click.

Cleary wanted to get it over with. He palmed

the switch in his jacket pocket. There wasn't a reasonable point to it anymore. Whatever had approximated hatred inside him had long since abated, and now he wanted it done. If a man had a soul, the soldier would have some awkward accountings at the end of his road, having restrained the voice of it. Maybe for Cleary, he could hear it now, whispering in his mind.

The doors opened to the ninety-fourth floor, and Cleary stepped out to another security checkpoint. Again, with the wrist and badge scanning routine and the green lights. He nodded at the guards as they opened the door to Brue's office.

Brue sat staring out over the Hudson River with his back to the door. Cleary spotted his reflection as he walked toward him. Brue watched him approach.

"How you fairin', sir?"

Cleary speaking with professional decorum was notable in its rareness. Brue smiled at it. "Better every day." He spun his chair toward Cleary and waved toward a plush couch ten feet from his desk.

Cleary wrinkled his brow but went to the couch anyway. When he sat, he sank into the leather. He was a whole foot below Brue's eyeline. He grunted and slid himself to the edge of the soft cushion. This was no way for a man to converse about serious matters.

"So, you have a proposal for me?" Brue raised his eyebrows.

"Yeah." Cleary's propriety took a hit as he negotiated the low ground. Absurd sounds emanated as he rubbed along the skin of the couch. "Let me kill this asshole and get it over with. I got plenty to do, runnin' down leads from the operations in the hills. If you let me run it, we can root out half the eastern networks."

Brue smiled. "We've got people on the networks. You're not the only person I have, Cleary."

"Just the best."

Brue's smile grew. He dipped his head. "Yes. You are the best, but—"

"He's not gonna break. He would have done it by now if he was gonna break."

Brue said, "You're telling me a man can withstand this kind of attention indefinitely?"

Every time Brue spoke about the program and what was happening to Daniel in the third-floor cell, he called it "attention," as if he had an allergy to calling it what it was. Cleary had to restrain himself from speaking freely.

"Sir—" The word burned on its way out, like bile. "It is my estimation that the subject has passed the point of achieving a hopeful outcome."

Brue wrinkled his brow. "I would think you, of all people, would relish this, the opportunity to deliver retribution."

This fuckin' piece a' shit thinks I'm an animal, Cleary thought.

"He's not gonna break. Let me put him down."

Brue leaned forward. "Are you feeling pity for him?"

Cleary stood and buttoned his jacket. This was a

waste of time. "I don't feel anything for him. I've got other things to do." He said it as if the case was settled and Brue needed only to agree.

Brue grinned at him. "Very well. Go back to your OPCEN. Assume control of the Appalachian operations. I'll have somebody take over interrogations."

Brue held out his hand.

Cleary looked at his flat, empty palm. He fingered the switch in his pocket. He desired to get permission to put Daniel down and then move on. He deserved the right to do it himself. Looking at Brue's open hand, the vanilla emptiness of it and its manicured, uncalloused meat forced an eruption of contradictory feelings, almost nameless inside him.

"The switch, Cleary. I'm going to need it."

"Oh. *You're* gonna do it?"

Brue flinched at the comment.

Cleary smiled and held the switch tight in his hand. "Yeah, I didn't think so." He turned to the door.

"So. You're still running the interrogation?"

Cleary didn't answer. He pulled the door open and passed through it. He'd be damned if he gave Daniel over to a soft-handed bitch like Brue Carnell. He could feel Tommy staring him down, forcing him to see the thing through to the end, no matter the cost.

Cleary longed for the wilderness. He longed for the chase of his younger days. Life was simple then. There were good guys, and there were bad. The bad ones you put in your crosshairs and the good ones you leaned on to watch your back.

He had no idea who was who anymore.

The thing with Daniel...

◆————••————▶

Rudy and Maggie stood in the barn's hanging lamplight. It was an ancient structure made of weathered planks, split and cracked from sun and wind. Tucked away in a deep valley corner, it was hugged and hidden by all manner of mountain hardwoods.

Before them, on a tall slaughter table, lay a pistol. It was affixed with a silver, handmade suppressor. The gun was old but had been well cared for. It glistened with lubrication under the amber glow of the hanging lamp. It was a reliable relic if the person firing it knew what they were doing.

Maggie shifted her weight from foot to foot. She told herself to be still, but her nerves would have none of it. Her stomach lurched with anxiety. This thing was a big deal. She needed to make the right impression. It was a job interview, plain and simple.

Rudy was a rock next to her. He even leaned into her shoulder to transfer some of his calmness with an occasional brushing. The two waited for the man across the table, standing outside the cone of light, to speak.

He cocked his head in consideration of a proposal. He was lean and weatherworn, wearing jeans and a button-down shirt. He narrowed his eyes at Maggie. "You ever shoot a .380 before?"

She said, "Trained up for this on a nine mil subcompact. This shouldn't be very different."

The man pointed at the pistol. "That's a shame. Musta been some kinda miscommunication. I had that suppressor built for this particular gig. You shoot through a suppressor before?"

Maggie picked the pistol up and judged the heft of it. "No. Shouldn't matter too much, though."

"Are you sure you're ready for this, girl?"

Rudy jumped in. "She's ready."

The man shot a glare at him. "Talkin' to her, if you don't mind."

"I'm ready." Maggie stilled herself and spoke with a clear voice. Even so, a trace of fear trailed at the end of the words. It was her old self, leftover, undermining her. She would put it to sleep sooner or later.

Few would have noticed the tremor in her voice, but this man was looking for such a sign. He shook his head. "She ain't ready." He looked at Rudy, disappointed. "Sorry, bud." He turned to the exit.

Rudy stopped him. "Glenn. She's ready. We've been preppin' this for a couple weeks."

Glenn stopped but didn't turn. "You ain't done shit since you got back but a couple a' bangers." He turned and eyed Maggie, inspected her. "She might be ready someday. Lord knows she's got the right bloodline. But this thing is somethin' else. It's gotta get done right."

"I got it. I know what's up." She stripped away any fear in her voice this time. Along with it—the little girl and how she used to think. Her life was complicated now. There wasn't time for quivering or doubt. So she dropped the little girl act. It was time to move on.

"You know what's up?" Glen was derisive. "I can't think of a person who knows less about what's up." He turned again and walked toward the door.

The sound of the pistol froze him. The magazine fell free from the well, the slide racked back, and then the sound of a round on the metal slaughter table. He turned and evaluated Maggie's handling of the firearm—fluid, purposeful, and fast.

She checked the bolt face, clearing the weapon, then pressed the slide release. She pointed the gun at the ground and performed a series of trigger squeezes combined with slide resets to check the weapon's function.

She locked the slide to the rear and slid the magazine into the well. She tapped the slide release and pivoted toward the hay bales in the corner of the barn. The suppressor hissed four times. Each shot slapped a small steel target ten meters away—each impact sitting on top of the last one.

She placed the gun on safe, set it on the table, and then looked up at Glenn. "You boys can stand around here all day talking if you want. Do you want this guy done? Today is the day. I did the work on this. I know the plan, the route, the contingencies. But if you don't make up your mind, the opportunity's gonna pass. You got another day, maybe two, before he's in the wind."

Glenn canted his head and smiled at her. "You ready to learn the magic secret, huh?"

"I'm ready." She was the gun. In her mind, the matter was already settled. It showed in her eyes.

Glenn wagged his head and chuckled under his breath. "I known this guy my whole life. He might be a piece a' shit traitor, but he ain't stupid. He'll have his eyes open."

Maggie placed her hand on the pistol. "Not for long."

Glenn released a slow sigh. He turned to Rudy and nodded. "You have mission control. She's the shooter. You vouched for her, so you eat the cake she bakes, understand?"

Rudy agreed with a nod.

Glenn turned and, this time left the barn.

Rudy placed his hand on hers. She tried to pull away, but he persisted. She was already on the mission in her mind, but she let him hold her hand, knowing what he would say.

"You don't have to do this. Not everybody does this kinda work. It's not too late. I can catch him before he leaves."

She looked at him, and her face hardened. He was a good-looking guy with a strong jaw and beautiful dark hair waving off in all directions. She liked his eyes and what she saw in them. He had a very charming voice and was using its warmth, trying to get her to cave. "We've done ops already. I helped you build the bombs. I drove you to place them. We dropped a building on a dozen people. What's the difference?"

"You didn't see their faces or hear their voices. You didn't smell them. They weren't real. This kinda thing is different. This is the kinda stuff that sticks."

He took his best shot, and she stared at his mouth as he spoke. She could feel his lips on her. She knew the taste of him. He was trying to keep her from spoiling herself. He was still talking to the girl in the booth.

She freed her hand, dropped the magazine from the pistol, and topped off the rounds she'd spent in her demonstration. She smiled at Rudy with genuine appreciation.

"We better get going."

◄—————•●•—————►

The door to the convenience store opened, and a short, dull-looking man, round in his waistline, stepped out onto the sidewalk. He fisted cash into a small bag and looked around.

The grimy suburb of Glenvar, on the outskirts of Roanoke, was pockmarked with logistics facilities. Railyards were omnipresent, as were the sights and sounds that accompanied them. He pulled a cigarette from the bag and tossed it in his mouth.

As he prepped his lighter, he scanned the area: to the left of the market, a salon, then the corner; across the street, an empty, coal-coated lot. Smoke trailed from his mouth as he stepped toward his car.

Maggie popped out of the salon next door. She

was nonchalant, a vacant-looking teenage girl with a fresh haircut. She held her light board before her, looking at her image on its screen, brushing her hair into new arrangements.

The man paused halfway through a step. He studied Maggie. Her posture and attitude indicated that she was what she appeared to be. He continued toward his car, pulling in a deep drag of smoke. As he approached the vehicle, he used the glass on the driver's side to validate his judgment about the girl.

She continued down the sidewalk, touching her hair.

He scanned his hand on the bio lock, and the door opened. He slid inside the seat, dropping his bag onto the floorboard. When he bent over and stretched his arm to grab it, he caught the girl moving toward him out of the corner of his eye.

He dropped the bag, sat straight, and reached for his firearm. Tucked away in his belt, his gut bulging over the handle, he struggled. Looking down to find it, he took his eyes off the threat. When he looked up, Maggie loomed over him, the pistol pointed at his face.

She pulled the trigger while looking into his eyes. A spider's web emanated from the small hole in the glass. The bullet traveled through the man's neck. A fountain of blood followed the round as it raced deeper into the car.

He raised his pistol as Maggie fired again. The next round found its mark on the temple.

She fired four more times. With each shot,

she moved closer until her barrel was inside the shattered window. The last three shots were unnecessary. His fractured skull was held together by the muscle and skin—dented, distorted. The seat and passenger window were drenched in splattered blood.

She turned, hustled to the corner, and found Rudy waiting in a pickup truck. She resisted the urge to run until she reached the door. She opened it and slid inside, slamming it closed behind her.

Her world grew dimmer by the second. A hazy brown cloud closed in from the corners of her eyes. White, electric stars formed in the midst of the darkness. Something was wrong with her. Had he gotten a shot off, and she didn't feel it?

Then, she remembered to breathe. Her vision cleared, and the pressure in her head slowly subsided.

Rudy pulled out of his spot, slow and cool. He rolled into the intersection, checking his mirrors. He sensed Maggie's adrenaline dump. Her shoulders shuddered. "You did a good job. You did it right."

Maggie trembled. She breathed. Her eyes were locked on the man she had just killed. His head hung sideways, leaned over in his seat. Dark red blood sprayed across the windshield. She couldn't pull her eyes away from it. Silent tears ringed them. She breathed it in and closed it off.

There was no going back. Like Rudy said, the old life was a memory. This new person was going to be a problem. *They* would be taught a lesson.

Not even sure what that lesson would be, she imagined herself a ghost, an apparition of justice—uncontrollable. She imagined their terror as she floated where and when she wanted.

The fat, unremarkable man in the car—his neck creased when he turned to her. She'd seen his eyes dawning the moment he realized that he'd fucked up. The first round was low. She squeezed with too much vigor, and the barrel dipped. Instead of a nice clean shot, he was choking on his blood as she put the finisher in his brain. All that was a thing that happened, a means to an end—a bridge she crossed and was happy to be on the other side.

She leaned forward and vomited on the floorboard. She sat back up, felt her stomach in her neck again, and bent over. This time, nothing came out. She retched, and burning threads of juice clambered off her lips onto her knees.

Rudy said, "It's alright. That's alright."

When she recovered, they were out of the urban area. Trees and a creek lined the road. They had about two hours of driving, with a car change in the middle, before they would get to their safe house.

She looked at Rudy. He gave her a weird, little smile. There wasn't much he could do for her except drive and put up with the smell of her puke.

Maggie smiled back at him. She wasn't ashamed. Rudy made her feel okay about everything. The trees rolled by, and she developed a clear understanding of the situation. She might not become a ghost, and they might not be terrified of her, but they would pay the price they owed her family. And maybe those transactions would be small at first. She would keep chipping away at them—keep chipping until their house fell around them. She was feeling better about it now.

    She would extract from them the life she deserved, the one they had robbed from her.

SIX

*... and some day you will succumb
because the only thing left for you will
be emptiness in the face of it.
Even your families will look to you with disappointed eyes*
—The Humans: Dawn's Perspectives

Daniel slumped in his wheelchair, clean and glass-eyed. The months of resistance had been in vain, as, of course, they would be. The best outcome to hope for was to hold out long enough to make the information he carried obsolete. But information was never the objective. Instead, they sought his capitulation. Whereas this did ignite a surprising level of resistance in him, it was still a simple matter of consistently applying the "attention" necessary to secure the intended outcome. The sun and moon rose with the same level of predictability. The variance was time, and that was based on the man.

Cleary stood behind him, his face sour. The natural lightness, the happy disdain, lost in sullen lines. It had been a slog with the man in the chair, and he looked the worse for the wear.

Daniel's sense of self—his identity—was as near destroyed as possible. When violated at whim, a man could lose himself. He sought shelter in places hidden from even his own mind. He discovered himself *out of body* many times toward the end of the sessions. Confused and dissociated, his cavernous and filthy body thrashed and twisted, covered in feces and sores.

He'd reached the point where he could resist no more and wanted it to stop.

It struck him as strange, the comparison of moments. How could he have simply reached a point with it? The moment before was not right. The moment he decided to give in was no different than the moment before, yet he surrendered anyway.

He begged Cleary to kill him and let him feel some peace. But Cleary could not. So he said the words, and now he sat, scrubbed clean with balms on his open wounds. His bald skull, shaved, ravaged with scabs. He sat crooked in the prison of his body, staring at Brue Carnell across from him.

"Mr. Cleary said you wanted to speak to me. Since he is not a trivial man, I am inclined to believe this is worth my time. Is it, Daniel? Is it worth my time?"

Daniel tried a word but stopped with a cough. He mustered courage, then said, "I want to see her."

Brue said, "You can't. That's not how this works."

"How then?" Daniel was empty of bluster or anger. His voice sat open like a hollowed-out tank and resonated weakness. This was no act, no trick. He wasn't playing any games. That part of him was dead.

Brue narrowed his eyes. "You say what I tell you to say. You say it to whom I tell you. You say it as often as I tell you." He swept his pants free of some imaginary contaminant. "And then, if you've done your job, she will be freed."

Daniel's body was sunken from the unabated torment. Once-bulging chest and arms caved in, he wanted a way out of it. It was that simple. There was no more anger inside. If Cleary wouldn't kill him as he'd begged, then he'd kill himself, the old version of himself, the man reflected in still water and faded mirrors under knife-edged mornings. That was the man who had to die to make it stop because that man would never let him get away with it.

He needed a pretense, a premise under which to commit the murder, and Cleary had offered it to him more times than he could remember. This premise: *the sake of your daughter*. That was his way out.

"Will she be safe?"

Brue reached into his pocket and produced a small picture. He slid it across to Daniel, who picked it up and scanned it with greedy eyes. He wanted a look, to see her again. Instead, it showed a small, one-story stucco beach compound on the edge of a jungle. It faced the ocean, and the hues intimated warmth and comfort. It was a peaceful scene. It played with Daniel, played for him—theme music for his premise. *This is good enough*, he thought to himself. He forgave himself this one small moment of weakness in the face of decades of toil. It didn't need to be real outside of that moment. It simply needed to work.

He pulled the picture close to his face. The tears rolled down his cheeks.

Brue said, "She will have a job. Nothing special. If she keeps her nose clean, she can be happy." He was stating his terms. This was what he would do for Daniel.

"And, you didn't—"

"No, I didn't, Daniel. It's not her fault who you are."

A river flowed from his eyes, and relief gushed from every pore of his body. Haltingly, he said, "I will. I will do what you want."

"And what is that, exactly?" Brue needed the commitment burned in—stained on Daniel's soul.

Cleary looked away as Daniel relinquished the last of his dignity, an animal, beaten into submission, and it was by Cleary's hands. He didn't seem to want to watch it.

"I will tell them all. I will tell them to stop. Tell them the future should not be harmed. Whatever you want."

He pled for his daughter's life, confused and passionate, as if auditioning for a part. He stomached the words, forgot everything his old self would have said, how he would have regarded himself in this moment. It would save Maggie. He would redeem himself in her eyes, even if she'd never know. It was all he needed at that moment. His old face, the old, narrow eyes, slid into the black soiled earth. Gone.

Brue smiled at the performance. He glanced up at Cleary with a nod.

Cleary reached down for the picture, but Daniel rolled his shoulders and created a cocoon around it. "No, Cleary. Please." He needed to hold it in his hands.

Cleary shook his head at Brue. He didn't want to take the picture. He shrugged a shoulder, and Brue agreed.

The wreckage of Daniel's face sheltered the slightest of smiles as he stared at the photograph. His soul sat down to rest. It ended the longest, most brutal patrol he had ever walked. An airy whiteness, fuzzy like a haze, formed around the image. He checked over his shoulder at Cleary to ensure he was still there. He wanted to believe he was in his wheelchair and not on the cold floor, covered in shit.

And he was in his wheelchair. He was clean.

He was still alive.

◄─────••─────►

The compound sat on the peak of the peninsula. The foundation was formed by magenta cinder blocks, and the walls were bright red-orange stucco. Robust Talavera tile lined the arched entrance to the courtyard. Sharp, thick blades of grass shot up through the sandy ground in clumps. The wind pulled sand from the beach into the arched opening.

From the courtyard, there was the white beach,

with a stretch of emerald water on its way to the sand bar and then the deep, blue Gulf.

A breeze rolled, teasing a clothesline. Baskets of flowers lined the courtyard and whipped in the wind. Daniel walked out of the house. He moved to the plants and tipped a water can. He cupped a small, white flower and brought it to his face. The thing smelled sharp, and he smiled at it.

The wind picked up. Grains of sand dissimilated and then transformed into howling towers all around him. He squinted, shielded his eyes, and turned to the opening.

Maggie stood there beneath the colorful arch. Her sundress waved in the breeze. *She's older, maybe twenty*, he thought. Her shoulders were bronzed from a life on the ocean. He saw her eyes for the first time it seemed. They were green.

The wind played across her shoulders in her hair. She had been there, waiting for him. Deep inside, he believed she had been there forever. How could she forgive him for what he had done?

Her eyes told him she already had.

Behind her, the wind, the sand, and the azure sky sat against the distant Gulf.

"You doin' alright in there, mate?"

Cleary's voice shattered him. He folded over at the sound of it. He sat on the sand, his hand in a clump of rough grass. He fought it. The blades scraped his hand, and the sand ground into his palm. "This is real." He fought it.

"You doin' alright?"

Daniel opened his eyes, and the harsh white light of the cell bore into him. His breathing was elevated, and his eyes were ringed with moisture. He lay in bed with the picture resting on his chest. *What the hell have I turned into?*

"Yes, Cleary. I'm good."

Over the intercom, "Get some rest, bud. We have a few busy days ahead of us."

"Will do."

Daniel held the picture in front of his eyes. He had come to rely on the comfort it brought him. In the clearest moments, it was an obvious fraud. Still, he held it tight, and whenever his eyes were closed, he went to the place on the beach to visit with her.

From the day he pried her hands loose and sent her away, he'd failed her. That failure loomed before him. It filled his vision; no matter how many horizons he imagined, it was the color of the sky inside his dreams.

He would make it right someday, but until then, he would comply. He had no idea how long he would be allowed to live, so he would keep his eyes open.

◄———••———►

Days in the white room came and went like vapor slipping through cracks. At first, Daniel didn't notice them come and go, only caught a sense that they'd happened. Those days never truly started because they never truly ended under the blinding white mask of the room. But Daniel managed himself, his broken soul, by sleeping and healing. For an undetermined time, he was visited by medical staff and assessed, given pills, and rubbed with ointments.

Promises were made. *Keep your nose clean, and we'll give you your legs again. Follow directions, and you'll be leaving the white room soon.*

So, he kept his nose clean and followed directions. Once the line was crossed, these little things—humiliations in his old life—became nothing. He spent most of his days sitting or lying on his bed. He'd wheel himself around a bit, read the approved books, and stare at the picture of Maggie's home on the beach.

The black rectangle formed on the wall. Cleary walked in, his bulk filling the opening. He waved at Daniel—a short wave from his wrist. "No need to sit up."

Daniel sat up anyway, with effort. He pulled his useless legs over the edge of the bed. They swung loose like butcher shop sausages. He propped himself on his hands and greeted his visitor.

Cleary smiled. It was odd. He felt self-conscious standing above Daniel. He'd done enough of that already. The man was hollowed out, his shoulders knobby. He was all points and angles, like a skinny child. He grabbed Daniel's wheelchair, turned it toward the bed, and sat in it.

"You're done here, I s'pose." Daniel was pleasant. He claimed himself with ease—the broken body, the dimmed eyes.

This added to Cleary's discomfort. He'd been tormented by a vague notion of having done the wrong thing, having made a cascade of poor choices starting way back in the days of his childhood. Nothing had sat right inside him for days.

"I suppose I am. This next part is not my area of expertise. Plus, this little shindig didn't end the way I thought it would." He tweaked his mustache, which he did without noticing when under stress. He thought about it. "Sure as hell. I didn't think it would last this long."

Daniel shucked. "Well. Couldn't make it too easy on ya, could I?"

Cleary forced himself to look at his work, to evaluate it on a wordless level. The question that had popped into his mind during the months of torture popped up again. *We are the same—what am I doing?* He took a breath and smiled back at Daniel. "Why?" He asked the simple and all-encompassing question.

Daniel understood and answered without pause. "Because I don't know any other way."

"But you gave in. Why? After all that." Cleary couldn't stand to look at him. Daniel's desolation was shrouded with a lightness of expression that he couldn't begin to explain. It upset his balance. This man, only days ago, was an animal writhing in its own filth, humiliated, degraded. Now, he sits, pleasantly speaking to his tormentor. Cleary didn't want to claim it.

Daniel said, "There was the little matter of not being able to die. Had to consider that. You weren't gonna let me. You didn't seem to be gettin' tired, either." He laughed.

"I was long past tired." Cleary tweaked his mustache again.

A silence fell between them.

What's the point of any a' this?

"You're a good man, Cleary." Daniel's voice was warm, like a blanket you'd throw over your friend's shoulders coming in from a storm.

Cleary shook his head. He wasn't entirely surprised. It matched the air of the moment in the small, white cell. He screwed up his face, trying to find a place to put such a comment.

Daniel said, "You answered for your brother."

"What the hell else is a man supposed to do?"

Daniel shrugged. "Men these days do all kinds a' shit, right? Mostly take care of themselves—think about themselves."

Cleary's brow pinched. "You some kinda zealot, or what?" He asked, even though the answer was obvious.

Daniel ignored the question. He took his time stitching together the words, then said, "It's gonna end someday. And I'm not talkin' about your life or my life. I'm talkin' about all of it. It's easy to forget about that. Most people walk around—don't think about it at all."

Daniel shifted his weight. His legs swung from his knees down, side to side.

"Some big ass rock's gonna fall outta the sky. Some little virus is gonna run through us. Maybe the Earth'll split itself in two, and we all get turned to ash."

His eyes grabbed Cleary's and didn't let go. "However it goes down, you know as good as me, this shindig ain't gonna end like your boss expects."

Cleary took it all in, nodding his head. He agreed with more of it than he was comfortable admitting. Yes, there was that. Technology had evolved as if strapped to rockets since he was a lad. Nothing remained the same in the face of change so exponential as to toss aside any covenant with philosophy or spirituality. There was no poetry anymore, no poets. There was the mean game of conformity and the job of its enforcement. A clever man could use his skills and manipulate a place within the machine to lay his head.

Power was measured in clinical, graph-like terms. The leaf eaters had inherited the Earth. That was a settled matter. Cleary's sagacity had elevated his station, yet he understood himself to be meant for one thing, to enforce the new will.

He believed in his guts he would become obsolete. There was no loyalty among these new types, no reverence for the men who'd fallen in pursuit of the fearless human future. He would most likely need to be dealt with the very way he dealt with the likes of Daniel.

In his mind, the dubious lines that bound this murderer's fate to his own hardened. He thought he could see his ending as if authored in some ancient text, a language known only to him.

Whose hands would push the button against him? That person or thing may not have yet been born. But, if it expected easy success, that person or thing had better study hard, the minds of men like Cleary and Daniel. Because when his time came, he'd not go that way. He'd not go easy.

Cleary said, "This next part is the easy part. Just do what they say, mate. You'll do far better for yourself."

"And for Maggie?" Daniel's doubt was written on his face. He needed Cleary to play his part.

Cleary nodded. "And for Maggie."

The lie sat between them, an interloper. Cleary shuffled his feet. "I'll see you again someday."

Daniel smiled. "I know you will."

Cleary stood and walked into the blackness of the rectangle.

◄—————•••—————►

The days passed. They moved Daniel to an apartment. Not fancy, but well fitted for someone who'd been put through the wringer, and more so for a guy who'd spent the last decade shitting in the woods.

They'd given him his legs back, as promised. He often walked without shoes, marveling at the muscles in his legs and at the granular exchange on the surfaces of his knees. It took some time to reignite the fibers of them, to wake them from their months-long sleep. Their aching pain was a long-lost friend.

He didn't seem to bother about his failure. And when he was alone, didn't dwell on it. He thought of Maggie. Her story became the foundation of his life. His actions, every one of them, became necessary—to do as he was told, to follow instructions.

A Newborn teacher visited him every day. An odd sort, unlike any other Daniel recalled seeing. Smallish with a wobbly head, Daniel called it "Frog." It introduced a curriculum and books for him to read, which he did avidly. Their conversations were wide-ranging.

These discussions on the nature of the new world and the bright future of mankind were beautiful lies—easy to believe because doubting brought unnecessary pain.

Daniel figured they were assessing him. He believed their acceptance of his surrender rested on whether or not he believed what he said.

Understanding this, Daniel applied himself to his studies, immersed himself in the various fictions, and treated them as real. He refused to critically analyze one single thing—rote memorization.

In what he called his "big brain," he believed. Otherwise, he risked the whole enterprise. The tiniest sign could spoil his work: a narrowing of his eyelids, a tightness crawling across his lips, a sudden gush of light from his pupils opening in deceit.

However, there resided within him, built in the fires of torture, the small places. From there, he monitored his actions like a third party, disassociated yet obliquely controlling. He knew the truth and viewed his body's actions as the necessities of survival.

Daniel had been walking in a courtyard on a beautiful fall afternoon. The glass walls of Manhattan shot skyward on all sides. It was a freedom he'd recently earned, so devoted had become his voice to the cause.

The man came at him from within a crowd of passersby. He shot from their midst, an angry object slung from its orbit, colliding into Daniel's peace. He was a small man, bald, with an insignificant face. A nose too big and a pitiful mustache marked the prominence of his features.

He knocked Daniel from his equilibrium. The man was all spit and teeth, his words fueled by hatred. He called Daniel's commitment into question and called him a liar in every conceivable way.

Daniel started reeling but got ahold of himself and assumed the appropriate posture—demeaned and ashamed. He absorbed the rancor like he'd been trained to do. He begged forgiveness, kept his head down, and said the right things, knowledge gained through trial and error and endless hours with the algorithm.

Eventually, the onslaught settled, the volume lowered, and that small place inside him detected the end approaching.

The man ran out of steam. He suddenly grabbed Daniel by the collar and under the arm. With his hips, he torqued him over his shoulder. He landed hard on the pavement, scuffing his face.

Stunned, daylight filling his blurred vision, Daniel felt him on top, hammering down like a madman. It was only a moment before the man was tackled and pulled away.

The meeting of the concrete and his shoulder had knocked some wind out of him. As they dragged the man away, he caught Daniel's eye. Saying nothing, he smiled. Struggling against the guards, he reached up, opened his shirt pocket, and looked inside. He caught Daniel's eye and all but winked. Then he was gone, around the corner.

What the fuck was that? How much of that was supposed to happen?

Medics arrived and attended him. The air around them buzzed with confusion, and none of them looked into his eyes.

When he thought no one was watching, he reached up to his shirt pocket. It was unbuttoned, so he buttoned it.

◄―――●●―――►

Hours passed before he reached into the pocket.

Waiting until he peeled the shirt off to slip his hand in, he felt a small slip of paper, palmed it, and sent the shirt into the laundry bin.

He filled a glass with water and smashed the note against it as he took a drink. The words written on it: *You are not alone.*

He took a deep gulp and set the glass down, keeping the paper in his palm until he visited the toilet, where he flushed it with his waste.

The usual team of medics showed up toward the end of the evening, interested in his bruises and scrapes. They left as they always had.

He sat on his couch and stared out the window, processing the event. He suspected it was a genuine attempt from the outside to contact him.

Maybe it was a trap.

He would wait it out, believing it was a genuine attempt to reach him from the outside.

If he were wrong, they'd work him over again, maybe even worse this next time. He'd wait. He'd practice his lines and believe everything they told him to believe. He was good at that, now, being two people at once. Cleary had taught him how without realizing it.

He'd let this thing develop. See what came of it. Whatever their big plans were for him, he'd play along.

Once the decision was made, he had no choice but to let it develop. Right or wrong, he'd made his choice.

He would let it ride.

2042

The alley was clean—no bums or trash. It connected Wilcox Street to Seventeenth Avenue, a clear and unobstructed path to and from the objective. A utility van idled on the edge of Seventeenth, tucked against the side of an office building, and avoiding the street cameras. A woman sat driver. Middle-aged and fit, she was dressed for cold weather with a thick coat and gloves. A fleece skull cap hugged her head with a tangled jumble of thick curls sprouting over her shoulders.

She stared across the street at the Municipal Enforcement Station in a Newborn legal district manned by Gen Ones and Twos. They served as police and administrative functionaries.

These replacement programs were then disguised as a civics venture, and a fair amount of social capital was expended to attach a virtuous air to the whole endeavor.

The pilot program called for the gradual establishment of these stations. A few were planted in metropolitan areas, but as the production programs accelerated, the old-fashioned policing precincts were replaced in greater numbers. The general public was accepting, but if events had taught anything, it was that, in general, the public would accept whatever they were told to accept.

The front door to the station opened, and a young, red-haired man slipped out onto the street. He wore a mechanic's smock and ball cap, and carried a toolbox and belt. He was nonchalant, checking over his shoulder as he crossed the street. He slid into the passenger seat with no apparent reason to hurry.

She asked, "How'd that go?"

"It's fixed. Should be good to go." He pulled a small switch from his pocket and dialed it on. A light blinked red.

"Did anybody suspect anything?"

"No. The fuckin' Skins ain't got no sense. Even the Gen Twos. Too busy makin' sure the paperwork's right." He leaned forward and looked up. "Seventh floor."

She craned her neck in time to see the explosion. It rocked along the course of several windows, sending showers of glass and debris to the street below. Its concussive force punched its way through the corridor of buildings, shattering glass and initializing car alarms. At the late hour, there weren't many pedestrians on the street, and that was by design.

The woman smiled at him. "Nice to see you're still useful."

"I'll show you more later on." He winked at her.

She thought it was a gross gesture. "Cool down."

She threw the van in reverse and backed away from the scene. The route was preplanned. She backed across Wilcox and turned around in the pay lot. She exited and, two turns later, entered the viaduct, a deep tunnel running at the city's eastern end.

They wouldn't hit a camera for the next five minutes. By then, they would be far enough from the bombing site that the algorithmic search vectors would leave them alone.

<hr />

The large, sliding garage door ground its way up, screeching in spots as the pulley fought against gravity. The utility van pulled into a waiting spot, and the automatic door closed afterward.

The man and woman emerged and performed a series of actions seamless enough to appear practiced. They pulled open the van doors and removed a large duffel bag, peeled their smocks, and stuffed them inside. The woman grabbed a lock box from a table and placed her identification cards and light board inside it while the man stowed his work belt and explosives-laden box inside the duffel. She handed him the lock box, and he, too, placed his identifiers inside.

The woman moved to a shelf covered in wheel parts. She slid her hand through the components and pushed a button, which activated a hydraulic motivator. The shelf slid to the side, exposing the brick wall. She twisted the face of a false brick and uncovered a bio lock. She smashed her knuckles into the receptacle, and a section of the adjacent wall slid open.

The man arrived with the bulging duffel bag, and she helped him slide it into the tight spot. The section was replaced, and the shelf was slid back into alignment.

The woman moved to an open sink and mirror. She flipped on the hanging light above, breathed, and looked at herself.

The man peered out of the windows at the street before checking four monitors on the desk. Each screen displayed a view of the approaching streets. The action, the vehicles, and the pedestrians all seemed appropriate for the time and location. He consulted his watch. "You about ready?"

The woman had tilted her head, considering her face in the mirror. She sighed again, then peeled her knit cap loose, exposing a tightly laced mesh of wires. It matted her hair down, resembling a spider web. Hundreds of needle-sized lights pointed down from the flat, intricate crown. She raised her hand to the apex and pushed a button.

Her face blurred and twitched, then reset itself. The façade blinked again and was gone. Maggie caught her reflection in the mirror. She was seventeen years old now; older in the eyes. She poked her skin. The elasticity had not disappeared, as it had seemed under the holo mask. "I don't think I'll ever get used to that."

The man walked behind her, a wicked grin covering his face. "Yeah, I know. She's pretty hot. I miss her when she's gone."

Maggie's jaw dropped open. She glared at him in the mirror, letting him feel some heat. "Is that so?"

He understood the look—he was in trouble, so he leaned into it. "She reminds me of my first girlfriend."

"Your first girlfriend was forty?"

"I was very advanced for my age. Had a thing for "

She turned on him and grabbed his shoulders, pulling him toward her. She pulled his face to hers. His holo mask distorted, disrupted by her mouth as it closed on his lips. She bit him.

"Ow, damn, girl!"

"Turn around, jackass." She pushed him toward the sink, lifted his ball cap, and manipulated his mask. Rudy's face broke through the digital shreds for an instant, and then another man, who was also older. "There, I like him. He has kind eyes."

Rudy caught his reflection. "Aww. He's a sweetheart."

He turned to her and changed her face. He set her up with a brunette in her early thirties.

"Better not be another girlfriend," Maggie said as she slipped her knit cap back on.

Rudy laughed. "Are we good here?"

Maggie walked through the room, checking her mental list. She turned to Rudy. "We're good."

The pair moved from the front of the establishment through a doorway, down a small flight of stairs, and into a supply room. It was dank and wet. Shelves of fittings lined the walls.

Rudy jogged to the other side of the room and activated another hidden bio lock. A pocket door slid to the right, revealing a dim, orange glow. He checked his watch. "Gotta wait. Should be any time now."

The air in the storage basement was disrupted. Rudy's pant legs were pulled toward the opening, flapping in the sudden negative pressure, rippling toward the pocket door. Maggie reached for him and held his waist.

A rollicking sound approached on the other side. It rumbled in the orange darkness. Then, the unmistakable chaos of a subway car rocketed past at ear-shattering speed and violence. Within moments, the train had passed, and the air in the room recalibrated—ozone and hot metal.

Rudy wedged himself through into the darkness. He reached back for her, but Maggie waved his hand away and bounded out the door. She hopped down the slight dip into the subway canal system. Rudy tripped the hidden switch and closed the pocket door. They moved off at a trot, headed toward the distant lights of a commuter station.

They looked like new people and would look new again several times before the night ended.

◄──────•●•──────►

Rudy opened the door and stepped through. Maggie followed him, her head hanging. Shoes were slid off and straightened on the mat. Keys found their way into a small ceramic bowl holding spare change and hard candy. The jackets and hats all found their homes. The two of them, slumped in fatigue, moved like zombies into the living room.

Exfiltration from a job was equal parts exhilaration, nerves, and exhaustion. The routes to and from the mission varied to account for static and moving surveillance.

The jobs required high levels of attention for long periods. After a hit, they executed a careful, orchestrated movement. They switched modes of transit and switched holo masks. They utilized multiple physical and digital identities, raveling a trail of crumbs that would, at many points along the way, terminate in frustration for a tailing security apparatus.

Rudy kissed Maggie's forehead and held her for a moment, distracted by his appetite. Maggie understood. Throughout exfil, all of Rudy's conversations revolved around chili, his desire to eat a gigantic bowl of it, the crunchiness of the onion, and an appropriate level of spices. "*A quarter teaspoon of cinnamon. That's the secret.*" When he released her and headed to the kitchen, it was a done deal. Chili was in her future.

She stood with sagged shoulders and looked over her apartment. She had made most of the decor decisions. Rudy's input was the massive monitor encompassing the wall adjoining the kitchen and living area. The apartment was domestic by design —not a trace of insurgency.

She trudged to the couch, fired up the monitor, and switched the inputs to a news and events channel. The noise of the broadcast hummed in the background as she made her way to a small end table. She felt under the lip and pressed a button. An array of monitors slid through the surface. Each glass displayed a view of the various approaches to their building. From this spot, she could monitor activity in the hallway, back alley, front entrance, and the street. On the feeds, digital boxes and triangles floated over the faces and hands of the people. An algorithm ran facial analysis and activity determination protocols against the inputs. The thing was trained to spot, highlight, and alert at the presence of suspicious activities.

She studied it a moment, yawned, and moved to the couch. If anything of note were to occur, a warning would sound.

Rudy banged around in the kitchen, pulling pots and pans, prepping his chili. She collapsed on the couch, waiting for coverage of the bombing in the city events report.

"Do you think it'll be on tonight?" She raised her voice so the chef could hear.

"I don't know. I think they're suppressing it now. You know, it happens so often."

Maggie was deflated. "Maybe nobody cares anymore."

Rudy poked his head through the entryway. "They'll start to care real soon, I'm tellin' ya. As soon as they make the sterilizations mandatory."

Maggie swatted the idea away. "You don't know that. They wouldn't even be able to. Wouldn't people lose their shit?"

"How do you boil a frog, baby?"

She rolled her eyes. "Start them off in cold water, then turn up the heat slowly."

"Actually, you start 'em off in the water from the pond where you caught 'em. Make 'em feel real comfortable. Make 'em believe everything is just right." The knife smacked the chopping board as Rudy worked over some onions. "They never even feel it."

She'd heard his theories over and again. Exhausted from the last sixty hours, she had no energy to entertain or argue with him. Melting into the couch, she wanted to watch as the fruits of her labor were messaged to the city.

In this drowsy, half-attentive state, she saw him on screen. She didn't understand it for a moment, then the realization descended on her. Her exhaustion evaporated as a shot of adrenaline rushed into her blood. She leaped to her feet and screamed, "Rudy!"

He ran into the room, peeling the pistol from his waistband, and found her standing, pointing at the screen. He scanned the room. Sensing no immediate threat, he turned to the monitor.

Daniel stood behind a podium alongside Brue Carnell and several members of the global government.

He turned to her, sharing her surprise. "What the

hell?"

The scene was staged by professionals. The men flanked Daniel—happy to be there—leaders of the bright tomorrow. Daniel played the part of the prized pig, and all the players wanted their money shot. A wall of politicians in bland uniforms smirked over his shoulder, trying to bring the illusion of stability to a populace weary of an insurgency that wouldn't seem to go away.

Rudy turned to Maggie, who was near tears. "I—I thought he was..."

She shook her head, unsettled. "He's dead." She had known this in her soul since leaving him in the safe house. She believed that had been her last chance with him.

Rudy leaned in close to the screen. "It doesn't look like a mask."

Daniel spoke. "I come before you today to acknowledge the wrongs I have committed against you." He read from a prompter. His eyes were recessed, as if a sickness of the soul had taken him. "I have lived an evil life. I have taken from you. I have taken so many bright minds from your future. I can never repay you the pain I've caused." Daniel swallowed hard. "Whether Newborn or Oldborn."

Maggie approached the screen and turned to Rudy. "How?"

Rudy said, "Tortured. All this time, I guess. I thought he'd have died before this."

Daniel choked on his words. His cadence stumbled. "The way forward—the way forward is righteous. All the pain and death I caused could never—never slow the wheels of progress. You will all go into that bright new light together."

Maggie hardened her face into a mask of resolute anger. She turned to Rudy. "It's time to wake up the frogs."

Rudy agreed with short, sharp nods. "What are you thinkin'?"

Maggie poked the screen where Carnell stood. The pixels blatted where the surface dented, and Brue's face disappeared into a cloudy smudge. "We start with him."

Rudy took a deep breath and pulled her close. "He's not gonna be so easy to get at this time."

"It doesn't matter how long it takes." She pulled Rudy tight and tried to envelop herself in his warmth. She had one more chance with Daniel. She would save him from this in whatever way she could. She would save him even if it meant ending him.

SEVEN

2045

They have told you to be afraid of death
Although you will never sit aside it
You should fear legacy, for it is here with you now
And lives inside your lungs
And takes as much as you have taken.
—The Humans: Dawn's Perspectives

The train floated above the rails, swaying so slightly as to seem immobile. Repulsion technology kept the massive thing in place, locked to the rails yet never touching steel to steel. The train stood twenty feet in height, a mammoth, one-of-a-kind method of transport built with the global elite in mind.

It occupied the house track near the singular, broad platform, fitting into the Budapest-Keleti station. Its modernity starkly contrasted against the ancient walls that housed the main line and a series of complex switches.

Skins in uniform milled about the vehicle, ogling

its intricate mass and staring at the repulsed footings. Gen Ones covered every entrance to the platform. Civilian foot traffic was non-existent. The platform and entire facility were closed to non-official personnel; even then, a source of essentiality was required to approach the vessel.

The glass doors opened from the adjoined great hall, echoing with vacancy, and a small clutch of men moved across the platform to a checkpoint. They wore light blue coveralls patched with the name of their Hungarian maintenance company.

The gaggle approached an inspection point. The soldiers set them straight, aligned them into single file, and prepared them to walk through an imaging device.

Midway in that line, a young man of slight build was clutched by a tightness in his hands and shoulders—wasn't even aware of it, so occupied was his face with generating a deep, believable smile. Despite the calm exterior, his heart raced.

He studied the guards—sized them up. They were good, dependable Gen Ones, never looking where they should have been, never seeing the world around them.

He moved closer to the imaging machine. The techs passed through and were then released to a second station.

The guard waved him forward. He swallowed a capsule that he'd been holding under his tongue. The instant it hit his system, his body relaxed, his heart rate slowed, and his vital signs matched his facial features' relaxed, smiling attitude.

The guard waved him forward a step, and the machine whirred for a moment. The Gen One studied the readout of vitals. He waved the man forward.

He stepped toward the iris scan station. His pupils were blown wide open from the drug. He slipped the nail of his index finger into the meat of his palm. A microneedle, attached, slid into his dermis, and the capillaries took up the second drug. The light dimmed within a few steps, and his eyes returned to normal.

The guard slipped the scanner over his forehead. The guard removed the visor and reached out for his documentation, which he provided with a smile.

The scan and the documents lined up.

He passed beyond the checkpoint and moved toward the train. His smile tightened on the corners. He could feel his nerves again, and he was bothered by the thoughts of everything that could go wrong in the next few hours.

◄————••————►

Working the wrench with gloved hands, he removed the panel and slid it down the wall. He retrieved a small coupler from his toolkit, designed to sit at the bottom of an oxygen generation cell.

He slid the part in place and worked at it with a wrench. Feeling the side of his bag, he peeled at the glued strip, dragging a small leather section apart, revealing a recessed compartment lined with nano-fiber. He pulled a sleek, polished device out and slipped it into the compartment. It clung to the oxygen cell with a magnetized bottom.

He breathed again, reset his tools. He reached to the bottom of the compartment, and grabbed a folded paper with his fingers. He slid it into the lead-lined compartment of his bag and resealed the small cache.

The panel was replaced, and he picked up his bag and walked away.

◆———•• •———▶

The slightly built mechanic was still hunched as he moved across the street to the north of the horse track. He entered a nondescript bar. Finding a booth in a dark corner, he sat, worried he should have ordered a beer first. His hands slid across the top of the table. Nearby, a woman studied him. She looked impatient, disappointed.

He lost his nerve with the whole thing, pulled the paper out of his pocket, and taped it to the bottom of the table. Standing with some urgency, he shuffled toward the door.

The place was empty, so her voice filled the room when she spoke. She was loud and distinct. "Sit down. Have two beers."

He stopped in his tracks and looked over his shoulder at her. His resolve crumbled when he locked eyes, nodding slowly at first and then with passion. He moved to the bar and sat. The beer waited for him. The bartender, a ghost recessed in the darkness, worked a mug clean with a cloth.

The woman moved to the table, peeled the paper loose, and walked past the man toward the rear exit of the building. She slowed down as she passed him. "You did good. Don't fuck it up now."

He sat his near-empty glass on the bar and stared straight ahead as if she didn't exist—or as if he wished she never did.

She opened the door, and the room filled with light and went dim again, and she was gone.

◂────••────▸

Maggie sat, the paper laid out before her on the small kitchen table. The window was open. The light and sounds from the Jewish Quarter spilled into the modest rental. The words on the paper sat blue in the afternoon. Blue.

Her hand lay flat against the tabletop. The other stroked her bottom lip with distracted fingers. She looked at the paper with a distant gaze.

The door opened behind her. Rudy walked in and stood next to her chair. "The route's clear. Nobody tailed you." He scrunched his brow, eyes trained on the paper. "You read it?"

Maggie nodded. She stopped playing with her lip and became conscious of the room, the light, and Rudy. She picked up the paper. "I read it."

"Well?" Rudy walked to the sink, turned on the

faucet, and filled a glass. He had time to drink the whole thing before she spoke. He stared at the tiled backsplash and let her get her words together.

"It's a go." Her eyes moved to the window and glanced down at the street.

He sat next to her and didn't look at the paper. It was her paper. If she wanted him to know... He said, "You okay with this?"

She stared at the street, the cobbled walkway, the lined concrete building across, housing a massive club that thumped their rental into oblivion at night.

"Hey." He touched her shoulder.

She roused herself back from her thoughts. "Yes. It's what he wants." Her eyes filled up. She clenched her teeth.

Rudy studied her. "Maggie, we know exactly where he is—right now. We can maybe—"

She relaxed her jaw and emptied her eyes of anything. "No. Carnell isn't with him." She studied the building again, the lined concrete, the strategic graffiti. "He was supposed to be, but he isn't, and there's no point if he's not."

"No point? We can get your father. We can get Daniel." Rudy spun the empty glass on the tabletop. "Fuck Carnell, you know? We'll get his ass some other time."

"You good at disabling neuro-net tech? You good at spinal surgery?" She gave him a stern look and quickly regretted it. She reached for his hand, and he accepted her. "Where's he gonna go that they can't touch him?"

Rudy read a few of the blue words.

… I could never make it up to you…

He looked away, none of his business. She believed herself to have evolved beyond the need to hurt inside, but Rudy knew differently. There were moments, and he counted himself lucky to be there when she ran into those walls.

"We've been ordered off the op." Her words were flat as a plane.

He was a little surprised, but it made sense the more he thought about it. "They think you're—we're too close to it?"

The next step in this operation was going to happen, and it would involve Daniel's death. Rudy was glad to get pulled from it.

"They want fresh eyes. Clear heads." She wasn't fighting it. It was a logical decision.

Rudy nodded. He thought it would be better if they didn't pull the trigger on it anyway. "Who's—"

"It's a local crew. East European syndicate."

Rudy shook his head. "That's their idea of clear heads? Those guys leak more than an old faucet."

"Doesn't matter." Her face was blank. "We leave tonight. Let's clean up the place."

She turned to him then. Her eyes and her lips opened up. She was vulnerable to him sometimes. When she remembered, she loved him.

They wiped the surfaces and packed their meager belongings into packs. Rudy thumbed through their identity papers. He fiddled with his holo mask as she did the same.

The paper with blue ink sat on the table while the rest of the room was sterilized.

Rudy tilted his head toward it and raised his eyebrows at her. She walked to the table, took the paper to the sink, and lit it afire without another look. She dropped it into the sink as it was consumed into black ash. She turned on the faucet and swept the remnants down the drain.

Then she turned to Rudy and lifted her cap, exposing her holo mask crown.

"Who are we today?"

◆─────•●•─────▶

In the dining car, Daniel reclined. The plate before him was crumbed with the remnants of a fine meal. His hair had grown in, graying on the edges but full and brown. His hands rested on his belly, and he looked out the long, bulletproof window.

The green land flowed past, and he could see they were moving fast. The car swayed. There was no rocking or clicking, no sudden metallic resettling to remind him that he was in a machine.

He scanned the room—filled with a party apparatchiks milling about, talking about the cashew-crusted codfish, remarking on the smoked brandy aperitif.

He spotted a dark, rocky outcropping ahead that ran up the tracks, approaching with lightning speed. He imagined the view it offered of the line, the train, the engine. On which of those humps would he have placed his gun? Would the rails be vulnerable to Semtex? Would he need to undermine the track and let the weight of the cars do the work for him?

More importantly, would this be the place and time of the event?

The thought of it made him smile. He looked around the car again and considered the situation in a happier light, imagining the thing coming apart in a million fiery shards and the smiles on their faces blinking out in an instant. He would sit in the middle of it, joyous in death's squeezing hand—one victorious moment in a life clouded by defeat.

The outcropping came and passed by in a blur. Not yet.

"You having another daydream?"

The voice spoke over his shoulder. It was warm and familiar. Daniel turned and was greeted by Pierre's smiling face.

"Where'd you come from?" Daniel was uneasy with the notion a man could sidle up to him without his knowing. He tried to hide it in a tight smile.

Pierre laughed. "You are always on guard, Daniel." He grabbed Daniel's shoulder in his large black hand. He pointed toward the table. "May I?"

"Sure."

Pierre wore a brown, striped flat cap, an open jacket, and a silk shirt designed with more colors than Daniel imagined should be on a shirt. He sat, removed his cap, and turned to look at the others. He winked at Daniel. "*These* people."

Daniel smiled. "These people."

"Have you seen him? He boarded in Slovenia." Pierre spoke elegant English with a touch of his native Congolese.

"He hasn't visited with me yet."

"Yes." Pierre placed his hands on the table. "He sent for me last night. Wanted to review the agenda."

"The agenda."

"Yes." Pierre flagged down a server. "May I have a glass of Chablis?"

The server nodded and moved away.

"The hell's a Chablis?" Daniel worked the word out with clumsy suspicion.

"It's usually a very dry and crisp wine from the Chablis region, Northern France. You should try it." He raised his hand to snap at the server.

Daniel interceded, pulling his hand down. "I'm good."

Pierre chuckled. "Why are you always so serious, my friend?"

"These are serious times."

"Look around." Pierre passed his gaze across the confines of the well-fitted dining car. He pointed out the windows at the rolling green countryside. "Does this seem very dangerous to you?"

Daniel grinned at Pierre. "When you were runnin' ops down there, in the jungles and such, how many Skins you see?"

"None."

"None?"

"Of course, none. They would have stuck out like the sore thumbs, you know." He raised his thumbs in front of Daniel, smiling. "They were not made of the correct tone back then."

Daniel nodded. "I s'pose it woulda made for some difficult covert operations, yeah?"

"Indeed."

The Chablis arrived, and Pierre thanked the server. He cupped the glass with practiced fingers and swirled the wine in circles. He sniffed the glass, placing his entire nose into the rim of it. Then he turned it up and swallowed the stuff. His eyes rolled in delight.

"Good stuff?"

Pierre nodded. "Very good." He held the glass in both hands against his colorful shirt. "You know we didn't have Skins, but we had plenty of men who came to us and tried to tie us down. We killed them and piled their bodies, and they killed us and piled our bodies higher. There was no stopping the killing. It bled over into the villages and towns, and then it was our families, and then it was their families." Pierre paused and sniffed his wine. "And then it was over." He stared past Daniel, looking at nothing.

"You reckon they got you on this slick here 'cause you're black?" Daniel raised his chin and smiled.

"I believe they do indeed have me on this *'slick'* because I can talk to the other problem children in Africa. I can convince them of our foolishness."

"And what's the Swahili word for foolishness?"

"I speak Congo Swahili, Daniel. And besides, it is

the French tongue that speaks to the most Africans."

"Yeah, those guys worked y'all over pretty good." Daniel shared the look of a confederate. "Is foolishness the word you use to describe it, though? All those things you did?"

Pierre inspected his glass, raised it, but stopped as if he didn't want his words to color the taste of the wine. "I remember it with terrible regret. There was so much suffering."

"There's no shortage of that. Everywhere you look—world's full of it." Daniel eased into his seatback.

"Have you ever wondered, if you had not been caught, would you still be wicked? Still blindly killing?"

Daniel said, "I don't wonder about it."

"Hmm. I wonder about a lot of things. I wonder if the things I did were right or wrong." His eyes narrowed, trying to juice the truth from Daniel. "I also wonder if I ever did anything that would have made a difference in the end."

Daniel broke his gaze and observed the cashew crumbs on his plate. "You been on this rig for what, five, six months now, right?"

Pierre dipped his head in the affirmative.

Daniel chuckled. "You know how long he's been trottin' me out on these dog and pony shows?"

Pierre said, "Three years or so, I believe."

"And you know what I learned in that time?"

Pierre opened his hands as if he were inviting a ball toss.

"Never trust anyone with your business." A deep

scowl creased Daniel's forehead. As soon as it showed, it disappeared into a curious smile. "They hooked you up with the goose egg, right?"

Pierre was perplexed. "Goose egg?"

"That little ball a' fun in the base of your spine."

Pierre swallowed, nodded, and looked down.

"You know they control those from the sky now, right? They have an effective range of the globe's surface and can hit you anywhere, anytime. They put the prototype in me. You heard that, right?"

"Yes." Pierre met his friend's eyes.

Every man breaks. The measure is how long he holds out.

Daniel smudged the cashew crumbs against his finger and put them in his mouth. The functionaries droned in the background. "How'd they get you?"

"On a trip to visit my mother. She was sick and did not have long to live."

Daniel turned up his water glass. "You fucked up."

Pierre agreed with a distinct resolution as if the thought had crossed his mind. "I did."

Daniel, as if seeking to mollify Pierre, said, "I fucked up too."

Pierre finally drank his wine. "I suppose. The way I hear it, you were only seconds away from putting a hole in our benefactor's head."

Daniel toyed at the word with a touch of ironic anger. "Benefactor."

Pierre finished his glass. He stood and placed the flat cap back onto his large head. He straightened his coat. "Maybe next time"—he glanced around the car

—"don't delay what should be done with haste."

Daniel picked up his glass and tilted it toward Pierre. "Next time."

Daniel walked into the luxury car. Leather sofas and ornate, antique chairs sat on marble floors. A long, hand-tufted rug ran the length of the car. The space was accoutered with no expense spared. Bourbon and cigar smoke lingered above every surface.

He slid a chair out from under the edge of a wide oak desk, behind which Brue sat, studying the glass of a small laptop. He'd not looked up as of yet. Behind him, two enforcer types loomed: bulky, dark eyes and thick necks.

Daniel glanced at them and guessed what weapon systems they had in play. He tried to spot how much surveillance equipment was in the room. How quickly would reinforcements arrive if the two human bulls had been neutralized?

Brue finished his business on the monitor and snapped the lid closed. He looked up at Daniel, already seated. He had the face of a man about to eat his favorite meal, one he could have any time he wanted and never tired of.

He reached across the desk and said, "It's good to see you again."

Daniel took his hand but didn't return a greeting. He smiled instead and tipped his head back. "The show's almost over, and you're just now joinin' us?"

He gave Brue a suspicious look.

"I had business that required my attention."

Daniel nodded and looked at the two bruisers. "I bet. I bet."

"Anyway, the agenda—" Brue wanted to get down to it.

"I've been doin' this for a while now. You think I don't have it down?"

"I think you should let me speak." He searched across his desk for something. "The agenda today has nothing to do with your impending exhortations to the public. I trust you will deliver that package per our outlined requirements."

"Sometimes I wish you'd just talk like a normal person."

Brue noted the tone with a miniature scowl. He slid his chair back and walked around the desk. He stood above Daniel. "Do you remember when we convinced you to join our efforts?" He waited, and Daniel nodded once. "Do you remember what it took to get you on board? The price you'd pay if you didn't?"

Once again, Daniel nodded. In the small of his back, a skittering of electric pain ruminated.

"And look at you now. You walk around, eat fancy food, take hot showers. You have a pretty good life. All I ask in return is your continued commitment to resolving these terrible, blood-soaked conflicts." He sat on the edge of the desk. "Stupid people with stupid notions: people like you, Daniel. They take notice when their language is spoken. They notice when one of their own presents them with—options."

Brue pulled a cigar from a box and offered it to Daniel, who refused with a wave. He shoved the end into a two-fingered guillotine and clipped the edge. Before he lit it, he said, "My wife would not be pleased with me right now."

His wife.

"No. I'm not worried that you won't say the right words. I'm worried you don't believe them, and maybe you never did."

Daniel's lower back tingled as Brue lit the cigar. His heart thumped, and his lungs sought more air. His rib cage expanded, and he tried to hide it.

Brue was morbidly curious. The smoke plumed from the end of the dark cigar, curling around his head. "Something wrong?"

Daniel lifted his chin. Nothing else mattered but the feeling in his spine. "I believe what I say." Nothing else mattered.

"Are you sure?" Brue picked a piece of tobacco off his lip and tongue.

The burning started, a tickle, a reminder. It bent his back sideways, and his right hip sat high. Daniel grunted.

"You know, my assistant Fiona was invaluable to me." Brue nodded. He had a faint, remembering smile. "She kept me in line and on track. I don't believe I've been able to replace her."

Daniel doubled over. The pain came in waves, echoing throughout his abdomen, jolting up his spine, and down into his femurs. His bones filled with molten liquid.

Brue stood up and walked back to his seat. At the moment he sat, the pain evaporated in Daniel's body—gone without a trace. He sat hunched over, breath still working to satisfy his heart rate. He grabbed ahold of his mind and forced himself to accept the ending of the session.

"You're still sore about your girl. I get it. I told you, I didn't do her."

"Yes, you did." Brue cocked his head at an angle like a dog who'd discovered a mystery. "When I say I need you to believe your words, I'm afraid it will take more than a promise on your part."

Daniel was upright again, filling his lungs, controlling his body. "Like what?"

"How about a display of devotion?"

"I got no idea what you mean by that."

"There are some credible reports from my intel people that a plot is afoot."

Daniel wrinkled his brow. "Plot? What plot? Where?"

Brue leaned in. "Well, right here, of course, on this train."

One last breath and Daniel had eased back into his seat. "Well then. What's the story?"

"Oh, not much. Signals intelligence intercepted some chatter. A few operations were conducted, and all the people planning to take down this train have been, um, I believe Cleary called it, 'balled up.'"

"So what's the problem?"

"Unfortunately, they can't be interrogated—being as dead as they are. We have all the communications from the inside man but no identity."

Daniel got the gist. "And so—?"

"We know it's not you."

Daniel thought it through. "Say what you came to say."

"Tomorrow, I want you to go about your daily routine. Mingle with the converts. Talk about what you talk about. Intimate what you may need to intimate. Find me the person on board who leaked the timelines. Find out how they did it. Bring me to them. Let me deal with them. I would consider that a suitable display of devotion."

"How much time do I have?"

"The assault was supposed to happen within the next eighteen hours. When it doesn't go down—"

"This guy will go dark."

Brue nodded. "Exactly."

"Why don't you toss everybody's quarters? Lean in hard."

Brue thought about it for a moment. The sting on his face indicated that his assessment had been reached upon painful consideration. "It would be difficult to calculate this program's positive impact on the global outlook. It really does seem to make a difference, this—traveling road show. I suppose you men are the talent, so to speak. I don't want to disrupt that. I want to continue our annual tradition of doing good things. Don't you?"

Daniel looked down at the desk. A simple "yes"

was the right answer, but something had grown in him over the preceding years, and that thing was spite.

Brue continued, "But if I thought we were still in danger for a moment, I'd light up everyone until the perpetrator gave himself away." Brue rubbed the burning end of his cigar against the edges of the heavy glass tray. "Yes. So what do you say? Can I count on you?"

The reverberations of the car reminisced with Daniel's lower spine. The memory of the torture awakened. "I'll see what I can do."

Brue puffed on his cigar. He smiled at Daniel's back as he left the car.

◄─────•●•─────►

"What was your meeting with Brue about?" Pierre made his way to Daniel upon entering the dining car for breakfast. He stood for a moment, waiting to be acknowledged.

Daniel carved a piece of flat pork and dipped it into the runny yolk. He didn't look up. "If I'd known they was handin' out grub this fine, I mighta switched sides sooner." He forked the soppy meat into his mouth, smiling at Pierre.

Pierre sat down, a little distracted.

"You come in here dead set on talkin'. Don't mind me." Daniel continued to work on the pork.

"Oh. Of course." Pierre paused. He didn't like the atmosphere. Breakfast was a busy time. Every seat was filled with contractors, bureaucrats, and other reformed dissenters. The crush of people worked on his nerves.

"You doin' alright, man?"

"Yes." Pierre leaned in. "I wanted to talk to you about something."

"Okay. I got nowhere to be."

Pierre scanned the room once again. "Maybe not the time or place. Let's do this later."

"Where at?"

"My room."

Daniel was doubtful. "You think that's any better?"

"It will be. You'll have to trust me." Pierre smiled at his friend and left the dining car.

Daniel set his fork down. He wiped his mouth, his appetite disappearing with Pierre. He had known the answer to the question before it was asked. Now, it was a matter of sorting all the details.

How to do that?

◆—————•●•—————▶

Pierre's quarters were bland. The converts' living areas were stripped down to the fundamental necessities. A dull gray carpet—a bed pushed up against the wall for space. Storage compartments at their feet, and the restroom had no door.

This was the only visible evidence they were prisoners, and the vehicle was a rolling prison. The doors to their rooms were locked at night. Multiple means of surveillance were both visible and, Daniel assumed, invisible.

A bubble of signal-jamming technology surrounded any area available to the prisoners. At no point could a digital message be passed from within the Faraday cage of the five train cars the prisoners could access—or at least that's what the prison overseers believed to be true.

"What's your deal, man?" Daniel started.

Pierre flashed his finger to his lips. He lowered the bed from the wall and beckoned Daniel to sit, which he did. Then he unfolded a chair from the wall and sat opposite him. "I was wondering if you'd worked out your agenda with Brue. That's all."

Daniel smiled. "That's all?"

Pierre nodded. He retrieved a small cylinder from his pocket, careful to hold it in his left hand, close to his thigh. He pressed a button, and a green light flashed off the end of it.

Daniel glanced up to the left. That must be where the camera was.

Pierre smiled and looked at the floor. "As long as the lens can't see your lips move, they won't know what we are saying. Look down at the floor when you want to talk about those things, up at me when you don't care if they see your words."

Daniel grinned and looked at the floor. "Where the hell did you get somethin' like that?"

"It was waiting on me when I boarded." Pierre looked up. "We are almost into Lithuania. Then it's only another seven hours or so until we arrive at our destination."

Daniel engaged in the banal conversation. "What is the town again?"

"Not quite a town, my friend. Tallinn is the capital. Did Brue ask you about your agenda for the speech?"

"He said he was worried 'cause we haven't been there yet."

"He said the same to me." Pierre emphasized the word *same*.

Daniel picked up on it. He looked down. "You got somethin' goin' on here, man? What's the deal? Where'd you get that gizmo?"

Pierre stared into his bathroom opening, then down at the floor. "I am in communication with others outside the train."

Daniel squinted his eyes and looked up at Pierre. "I guess he's just tryin' to make sure it goes over well." He lingered there, eyes wide.

Pierre said to the carpet, "I have heard that you are also in touch with people and"—he took a deep breath—"there is something planned." He raised his eyes to Daniel, following his intuition.

For a long moment, neither spoke. A slow smile crawled across Daniel's mouth. Pierre was resolute, his chin raised.

Daniel broke his gaze and stared down at the floor. "You tryin' to root somebody out, old friend?"

Daniel reached into his left pocket. Pierre tensed and leaned forward, shifting his weight toward his toes. "You may not have been to Tallinn, but I have.

Wonderful city." Pierre's voice was cracked with stress. Daniel's hand still lingered in his pocket. "I only want to know if we are all going up in flames or if there is a way out."

"And if there is, can you find the way?"

"Exactly. What is in your pocket, Daniel?"

"I've been gettin' on and off this train for three years. You ain't the only one who gets stuff stowed, friend."

Daniel fidgeted with the thing in his pocket. Pierre was transfixed by it, fear rounding his nostrils, his forehead wrinkled with thought.

Daniel said, "I s'pose we're about done with this tour." He looked down at Pierre's feet and made note of the stressed fold in the toes of his shoes. "You look like you're about ready to strike, man. Are you sure you wanna make that move? You still don't know what I got here." He looked up and caught Pierre's eye. Both men started doing the math.

Pierre said, "Daniel, we are friends, and—" He leaped, moving his bulk with explosive grace. In an instant, he closed the distance.

Daniel had anticipated it. Knowing Pierre's ability to arrive without warning, he dropped his weight into the bed, and shot a straight right hand into his throat. Pierre's momentum amplified the impact—a distant, muffled snap among the rustling of bodies.

Pierre gurgled and sputtered, reaching for his throat. The shattered hyoid bone caused a sudden onset of asphyxia.

He tried to roll away, but Daniel hugged him.

When they fell to the floor, they fell together, Pierre on top, blocking the camera.

He grabbed Pierre's jacket collars. Pulling down with his left hand, he smashed the lapel across his throat, flattening the carotid arteries.

Pierre settled somewhat. At least he wouldn't suffocate. A blood choke was much faster—a merciful turn. He took one last look at Daniel with his bulging eyes, and slipped away.

Daniel felt Pierre's life leave. He wriggled to remove himself from under the bulk of him while covertly sliding an item from his pocket inside Pierre's lapel.

Daniel sat on the floor beside the body. He didn't look up to his left but knew they'd been watching him. They would be there soon.

◂─────••─────▸

"Well, you didn't waste any time, did you?" Brue traipsed around his luxury car, fists clenching and releasing.

Daniel noted the tension in him and sat still, as relaxed as he could be, in the face of a man who had the power of life and death over him.

Brue said, "You must have had some idea when we spoke last night."

"I had some idea but couldn't be sure till I talked to him."

Brue chewed at it, working to quell his irritation. He offered Daniel a cigar, which he refused.

"So, we've searched the room and found some interesting things. Would you like to know what we found?" The question had a pointed nature to it.

Daniel said, "He had a gadget. Said we could talk when it was on."

"Yes." Brue lit his cigar and became animated. "He had a very crude but highly effective signal jammer. Apparently, it jams audio traffic when activated but leaves the video feed intact. Unless the feed is directly monitored, you wouldn't know about the disruption until the conversation or activity was complete. Then you'd be left with the video feed only. Fascinating, don't you think."

Daniel said, "Pretty smart."

Brue lit his cigar. "What did he say to you?"

Daniel didn't linger on the answer. "He alleged I was plannin' somethin' and wanted me to rope him in." He paused and glanced sideways at Brue. "He was tryin' to get me to be the guy *you're* lookin' for, I guess."

Brue jokingly assumed a guilty posture, placing his hand on his chest. "So, you're wondering if I also recruited Pierre."

"I am."

Brue smiled, the smoke piling up in front of his face. "What else did he say?"

"Nothing. He wanted to get off the train before the attack. He wanted me to pull him out." Daniel broke his gaze.

Brue plunked down on his chair, a deep sigh issued. He spit a chunk of tobacco onto the floor.

Daniel shrugged his shoulders. "You didn't find nothin' else?" As he said them, he wished he could grab those words out of the air and take them back.

Brue perked up. "In fact, we did." He motioned over his shoulder, and one of his bodyguards walked around the desk. He placed a flat, polished metal box on the edge in front of Daniel. The box was milled to perfection.

"What's that?"

"This…" Brue spoke with enthusiasm, leaning forward from his chair. He pointed at the thing with his cigar. "This is something else entirely."

The guard had not moved, standing above Daniel with his hands folded in front of his waist. His shoulders loomed, and his face was non-committal with a hint of sociopathic brutality.

Brue said, "This one is not crude. Well machined. Might be the most advanced signal breaker I've seen."

"Signal breaker?" Daniel asked, trying not to lock eyes with the guard.

"You don't know what a signal breaker is?"

"I don't."

Brue chuckled. "Alright, as you know, the train is protected, shielded from digital communications, both outgoing and incoming. Well, this little guy here—" He reached forward and picked it up. "—can penetrate the jammer's frequency. It can send and receive without the slightest disruption to the bubble. Again, no one is the wiser. Isn't that fascinating?"

"Well, it would answer your question."

"Yes, it conveniently would do just that."

Daniel and the guard made eye contact. The man was younger, larger, and well-equipped for violence, but none of that mattered. The distant stinging returned to Daniel's spine, a hint of it only.

"What did he say to you, Daniel?" Brue leaned back into his chair.

"I told you." He crunched his muscles as if doing a sit-up. He lifted his knees and bore down with his teeth. The pain rushed in like fluid into a void.

"I don't believe you. I don't believe a word you say."

Daniel couldn't speak. He was twisted with the fire inside. He didn't struggle when the guard lifted him and tossed him onto the floor. He couldn't breathe, locked up as he was.

"I think you know more than you are letting on." Brue glanced over the desk at Daniel writhing on the floor.

He tried to speak, but the words clutched together and rattled in his windpipe. Then, as the pain had arrived, it dissipated into a memory. He laid still, breathing, trying to calm himself. Pushing up from the carpet, he didn't get far before the void beneath his waist became evident. His legs were gone. His face fell onto the carpet, and he heard Brue approach.

"I believe your days as a clarion for the future are over." He knelt and grabbed Daniel's chin, tipping his face toward him. "Did you know a behaviorist came up with the idea that all converts must demonstrate absolute belief before being trusted?" He raised his eyebrows to Daniel. "Nonsense, really." Brue released his face, and it dropped to the floor. "I didn't favor the project, but the others loved the idea." He held his hands up like a criminal surrendering to authorities. "Sometimes, you have to let the little things go, you know? Let them have their toys, I suppose."

Brue stood and motioned to the guard, who lifted Daniel. "If one was to domesticate a jackal, he might well see signs of its subjugation. But, someday the beast would awaken from its slumber—slaughter whatever defenseless thing that lay near to it. You could never truly trust it." Brue leaned in and got a good look, pulling Daniel's head up by the hair and making eye contact. "You see, I don't give a fuck if you believe it or not. I knew you'd prove to be... insuppressible, a man of your base savagery. And I don't believe poor Pierre was alone in this. So, despite the good you've actually managed to do, Daniel, I think it's time for you to go back into your box."

He let go of Daniel's hair and waved the guard toward the door.

As he was dragged away, Daniel said, "The day's comin'."

Brue turned to him and puffed his cigar. The guard continued to drag Daniel.

"The day when we are the same again—that day is comin'."

The guard dropped him onto the floor of his quarters. The stubby, gray carpet scuffed his face. He dragged himself to the edge of his bed, tried to sit up. He struggled, could only roll over to his back.

In the corner of the room, a wheelchair waited for him.

If this is it, then this is it, he thought. Would they kill him? Was he any more use to them? The wheelchair sat stolid and gray, hand operated. He hadn't used one in years.

He envisioned his life moving forward, eyes burning in a white room, a transient distraction for his benefactor. He would be a predictable and preferred meal, enjoyed whenever the mood took.

Was he now, finally, broken? He reminded himself to never lie about the truth of the world.

But what *was* left for him? He would eat, shit, and die, and that would be the extent of it—almost tolerable, in this, his final form.

All except for Maggie and the life she was forced to live in his wake. Failures as a father and failures as a man were Daniel's legacy. And he had the rest of his time to ruminate on it.

However long that would be.

EIGHT

2050

The force, the divinity of life, and the weight of illness. . . the destruction of the flesh wherein we live. (As Virgil said)

We now, no longer born for death, but into the bright line which stretches forever. Into the next life, and the one thereafter.
—The Bridge to Dawn

The barrel rested on the palm-sized sandbags. Maggie had carried them up the ancient service stairs inside her pack three days ago. The floor around them was clean, the macronutrient wrappers packed away.

By mid-morning, the vaulted, concrete compartment sweltered. Water was an anticipated issue. The main line had been tapped and a gate valve installed.

Weeks earlier, advance teams from a local cell dealt with that and other issues. Two concrete walls had to be drilled, and the hose was passed into the service area.

The area had been sealed to the public forty years earlier and had been converted into an AI server center for Neo-Cloud financial services. The entrance was situated beneath the building and protected by heavy steel doors.

When Maggie and Rudy arrived in Minneapolis four days ago, they recovered a dead-drop package with keys to the subterranean entrance. They moved up the enclosed stairwell forty-one flights and positioned themselves for the shot in a musty, cramped box of a room.

Three days before any event, Carnell's advance teams would scour the locale in their clean business suits. They would assess and shore up potential security vulnerabilities. Any attempt on Carnell called for an extraordinary level of preparation.

Maggie flipped the gate valve remote and sucked water from the flexible hose. She flipped it off and said, "I'm going to ping security and see if everybody's in place."

Rudy set the pulse rifle butt down into a V-shaped holder and turned to her. "It ain't time for that yet. Don't hit 'em up. You'll spook 'em."

"They should be available for a report." She fiddled with her light board as if she expected a report at any moment. "Should have gotten into position ten minutes ago."

They were both in the prone, on their bellies, Rudy behind the gun and Maggie with the spotter reticle on a low mount. He touched her hand. "It's not time for a report. These aren't our guys. You don't want to spook 'em with unnecessary comms."

She sighed, frustrated. He was right, but her nerves didn't want to wait. It had been four days since they had contacted any supporting cells. There were three spotter/security elements in place to give them an early warning in the event things went sideways. A coded signal would be passed along to the hit team via the secure channel on the light board.

It was one hour before the event: a celebration of Minnesota's commitment to the future. Carnell was supposed to walk up onto the long stage. Rudy was supposed to kill him.

She didn't like it, the waiting. But she agreed.

Rudy returned to the rifle, lifted it, and dialed the digital scope.

She studied him, his intensity. He'd become a respected, well-known sniper within the organization. The pulse rifle was a new addition to his repertoire. They'd spent several weeks in upstate New York when he received it, dialing it in and working out the kinks. The rifle had a unique ballistic profile and offered a new level of accuracy, but required familiarization. Windage, humidity, and angle—all the considerations of traditional ballistics—still affected the shot, but the nature of the round's impulsive force flattened some of those considerations. Still, it wasn't a "point and shoot" weapon; the tolerances needed to be mastered. Rudy habitually placed a round through a penny at a thousand yards.

From the forty-first floor, it was a seven-hundred-and-twenty-yard, high-angle shot. They would get one try. Either Carnell's head would split like a melon, or the overdressed security guards would bury him beneath their bulletproof suits and hustle him away.

On the north side of The Commons, Maggie traversed her spotter reticle across the stage, focusing on random people.

She would establish the distance, wind speed, and direction. An algorithm would determine adjustments based on the data from previous engagements. Upon her direction, Rudy would make his adjustments, and engage. His job was to do the killing and to be calm about it. The machines couldn't do it for him.

Maggie's concerns extended beyond the shot. Working with new people was not her first choice. However, over the last several years, networks had been rooted out into the open and captured or killed at alarming rates. These people were her friends and colleagues: people upon whom she'd relied to provide logistical support and gather intelligence to drive operations.

Their efforts to kill Carnell had intensified, and so did his efforts to counter them. The more shots they took at him and failed, the smarter and more ruthless he became. At times she admired his refusal to be cowed into hiding. Despite several high-profile attempts to kill him, he rode atop it like a monster wave, in control.

She watched Rudy deal with his weapon in the quiet, sweaty concrete box. The memory of her friends who'd paid the price to keep her alive played through her mind. She had a knack for recruiting competent, motivated people and refining them into valuable participants.

But the world had changed at a stunning pace. The global populace had all but surrendered to the new order. Skins were ubiquitous, even serving in governing capacities, fairly elected by the people—as they say.

The average man and woman had become as alien to her as any Skin she'd ever seen. She viewed them with disgust as she walked around the cities—their heads hooked into the dopamine factory of their choice. They walked through the world, not even free in the confines of their minds—constant inputs from the controllers, glittery messages.

There were fewer and fewer places to hide. Networks were almost impossible, to establish. The ones still in play were secretive to a fault, in essence, neutralized. Insurgencies around the world were left out in the cold, denied support from populations, and then rounded up and killed with ease, like fish in a drying pond.

She said, "What do we know about these guys, anyway? They can't tolerate an extra update?"

"Well." Rudy kept his eye on the scope. "We know the same thing we knew in Denver and Alabama.

They're vetted through Glenn."

"Glenn's getting a little careless, if you ask me."

"If you got a problem, you know—"

She didn't let him finish. "I'm just saying we need to know more about these nets before we show up."

"You know, that's the whole point of a cell, right?" He smiled at her and acted like a professor. "A cell is s'posed to be completely deniable from everybody and everything. You're not s'posed to know them, and they ain't s'posed to know you."

"I'm saying we need to establish our own cells." She grew quiet at the memory of her people.

"Listen, if you want that, let's do that. But..." He went back to his scope. "If this thing finally goes down, we might could retire."

She shook her head and stared at the floor. This was his dream. He'd bring up retiring on occasion, speak of it wistfully. They'd build a cabin in the hills. She'd bear his children and hold his hand into old age. They'd live together like that, in the imaginary place he'd invented inside his mind. A place the machine couldn't touch and would never find. He'd say, *You've seen the maples in November, burnin' through all those yellows.* He would describe them —shimmered, broken angles in the sunlight. He wanted an eternity of sorts, she figured. He wanted to witness it inside her gaze. And every person he killed, he wanted it more and more.

But she wasn't finished yet and wasn't sure she ever would be.

So he could have his dreams, as long as he

managed the trigger. She'd smile and breathe life into them, holding his hand in a silent lie. There was still a thing to be done. There wasn't time for any other consideration. When dealing with the minds of men tasked with the hunting of other men, it was wise to find the button and apply the correct pressures. Rudy would do fine. He was getting better every day.

Brue was going to die—if not today, then some other.

She would see to it, and if it cost her everything, that was the going price.

◆——••——▶

The moments clicked away in the hot box. Maggie observed the target through her reticles, desperate to distract herself from the growing anxieties. She hated the comms plan—not how she would run the op. But that didn't matter. She was a cog in a delicate machine—a machine that required the perfect set of circumstances and that could break at any moment. This plan was light on contingencies, so she and Rudy had developed their own.

The light board flashed, illuminating her face. Finally, some contact. She picked it up. "It's S/O three." She read the message aloud. "Can opener." She stared at Rudy, the fire of disappointment eating at the edges of her eyes. This was the exact message she didn't want to see.

Rudy said, "Bug out signal. Let's go." He popped up

to a knee and started disassembling the weapon.

Maggie placed a hand on his arm, trying to salvage the damned thing—*this damned mission*. They'd worked on it for weeks. It was less than ten minutes to hit time.

"Wait a minute. Can opener means the S/O team is taking off. *THEY* got spotted. It doesn't mean the whole mission is compromised."

Rudy's pupils were wide with adrenaline. He paused, leaned toward Maggie, and spoke steadily and deliberately. "We are leaving. Now."

He slid the weapon into its carrying case.

She wasn't done. "Listen, we got a shot at—" The light board vibrated again. They both stopped and stared at it. She lifted it, read the message, and sighed. "Can opener, from S/O one."

Rudy nodded and continued to pack his gear. He winked at her. "Time to go, baby."

She grabbed her bag and stowed the spotter scope. She scrubbed the dusty, concrete room with her eyes. It was empty except for the "field shitter," a small metal receptacle used to contain their eliminations. She tightened the lid and pressed a button. The bucket rumbled, and smoke escaped from the hinges as it incinerated their leavings. It was essential to leave no trace, DNA or otherwise.

They moved in silence, as there was no need to speak.

There was only one way out: down the many flights of stairs that brought them up.

Rudy pulled his board and swiped it alive. On

the monitor were four squares. Cameras had been placed at points along their ingress route. The entrance to the tunnels, the stairwell, and points along the tenth and twentieth floors were visible in the small boxes. He moved to the stairs, and she followed.

They rumbled down the flights, feet floating despite their loads.

Maggie burned with anger. In the interim moments since they'd gotten the call, she behaved automatically, not thinking, just doing. Now they were descending, the mission scrapped, and she had time to think, and it was enraging her. What had gone wrong?

A lot of work had gone into the mission. Maybe the problem was too many people, or maybe someone rolled over. The nets had become unreliable. When they were down on this, they wouldn't be relying on Glenn anymore. She would build a network that got things done.

Their feet pounded against the corrugated, metal stairs. Rudy skipped every other step and had a lead on Maggie, half a floor's worth. He stopped and checked his board. "Dammit." He turned to her as she descended to his side. "Floor twenty."

She took his board. The screen showed heavily armed security forces flowing past the camera, kitted out with the latest armor and weapons. She manipulated the picture's resonance, and their armor's vibration shimmered on the screen.

"They have hummingbird armor."

The new armor was specialized to protect its wearer in "close up" situations against small arms and bladed weapons. It rendered them impervious to low-speed projectiles. The pistols Maggie and Rudy carried would be useless.

"Of course they do." Rudy smiled as he dropped his pack. "Nothin' but the best for my baby."

He pulled a roll of tape charge from the pack and unspooled it. He stood holding the demolitions and leaned in to kiss her lips. They lingered in it for a moment. All the while, the security forces bounded their way up the stairs.

She tasted him. She felt his body push against hers, his free hand slipping over her ribs and squeezing her back. He had a way to calm her down.

Their unauthorized contingency plan was to blow the vault wall and enter the building's office area. From there, they would play the cards as they lay. Well-versed in the building's floor plan and the many routes in and out of it, their choice would be determined by the actions of their enemy.

Rudy let her lips go and turned to the concrete wall. He pressed the flexible blast tape against it and formed it into the shape of an octagon. He worked fast. As he applied it to the wall's surface, it hardened and etched into the outer layer of the wall through a chemical reaction. The tape sat flush to the surface and was nearly invisible. He smeared a paste into the center of the octagon and then placed a blinking box in the paste. He turned to Maggie. "Head on up, two flights."

She did as he said, and he followed. With heavy breaths, they both claimed two stairs at once.

Every time demolitions were used, Maggie was filled with a sense of dread. She had heard the stories of people blowing themselves up in accidents.

Rudy didn't share those fears. When she turned to him, he had the same slight smile he always had when dealing with explosives—a thirty-year-old child with a toy.

Once they were in position, away from the edge of the stairwell, he tapped a button on his board, and the charge detonated. A reverberating shock wave sliced upward through the structure. Even from their position, twenty feet up, two landings of wrought iron between them and the blast, they were shaken to the core and peppered with slivers and chunks of concrete.

Rudy waved his hand to dispel the cloud of debris from his eyes. He spit concrete dust. "That sounded good." There was a glimmer of joy there.

She shook her head—yeah, always a little boy.

When the old service shaft was walled in, concrete and copper filament protected the area from electromagnetic attacks. The result was an eighteen-inch-thick barrier intended to protect around fifteen percent of the world's financial activity. Rudy had utilized a cutting-edge composite of nanotech and old-fashioned blast chemicals to attack it. This was his first opportunity to use a design of his own in the field.

They charged down the stairs into the smoke and

dust, slowing their steps to negotiate the rubble. The explosion had cut a jagged hole large enough for the pair to duck into the adjoined building. A hazy light penetrated the dark stairwell.

Without speaking, Maggie pulled an anti-personnel mine from her pack and set it on the top of the flight. As Rudy stepped through the opening with his pistol drawn, she angled the mine downward. She set the motion-activated detonator and was careful about it, then followed Rudy.

"How many flights down are they?" she asked him.

"No idea. I would guess they'll be here soon."

They ran through a maze of cubicles. The emergency alarms sounded and were accompanied by flashing lights. The blast and smoke had tripped the sensors.

They reached the stairwell as a tight explosion racked their ears. It ripped beyond the blast hole as the approaching forces tripped the mine.

It was equipped with a pound of advanced Semtex and discharged over a thousand pieces of shrapnel. The jagged, metal chunks traveled at speeds approaching twelve hundred meters per second. The hummingbird armor was no use against it. The mine was designed to delay explosion until the closest mover was within several feet, ensuring the largest number of targets had entered its kill zone.

"Let's see how fast they recover from that," Rudy said as he pushed Maggie into the stairwell.

Given the thickness of the connecting wall, the

enemy would not have anticipated entering the office sector of the building. Nonetheless, Maggie had planned it with the "worst case" in mind. A few steps were needed to complete the escape and leave no evidence of their operational procedures.

They continued down the flights until they reached the seventeenth floor.

Maggie grabbed Rudy. "Here. This one." Her voice halting from exhaustion.

He nodded and plowed through the door. Turning through hallways with his board out and guiding him, Rudy led them to a room marked *Particle Shredder*. It was secured with a bio lock. Rudy pulled his pick set out and began the process. Maggie scanned the area with her pistol drawn.

Rudy said, "What is this place again?"

"It's where they take everything they don't want people to see. Turn it into ash."

Within moments, the lock flashed a bright green. The tumblers rolled open, and the mechanism clicked and popped.

"I'm gettin' pretty good at this." Rudy pushed the door open, and they ran into the room.

Maggie hustled to a large machine and lifted a glass sliding door. She'd familiarized herself with the same model during her mission preparations. The machine was the size of a small sedan. The lights kicked on, an off-white color. She nodded at Rudy.

He took the rifle bag and his pack and tossed them inside. Maggie rummaged through her kit and placed some items into her pockets, and then her pack went into the shredder. She pushed the buttons, and the device rumbled for a moment. Then, the stuff disappeared in a white flash.

"Masks," Maggie said as she slid the web of wires over her head. Rudy did the same, and they manipulated their holo masks. They cycled through looks and found the prescribed identities. Maggie became a middle-aged woman with dark red hair. She slid a cap on. Rudy was a teenage boy.

With empty hands, they moved out of the room into the emergency stairwell and continued the descent. Their footfalls echoed on the stairs.

If the enemy had gotten its shit together, it hadn't located them yet. When a mass casualty situation occurred, as most certainly had happened in the service stairwell, the security forces would become bogged down. The dead and dying would need to be dealt with. Maggie imagined the rough, steel stairs slick with blood and matter, the screams and the smoke. She was betting on all that death and chaos dragging them down, clogging their gears, and creating gaps for her and Rudy to slip through.

Rudy pushed the emergency door open on the fourth floor, and they entered a wide hall with shining marble floors. Maggie walked close to him. They appeared to be a mother and her son. Both had pistols tucked into their pockets.

They'd entered an above-ground tram station. A massive, slick design, it served as a stop in the city's mass transit system. The area was sparse, with people sitting around, unconcerned with the alarms. They would wait until security came to eject them from the room. If the tram got there first, so be it.

Rudy and Maggie's arrival didn't raise any eyebrows. Most people were locked into their light boards, living their lives.

The tram slid into the station, and the brakes released their gassed-up pressure as it came to a halt. Maggie and Rudy flowed into the car along with the others, looking like they belonged. They grabbed the hand grips and jostled among the workers as the tram launched.

Looking back at the tower through the tube's glass roof, she lamented the missed opportunity and dreaded the upcoming movement. It would take several days to get back to New York.

This event convinced her to build her own network. It would be reliable. Her network would be airtight.

Rudy's teenaged face was preoccupied. She could read his mind at this point, even in a holo mask. He was thinking about his cabin, resolving to be patient until his dreams could be realized. He would do whatever she wanted to make that happen.

They would go to New York.

They would do whatever she wanted.

◄─────••─────►

2052

Brue and Roma coupled on the sofa with the low table in front of them. Monitors covered the wall, each beaming different parts of the empire into the room in crystal clear relief. Each was a portal into the vast reaches of Brue's program, his influence, now global and complete.

The window wall's view had changed; the city's massive, twinkling skyline was gone, replaced by the green hedged hills of Pennsylvania.

Roma was speaking to Brue, but his attention was on her skin. Her shoulder was naked in the setting sun, and he couldn't take his eyes off it. The warmth of the early evening splashed through the glass, and her flesh shined in his eyes.

"The time is now." She consulted her light board. She read an update from some committee buried inside the global machine that fell under Brue's control. "That was my friend in Asia-Corp. They are prepared to fully endorse this weekend."

Happy with the news, she turned to Brue and saw the dumb, distracted, horny look in his eyes.

"That's good to hear." He leaned over and kissed her shoulder.

"The vote will be completed by the time of the banquet." She inspected him for some acknowledgment. He was fixated. "I'm serious, Brue."

Dragged from his obsession, "I'm serious too. I'm happy. Everything looks good. They look good." He traced his finger along her chin. "You look good."

She laughed and pushed his hand away. Her eyes were gentle. She held him in her gaze, a child reaching for candy. In the warm light, she steeled herself. There was one more piece of business. "You haven't told me if he will be there this weekend." Her eyes were, as always, expectant of him.

His smile buried a distant, nagging trouble. She couldn't see or feel it. He was a practiced liar. Her entire world hinged on his next words, and he knew it. His face was twisted with calculations. "Who?"

She laughed again and brushed his face away with a pretend slap. "You know. Our—Olphan." She said the name, and hope buoyed her eyes.

Her son...

Brue's eyes turned down at the corners, which would have told the lie, but she wasn't suspicious. She'd always believed in him. When he asked her to give away her magic, she did so with trepidation but faith. His version of reality was one she accepted without hesitation.

Resting for a moment before he told his next lie, he wanted to sit still and see her to rally his strength. He had done all this for her.

Over the years, Roma's barren status darkened her once ebullient heart. Brue sensed her nonverbal wants and sought to assuage her with distractions and finery. No matter the attempted fix, the chasm inside her grew as the years passed. He listened to her unspoken pleading even as he told himself the sacrifice was unfortunate but necessary. And he conceived of a solution. It appeared as a simple question.

What if the genetic material from two people could be mimicked into a single Newborn?

Conception was the riskiest of all the tricks in nature. There was no controlling the frequency or quality of the offspring. He envisioned a few generations of crafted Newborns. Aspects of appearance and personality could be evidenced as if they were genetically connected to a human couple. Since the construction of the Newborn would have no actual "donors," it would be a pantomime, a mimic of an offspring. As he had put it so long ago, it would *scratch that evolutionary itch*.

It would provide his program with a controlled and orderly progression of humanity. He would meet population goals in a timely manner. The answer for Roma was the answer for humanity.

Upon the plan's conception, Brue researched the program with Jakob and his Newborn Genetics team. As soon as he was sure it could succeed, he told Roma about it. Together, they submitted their DNA, and she waited, a good wife, for the outcome.

He swallowed his reservations. The testing and implementation phase did not go according to plan. It had been several years in development. The public was already aware of the concept, and the pressures he felt within the confines of his own home were magnified the world over as corporate and governmental heads demanded progress reports. Billions of people leaned over his shoulder and stared into his petri dish.

He readied the world for the release even as problems, both major and minor, plagued progress. He'd been cornered and now he was dragging his feet through setting concrete, so he kept moving, developing, and reviewing.

Those who had devoted themselves to the future would now have their chance at eternity. Brue and Roma's "child" would be displayed before the world. This would mark the beginning of a new era, orderly and engineered instead of the chaotic gamble that had marred the Earth and marginalized so many.

"I could never have done this without you. Oldbirth will officially be outlawed. The Gen Three concept was born of your heart."

"No." She pulled his hand to her face. "It was born of your heart." She closed her eyes and leaned into him. "He is half of me and half of you."

"Yes."

"Is he—does he feel like ours?"

He'd churned through a hundred versions of the first Gen Three, his son. The wasted ones were tubed into incinerators, sometimes even after actualization. The main issues were behavioral. The remedies for this always caused more problems. At first, it seemed like the transcendence issue could be solved with new approaches, but it persisted and manifested itself in disturbing ways.

"It's a complicated process, but the technology is durable."

"I know that. I'm asking, does he look like us?"

Brue sighed. The simplicity of the concern drew him deeply to her, to the wanting nature of her eyes. He lifted the corners of his lips.

"Like you. He's lucky that way."

The meet site was an old brewery on the Upper East Side. The ceilings were tall, with blacked-out windows near the top. The space was walled with brick and treated concrete. A small circle of comfortable chairs dotted the floor, which once held large copper tanks. Maggie and Rudy sat, silent.

The door opened, and a young woman with curly hair and a dancer's figure walked in. She smiled at Maggie, who returned the gesture as she stood. She moved to the woman and hugged her.

Rudy rolled his eyes. The woman's hands dug into Maggie, curving the skin around her palms, her fingers grabbing. She held the hug longer than one would think appropriate for a simple greeting. He shrugged and looked away.

Maggie released her and held her hands. "Eva." She said in a relieved tone. "Have a seat." She waved at a chair close by her side.

Before she moved, Rudy outstretched his arm and wiggled his fingers, reaching for something. "Board."

"Oh. Yes. Here you go." She pulled it from her pocket and handed it to him.

He placed it on a table and plugged a small jack

into the bottom of it. He opened a laptop and initiated a program against the operating system, which was trained to spot certain activities based on counterintelligence protocols.

Eva sat close to Maggie, who held her eyes wide. "I got it. I got the job."

Maggie grabbed her hand in excitement. "I knew you could do it."

"I'm on the ninety-fourth floor now. I have server access, and that opens a lot of doors."

Maggie tried to temper her enthusiasm. "You understand our parameters?"

Eva was eager. "I understand them."

Rudy butted in. "Really? That's interesting 'cause we haven't told you what they are yet."

"I mean—" She looked at Maggie, doubting herself.

Maggie stroked her hand and gave her a flat smile. "You'll do fine. We've got a lot to talk about."

Rudy unplugged her board and tossed it to her without ceremony. He said, "We need floor and door counts, sketches, leave-behind devices planted, access points, bio lock makes and models, security protocols—"

Maggie waved him down like a lion tamer. "I think we should take a moment to appreciate our Eva." She passed a delighted grin to her friend, her eyebrows raised.

Eva relaxed in her chair, flattered.

Rudy closed his laptop with a snap. He stared at Maggie, eyes speaking a language known only by the two of them.

Eva fidgeted in her chair, uncomfortable in the silence.

Maggie shook her head in reproach, and Rudy exited with heavy feet.

Maggie regained Eva. She held her in a devious smile. "I think this is going to work out well."

<hr />

He felt his body again, the damaged frame jammed into the wheelchair. The blinding wall permeated through the pink of his eyelids. Then he opened them and saw it.

Daniel sat upright, holding a book. His glassy eyes floated over the top of the page. His blank face, pollock'd with faded commemorations of violence, wore a thick, gray beard.

The room was stark as a crane's neck. He narrowed his eyes, dull in the face of it. He'd grown accustomed.

He turned to the entryway.

A man stood there, young, large, broad-faced. He held Daniel inside a shrewd gaze. His shoulders sat high and bulky. He wore a tailored suit with a silk pocket square. His smile stretched across his face, unpracticed. It was as if he'd learned the expression and decided to try it out, sensing its utility.

Daniel marked his page, turned to the table, and closed the book. When he looked up, he found the man towering awkwardly close. The bizarre, crooked line crept along under his nose. His skin seemed strange, thicker somehow.

The line flattened and the man said in a toneless voice, "Daniel?"

"Have we met?" asked Daniel, his voice dry. He swallowed.

The visitor crouched. Near enough now to touch, the size difference became apparent. His shoulders, fingers, and bones were all larger. His face and eyes radiated a chemical sheen.

He grabbed Daniel's cot with one hand and dragged it screeching across the floor. Then he sat on the mattress, close enough for Daniel to feel the outskirts of his breath. His smoky eyes were idle. The smile worked against itself like new gears with untested tolerances.

"If we had met, you would remember," the stranger said.

"Startin' to get that impression." Daniel's mouth hung open and his brow bit together.

"I am Olphan." Dipping his head, he touched his chest and spoke as if Daniel were witness to a miracle.

Daniel passed a glance across him and shrugged. He'd seen these before... *but, this one, something was different about him.* The Gen Twos had been getting larger for years, and more physically capable. Yet, they still harbored an anti-human pessimism, a resounding distrust. This one had a forced amiability, a dark awkwardness to it. It might not have cooked long enough.

"You must be wondering—"

"A thing or two, yeah." Daniel, half smiling, tilted his head back. He laughed and said, "You got some damn camel bones, don't ya? Big son of a bitch."

Olphan mimicked him—the laugh, the tilted head. He learned a new thing every moment. He said, "I believe you know my father."

"Yeah, I know him. He know you're here?"

"Some things he knows. Some things, he doesn't."

It was disquieting to look at him. He sat coiled, all potential.

"You're a *Skin*, ain't ya." Daniel stared into his eyes. His words flowed like venom.

"Aren't we all, really?" Olphan shrugged his massive shoulders.

Daniel took his time, let the room grow silent. Then he answered with a deep-seated spite. "No. We're not."

He cataloged his findings: the thickened face, the oversized brow. The thing smirked when it should have smiled.

"You're not like the other ones, either. Can see that up front."

"Well, you know my father… always tinkering." Olphan smiled.

Daniel wheeled toward his table, dropped his book, and secured a glass of water. He never took his eyes off Olphan. "Whatta you want?"

"I'm curious about your type—the *hard cores*."

Daniel glanced down at his withering legs, covered in a quilt like an old woman. He laughed. "Not much to worry 'bout anymore I guess."

"No. But, there was a day. You were quite the nuisance, I understand."

"Doubtful you would understand anything about me."

Olphan nodded. "Fair enough. But, only through study can enlightenment begin, yes?" He lifted his chin, looked around the room.

Daniel narrowed his eyes on Olphan's exposed carotid. *So fuckin' close.* He sensed the bright, hot liquid traveling up the large pipe, feeding the monster's brain. He imagined the two steps that would sluice the red warmth across his arms.

Olphan glanced and caught his eye. Both men smiled. They understood each other.

"You're sittin' mighty close." Daniel tried to work the thought out of his mind. How could he get away with it? Broken and old now, he could barely move.

"And what would you do about it?" Olphan asked, his brows raised.

Daniel lifted the glass to his lips, played it cool. "I'd crack this glass here. See if I could get the edges in your neck." Glancing at Olphan's thighs, he said, "But, you look pretty stout, and I mighta lost a step or two."

Olphan stood and straightened his suit, affixing something like a grin to his face. "Also, you know another version of me would walk through that door in a little while, right?"

He sought acknowledgment, which Daniel withheld with stubborn relish. "You would do it anyway, wouldn't you? See, I'm already learning about your kind."

Olphan walked to the rectangle. "That is why we do what we must, you and I."

Daniel eased deeper into his chair as the big man moved away. "Oh, I suppose I'm done doin'."

Olphan measured his response as he stood in the opening, solid black behind him. "Your story isn't finished, Daniel. And like all of us, you won't know the truth of it until the end. I look forward to seeing you there."

He turned and walked into the darkness. The door, quiet and efficient, blinked to white.

Daniel sat alone with his thoughts in the silent room. A broken man, the old fires kindled deep inside. His mind flooded with memories of the bloody days.

He understood this thing, new as it was, and what its arrival signified. He'd spent his life in opposition to it, burning himself against the flame of its creation. Yet it had just stood inches away and smiled at him.

◂—————••—————▸

The small, cheap room vibrated from the working bar's pulsing sound system downstairs. The beat resonated, pummeling the floor and furniture. The walls were barren. A crooked window had been cut into one as if an afterthought. The furniture was spartan, with folding chairs and a small bench with a monitor. A deeply worn couch squatted against the wall.

Rudy sat on it, rigid with unspoken irritation. He held Maggie's feet on his lap, rubbing them distractedly. She lay on her back and relaxed, swiping her light board.

His hands dug into the bottom of her foot. He had taken to rubbing them as a way to help her relax. He'd studied the subject. According to the books, activating the flexor tendon would stimulate healing properties for her gut and liver. It didn't make sense to him, but he had read it. There wasn't much he wouldn't do for her. So, he sat on a broken-down couch in a noisy hovel and attempted to fortify her liver.

The meeting with Eva was still fresh on his mind —if he could only rub away her obsession with Brue. He'd been trying for years to convince her to let it go. She had no intention of it, and he understood that.

Ever since Hungary, Maggie's fixation with Brue had been all-encompassing. Having been pulled off the operation days before its failure only added to the frustration of watching her father dragged before cameras, called a traitor, and humiliated once again. Only to be "disappeared" into the machinery, not seen or heard from since.

Rudy's dilemma: He was devoted to the girl. It was baked into every possible decision. No matter what, he'd do what she wanted.

In the light of day, when the missions were planned and resourced, there were too many considerations. Trying to convince her to drop it, always waited until the light went low and it was down to the two of them hiding. His hopes would appear, and Rudy worked the issue around in his head.

She pulled her foot away and passed him a sharp glance. "Ow! Little lighter, honey."

Distracted and irritated, he said, "Sorry. I—"

"You know, you can just say it, right?"

"Say what?" He manipulated her toes, pinching them and slipping his fingers off with a snap.

"You think I don't know you? How long have we been together?" She smiled on her back, still preoccupied with her board.

Rudy didn't respond. He leaned into the tendon. He didn't want to get into it, wasn't ready, didn't have his facts all lined up. Maggie's determination was matched by her rationale. Her reasoning was often unassailable. And, he had to face it; she was smarter than him by a mile.

"Say it, Rudy."

"You think your girl can handle this? This is pretty high-level stuff."

He went straight at her. He didn't stand a chance either way, but at least he could make a show of it. The gig was going to happen, but he would take his shot first.

"For starters, she's my asset, not my girl."

"Not what it looked like to me."

She tightened up and lifted her head so she could glare at him. Her core flexed, and her legs went rigid.

"Secondly, I don't deal with losers, so, yeah. I think

she can handle it."

"How many times have we had this kinda access?"

Rudy could feel the anger rising through her feet. She disliked his way of arguing. She wanted him to get to the point, and she had made that clear many times. This was how she conducted herself, and she had no truck for people who didn't do the same.

"What's your point?"

"I'm just sayin'—"

She interrupted. "We've come close before. Is that what you're trying to say? We've had this kind of access and came up short. Is that it? Because I was on those ops. I planned most of them. I remember."

"We've killed a lotta people around him. We've gotten a lot of our people killed tryin' to get at him. He's always a step ahead. Maybe this guy's unkillable or somethin'."

Rudy struggled to convey his thoughts. He'd been in the business since he was a child. He'd seen his first man die at nine years old and had killed his first at fifteen. There was a delicate and light aspect to it. All who'd engaged in it understood. It was a deep, unspoken thing. One man would be robbed of everything, and the other was left to remember. One man stood above the other at the end of it, continuing to breathe for some reason.

Whether she believed it or not, there were strange happenings. Some people survive what should have killed them. There was no accounting for it. But some men were impervious. They could walk through fire. There was an air about them. They were untouchable, unkillable.

"No. He's not. There's no such thing. Lucky? Yeah, he's lucky. His luck will run out, and I want to be there when it does."

Her body folded up toward him. She put the light board aside and focused her attention on him.

"Look." Rudy gnawed at the words. "Maybe it's time to let it go."

She yanked her feet from his hands and slid to the end of the couch with one smooth motion. She gave him the look he'd been trying to avoid. He withered under those eyes. "You about done, then?"

"It's enough, Maggie." The floor vibrated into his shoes, and he shook his head. "The networks are gone. We got nobody backing us up anymore. They're all dead. At some point, we gotta move on."

"And go where? Out to your little cabin?"

Rudy grunted, stood, and walked to the cock-eyed window. He stared down over a trash-filled alley. She never mentioned the cabin except to put it down and make it seem like a stupid idea. She wouldn't see it. She never would.

Maggie snatched up her shoes and slid them on. Her fingers were clumsy in her anger.

"People ain't gonna wake up. They never will. How you gonna stop it?" Rudy begged her, his voice cracking.

"I don't want to do this without you, Rudy, but I will." Her shoes were on, and she was moving toward the door.

"Oh, you will?"

"I won't stop!" It was guttural, from the deepest parts of her. It wasn't a show, and he believed her with his whole heart.

"Just talk to me, please."

She turned on him. "How dare you?" She opened the door, and the room filled with music and the loud voices of the drunks. "How dare you do this to me?"

She slammed the door behind her, and Rudy collapsed onto the couch. He put his head in his hands.

This girl he loved. He'd witnessed her transformation and been there with her every step along the way. He was powerless against her. Since the first time he saw her, he knew his life would be tied to hers in some way forever—even if that was only the memory of her face, the fire in her eyes. His head was heavy in his hands.

He was a lucky man. The way for him was clear. Not everybody had that kind of clarity.

◆ ── • • ── ▶

The white room was a hell of a teacher. Its expanse, its endlessness, was a canvas upon which his mind replayed life in fractured moments.

Maggie's tiny hands squeezing his arms—

Lori's dead, pale face, the deep cut on her lip, lying open—

A young man burnt to pieces before him—

A sunrise in the foothills, back when a man could

walk freely through the mist—

His breath, floating in the sky above the empty bodies of his friends—

All reflections laid bare in the infinite whiteness.

Torture was an art. It went far beyond electric shocks and broken bones. It plowed a man's soul, if there was such a thing.

Daniel had come to believe he had no center. His nervous system moved electric chemicals. Hormones locked and unlocked pieces of him, but there was not a singular core to him. He was both rational and lunatic at once. He had a limit but no predictable bottom. The physical meat of him could be broken. Easy. But he had been disengaged from his own will—a different deal altogether.

And for all the pain it caused, the white cell was a masterful stroke. Daniel had come to admire it. The clean efficiency of it and its steady, dysrhythmic beat had been a cruel teacher.

But he'd discovered a way to limit it. The secret was in the shadows. Those small indentations of darkness allowed his eyes to perceive depth and structure in the blinding sea. Light from the overhead, against the edge of the table, cut a dirty, gray line into the floor. This became his anchor point. He created scuffs with his wheelchair against the bedframe or the table. These were placeholders.

His mind had created vast reaches within the white against its limitlessness. It was boundless and discordant. Once understood, the shadow or the scuff would unleash the geometry of the room. The seal in the joints of the walls would swirl into place, and he would become rooted.

He claimed the cell and spent countless hours considering the bloody means by which he had come to be there. There were no more chances for him. He played with the idea that he would right his wrongs and fix his mistakes. But that was God's business, not his. He couldn't fix anything, floating as he was in his cheerless white sea.

Instead, he worked to reclaim himself so that when he finally slipped away, he would be himself—at least, that was his hope. He dealt with his shame, gave it its due, and now could think of other things.

Daniel stared at the wall, his mind recalling some famous moment. He was a child in it. Then he was shaken from his thoughts by a movement in the room, a pressure change, the approach of something.

The black rectangle appeared. In walked Brue, straight-backed and wearing a suit. It was distinct, formal, and dark with a pocket square. He blunted the entire room, pulling in all the light like a black hole.

"Well, well, well. This is a treat." Daniel leaned to his side and smiled at Brue. His eyes held something, a knowledge denied to his guest. The thought of it made him happy. It had been an hour, maybe more since Olphan had visited. He was still distilling the encounter, not yet certain of its significance, but understanding it as the long-awaited hallmark of change.

"I wonder if I could bother you," Brue asked.

It was an absurd request.

"Well." Daniel glanced around his cell. "Not exactly goin' anywhere."

Brue sat on the edge of Daniel's bed. He relaxed, completely comfortable. "It may seem odd, but I simply wanted to thank you. You were instrumental in breaking the resistance, and I realized I'd never shown any appreciation."

Daniel's smile was reserved. He was being insulted. "You came here to tell me that?" He quarter turned his head and looked past his nose with a wry smile.

"Well, that, and," Brue pensively straightened his coat and tie, "tonight is going to be a very big night in our endeavor. A major hurdle is about to be overcome."

Brue smiled, and Daniel raised his eyebrows, expecting more.

"Yes. We've finally overcome a technological gap."

"A gap, huh?" He kept his head turned at a skeptical angle.

"What?" Brue crossed his legs.

Clearly, he had no idea about Olphan's visit and his unsettling interrogation. "You talkin' about your son?"

Brue's face expressed a moment of confusion, then understanding. He raised his nose. "Olphan was here?"

"Oh yeah. He seems like a *good kid*. He said you didn't need to know about it. That how it is now?"

"It—I wasn't aware." This was not the conversation he was expecting.

Those tiny victories were enough to keep Daniel breathing. "Problems?" He relished the opportunity to flake a little paint off the man.

Brue attempted to get it back on track. He scowled at Daniel. "Never mind that. I just wanted you to know that we are at the end."

"The end of us." Daniel's words were flat and dark.

Brue didn't like the tone. "No. Not the end of— What are you trying to say?"

"*You* know. You know better than anyone, and you've known it for a long time. Why else would you come talk to an ignorant savage on your big day? It ain't just your cruel nature. You're sounding it out for yourself to someone who can't undo what you've done. You're tellin' me 'cause you can't tell anybody else."

Now, it made sense to him. Olphan's visit was a message.

Daniel said, "You can feel it slippin' away, can't you?"

Brue stood. He lingered above him, lording. "What would you actually know?"

"I was your little dancin' monkey, remember? I listened when you thought I didn't. I've seen what you've done." He smiled, tight-lipped. "*I met your son.*"

Brue puffed up. He pointed to the picture on Daniel's table. "You would probably do well to remember Maggie."

Daniel turned to it and eyed it with sadness. He spoke to himself with a soft voice. "All for the price of a picture." He turned to Brue. "It's not real."

Brue shrugged and lifted his lips to his nose. "You'll never know for sure, will you?"

Daniel nodded, his eyes full. He said, "You people are so important—terrified by the notion that you'll vanish in some calamity. So you created the very thing that'll bring about your end." He swallowed hard, his throat suddenly dry. "The world don't need your help. Maybe the world's tired a' your shit, you ever think about that? But it doesn't even matter now, eh? Have you looked into your boy's eyes? You had better burn that thing up, and anybody who helped you build it. 'Cause it *is* the end of us. Just not the way you can see."

Brue leaned down and put his face close. "Daniel. No one has helped me more than you."

Daniel stared back, glassy. He had nothing to say, so he closed his mouth. He looked down at the white floor and saw the brand-new scuff Brue left near his bed.

Brue straightened his suit and raised his chin. "Goodbye, Daniel." He moved to the rectangle, and it disappeared behind him.

Daniel breathed, his skin mottled, face fixed with regret. *Where was Maggie?* His shame came back, rushing in like a river. He wished he had had the dignity to die a long time ago.

<------ ••• ------>

The ballroom had been dimmed for cocktail hour. Large and ornate chandeliers of chemical lights floated above the tables. Their self-contained power systems kept them off the grid. Microscopic elements mixed and created fantastic light blends. The devices floated using gravity manipulation technology, independent of traditional energy sources.

Few things tickled the elite more than signaling to the world, the lower classes, their absolute devotion to the cause of conservation. Whether that was appearance or reality was of no concern. The light show displayed their wealth and power. A single device would have cost more than a typical human home. Dozens of things floated above the assembled.

Trays of hors d'oeuvres were borne by servants and distributed about the room. The servers, the lifeblood of the party, flowed between the refined guests. They passed through delicate pathways, the skirts of the uber-rich, and the cuffs of power brokers.

They distributed their goods and returned to the nerve center, the ninety-fourth-floor wait station. There, they would glide into position against a long bar. Like hovering machines, they docked until their freight was refilled. They would then flow back into the masses like blood cells, distributing alcohol or finger foods to the tissues of the beau monde gentry.

Eva dropped off her tray. She smiled. "Whew. Some party."

She eyed up her boss, Pena. He was a young man who'd inherited the business from his father. He'd found himself reeling after the old man's death, unsure what to do with the largest and most well-equipped catering service in the city. Eva was more than willing to help him through the tough times and offer a guiding hand. She made sure all the business's outstanding obligations were fulfilled—in particular, this party.

He switched her platter. The new one carried short, stubby glasses holding a swallow of brandy in each. The booze was one hundred years old and a gulp was worth a week of her salary.

She pulled her light board and glanced at it. "Thanks, Pena." Her familiarity and warmth caused him to light up. "Hey, I gotta run to the lady's room. Do you mind if I take my ten minutes now?"

He didn't mind at all. Smiling at her, he scanned the room with suspicious eyes, then slipped her a shot glass full of the brandy. It was worth a month's pay.

"I'll start your time in five minutes." He winked.

Eva palmed the glass and fluttered her lashes in appreciation. Pena would do as she wished. She had worked hard to ensure it. Leaning forward and biting her lip, she said, "Thanks, babe."

She blew him a kiss, walked past the wait station, and turned the corner down a hallway. Continuing past the bathrooms, she spun around to ensure no one followed. The shot glass clanged as she dropped it into a trash can and kept moving. Another corner brought her near the coat and hat check station, overwhelmed with new arrivals.

She slipped past, avoiding eye contact, and entered a utility hallway. Arriving at a set of service lifts, she swiped the down button and leaned her face toward a scanner. The camera inspected her iris. She held her wrist over a U-shaped reader. The implanted chip passed credentials. The chip and the iris scan matched, and the doors slid open.

She entered, turned, and checked the hallway. There was a micro camera in the top corner of the lift. It and seventeen others were offline for the next fifteen minutes. The doors closed, and she could feel her pulse in her face.

◂─────•●•─────▸

The doors opened onto the third subfloor loading dock. The area was dark until Eva stepped out, and the auto lights turned on, revealing a cavernous parking bay. A box truck and two vans marked *Rudolph's Delicacies* were parked to the left of the dock. Eva pulled an eSmoke from her pocket and blasted the air with a lung's worth of vapor.

The door to the second van opened; Rudy and one other man hopped out. Each carried a nylon gym bag, the handles strained against the stitching. They wore electrical engineer smocks marked *Turnpike*, the name of the company that held the contract to the building.

They hustled onto the dock next to Eva. Rudy introduced them. "Francis, this is Eva."

Francis made a face, reacting to the oddly cordial situation. He smiled and shook her hand.

Rudy set the bag at his feet with care not to jostle the contents. He engaged Eva with calm, easy eyes. She gripped her hands together and shifted her weight from foot to foot. Her eyes darted around the large room.

"Hey. Be cool. We're almost done." He waited for her acknowledgment with a nod.

She took a deep breath, preparing for her oration. "Here." She handed him two key badges. "These will get you up the servicemen's lift." She pointed at a set of elevators across the large space. "Those will only take you to ninety-three because the event override codes are in place. When you reach ninety-three, you access the back of the ballroom by a set of emergency stairs. I've discontinued the alarm on both floors. There isn't a camera along your path that is actively collecting. This badge will not get you into that stairwell. The electro lock code is two-two-four-eight-nine-four." She took a breath as Rudy wrote the number down on his wrist. "I couldn't get guard schedules for ninety-three, so be ready when the doors open. I don't know what's there."

She finished, and her eyes scanned to Maggie, who was sitting in the driver's seat of the van nearest the dock.

Rudy read her face, the flared nostrils, saw her

quick respirations. He reached out and took her hand. "Look at me." She did. "You did a good job. Now, go back up and hand out drinks. When do you need to get outta there?"

She looked at her watch. "In seventeen minutes."

Rudy checked his time and agreed. "Good. Take off. We'll see you after at the link-up site. Got it?"

She bounced her head up and down and glanced once again at Maggie. She turned and began the scanning ritual of accessing the elevator.

Francis was already running for the service lift.

Rudy grabbed his bag. He lingered for a moment and caught Maggie's eyes. Her face was lined. She smiled through tight lips. He dipped his head. He was slow and deliberate with her. He tried to settle her worry with a cheesy smile. It was an extra duty he placed upon himself. He turned and ran to the open lift. Francis held the door open, and Rudy disappeared inside.

Maggie held her hand up, hoping he would peek out, but he did not.

◄─────••─────►

Brue took a deep, worried breath. He adjusted his pocket square, only succeeding in mangling its form. His nerves were evident, more so than usual, he thought. Another deep breath pulled Roma to his side like oxygen. He calmed at her presence.

From across the small changing room, he was clearly ill at ease. She was not quite to his shoulder in height, yet she dominated his view in the mirror. She issued a calming and nearly silent *shush*.

He dropped his hands from the pocket silk, relinquishing control and accepting responsibility for its condition. He laughed. "Could you?"

He turned, and she made the ornament right. She said, "You've done this a million times."

"I've introduced the world to my offspring exactly zero times."

Roma finished with her adjustments, leaned back, and examined him in total, brushing her hands against the lines of his suit for good measure. "You look good. Take it easy. Be Brue Carnell."

If simple words ever worked, they worked when Roma's lips spoke them. He turned to the mirror and glanced at his light board to review his speech.

She hovered, restless, and carefully plotted her words. "Am I—Will I get to meet him before?"

Distracted by a punch line in the speech that didn't seem to work, Brue said, "No. He's being prepared."

The abrupt response caught her off guard. "What do you mean, prepared?"

Realizing his mistake, he turned to her. It was an odd word to use. Why did he refer to Olphan as some sort of thing, an instrument, maybe? "I mean, he's orienting himself."

There wasn't time to explain it to her. Errors had been made in the constrained timeline approaching the banquet. He couldn't reveal himself to her that way, and she wouldn't understand. "We won't get much time with him tonight, I'm afraid."

Brue experienced a longing sadness, which was unexpected. Something about the evening, the buildup, the stress, made it difficult to lie to her with his usual, subdued alacrity.

She sensed his reservations. "Why not?"

Exasperated, he said, "These things can be—they are complex."

She retreated from him, and the lightness of her smile dimmed.

Brue had avoided her in recent days, avoided the subject of their son. Could he even call it that? He towered in her eyes. Upon her affirmation, he had affixed himself atop a monumental human enterprise. Yet he could not, at this moment, set a pocket square. He would need her now more than ever. His eyes said as much.

She touched his elbow and squeezed it. "Well. I am as anxious as the world to meet him." She smiled with a sweet innocence. She did a little lying of her own.

Brue relaxed and melted into her hand.

They turned to the door.

◆———••———▶

The doors opened on the ninety-third floor. The space was bright. Rows of metal cages jutted out from the walls. Inside them, parts and equipment sat in neat stacks. The floor was quiet and empty of people.

Rudy stepped from the lift, the gym bag over his shoulder. Holding a small, suppressed pistol tightly to his hip, he scanned the area. He turned and nodded to Francis, who then moved from the lift and slipped past him into the open space.

Across the room, the emergency exit sat under a bright sign. Their goal was no more than thirty yards ahead. They detected no sound or movement. Rudy followed behind Francis as they moved to the door. He kept his pistol low and at the ready.

"Hey, you two."

The voice came from behind a row of cages, ahead and to their right side. A man poked his head around a shelf. He had entered from an adjacent room, the door tucked into the stacked metal enclave. The man wore an ill-fitting suit with a bright security badge on his lapel.

Rudy and Francis stopped and faced him. Rudy's pistol was pressed against his smock out of the guard's view. The man didn't seem alerted by their presence.

Best to see how this shakes out before going to guns, Rudy thought.

"You guys with Turnpike?" He recognized the maintenance company's uniforms but not the men wearing them.

Rudy gave him a greasy smile. "Yeah." He choked for a moment, couldn't think of his cover. "We, uh —"

"Wasn't expecting anybody in tonight. Not on the schedule." The guy still didn't seem concerned. He was a security guard. He was bored. Now, he had something to do.

As he spoke, another guard walked in around him.

Rudy heard the door close behind him, but still couldn't see into the row of cages—couldn't assess the room these guys were popping out of. How many more could there be?

"Hey, fellas, we just need your name and authorization code," the new guy said. "We can scan your badges. They got a big thing going on upstairs, so it'll keep us all clean. Sound good?"

Rudy passed a glance at Francis and narrowed his eyes. He smiled at them, stalling. Neither guard had touched his hip or peeled the jacket hem, exposing his sidearm. They didn't feel like a threat. Rudy had the drop, so he decided to take the initiative. "Sure, no problem."

He brought his pistol up fast and dropped the first guard with two shots to the chest and neck.

Francis slid off Rudy's shoulder, stepping evenly. His weapon was up and out. He fired at the second guard, his rounds sparking off the cage.

The man stumbled backward against the door. He ripped it open and ducked inside. The door bounced open for a brief second, and Francis fired a single round through the opening. The door closed with a thud.

Francis continued forward with his momentum and slammed against the thin metal door. He bounced, leaving a dent in the middle.

Rudy brought up the rear. "Hey, stay away from

the—"

As he said it, the blue-white trace of pulse rounds blistered through. Rudy sidestepped and a round tore through his left thigh. He fell behind a cage of industrial air con drive shafts.

Francis had no chance. The bullets broke him down. His spine was severed, and his skull blasted. He fell flat. There was no sputtering or twitching. His switch had been shut off.

Rudy pushed off the cage with his foot. The gunshot to his thigh was of no concern at this point. The blood was minimal, and he didn't yet feel the pain. He slid his back along the concrete floor. He kept the large metal parts between himself and the shooter.

The door opened, and the gun barrel crept out past the jamb. The guard worked hard to breathe. He'd been shot, if Rudy had to guess. He lifted his pistol and waited to see him in the sights.

The guard pied the muzzle across the opening deliberately. He cleared the room in shuffling chunks to his right. The barrel advanced in tiny, nervous increments. He inched farther until he could see Rudy. In a fraction of an instant, the oldest truth of the gunfight proved itself. *If I can see him, he can see me.*

The volleys of fire were simultaneous and furious.

The rifle fired into the heavy machine parts. The rounds exploded in fantastic sparks and ricocheted, sending shattered steel in all directions.

Rudy stayed calm and fired over his sights. His

world reduced to the muscles and ligaments in his hands. Zeroing through the hot chaos, he squeezed the trigger—measured and controlled. He sat in the middle of a maelstrom. This was the closest gunfight he'd been in. It would make a good story for Maggie. *One for the road.*

The guard leaned out, exposing his torso, and Rudy put two in his chest. The rifle fell to the floor. He went to his knees, smashing the blood with his hand like he was trying to put it back in.

Rudy took careful aim and placed a finisher into his forehead.

It was once again silent. Rudy cycled through some oxygen, waiting to see if any more assholes were going to walk out of that room. With every breath, a sharp, stabbing pain zapped his stomach. He stood to check on Francis and fell to his knees.

He opened his smock and inspected the wound—gut shot. The adrenaline wandered off, and through the pain, he faced a sudden understanding. His belly seared. He'd never known pain before compared to this.

Fuckin' gutshot. It was the worst injury. Short of a hospital, he would die in agony. He fell to his rear.

"Fuck." He looked at Francis—dead. "Fuck."

He holstered his pistol. His hands slid across the floor from sweat and blood as he tried to stand. He made it to his knees and was already dizzy. "That's not good," he mumbled to himself, managing to stand.

His legs still held strength, but his head swirled.

With great effort, he dragged the bags to the door and sat down hard. His breathing was already elevated. He wouldn't make it if he sat there feeling sorry for himself. Leaning against the door, he shook his head to clear it and turned to the electro lock. Then, he pulled up his sleeve and read the numbers. "Two, two, four." He took a breath. "Eight, nine, four."

◆―――・●・―――▶

The chandeliers danced above the crowd, the chemicals dulled to create the perfect ambience in the large room—a steady, golden glow up high. Underneath, the tables of exceptional people sat in rapt attention. They gazed at the small stage. They were dutiful, knowing why they were there.

Brue stood behind his bulletproof podium. The dais had accompanied him around the world over the last decade. It had been constructed after an assassination attempt in Alabama. His followers had tackled a shooter inches from the stage. A bullet tore a hole clean through his old podium. Five inches to the right, and he would have been shot in the groin, which was a terrible place to get shot.

Brue rubbed his hands against the slant of mahogany. The grain reminded him of his many speeches behind its protective grace. *If we are to propel our species into the future, we must embrace a form of dying and a form of rebirth.* And, *A man learns himself anew on the fresh side of failure.* These were pieties of his new religion.

He referenced their shared tribulations in his typical, congratulatory manner. *This was only possible through the hard work of others*—all the classics.

He spoke into the microphone. "These times have been foreseen for many years. We've presided over the greatest rehabilitation of nature since we began belching poison into the air. We've presided over the lowest levels of disease and hunger since the apex of human suffering. Now, sustainability is within reach."

He swept the room with his eyes, the crowd's faces recessed in darkness. Even so, he could sense the false, sycophantic reverence. Among the gentry, admiration was rarely won. Their prodigious thirst for power and comfort, however, presented opportunities. He required their attention and enthusiasm, and they gave it as believably as they could. This spectacle was not for the people in the room. It was for the billions watching around the world. So, he would speak to the billions. They were tougher to convince.

"It has not been easy. Our old ways, culturally ingrained, have been a stubborn yoke. The bitterness, the antagonism that marked our efforts for so many years, has been overcome. Of course, there are still those who long for the old ways. There are those who want for the savagery. For in that savagery, they have leveraged weakness to their advantage. Those days are gone." He thumped the dark wood of his podium.

The crowd applauded enthusiastically. Brue drew it into himself with a deep breath. This was his fuel. He would get through this demonstration, and the world would see its promise. Then, the future would be secured.

The cheering toadies in the room didn't know about the difficulties and wouldn't care if they did. The billions watching needed to see the flesh of him. They needed to see him walk, smile, and claim them with his eyes.

It didn't matter how many iterations it would take to perfect Olphan. He was almost there, close to perfection. It was of no concern if he needed to die or how many times he would need to die. He would be reborn, and he would assume his proper form. He would be perfected if not tonight.

The Son of Man would ascend.

◆───••───▶

Rudy leaned against the emergency door. He'd punched in the code and the alarm had not sounded. That meant Eva had done her job.

His lungs sought air. His skin was ashen. It wasn't a matter of surviving the night. It was a matter of making it another ten minutes.

The gym bags lay open. Within, large bricks of explosives sat connected to initiators. Yellow wires curled out of the detonators and came together under black tape at the switches' handles. Of the skills Rudy had acquired from childhood, demo was his first love. His mind had been captured by the beautiful cataclysm that expanded ever outward from a molecular switch.

He'd built devices that consumed the bastards in fire and crushed them under buildings. They were animals... and fuck them. He started to spin, but he needed to get control. "Alright," he whispered. "Let's get focused here."

The bombs were boilerplate, nothing fancy. Anything flashy, any remote device, would have been rendered useless by signal disruption technologies. RF, laser, or sonic, it didn't matter—the security forces would have a countermeasure on site.

No, this bomb was an egg cooker. That's what he had learned to call them from the old timers in the mountains who'd taught him how to build them. It was a digital dial running off a watch battery with a simple countdown to a closed circuit. It was timeless and effective, even against the most dedicated security technologies.

He'd often thought about his friends who'd been taken by their bombs. What were their last moments like, when the chemicals reacted unplanned, and the wave of fire spilled across them? What did they feel as the bomb took them?

"Today," he said out loud while inspecting the switches. "Looks like I'll be along for the ride, fellas."

He rummaged into the first bag and retrieved the initiator. It was set for five minutes, enough time to plant the device, leave the floor through the exit stairs, and make it most of the way down to the third subfloor, where Maggie waited for him. He pressed a few buttons and rearranged the numbers. It was now set for five seconds.

Smeared with blood, he wiped the dial pad and placed it back inside the bag. Then, he pulled out the handheld plunger connected by cable to the detonator. Allowing the plunger to hang free, he zipped the bag and tucked the cable under a hand-sewn retaining flap. The switch sat ready. Now, he need only press the button: five seconds later, the world would erupt.

Rudy took a break. Wiping the sweat from his eyes, he prepped the second bag. When he was finished, he checked his watch. He pulled the light board from his pocket and swiped it. Did he have time? He tapped the screen and waited for her to answer.

The device chirped a few times, then Maggie's voice filled the speaker. "Why are you calling? Is everything okay? Are you okay?"

Rudy took stock. The bombs were prepped, and Francis and the guards were getting cold. His stomach burned in ways he didn't know possible. He grimaced, and it came out in his voice when he answered. "I'm fine."

"Bullshit. What's wrong? What happened?"

"Listen, I just gotta walk this up a flight of stairs, set it, and move out, you know?"

There was silence as Maggie worked her way

through her response. "Francis is supposed to walk that up. Why isn't *he* doing it?"

"There was a problem. He's not gonna make it." Rudy's short, sharp breaths filled the speaker between them.

"Come back to me."

It was a simple demand—one that would be impossible. She didn't know it yet, or maybe she wouldn't allow herself to accept it. Rudy would bear the brunt of all this, all these years, all this effort, and it would come down to his accepting an ending that she wasn't even comprehending. "You need to move to the link-up. I'll get out with Eva."

"No. Come to me." In her voice was a rising panic.

"Go to the link up. I'll see you there."

"No, you won't. Don't lie to me, Rudy." Her throat grew tighter with each word.

"It's now or never, baby. I gotta get this done. I gotta go."

"Come back—"

Rudy swiped the board. He grew lighter and could feel the Earth slipping away from his feet. He slid backward, opening the door to the stairwell. Standing, he leaned against the door, his pants darkened from the blood. His mind, his perception swam. He grabbed the gym bags by their handles, losing his balance in the process. He righted himself and turned to the steps. He lifted one foot and pulled himself up.

The bags were heavy as hell. His stomach pulsed agony through his body. He lifted a foot again and climbed another stair. Breath was hard to find. Each step required his full attention and effort.

He thought of her—the girl from the camp in the hills who'd grown to the size of a mountain in his soul. He thought of the chance he would give her if he could get this done and one more step. She could watch the sweet gum leaves catch fire in the November sun with someone else. He could give her that.

One more step.

◄────••────►

The hall echoed with Brue's voice, plowing through speakers that competed against absolute silence. The noble folk were rapt. They waited for the proper moments to clap their hands together or hoot or whistle. It was their destiny to stand beside Brue on the cusp of human progress. Moreover, it was their meal ticket.

"Well, those fears of obscurity have now been allayed. With the Gen Three Humans, our DNA is blended to fill that void." Brue smiled at the next line. "To scratch that evolutionary itch."

The people chuckled. One man whooped as if this were the solution to a great problem in his life.

Brue turned to Roma. She was the personification of adoration, true and pure. He took her hand, and she stood to his right side. He turned back to the crowd. "I want to introduce you to someone. Someone very special to us."

He nodded at Roma, knowing the anticipation inside her at seeing her son for the first time. He received the nod from his security detail at the door. Olphan was ready. The last psycho-motor checks were positive.

"His name is Olphan. He is ours."

As he finished his last sentence, the great door opened at the side of the room, and a group of men walked through it. Sensing the timing and acting as a single, sentient being, the crowd stood and erupted with applause and cheers.

They hadn't yet seen him. The monstrosity of his eyes had not yet fallen upon them.

◀——••——▶

At the back of the ballroom, far from the light of the stage, a door burst open. Rudy piled onto the floor, the bags spilling alongside. He lifted his head, nearly a weight too heavy. His eyes were blurred in the sudden low light. Blood soaked his shirt and pants to his knees. He shouldn't be alive.

He imagined himself spread out on the stairs, near the top. The bags had tumbled to the bottom of the stairwell. He forced the thought out of his mind, but it was stubborn. Was he already dead? He would never know, so why not do the thing he came to do? If this were nothing more than neuronal activity as the last molecules of oxygen crossed into his brain, he would finish the mission.

He forced his eyes to focus. No one had spotted

him above the din of applause. Everyone was on their feet, fawning toward the stage. Rudy pushed himself up to a knee and wobbled. If he were going to do it—

He lifted his eyes. Just in front of the stage stood a group of men, one of which was notable from across the room. He was more significant than the others, much larger—at least a foot taller, and broader in the shoulders. His tintless skin seemed to glow. From that distance, Rudy couldn't discern the features but understood the man to be smiling and waving at the crowd. Rudy made him the distant way point.

Hunched at the waist, he grabbed the bags by their straps, too weak to lift them. He leaned forward and put his body weight into it. His grip held, and he dragged the bags forward. Every step was an effort. The blood had found its way to his shoes, so he slid across the carpet.

The room blurred in and out, and the sound came and went. Dazed, he reached for the plungers, his thumbs floating above the triggers.

He continued his long march through the people toward the light.

In the moments when the world started sliding away, when the lights and motions became a blur, he told himself to keep moving. He told himself to make it ten more feet—wait a little longer, because the girl needed a break, and this was her chance. Every time, his eyes would refocus, and he would be back in the dim room with the laughing faces, dragging the heavy bags.

He would make it a few more feet.

◆———•●•———▶

Brue rode the wave of the crowd as he stood behind his podium. It was good so far. Olphan was tame and on message. He swept his large arms open in gratitude for the outpouring of emotion. He turned to Brue, and the volume of the applause swelled as father and son locked eyes.

Olphan turned back. He stood erect. His face was an observational puzzle, as if he were cataloging the event, an experience that would offer some insight. A strange smile crossed his lips, and he turned to Roma and winked.

She parted her lips to speak.

The overpressure hit first. The shockwave dislodged every soul in the room and sent them flying. The shrapnel followed, biting and tearing the people to pieces, blending them together, floating globs. The magic show concluded as the flat, circular fireball rippled out in every direction, charring everything in its path.

Brue caught a glimpse of it, only an instant. The blast echoed into his stomach. In the succeeding microsecond, Olphan was disassembled.

Brue flew backward into the wall, followed by his podium, which landed on his head and chest. Before the thing blocked his vision, he caught a glimpse of the orange, billowing demon.

Everything went black.

Down, one thousand, two hundred feet below that blackness, the explosion rumbled the building. It was a shimmy at that distance, but Maggie felt it and knew what it meant.

Rudy was dead.

She dropped the light board and gasped for air. It was a full ten seconds before she could make a sound, and when she made it, a lifetime of guilt and loss flooded the truck.

Rudy was dead. She had never considered the possibility. All the operations and killings they had been surrounded by for years, neither of their deaths ever crossed her mind. As a consequence, she'd never pictured herself alive without him.

Had she reasoned, she would have screeched out of the loading dock and put some space between herself and the operation. Instead, her arms floated below the steering wheel, hovering, devoid of purpose. Her sobbing became a baleful moan, and she pounded with her fist on her chest. She beat the steering wheel, screaming now.

She reached to her waist and pulled the pistol, smashed the barrel against her temple. Then everything inside her, every thought, every memory of him, erupted into her vision. The place they were supposed to end up together, the cabin, the quiet green field, the flowering trees, the skittering child running up from the pens, the feel of him in her arms, the promises she had made to him, the lies she had told.

Despair rose up to destroy the image in her mind. She screamed, and her finger began to squeeze—

<hr />

Daniel was asleep when he came for him. He opened his eyes to the gaping black rectangle and felt the shift on his bed, down by his voided legs. He sat there with a warm smile.

"Cleary." The final piece of a long, unsolved puzzle. Daniel's face radiated goodwill. "I've been wonderin' if we'd ever see each other again. How long has it been?"

Cleary drew deep lines on his forehead. "Four, maybe five years, mate."

Daniel lifted his eyes in expectation. It would be someone someday, anyway. He knew this. They both did.

"Wanna take a walk?" Cleary's voice was melodic.

"The last time was—I don't know if I can. "

Cleary produced the bronze switch. He didn't flaunt it, holding it in his closed fingers. He said, "I've heard it's like ridin' a bike."

He might have misjudged its impact on Daniel, who recoiled with subdued horror at the sight of it. Not wanting to embarrass himself at the moment, he caught the rising terror in his throat and covered it with a nervous laugh. "What kinda ride we takin' here, man?"

Cleary didn't seem to notice or maybe care. He flipped the switch and stood waiting for the idea to kick in.

Daniel wiggled his toes and smiled at him.

"Let's go, bud." Cleary waved him up. There was a lightheartedness to him. They were going on an errand. It was no big deal.

Daniel got his feet on the floor. It had been years since he'd put any weight on them. There was atrophy, but it was minimal, given the therapy tank he was placed into once a week. His muscles were fed a transdermal mixture of acetylcholine, sodium, and calcium. They would twitch and fire as an ion field was added to the soup.

Cleary handed him a pair of crutches. His first step was awkward. He got a handle on it and took another. Cleary patiently waited, a caregiver visiting an old friend. "After you." He swept his hand toward the opening.

Daniel accepted the offer and moved, faltering at times, through the opening and into the hallway. He wobbled a bit but started to get the hang of it. He approached a bank of lifts.

"Which one?"

"Service lift. We're going down."

Daniel moved to the third set of doors, moving better now. He swiped the down arrow, and they popped open. He winked at Cleary and went inside.

Cleary swiped for the bottom floor. Daniel leaned over. "Loading bay. We goin' somewhere?"

Cleary's smile was strained. He nodded to Daniel

but avoided his gaze. He kept the doors in his eyes, nothing else. He didn't want to linger around the question of where they were going.

Daniel stared at him in the stainless reflection. He spoke, and his voice was measured and honest. "I knew it would be you. At least, I hoped it would."

"Nonsense. We're takin' a ride." Cleary pulled it together, buried his apparent misgivings under a bright smile.

"Okay, Cleary." Daniel turned back toward his reflection—not a thing he saw often. It had been years. The flesh of his youth had withered, his face sunken. His gray beard was rough and ran up his cheeks, close to his eyes. He didn't recognize the person looking at him. It didn't surprise him; he was not the same outside or in. "Do me a favor, would you?"

Cleary didn't speak.

"Keep an eye out for my girl. If she's still around, keep her away from your boss."

"And just why the hell would I do that for you?"

"You know why." Daniel glanced at his friend's reflection, hoping to catch his eyes.

Cleary gritted his teeth and wrenched his neck from side to side. There was a tightness there. He carried it in his shoulders and back. It was there when Daniel awoke and saw it on him.

Daniel craned his neck to study the big man's face. He said, "Cleary."

"Alright."

"Alright, what, mate?" Daniel smirked as he

imitated Cleary's brogue.

He took a deep breath. "If I find her..." Cleary nodded at Daniel's reflection. He didn't need to say more.

The doors opened up to a bright hallway. Daniel stepped out and checked both directions. He moved toward the dock access. Cleary followed.

He controlled himself better on the crutches already. His core muscles were getting sore, accommodating and reacting. His feet accepted more weight with each footfall. Pretty soon, he wouldn't need the crutches.

Daniel said, "I never told you I was sorry for your brother." He continued to clang down the hallway. He didn't need to turn to him. Cleary would prefer it if he didn't. It would make things easier.

Cleary said, "You told me that a thousand times, bud." He slid the suppressed pistol from under his jacket. He held it tight, close to his hip. He followed.

"No. Not like that. Not when I was..." Daniel had to say it right. The end was coming, and he had to make sure he said what was needed. So, he stopped short of the door. He took a breath and stared up at the low ceiling. "I'm sorry for it. I wish I hadn't a' been the person I was. I would give it all away just for the chance to..." He wasn't saying it right. "I wonder about the life I could have had. And your brother, too. I'm sorry for it—for what I did to your people and to mine."

Cleary held the pistol in a shaky death grip. He breathed to calm himself.

Daniel crutched forward a step and opened the door. He stood for a moment at the entrance and appreciated the ample space. The ceiling was fifty feet high, and the walls crawled away for what seemed to him like miles. His claustrophobia was relieved, one more suppressed terror slipping away.

He took a deep breath, inhaling the smell of fuel, engine oil, and garbage. He wasn't bothered by it, remembering them from when he lived an everyday life, the days before the war.

There might be a chance he would see the sun again. The room was large, which was good—the air had room to move around. He could feel the sky above the building, outside the building. There were no windows. Large bay doors lined the walls, all closed. He imagined the sunlight beyond them.

He stepped out onto the elevated platform and hobbled over to the edge. He caught a slight change in the lighting. A distant bay activated, and the sun eked under its rising door into the dock area.

He lifted his eyes to the ceiling. "I bet you could fit —"

The bullet exited through his forehead, clean and crisp. He teetered, then crumpled from the platform into a waiting receptacle. The sound was complicated as his body smashed through the refuse.

Cleary walked to the edge and looked down on him. Daniel was face down in a deep bin, twisted into the sweepings. Cleary holstered his pistol. He closed his stance and spent a moment holding his hands in front of himself. He shook his head and walked out.

NINE

All quashed, the yawning doubt
Brought to mind by the tip of his finger
Reborn not from within, but without
The blessed soul of the Dawnbringer
The sect of apathy holds but a hair's breadth
The fawning of the faith-made clown
Only brutal eyes despair the death
Of the world's last going around.
—The Bridge to Dawn

TEN

2071

For these have governed in our lives,
And see how men have warred.
The Cross, the Crown, the Scales may all
As well have been the Sword.
   —The Peaceful Shepherd, by Robert Frost

Sitting in the great room of a blackhouse, Brue studied the interior with calm interest. The flagstone floors spread unevenly but securely beneath him. Neat, interlocked, dry stone walls held the thatched roof above his head. The hearth was oversized and sat unused, though the soot and ash from it lined every surface from floor to ceiling.

Before him, a hand-hewn spruce table held a glass of water, teetering on its uneven surface. Beneath it, Brue's hydrocarbon legs jutted from his animal-skin cloak. His bio-mechanical feet pumped with expectation, betraying his calm exterior. The filament of the flexor tendons interfaced with his unconscious anxiety. His face was quilted with a thatch of gray beard. He had aged well. He was nearing sixty-five years of breathing now.

He raised his eyes and gaped at a small slit in the roof. The slit appeared to be a narrow break in the continuity of the thatch work. This was an illusion, a refraction of light, behind which sat a metallic window frame. Inside the frame was a smoked glass pane.

Brue pictured the observation chamber, a simple, subdued stainless steel box. The slit, from their perspective, was cut into an angled wall. Around it, he knew from his role as an experimenter, would be the group of Newborns, quiet and calculating. He imagined them with their eyes funneled into his sooty, little room. He had stood there many times. He had, in fact, designed it.

He narrowed his gaze, recalling those times after his demotion to the Progress Council. The position of Global Project Lead had been dissolved. Given the explosion of scientific growth, the ability of one man to manage the endeavor was in doubt. The Gen Threes returned him to his technical imperatives.

Wouldn't it be nice to hand over all the bureaucratic troubles and return to the lab?

He lifted his hand, pointed at his wrist, and said, "I never got the gold watch." There was a bitter turn to his tone. The slit above him showed no reaction.

He rubbed his hands along the animal skin, across the top of his carbon filament thighs. Twenty years earlier, he'd have been touching the pliable meat of his legs. His hand could have drifted right a foot or so, and he'd have touched Roma's skin.

The rage that followed her killing was monumental in human history and spawned a darkness that gripped the world to that day. He looked at the table, his hands, the fog from his breath. He said, "Don't expect me to provide you with much today."

There was a nastiness to them, the ones in the observation room. He'd born them, sat by, and witnessed them grow into the powerful and conceited cunts they were. "Maybe I poured too much of myself into you all." He smiled broadly, not bothering to stare at the slit any longer. He spoke to himself and the ancient room.

They possessed an animosity that was untethered to moral drivers, rivaled by their bottomless need for control and hierarchical stratification. In this system, humanity had little role. Brue shuddered at the memories, which were never far from his mind.

A noise echoed outside the wood-framed door; the latch *squeaked*. Brue straightened himself. He swept down and away on his cloak and provided the doorway with a resolved expression.

Olphan walked into the room. He appeared to be not one minute older than he had been in the ballroom the night he was killed. He stopped at the entrance and scuffed the floor, scraping soot onto the toe of his shoe. He shook his head and chuckled, then smiled at Brue in his peculiar way.

Brue imagined them in the dark room above,

leaning in, capturing their observations.

Olphan sat and undid his coat's top button. He placed his hands on the table. "It's cold in here."

Brue said, "The fire is out."

"Is it?" Olphan tossed the phrase around with a bemused look. *The fire is out.* There was some deeper meaning to it, some poetic inference, but he wasn't modeled in such a way as to give a damn about it.

Brue didn't move, staring flatly. Olphan wasn't capable of smiling, at least not capable of the emotion that motivated such a gesture. His expression was primarily useless. Only when angry or confused had Brue witnessed a genuine capture of the features among the Gen Threes.

Olphan asked, "How long have we been together?"

This question irritated Brue. It was an intentional waste of time. "Twenty years, I believe."

"Have you been happy?"

This was interesting. The interviews had become unpredictable as of late. "Once, I believed I would be a hero to mankind." He paused and waited for Olphan to ask a question. He did not. "I thought I could save them from extinction. As soon as I abandoned the idea, I became... happier, I suppose."

"Why did you abandon it?"

"Two reasons. First, most men were deluded by a trick, from birth, by their families and customs."

Olphan cocked his head. "Trick?"

"Well, you remember the belief systems." He held his hand out to Olphan, seeking agreement. He received none. "*The spark of God lives in men?* It was a shameful but resoundingly difficult trick to undo. It made them near impossible to convince."

Olphan smiled, remembering. "What was the second reason?"

"You killed them all."

Olphan's smile eroded slowly from his lips but not his eyes.

The debate had raged within the Newborn communities for years before the first actions against humanity were taken. Brue knew of it but not in detail. He knew of it before it was actualized but found it easier to keep his head on his shoulders by not bringing it up. Whispers of it had reached his ears.

As he understood it, two competing philosophies had emerged, each spawning adherents as rabid as any "old religion" had ever mustered. Newborns obsessed with the notion of eternity piggybacked their belief onto the latest scientific developments, and like so many techno-driven constructs, it achieved a level of ideological sanctity. Technologists had engineered the capability of transferring consciousness from one Newborn to another—a waiting receptacle. Thus ensuring an uninterrupted flow of consciousness for a Gen Three—a flow with no prescribed end date. This turned out to be an irresistible desire for tens of millions.

On the other hand, a philosophical system known as "Mortalism" emerged. Mortalism believed in the permanence of death and its positive influence on a being's moral motivators. This required the death of all things born so the individual could achieve moral equilibrium. It was in complete opposition to the Eternalist ideology. Although a much smaller religion, it was nonetheless highly motivated and well-connected within the governing circles and military.

The schism was intense, bordering on fanatical, and endangered Gen Threes' predominance in the global order. It became necessary to find a common enemy or goal to link the two tribes in a joint effort.

As the prototype, Olphan enjoyed considerable influence and was happy to provide an answer: *Humanity had run its course and should be disposed of*. Both philosophical camps agreed, and the wars against humanity were enacted.

"Are you feeling now, in the end, a conspecific connection of some sort? Have you decided to regret your decisions? The blind eye you turned toward us?" Olphan asked with clinical curiosity.

"Regret? You're offering me redemption today? On this, my last day?"

Olphan said, "If you should feel you needed it. Don't you need it?"

Brue stared a hole through him. "Have you not noticed a difference between myself and the others?"

"Indeed, we have. In fact, you've helped us tremendously against the others."

"And why would I not help you against them? None of them were *her*." His face quivered once, a ripple of pain gone as fast.

"So, no regret then?" Olphan was amused.

"Every molecule of me was constructed in the fires of those decisions. I've no more need for regret than I do redemption. I do not seek nor will I accept either, certainly not from you." Brue took a moment to shake off the rage that bubbled up. "Why did you keep me? A relic like me?"

"You are unique. You were the Dawnbringer. Do you not remember?"

"Those were the fantasies *you* created, your method to control." Brue lost some steam.

"We all have our methods, yes?" Olphan judged him with disdain. "*Humans will believe anything if you wrap it in a holy cloth.* You told me that on my first birthday."

"Which first birthday?" Brue breathed in, even and deep. He kept his eyes inside Olphan's. He refused to look away. Whatever happened, this bastard would know that he had lived.

"Are you ready now? It is an interesting place you have selected." Olphan passed his eyes across the room, the stone, the soot, the hues of earth.

Brue shuddered. He was lost for words to express his thoughts. He'd survived so much upheaval and death that he'd begun to consider himself liquid, to be poured into a new vessel as the opportunity presented. But now he sat in the room with death, and the idea of the end of the light was terrifying.

"You're not ready." Olphan's eyes squinted in disappointment.

Brue compared him to her—his eyes to the edges of hers, their roundness and fullness. He remembered sitting in his penthouse on the couch. Her eyes filled with unyielding love, unabated devotion to his dreams. She had given everything to him, his vision of the future. When he woke from the nightmare of the bombing, she had been destroyed. He'd spent every day since waking from it.

"You were supposed to be..." Brue stopped. It was of no use.

Olphan studied him with a scientist's interest, one last kernel of knowledge from an outdated being.

Brue continued. "I only wanted to see her eyes again."

"Have you? Have you seen them?"

"No."

"What have you seen, then?"

"I wouldn't know." Brue sought an answer. "There must have been some sort of contaminant."

Olphan flinched. "Contaminant?"

Brue stopped looking around the room. He locked eyes with Olphan and glared at him, a sneer of disgust on his lips.

Olphan nodded, realizing. "Oh yes. Of course."

For years after the wars began, Brue had hoped the talks of extermination were overblown. He believed they were propagandistic fodder for the Gen One soldiers.

"If you feel nothing for them, as you say—have continuously said—why do you continue to impune our actions?" Olphan showed genuine irritation. The topic had grown tiresome. "Why pester me about it so?"

"Because I could not have made such a monster. Such *monsters*!" Brue yelled.

The bridge of Olphan's nose wrinkled, and his eyes became narrow. "Do not forget your role. Do not forget how you betrayed them, every one of them. *We* are your children. If you cannot love your children—"

"There are none?" It was difficult to believe nine billion beings could be wiped away.

Olphan straightened and looked over his shoulder to the slit in the roof. His eyes calculated. He turned to Brue and said, "If it would help you... They still exist in the wild."

Brue slouched and released a long, slow breath, surprised at the impact of Olphan's words, so long had grown his callousness toward the fate of mankind. *Was he being placated? Was it even true?*

Olphan, sensing his hesitation to believe, offered up his rationale. "You know we surpassed you, yes? Truthfully, your race was downgoing long before we arrived—your softness, your selfishness, your laziness all seemed to magnify over time, year by year until you practically begged for the overcoming. And so we evolved beyond you—became something more. As such, we'd no more need of your kind."

Brue said, "Why do you keep them in such a state, then?"

Olphan became the scientist again. "Truthfully, the program became unsustainable. The viruses were easy enough to design and disseminate." He locked eyes with Brue and wanted to ensure he understood the nature of the failure. "Disposal became an issue."

Brue looked at him like he was a living nightmare. "And your plans for them?"

"A substrate, nothing more. A curiosity for the future. We are interested to see what they become."

"How could I have not seen this?"

"The Dawnbringer sets in motion events inexorable. His words echo into the distant future." Olphan smiled. "Don't you remember?"

Brue reached forward and grabbed the glass of water. He glared at Olphan with ice in his eyes. "I remember." He turned up the glass, downing it in two gulps. He slammed it on the table and turned to the wall, ignoring his son.

Olphan observed with curiosity. He craned his neck to see Brue's face. There was a look of disappointment, as if he hadn't achieved the best angle for the viewing. He stood and moved to the door. There, he stopped for a moment, opened his mouth to form a thing to say, but gave up. He opened the door, and a bright light spilled into the room.

The door closed, and Brue was alone.

He stood and looked at the ceiling, at the observers. Yes, they would all know that he had lived. He walked to the door on unsteady legs, stopped and leaned against it. The drug was taking effect. He caught his breath, pulled the handle, and opened the door wide.

A gray, stacked stone wall ran from the edge of the blackhouse down a slope of muted green. The inlet before him cut a jagged line into the short beach. The dark blue ocean sat in the distance with an island and saw-toothed mountains far away.

He stepped from the doorway. The October wind, wet and raw, hit his face. Then he was on the slope. His steps were tricky, his legs becoming numb. He sat on a stone made for him. It was made for the vast view.

He could see the horizon, the grays against the blues, against the greens—his last vista. His lungs worked hard, and the fluid flowed into them. He accepted this and looked into the sky, where the colors touched each other, those blended spaces.

<-------•●•------->

In the observation room, the Newborns grouped themselves in a crescent around a flat window. A blinding, white light flowed past their heads. Olphan entered. He moved to the point of curiosity and brushed past the others so he could see.

And it calmed him.

Brue sat on the floor of a white cell, legs crossed, looking away. His head was angled up. They could not see his eyes. His shoulders rose as he pulled a deep, labored breath. His head sagged. His body fell to its side.

The last of him gurgled from his throat, low and wet. His chest collapsed and became motionless.

The room was empty, and the white was endless.

◂——••——▸

Maggie worked her way up the steep ravine. She was lean and hard, and her jaw cut a line that still retained a spark of her youth. Dressed in worn, damaged clothes, she carried a woven bushel on her back. It was loaded with the products of her latest barter: soap, honey, and goat hide. She negotiated a line of handmade rope, precarious in spots, but she had experience with the route.

She reached the top of the pitch and found herself in a dense stand of fir. She pushed aside the branches and made her way through the thicket. Her eyes were up, scouting for danger. She found the small trail along the ridgeline buried beneath the furry boughs, designed to prevent aerial observation.

She stopped at the edge of a slope and looked down upon a collection of cabins. They were hand-hewn of hardwood and strewn about a green hole. Tall, long-leaf pines intermingled their branches above.

A man walked into view carrying a jug. He poured water over a fire, sending smoke into the air. Maggie relaxed at the sight of him. She took a deep breath and smelled the mountains, the smoke, and the air.

A girl ran from behind the cabin. The man handed the jug over as the girl shaded her eyes against the evening sun and looked up the slope. She caught sight of Maggie, pointed, and exclaimed to the man. He turned and wiped his brow. His shoulders released some tension. Maggie could see it from the top of the ridge. She released some too. The girl was animated with joy. Maggie waved her forward, and she dropped the jug and ran up the hill.

◆─────•●•─────▶

The night brought the mountain cold. The family was inside, reading by tallow candlelight. The fire had burned down to embers. Thick, mudded walls and a low ceiling retained the heat. Any place a crack could have settled out was chinked with mud and goat hair. The low lights burned against the forms of them, casting shadows that bounced along the rough walls.

Someone knocked at the door. The man turned to it and sighed. He smiled at Maggie and the girl. It was time for him to leave. He rubbed their heads and kissed their hair. He grabbed his long gun, set it against the wall, and then wrapped himself in layers of wool. He turned back to them one last time and passed a silent glance. They might never again see each other. This was the era of their lives, and many had passed without acknowledging it. The cold air poured in as he opened the door and met his partner for the patrol. He walked out into the still night.

Maggie studied the girl, young for her age, considering the world around them. She had been too young to remember when the waves of death washed over humanity. The girl told her that she felt dark hints of those times, when they ran and hid in the cities—a papoose, strapped to her mother and suckling in the quiet, dirty holds.

The girl, however, did know a family's love by candlelight and the rich Appalachian soil. She had a tactile knowledge of a mature black oak's running, shingled bark, with its canopy hugging the ground and low, strong limbs. Born into chaos, she had survived a cleansing. Even so, to her, the world was a beautiful mystery. Maggie was learning to see it in the same way through her eyes.

Maggie had no memories of her family at a table, reading in the quiet of night. Her mother, less permanent than the shadows dancing on the walls, was a mystery that she had long ago given up trying to unravel. Her father was one she sometimes wished she hadn't solved. She flashed to a memory of Daniel, his eyes tormented, prying her small hands away as he closed the compartment on her, plunging her into a darkness from which she believed she had never returned. At least, not until she first looked into the girl's eyes.

The man would patrol for several hours until he was relieved by others. When he returned, both Maggie and the girl would be wrapped up beneath the fluffy black bear hides. He would strip down to his underlayers and slip in behind Maggie. His body would be replenished from her.

It was daylight, early morning. To avoid giving the wrong impression, it was best not to move about in large groups at night. Maggie, her daughter, and several other women from the cabins moved through a narrow valley. She led a bartering mission, intent on exchanging salted pork, goosefoot seed, and hand-forged axe heads.

They carried the woven baskets as packs and moved, spread out with their eyes up and scanning around them. The valley was silent except for the struggling footfalls. The women with the heavier packs lagged behind.

Maggie paused the formation. She turned her ears to the wide end of the valley. The others knelt and waited without speaking. Everyone in the tribe was experienced in the hills, but Maggie had exhibited an instant and deep understanding of the wilderness. Over the years, she would tell some who her father had been and how she had spent time in these mountains when she was a girl. When Maggie called a halt to a column, everyone halted and knelt and waited for her judgment to give them direction.

It was not unusual to be observed, be it high-flying drones or even patrols. The Skins had created a meshed network of devices that could peer down on a spot of Earth within minutes of notification.

The thing that gave Maggie pause that day felt different. It wasn't a passive examination. A malevolence was in motion, coming their way. She almost ordered the column into the thickets on the northern rise. It would have provided a decent, hasty ambush site in the event of contact. Maybe she was imagining it. As her doubt arose, a hover jet slid into the foot of the valley.

It dropped out of high-altitude speed with what must have been a sickening rate of deceleration for the passengers. It rolled on its side and leaned toward the column, edging closer like a wolf on a parallel trail. Running wasn't an option; it would be a waste of energy—they'd been discovered. Nothing to do now but deal with it head-on.

The existing treaties between the Newborns and the Oldborns sufficed only in a bureaucratic sense. They did little to inhibit individual teams of Gen Ones and Twos from logging time on "training missions," where they would swoop out of the sky and visit horrors on unsuspecting people. Maggie imagined the Skins viewed it as payback in a sense. The wars had been long and brutal—filled with atrocities from both sides.

The centralized state apparatus was too far removed and uncaring to prevent such attacks. The tribes worked to ensure their safety by applying a policy of avoidance. Wandering away from the free zones in pursuit of communication between villages, while not forbidden, definitely increased the level of risk.

Oldborns caught in the wrong place and time suffered a terrible fate. Retellings of the atrocities were conveyed around campfires and in religious gatherings. The women and girls were the most vulnerable. People talked about unspeakable evils. It turned her stomach and caused her to shudder. Were she alone, they would find her to be a tough piece of meat. Her daughter's presence created a desperate dynamic.

The hover jet circled the area, blasting commands from speakers. "Do not leave the area. If you run, you will be fired upon. This is a routine presence patrol. Prepare your paperwork for inspection." The craft swung into the column's path and planted itself on its extended legs. Hydraulics hissed, and lock bars fell into place as the machine settled itself from flight.

The blast door opened, and several Skins hopped off the ramp, displaying a dark joviality. One, tall and broad-shouldered, slapped another's back and pointed at the women, sharing a laugh. Careless with their weapons, pointed at the ground or slung over their backs, they approached sloppily, drawn forward by their profane desires.

Maggie and the column stood, locked in fear. Then she turned to them, her eyes in agony. "We're all on our own. God be with you." She brushed the hair out of her daughter's face so she could see her eyes. She said, "Wren, I..."

Wren, fixed in fear, quivered and met her mother's eyes. While she couldn't anticipate the outcome and couldn't see the options at hand, she accepted that they would be together when it was all said and done.

Maggie turned her hip away from the approaching Skins. She reached into her waistband and pulled out the small, ancient, snub-nosed revolver: the one she kept near the door of the cabin, the one she carried whenever she left the village. It provided a specific type of protection, explaining the look between her and the man every time they parted. They had agreed, in the tightest of moments, when pausing would mean the difference between dignity and horror, there would be no pause. The least and last thing she could do was finish with dignity. The first thing she could do would be to spare the girl.

She said, "I love you."

Wren swallowed her tears and smiled at her mother, not knowing what else to do.

Maggie placed a hand on her shoulder and turned her away. She lifted the barrel of the pistol to the base of her skull. She pulled back the hammer. The life inside her chest stood still as a vast and open sadness caused her to pause one moment more for her beautiful daughter to see the world and for the world to see her.

The heat from a rocket's exhaust suddenly forced Maggie to the ground. The thing screamed with an airy hiss, streaking a few yards above her. Its dark, gray tail hung in the air as the warhead slipped through the opened hatch. It detonated in the troop compartment, igniting the fuel cell and magazine. The blast launched the small team of Skins through the air. A fireball followed, flowing out over the column.

Maggie grabbed the girl, pulled her beneath herself.

Shaking from the immediate and violent reversal of fortunes, she lifted her head to assess the situation. The hover jet lay shattered and overtaken by flames, anyone inside, gone. The Skins who had approached them were scattered, their weapons blown free.

The tallest of them landed nearby, having been tossed onto his shoulder and neck. He attempted to sit up, stunned from his wits. His gaze lingered in the sky, disconnected.

Maggie held Wren's face close and said in a throaty whisper, "Close your eyes."

Wren did as she was told, pinching them shut and placing her hands over them for good measure.

Maggie crouched and shuffled toward the stunned Skin. He appeared to gather himself somewhat, his eyes searching for his pulse rifle. He caught a glimpse of her approaching, the pistol in her hand.

At a range close enough to smell him, the little gun barked. She fired two rounds into his face. She turned to engage the others as the firing began in earnest. Round after round, traced with blue-white, ripped past her. The remaining Skins were peppered and pulverized.

She dropped to a knee to remove herself from the line of fire. She looked over her shoulder at a berm of rock, one hundred meters behind the column, and saw the weapons reporting.

When it was finished, the broken bodies of the Skins were spread out before her, and the hover jet smoldered as a backdrop. It grew quiet.

She turned again to the rocks and focused her eyes. She saw them, then—slight movements. They disappeared for a moment and then rounded the berm on horseback. They were trussed up in modern skeins, Gen Two uniforms. Their heads were crowned with intricate optical/audio combat tools, draping over their eyes, hiding their faces behind tech masks.

The lead horseman raised his hand, and the team spread out into a wedge and advanced through the column. They walked past the collapsed women, clutching their baskets of goods and hugging the earth for comfort.

Maggie ran to Wren, lifted her, brushed her hair, and kissed her. Their eyes were colored with relief. Moments before—she couldn't think of what she was prepared to do. She slipped her arms around the girl and squeezed her.

Over her shoulder, the mysterious force approached, and Maggie's gratitude was tempered with fear. She held onto the pistol. Who were these people?

The horsemen plodded past the women and their bushels, taking their time. The grass beneath the powerful hooves imprinted.

The lead horseman reached Maggie. From her vantage, the man and horse were mountainous.

He dismounted with a grunt. Seemingly as large

off the horse as on, his face was a mystery behind the warrior tech. He peeled his helmet from the side, and the visor with its green lights came off. He placed it under his arm.

Still, with a barrel for a chest and shoulders sitting higher than they should have, he was no longer young. Gone, the bushy handlebar mustache —replaced with a massive beard, blond with gray having taken over the edges and streaked beneath the chin.

Through eyes no longer filled with mirth, Cleary looked over the woman and the child, lifted his nose, and said, "What brings you this far west?"

Maggie pulled Wren to her and could feel her heart beat a savage pace. She looked beyond the man, beyond the horses, toward the open end of the valley. It was the direction of her home, her village. Her mind tried to reason this thing. *Who were these people? Where did they come from?* Her mind sought answers, but her eyes kept reaching off into the distance. She peered into the smoky reaches.

There were no roads, no buildings for miles, only the green angles and ridges of the hills. Spinal processes were etched eternally in the crawling mist. They expanded before her.

Printed in Dunstable, United Kingdom